THE TREEHOUSE

THE TREEHOUSE

RANDI TRIANT

SAPPHIRE BOOKS

SALINAS, CALIFORNIA

Editor - Heather Flournoy
Book Design - LJ Reynolds
Cover Design - Treehouse Studio

Sapphire Books Publishing, LLC
P.O. Box 8142
Salinas, CA 93912
www.sapphirebooks.com

Printed in the United States of America
First Edition – March 2018

This and other Sapphire Books titles can be found at
www.sapphirebooks.com

Dedication

For Fiona Sinclair and Maria Flook

Acknowledgments

Many thanks to Chris Svendsen and Sapphire Books for taking a chance on this first-time novelist.

To Heather Flournoy for her editing wisdom and prowess, and for making me laugh through every nip and tuck.

To Ann McMan for the cover design.

I am very grateful to Christine Destrempes, Ailish Hopper, and Sarah Anne Johnson for reading early drafts and offering invaluable feedback that moved the story forward.

Thank you also to my brother, Richard, and to Wendy, Jessica, and Nicole for their unconditional love and support.

I will be indebted forever to Fiona Sinclair and Maria Flook whose faith in me and this book never wavered. I could not have asked for more loyal companions on the journey, nor could I have done it without them.

Day One

Camilla

Camilla had not seen her son for almost two years. Not since she walked out on him when her girlfriend forced her to leave. One Saturday morning, just before dawn, she drove to the old neighborhood in the next town over. On the street where she had lived with Allison and Nico, she cut the engine. She flicked off her headlights. She went dark. Coasting to a stop, Camilla parked the car several houses away.

The back of her Mini Clubman was jammed: a pile of pressure-treated plywood panels, a slew of small cedar boards tied together, a wooden spool of heavy rope, cans of paint. On the passenger seat there was an old fishing creel filled with two hammers, boxes of lag bolts and roofing nails, a nail gun still in its plastic housing, and several pages of instructions, "How to Build a Treehouse," printed off the web. Roped to the car's roof was a fifteen-foot metal ladder, with its warning sign on the top rung, "Not a step."

A few minutes later, Allison appeared, leading Nico by the hand to the driveway gate. Opening the gate, she walked with him to a SUV in the driveway. Allison lifted Nico into his car seat in the back, buckled him in, and she slid into the driver's seat. After the SUV backed out, Allison re-latched the gate. Camilla watched as they drove away. She whispered, "Mister, mister," just like her four-year-old son used to say it: soft, incantatory. Camilla hoped he might turn around. He might wave. She felt a familiar pinch in her chest. *Turn around, turn around*, she thought despite her fear that he would. Then the SUV disappeared down the hill and the street was empty.

A light drizzle started up, surprising Camilla. The forecast for the week had been a slot machine of sun emoticons. She clicked open the driver's door and stepped on to the graveyard-quiet street. She unlatched the driveway gate, ran back to the car, backed the Mini in, and then closed the gate again.

❧❧❧❧

They had met at a club. Camilla was at the bar buying drinks for herself and her best friend and ex, Taylor, to celebrate an upcoming trip to Mexico, when she turned and almost dumped both frozen margaritas on an attractive woman. Her hair was a sexy mass of soft red wavy tendrils that curved to her shoulders. Dressed in an expensive pantsuit, Allison was wearing thin heels that gave her three inches over Camilla.

"I'm so sorry," Camilla shouted over the numbing bass of the electronic dance song. "Did I get you?"

Allison wiped away a dribble of the icy green drink that had landed on her white silk blouse. She laughed warm-heartedly. She smiled.

"At least let me buy you a drink," Camilla told her loudly over the music.

While they waited for the bartender to come back with Allison's Cosmo, they talked. Camilla learned that Allison was a doctor and about her horrible morning.

She'd lost a patient and had already been at the club two hours with her colleagues, trying to forget the sweet seventy-year-old whose run-of-the-mill bladder surgery had gone south quickly. She'd been sent to retrieve the next round of drinks.

"What do you do?" Allison asked as the bartender handed her the red drink and Camilla paid. Camilla wondered if the doctor had chosen the drink unconsciously for its blood-like color. Allison leaned into Camilla, next to her ear so she could save Camilla from shouting to be heard over the thumping bass line. From then on, they alternated leaning into each other's ear when they spoke. Something about the gesture made Camilla feel as if they were old friends who hadn't seen each other in a while. Camilla smelled expensive Chanel perfume on Allison's neck.

Camilla shook her head. "Nothing as important as your job. I teach. At Tolland. Humanities. A course on Dickens."

Allison's perfectly waxed eyebrow arched. "*Really.* I was a Humanities major as an undergrad." Her eyes focused more intently on Camilla's face. "Not many of us left. We need to stick together." She smiled again. "Look, I have to get back to my friends, but here's my card and a pen. Give me your number. Maybe we can get together sometime and talk Socrates or something." She uncapped a cigar-sized fountain pen that was the same red velvet color as her hair. Reaching up, she tucked a coil behind her right ear. She handed the pen to Camilla. The gold pointy nib gleamed like a knife in the dark club. "Careful," Allison said in Camilla's ear. "I'm off duty so I can't stitch you up."

Maybe because Camilla hadn't been with anyone

for years, not since Taylor, or maybe it was the margaritas, but she wrote her number on the back of the hospital-issued business card and handed it back to Allison.

"Bye, Humanity," Allison said, and then she slipped through the crowd before Camilla could say, "Good-bye."

A month after she and Taylor returned from their trip, Camilla fell ill from giardia, a parasite that she'd picked up in Mexico along with most of the bar tabs Taylor had started. Camilla was renting a studio apartment, right around the corner from Taylor's apartment in the South End. She'd spent another bad night, vomiting for an hour before she'd passed out on her bathroom floor. By the next afternoon, the nausea had passed. She knew from the cycle she'd been experiencing every week since they'd been back that she'd be able to eat, but only miso broth or rice. There was a Japanese takeout a few blocks away. She was starving, but didn't have it in her to make the trek.

Camilla called Taylor three times before Taylor finally picked up, her voice sleepy and cracking. It was obvious that Taylor had been up all night, too, only having fun while Camilla had felt like she was going to die.

"Can it wait a few hours? It's probably better for your stomach if you do anyway," Taylor said.

Camilla said she was probably right as fast as she could so that Taylor wouldn't hear her crying. She was so worn out from the month-long parasite roller-coaster ride that she cried over the smallest thing. Maybe Taylor was trying to look out for her by making sure that when she'd eat she'd be able to keep it in. But Camilla sensed that wasn't the case at all.

As soon as she hung up her cell, it rang immediately. It was Allison. They hadn't spoken since their meeting at the club, and it was the first time Allison had called her. When Allison heard Camilla's cracking voice, she asked, "What's wrong?" Twenty minutes later, Allison was at Camilla's door, holding a white take-out bag. Camilla remembered it was pouring outside and Allison stood there, making sure that the umbrella was covering the paper bag more than her. That's how it all started between them, with Allison coming to her rescue, still dressed in her white medical jacket from her shift, and acting as if Camilla was the only thing that was important to her in that moment and every moment to come. She could be depended on. Taylor, however, was never reliable. It was a lesson that Camilla wouldn't forget.

୬୯୪୭୬

Within six months, they bought a condo in Boston's Back Bay and moved in together.

"Just like every other lesbian who pulls up on the second date with the U-Haul," Taylor groused at Camilla when she heard the news. She was acting the part of the aggrieved ex. Camilla shrugged it off. She liked that she and Allison were both nesters. They filled the two-bedroom-plus-study condo with custom, deep-cushioned chairs and sofas, and beds with cashmere-infused mattresses covered with soft cotton sheets and comforters. They hung paintings and scattered sculptures that they collected from galleries and shops devoted to Asian art. The condo whispered calculated comfort at every turn. Allison wasn't afraid of commitment, either. She seemed to thrive on it. She worked long hours during the week at the hospital, but checked on Camilla constantly between her patients. Sometime around ten o'clock at night she'd come bursting through the condo's front door shouting, "Where's my humanity?" One night, as a joke, Camilla ran as fast as she could from the back of the condo into Allison's arms, yelling, "Here I am, here I am!" Because Allison loved her so freely, so constantly, Camilla felt that she could let herself go with such childlike games. It became a joke between them that was reenacted every time Allison walked through the door.

Weekends were spent shopping for groceries and then cooking nonstop: large pots of mild chili or ratatouille in the winter months, marinated salmon or barbecued chicken on the patio's grill in the summer. Nothing that tested their epicurean boundaries or their stomachs, just good, solid food that could be counted on. They agreed that they could never understand those people who try a three-alarm taco as proof that they were adventurous. "They're the ones driving up our medical costs when they show up in the ER with a bleeding ulcer," Allison told her.

"Aren't you sick of the Kool-Aid yet?" Taylor asked Camilla over the phone one night after Camilla and Allison had been living together two years. "I never see you anymore. Have you noticed you've been MIA?" Taylor often spoke in military speak, a consequence of her being raised by two career Army parents. They had no idea that Taylor was a lesbian, that she freelanced as a graphic designer at the local gay newspaper, or that she recently curated a loft art show whose theme was A Bloody Business: What War Leaves Behind. Even so, Taylor couldn't kick the childhood habit of military jargon. Although they had been friends for twenty years and lovers for the first three months of those, Camilla still had no idea what she was talking about sometimes.

Taylor was right, however. Camilla had been missing in action. She missed Taylor, especially during the summer months when she wasn't teaching at Tolland College and had lots of free time. But if she'd try to make plans with Taylor, something else would suddenly come up that required Camilla's presence. Allison had scheduled, without telling Camilla, painters to redo the living room walls that week, and Camilla needed to be on hand to make sure they didn't steal the furniture. Or Allison needed Camilla to do an emergency dry-cleaning trip that particular afternoon to wait for Allison's favorite suit to be steamed and pressed because she'd just been informed about an important meeting the next morning with the hospital wonks.

"Oh, no," Allison told Camilla one morning as she was rushing around the kitchen, pouring coffee into her to-go silver bullet mug, racing to get out the door for work. "I didn't realize you were going out *tomorrow* night with Taylor. I already invited the team over for dinner." "The team" was three of Allison's male colleagues and their wives. It rankled Camilla a little when Allison would call them "the team." She wasn't their boss. The phrase was also a little too "cheerleader" for Camilla's tastes.

"I told you, remember?" Camilla chaffed at yet another time she'd have to cancel on Taylor. "That new sushi place on Washington Taylor wants to go to? I did tell you."

"I can try to reschedule it," Allison said with her back to Camilla as she screwed the lid on the travel cup. "I'll try to talk to the team in between patients today, I guess," she added, sighing.

"No, I'll call Taylor. You have enough to worry about." Camilla didn't want to give in. She missed Taylor. She couldn't remember the last time she'd seen her. But, Camilla's schedule seemed so undemanding next to Allison's: summers off and only three classes at most each semester. If she stuck to her plans she knew she wouldn't enjoy having the dinner with Taylor anyway, the taste of the Spider Monkey and California rolls made rancid by the acidic drip-drip of guilt from not supporting Allison.

"What would I do without you?" Allison said, smiling. "I left you the shopping list on the table." She kissed Camilla and then rushed out the door.

"You need to unionize," Taylor told her when Camilla phoned to cancel. "I hear personal assistants get what? Sixty grand these days? Health and dental. Maybe even worker's comp."

"You don't understand. *You've* never been in a relationship."

"Blah blah blah. I've never been a slave either, but I know what shackles feel like."

Camilla knew it was useless to talk to Taylor about how it felt to be needed by someone. To be so utterly loved and depended on. How it was sometimes small moments that kept a relationship afloat. Like the afternoon when Allison unexpectedly started dancing in the kitchen to a bossa nova number playing on the stereo as they chopped bok choy and broccoli together at the kitchen island. How her hips moved so seductively as she spontaneously grabbed Camilla, the knife still in Camilla's hands, tugging her into the dance. Or the night Allison woke her up at midnight during their first winter snowstorm after she'd come home from the hospital, and cajoled Camilla into going outside and making snow angels in the fresh powder on the brownstone's backyard patio.

"Put your arm through, honey," she coaxed a sleepy Camilla as she pulled a silk underwear shirt over Camilla's head. On the bed were Camilla's crisp snow pants and parka. "Let me put your socks on before you stand up." She was giving Camilla the full doctor treatment.

Camilla protested at first. It was too cold. She wanted to sleep. But once outside, the sheer beauty of the knee-high landscape of unmarked white and the quiet stunned her. Their cloudy puffs of breath intermingled as the sides of their fleece hats leaned in and touched. They were the last people on earth. Allison held her hand as they plodded their way through the drifts toward the center of the patio. Finally, they both lay down and swished their arms and legs back and forth in unison, laughing with abandon. When the condo owner on the second floor came out on his deck to see what the hubbub was about, Allison called out to him to come join them.

"It's a little late," he called down, clearly miffed that they'd awakened him with their childish game.

When he went back into his condo, Allison called after him, "Philistine!" And although Camilla was embarrassed that they'd been caught and felt a little guilty, she loved Allison for her word choice and spontaneity.

Sometimes, though, Camilla saw that treasured impulsiveness slide into something else altogether. In the first two years, they fought occasionally. They were nothing more than spats really, Camilla thought, like every other couple tiptoeing their way across emerging fault lines. Why didn't Camilla stack the pots in the cupboard according to size rather than in the hodgepodge tower that fell out on Allison's foot when she opened the door? Did Allison really have to talk on her cell to one of her colleagues as they watched the Sopranos finale?

The third year, that changed. In addition to her increasing surgical load, Allison received a million-dollar grant from the National Institutes of Health to study quality of life in five hundred women pre- and post-hysterectomy. They celebrated with "the team" sans their wives at an expensive steak place where they drank two-hundred-dollar bottles of wine and ordered a round of filet mignons, except for Camilla who ordered the haddock because she'd eaten a hamburger on campus for lunch that day.

"You're a fish out of water," one of "the team" quipped, and everyone at the table laughed. Camilla didn't think it was particularly funny, but she knew the celebratory dinner was important to Allison and so she laughed, too. She'd wanted to stay home and for Allison to celebrate on her own with "the team," but Allison had insisted that she come even though none of the other wives were there.

The entire discussion during the meal was focused on how Allison could cajole sweet biddies into not only losing their uteruses, but also opening up about their sex lives before and afterward for the research project.

"I hate that word, hysterectomy," Camilla mused later that night as she and Allison brushed their teeth in their hers-and-hers bathroom sinks before going to bed. "You know where it comes from, right? Male doctors in the seventeenth century thinking they could cut out what they saw as feminine madness." Here she did air quotes, still holding her toothbrush in one hand. "*Ectomy* is from the Latin, meaning to excise or cut out," she said, slipping into her professorial voice as she waved the toothbrush like a pointer. "*Hysteria* meaning madness. Cut out the madness."

Leaning over her sink, Allison spat the toothpaste from her mouth. She stood up, glaring at Camilla.

"That's just like you to criticize something I've accomplished. What have you done lately that's so great, huh? At least I get off my ass and do something more than read a book."

Camilla was speechless. "The team" had downed Champagne followed by those horrendously expensive bottles of wine. Camilla had driven home because she'd stuck pretty much to Diet Cokes. But, she wondered now if Allison was more drunk than she'd thought.

"I wasn't—"

"Yeah, right," Allison seethed, throwing her toothbrush into the cup holder. "Oh and by the way, *Humanity*, hysterectomy is from the Greek *hystera*, meaning uterus. Excision of the *uterus*. And you teach college. Christ."

Then she walked into their bedroom, closing the door behind her. Camilla slept on the couch that night although she didn't really *sleep* at all. She relentlessly kneaded over what had happened, gradually sifting into a doughy mixture of hurt and anger at the thought that Allison must really be stressed to lash out like that. By sunrise, Camilla was up and making Allison a double cappuccino and her favorite chocolate chip pancakes. She carried a tray to their bedroom and, tapping lightly on the door, hesitated but then went in. Allison was sitting up in bed reading an article in *Lancet*. She looked pale and tired. She lowered the journal.

"Oh, how nice," she said. "What's the special occasion?"

They never spoke about what had happened. Camilla was relieved. Far easier to chalk up Allison's behavior to work stress than to perform an *ectomy* on what really lay beneath it. It was a one-time thing, that was all.

But, it wasn't. Once that initial sighting of Allison's temper had happened, flocks of it appeared, like when one bird on a wire is suddenly joined by two of its feathered friends, then a third, then more and more. It was like that famous scene in the Hitchcock movie when Tippi Hedren watches in horror as the crows, one by one, gradually cover the jungle gym on the school playground.

Sometimes these flare-ups were like that first time, with Allison spontaneously combusting and sniping about what she considered Camilla's easy life. One Friday night, Allison came home to find Camilla so entrenched in editing the final draft of an essay on the dying words of famous writers that Camilla had forgotten to start preparing their dinner.

"Is it too much to ask that dinner be ready? When you add it all up over the entire year, do you even work an average of ten hours a week?" Allison sneered. "Lifeguards work more than you do. Oh, and by the way, I lost a patient today. But what's that compared to what Dickens did or did not say when *he* died? I could forgive you if you were writing something that someone will actually *read*."

The following afternoon, though, was the bossa nova impromptu dance and Allison acted as if she hadn't said those horrible things, and instead she swept Camilla across the tiled floor. This dynamic was ingrained by the fifth year they'd been together: Allison lashing out, followed either by Allison performing some spur-of-the-moment, romantic act, or by Camilla contritely making sure that the house was spotless, the laundry washed and folded, and Allison's favorite dinners ready as soon as she walked through the door. Allison rarely apologized, although Camilla often did, even when Allison's verbal tirades began to be coupled with physical acting out. A coffee cup could be hurled at a wall, or a stack of Camilla's research papers angrily brushed onto the floor. Once, when Camilla had taken refuge from the shouting behind the locked door of the bathroom, Allison had punched the door, not hard enough to splinter the wood or hurt her hand, but the abrupt thud was enough for Camilla to worry about what else would follow.

"No apology, no surrender. That's her philosophy in a nutshell," Taylor told Camilla one night after an especially brutal fight. "That girl needs help. And I don't mean the domestic kind."

They were sitting in Bukowski's, their favorite dive bar from their undergrad days at Boston University, because the drinks were cheap and the girl who bartended was one of Taylor's exes and let Taylor illegally smoke her cigarettes in a back booth in defiance of the city's clean air ordinance. The fight had ended with Allison removing one of Camilla's bureau drawers and emptying it out the third-floor window onto one of the box hedge sentries perched in a metal urn on the patio below. The wood drawer had obliterated the hedge.

"You don't understand," Camilla said, shaking

out a cigarette from Taylor's Lucky Strike pack. Every single one of Taylor's exes were now her best friends, including Camilla. Even the exes of her exes were her best friends. None of them had ever dumped a bureau drawer out a window. Women instantly wanted to spend time with Taylor, over dinner or at a Laundromat. It didn't matter where it was. Taylor often chided Camilla, "Don't get attached. Even the Dalai Lama tells us that. Attachments are no good unless you're an earlobe." Sometimes when Taylor really wanted to make a point about Camilla being too possessive, she'd call her Earlobe.

At the bar, Taylor's fingers enclosed Camilla's hand and the bull's eye on the cigarette pack, stopping her from lifting the cigarette to her lips. "What are you doing?"

"Fuck her," Camilla said, shaking Taylor's hand off and lighting up two cigarettes, one after the other. She passed one to Taylor. "I don't care if she smells it on me. She chucked my clothes out of a window for God's sakes. What more can she do anyway? Ground me? I do everything. *Everything.* Listen to me. Shit. I sound like she's my parent."

"She needs therapy, Milly."

Camilla shook her head. "Not going to happen. She tries. She really does. You have no idea the kind of pressure she's under. She saves lives."

Taylor scrunched up her face. Camilla knew coming to Allison's defense was often too much for Taylor to stomach. Taylor laughed and wiggled her fingers at Camilla. "Ooh, she saves lives. Please."

Camilla took a long drink of her Scotch. She shouldn't have had that third one, yet alone this fourth. Now, she'd end up crashing at Taylor's, too shit-faced to go home and face Allison and the bureau drawer, which undoubtedly had been left on the patio for Camilla to clean up. She was making matters worse, but she was too worn out to care.

"No, listen," she told Taylor. "She's on call twenty-four seven. You have no idea what that's like. I don't either. People dying because of something we did or didn't do. Wondering if someone is going to sue us."

Taylor's head drooped onto her chest as if she was sleeping. She jerked her head up.

"Sorry, what were you saying? Enough with the do no harm lesson, Professor. She's crazy, pure and simple. I'm getting the next round." Standing up, Taylor made her way through the dense crowd of wannabe Beats, Goth punks, and people who looked like they hadn't changed their clothes in a week. They were at least fifteen years younger than her and Taylor. *What are we doing here?* Camilla thought.

She took out a small pearl penknife from her jeans pocket and surreptitiously started to carve her initials into the wooden bench she was sitting on. It was an old habit. Making tiny grooves in the oak helped to calm her down.

Camilla wanted to call after Taylor as she walked away toward the bar that it wasn't pure and simple. Not at all. Camilla never knew what she would find when she returned home after teaching. She wondered if the push-pull of the relationship was what kept her in it. She loved Allison and months would pass without any eruptions. And the biggest outbursts would usually be followed by beautiful acts of love on Allison's part.

The next morning when Camilla returned home, she found the wood floor hallway that led from their condo's entry door straight back to their bedroom, was covered in rose petals. Allison was waiting in bed, naked.

"How long have you waited like that?" Camilla asked her, astonished, almost forgetting the reason for her showing up so late.

"Forever," Allison said, smiling sheepishly. She lightly patted the bed next to her.

Camilla didn't know if she meant it had felt like forever or she was alluding to the future. She was glad that Allison wasn't going to yell at her for staying at Taylor's. That they'd simply jumped into the makeup stage.

On her pillow was an envelope with First Class airline tickets and two entry tickets to Charles Dickens house in London.

"This is unbelievable. I don't know what to say," Camilla said, fingering the tickets. "Thank you so much."

Allison laughed and, pulling Camilla down toward her, told her, "Oh yeah? Show me *how* much."

Camilla knew Allison, of course, hadn't forgotten about the bureau or that Camilla hadn't come home all night, but maybe the love petals, the London trip, meant Camilla had been forgiven at least.

A week later, she told Allison she was meeting Taylor later that morning for coffee.

"Oh, I don't think that's such a good idea, do you?" Allison said, a tight smile forming on her face. "Besides the house needs to be cleaned and you"—she pointed at Camilla's chest—"need to start making a to-do list for London." She brushed her lips on Camilla's cheek. Then she walked out of the condo for work. From then on, it was difficult for Camilla to see Taylor.

☙☙☙☙

Five years skidded into seven. Any flare-ups that were not doused by acts of contrition, Camilla extinguished by the convincing thought that Allison would love her forever, would never cheat on her, could always be depended on just as she had that first time she'd shown up on Camilla's doorstep with the rice and miso. Camilla rarely saw Taylor anymore. Talking on the phone was easier than talking Allison into letting her go out. She didn't see very much of anyone except her Tolland colleagues when she was on campus.

They bought the house in Wilbur when Allison was made Associate Chair of Surgical Research in the Urology Department after she received three other NIH grants.

One day, after they'd been in the house a year, Allison came home from work and announced in the kitchen as she was pouring herself a glass of wine that she wanted to get pregnant. Camilla was forty-two years old, Allison thirty-eight. Camilla felt something akin to a low-grade earthquake or sudden fever. Dizzy, she sat down on the nearest piece of furniture, a very old, wobbly Mexican stool that she knew she shouldn't depend on if she wanted stability. The floor would've been a safer bet.

"What?" Camilla said. "What?" she repeated as if she were suddenly hard of hearing.

"I said I want to get pregnant." Allison looked at Camilla. "I can't wait much longer." She sipped her wine. She smiled.

Camilla should have the noticed the "I" of it, the

non-existent "we," but she didn't. She should've asked
her about that. Instead Camilla asked her, "How are
you going to work?"

"That must've been met with some incoming
fire," Taylor said on the phone the next day.

"It was probably a shitty thing to say," Camilla
agreed.

"You think?"

Up until that day, though, Allison's life had
increasingly revolved around her work. Except for
an annual Fourth of July vacation with "the team"
on Cape Cod, their own vacations could be put on
hold because of sudden turns in Allison's patients:
the mesh sling she sewed in to support the patient's
bladder neck unexpectedly disconnected itself from
the woman's abdominal wall like a wire snapping from
a telephone pole; or a sudden high fever indicating
infection had set in after a surgery. A good chunk
of their social calendar was laden with dinners with
"the team." Dinners of stuffed Cornish game hens
or prime rib marinated for hours, with fingerling
potatoes and roasted vegetables, all of which Camilla
was responsible for cooking because Allison would
still be at the hospital, arriving home minutes before
everyone else. Camilla loved to cook, but still, as she
sliced heads of cauliflower and snipped the stems off
Portobello mushrooms that reminded her of parasols,
she often found herself wishing Allison was there to be
her sous chef or at least to be company, like in the early
years. *How did we get here?* she'd wonder as she tugged
the vein free from the belly of another Haricot Vert.

The dinners had become a death pit for Camilla,
filled with talk of the pros and cons of a dizzying array
of surgical options with names that sounded like they

were parts of a car engine, like the transobturator, or a new feminist movement, like the retropubic.

Now, Allison nonchalantly sipped her wine. "I want us to have a baby," she repeated, substituting the "have a baby" for "get pregnant" as if to drive home the final outcome.

Although they'd been together eight years, Camilla was still unsure of whether there actually was a "we," an "us." The fights seemed to be happening every other week now. *You have no idea what it's like to live as she does*, Camilla often chastised herself after their fights. No idea what it feels like to be responsible every minute for someone's life as Allison was at the hospital. What it was like to have your emotions steer your life like a roller-coaster ride gone awry, a wheel bolt snapping, sending car after car into one monumental pileup. Camilla had never been an anxious person, like Allison. Not at first, but she was now. Always waiting, as her father would say, for the other shoe to drop. Maybe Allison's mood swings would slow to a standstill if there were a child to take care of, to love. Something, *someone*, else for her to focus her attention on.

"Great," Camilla forced herself to say to Allison. She clinked her wine glass against Allison's. "Let's do it."

❧❧❧❧

Saying she wanted to get pregnant and actually accomplishing that was harder than Allison thought it would be. They agreed that they wanted an anonymous donor who had filled out the required Boston Cryogenic forms and checked the box stating that he did not want to be part of the baby's future or contacted by any means. No matter what. Ever.

They studied the binders full of donors' medical and family histories, and pored over the toothy childhood photos that supposedly gave you a glimpse of what *your* child could look like with this match. Looking for Mr. Perfect and the weight of choosing the wrong one grew heavier with each new profile Camilla and Allison read. They decided to individually sort through them, putting their top picks in one pile. The first time through the hundreds of pages they ended up not choosing any of them. Each had an imperfection or a worrisome trait. Asthma on the mother's side. Heart disease on the father's. Trauma from a much-beloved sister dying in a car accident that the donor had survived. Employment listed as pizza delivery man for ten years. All of them went into the discards.

Under the question *How do you like to spend your free time?* one donor had answered *Playing rugby.*

"What's wrong with that? He's athletic," Camilla said, taking his profile back out of the discard pile. "His medical history is great."

"I'm not having a misogynist, who glorifies bashing someone's occipital lobe, passing his DNA to my baby," Allison told her and slid the pages back onto the heap. "Besides, no one's medical history is *that* good, especially someone who plays a blood sport."

"It's either an immaculate conception or you have to lower the bar a bit," Camilla told her.

The second time through they chose two men. Both had good medical histories, both touted being raised in loving families. Both had graduated from college, although one of them was now in medical school while the other was an accountant in the Midwest. Camilla wasn't surprised that Allison wanted the med student. She was leaning toward the accountant.

"You're just saying that to start a fight," Allison said. She stood up from the kitchen table, opened the refrigerator door, and stared inside. "I thought you said you did the grocery shopping."

"I did."

Allison shut the door. "Well, I don't see any iced tea in there." She sat back down at the table in a huff.

"Do you think the sperm bank brings them in on a private plane?" Camilla asked her, trying to lighten the tension that was on the verge of imploding.

"What are you talking about? All of them *whom*?" Allison sniped at her. "The donors don't fly all the way here to jerk off into a cup. They can more easily do it in a lab in whatever godforsaken place they live in. Why in the world would you want the donor to be from the Midwest anyway? Jesus, wasn't it enough they gave us Bush for eight years?"

Camilla laughed out of nervousness and because it was so absurd. She wanted to make a joke about DNA not being linked yet to state of origin or political party, but she didn't dare. She didn't mean flying the donors in. She'd meant the sperm, the donations, the…what did the instructional booklet call them? The specimens. From the Latin, *specere*, to look. It really wasn't the right word for it, was it though? They weren't scientists examining whether the tiny tails were swimming under the microscope. Was it really that important to her? Both candidates were fine. Wasn't it all down to *their* parenting skills anyway? Better to give in on it.

"Look, I don't really care who we choose," she told Allison as softly as she could. "You choose."

Allison stood up, shoving the pages back into the binder and snapping the metals rings closed to punctuate the end of every sentence she said. "That's great." Snap. "*You* don't care." Snap. "As usual." Snap. "I'm the one moving us forward, making the decisions." She grabbed the second binder. "Wanting a future for us." Snap. "But you." Snap. "Don't care." Snap. She closed the binder.

"Allison—"

"Nope," Allison said, shaking her head. She hugged the binders close to her chest, like a baby. "Fine. I'll pick. I'm paying the five grand anyway. I'm the one getting pregnant. Who *wants* to get pregnant. You're right, I should choose."

Later that night in bed, while Camilla was listening to Allison's breathing as she slept, she wondered if their argument was a sign of some deeper fissure between them. That she'd been wrong, that the small fractures caused by years of direct hits could not be mended by the love for a child. Maybe she was making a mistake. What if the fighting escalated even more? She'd never be able to leave if they had a child.

But, in the morning, there was Allison at the kitchen counter, enthusiastically showing her a catalog of hip kids' clothes. The cover showed a beautiful, blond mother and father with two equally stunning children hugging and laughing atop a faded blue vintage Land Rover, an African savanna sunset in the distance.

"That could be us," Allison told her, pointing at the parents. "On top of the world."

They made the appointment for the IVF procedure that morning for the following Saturday.

≈≈≈≈≈

Allison didn't get pregnant right away. Not until she'd spent a fortune on four IVF procedures and her thighs and butt had become pincushions from the hormone injections. Her mood swings were worsening and she lashed out at Camilla whenever their daily rituals weren't strictly adhered to. One night, Camilla was busy grading student essays when she heard Allison come home earlier than expected from work. When she walked downstairs, Allison was in the kitchen pouring herself a glass of wine, clearly upset.

"What's wrong?" Camilla said wearily. She was tired from the grading and exhausted from what she used to tell Taylor was the hamster wheel, meaning Allison's tirades that went nowhere, were never solved, had no end. Simply went round and round.

"It would be nice if you at least faked that you were glad I was home after I just worked ten hours," she told Camilla.

"Allison—"

"I have to go now and stick a needle in my ass so we, you and I, can have a family." She walked toward the stairs, carrying her wine. She locked the front door. "Don't forget to turn out the lights."

Camilla stared at the front door. It beckoned to her. What a relief it would be to shut off the lights and walk through that door right now. Was this it for her? All that life would be? She ached to call Taylor. She hadn't spoken to her in weeks, not since Taylor had told her over the phone, "Look. I can't take another phone call about sperm and specimens and Allison's shooting up enough estrogen to get a yak pregnant. I just can't." Camilla was hurt for weeks. But now, she wanted to get in her car and drive straight to Taylor's South End apartment and tell her that she wanted a baby, but she didn't want a baby. That she loved Allison, but she didn't love Allison.

All of that ambivalence, though, disappeared for Camilla the second Nico came into this world and one of Allison's OB/GYN colleagues slid him onto Allison's chest: his unruly mess of black hair, his dark eyes intent and shining, his wailing mouth immediately slipping into a lopsided smile.

"Look at that," Camilla said as she lightly touched his dimpled cheek and then his tiny palm with her index finger. His fingers intuitively wrapped around hers. And she thought: *reinforcements.*

❧❧❧❧

She was wrong about that. Not at first, but later.

At first, the three of them hunkered down for the winter. It was the snowiest, coldest winter on record. Wilbur's schools were closed so often that the school council had to extend the school year to the following July.

In some ways, it felt to Camilla like the early honeymoon days after she and Allison had moved in together. They were gentle again with each other. Allison had had a rough delivery and Camilla carried meals to her and read aloud to her and Nico the children's books they'd received as gifts, although it was always Allison who would choose which particular book. *The Very Hungry Caterpillar. Guess How Much I Love You. Brown Bear, Brown Bear, What Do You See?*

Within a few weeks, Allison joined her in the kitchen. They cooked together again, a return to simpler meals, with Nico in a small portable bassinette on the kitchen table. The house was filled with the smells of stews and soup cooking on the stove in large Le Creuset pots, or of roasted chicken, carrots, and rosemary potatoes in the oven. Gone were the five-course meals Camilla used to prepare alone for "the team." In fact, "the team" was nowhere to be seen. They saw enough women laid up in the hospital; they didn't want to see one of their own like that. No one else came to see them, either. Allison begged off any intrusion into their lives with complaints that she was still healing from the rough birth or was too tired.

The snow continued to pile up outside in record amounts. Although their snow service kept their pathways clear down to the garage, Allison said it was too cold for a newborn to be outside, that things would be different in the spring.

"Humor me," Allison told her one day as they watched Nico sleeping between them on their bed. "Let's treasure these days with just the three of us before I have to go back to work."

"You have three more months," Camilla told her, laughing.

Allison's face hardened. "That's easy for you to say. You're on sabbatical. You'll get to see him." She kissed Nico's forehead. "It's so unfair," she said under her breath. "I was the one who wanted you."

"*Allison.*"

"Well, it's true, isn't it? You'd prefer to get out of here and meet Taylor in some bar rather than—"

"All right, all right," Camilla whispered at her, worrying that their back and forth would awaken him. "You made your point. Just the three of us. *Contra mundum.*"

Contra mundum. It's what Charles Ryder in *Brideshead Revisited* tells his friend and great love, Sebastian Flyte, when Sebastian accuses Charles of choosing Sebastian's family over him. "I'm with you,

Sebastian. *Contra mundum,*" Charles assures him.
Against the world.

It was later that night, when Allison was fast
asleep with Nico and Camilla was in the living room
nursing a glass of wine, that Camilla remembered that
contra mundum became a sort of smothering isolation
that ended with Sebastian dying of alcoholism and
pneumonia after Charles had rejoined the world
and all that it offers. It wasn't a rallying cry for their
relationship. It was a death knell.

❧ ❧ ❧ ❧

Within a few months of their being shut off from
everyone and everything, Nico became another thing
that Allison could withhold from her or give to her on
a whim, as punishment, or from a heartfelt place of
wanting to share. When Camilla was an adolescent girl
her older brother used to play this game whenever he
was driving and he'd happen to see her walking home.
He'd pull up his Camaro alongside her and yell for her
to get in, but as soon as she reached for the passenger
door handle he peeled off, his tires leaving rubber. A
few yards away he stopped the car, waited for her to
walk up, and do it all over again. This would go on
three or four times, her fingers just reaching the cool,
silver handle when he screeched away again, before
she'd finally stop taking the bait and ignoring his fake
promises that he wouldn't do it again. She'd end up
obstinately refusing and walking home the entire way.

That's how Camilla looked back on most of
the two years she spent with Nico. There would be
Allison, holding him straight out to her, saying "Take
him, take him," his fingers opening and closing in
anticipation, but the moment Camilla reached out for

him, the moment her fingers grazed his skinny torso, the moment he gave Camilla his lopsided grin, Allison would snatch him back. Sometimes she honestly did it as a game. Sometimes he even squealed with laughter. But it always felt the same way to Camilla. Always there was the thought worming its way in: *If I had only been faster.*

❧ ❧ ❧ ❧

Three months later, Allison went back to work. Camilla and Nico would be alone five days a week during Camilla's sabbatical. No matter how badly her relationship had deteriorated with Allison, how unsure she was about whether she could survive another claustrophobic month, Camilla loved Nico more than her own happiness. It took her completely by surprise, this love for such a tiny being whose soft hands held on to her neck whenever Allison allowed her to hold him, or whose funny attempts when he first began talking—a mixture of mumbo jumbo, a kitten mewing, and a parrot shrieking—cracked Camilla up. During the weeks leading up to when Allison would be gone and it would be just the two of them, Camilla felt giddy with relief. She'd read to him whatever book *she* chose. They'd go on adventures together to the museums in Boston, to the nearby playgrounds, to visit Taylor and other friends that Camilla had lost touch with, like Sofia and Linda, artists that Camilla and Taylor had gone to college with who had a baby of their own. She'd bring Nico to Tolland and let her colleagues ooh and aah over him like every other baby brought by one of them over the years. He was six months old and hardly anyone had seen him—or Camilla, for that matter. The months of isolation would come to an end finally.

All those dreams were shattered, however, on the very first day that Allison went back to work.

"I want you to write down everything he eats and when he pees and poops in this book," she told Camilla, pointing at a spiral notebook on the kitchen counter. She was ready to leave, but still holding Nico. "And what time he does it. The *exact* time. Maybe I should stay home one more week," she said, but she said it to *him* as he reached out and clutched some of her hair.

"I'm not his nanny," Camilla said defensively.

"This isn't easy for me," Allison told her. "Do you have any idea how hard it is for me to leave him?" When her eyes began to fill, Camilla relented.

"Okay, okay, I'll write it all down. You should go. You're going to be late."

Allison hugged Nico tightly and then reluctantly handed him over. "I'll call you to see how he's doing." She started to gather her coffee and leather bag.

Camilla propped Nico on her hip as she walked over to the refrigerator and then gave him a frozen teething ring from the freezer to soothe his painful gums. There was the tiniest white stub shooting up smack in the middle of his lower gum.

"Call me on my cell in case we're out," she told Allison nonchalantly over her shoulder. She smiled at Nico gnawing away. "We have plans, don't we, mister?" she said to him as she smoothed his dark, curly hair down. Camilla touched her nose to his and rubbed it, the teething ring wobbling in his mouth between them. Her lips kissed his hand holding the ring, the pressure shifting it from left to right in his mouth. Instead of being angry that she was messing with his icy relief, Nico chortled.

"What's the matter?" Camilla joked with him, faking that she was going to pull the teething ring out with her fingers. She lightly tugged on it. "Uh-oh, hold on to it, mister. Watch out. I'm gonna get it!"

Nico laughed harder, and shoved the ring back in, covering it with his fist.

Allison dropped her bag back on the counter. "Don't tease him," she told Camilla. Her voice rose. "And stop calling him mister. His name is Nico. What do you mean anyway? Where are you going?"

"I don't know. Nowhere. Somewhere. I don't know," Camilla said nervously.

"Christ. Can't you just stay home this first day?" Allison hesitated. "He needs to be in his home. It's traumatizing enough for him that I'm not going to be here. You know what? I'm going to tell them I need another week."

"No, don't. We won't go anywhere," Camilla said quickly.

That set the course, Camilla would realize later.

"You buckled," Taylor told her on the phone when Camilla called as soon as Allison left. "You're like one of those fishermen who gives in when the captain is yelling bloody murder to get on the boat in the middle of a storm. It's easier to just get on the fucking boat than take on a raving maniac. Am I ever going to see you again?"

"Of course you are," Camilla said quietly, but deep down she knew that it was a lie.

Pecksniff

Camilla's plan for the treehouse came about simply. One Saturday, eight months after Nico was born, Allison was lamenting their choice of house.

"Kids can't play in gardens," she said as she looked out the kitchen French doors to those very same gardens she was criticizing. They'd just finished their breakfast of waffles and warm, gooey syrup. Nico was sleeping upstairs in his crib. The baby monitor on the kitchen counter broadcasted his breaths and gibberish murmurs.

"What kids?" Camilla asked.

Allison turned in her chair and looked at Camilla across the table. "Me, for one. My parents never let me play in the gardens." She faced the glass doors again. "Look at it. It couldn't say 'no kids allowed' any more loudly than if we had put a sign out there."

Their entire "backyard" was a hill leading down to the house, covered during summertime with all the flowers they'd planted: lilies, irises, azaleas, rhododendrons, and hydrangeas. Two peony trees were there too, the only plants they'd kept from the prior owners who otherwise believed in low-maintenance scrub bushes and hostas.

"The park's right around the corner," Camilla said, trying to jettison the conversation, which she saw taking off into them tearing up the entire garden that had taken them years of hard labor to birth, and now laying down a sod slope for Nico to roll down. Except there wasn't enough room for that. The slope wasn't long enough. It made no sense; he'd no sooner get some speed going before he'd crash into the back family room.

"So every time he wants to play outside we have to take him to the park? What kind of childhood is that?" Allison answered.

"He could have a treehouse in the oak."

"When can you start?" Allison asked. She walked across the kitchen and opened the screen door as if to say, "How about now?"

But Camilla didn't start then. She researched the internet on how to build a treehouse. Then, there were the weeks spent drafting a simple construction plan, which sat on her desk for another month. By then, she and Allison were fighting almost every day about everything.

They fought about which pajamas Nico should wear that night to bed. "Are those warm enough?" Allison said, questioning whichever ones Camilla picked up.

They fought about what to do when he woke up in the middle of the night in his crib, seemingly endless battles arguing how long they should let him cry before they walked down the short hallway to his bedroom and picked him up. Who should pick him up. One night, Allison protested, "I'm his mother. I'm the one who went through twenty-three hours of labor. You didn't even want him. I should be the one to get him."

When Nico was around ten months old, Camilla asked Allison if they could come up with a schedule to share who was "on duty" each night so that at least one of them could get some sleep. He'd been sleeping through the night in his crib for several months, but suddenly he was awakening every night, demanding and crying out that they come and get him. No amount of cajoling or holding or ignoring could break the pattern. Their pediatrician told them he was experiencing a touchpoint, a time when babies are about to achieve another developmental milestone but they regress in an area they've already mastered to compensate. "They only have so much brain power and energy," the peds expert told them. "He's getting ready to walk, so he's forgotten how to sleep for the moment. It'll pass."

Camilla proposed a schedule so that whoever was "on duty" would sleep in the guest bedroom, which was on the second floor next to Nico's bedroom, down the hall from the master. But the plan backfired on Camilla a few nights later. It was Allison's turn to check on Nico if he woke up during the night, but she insisted on staying in the master bedroom, claiming that after a day on her feet in surgery, the bed in the master bedroom would be better for her back. Around two in the morning Camilla was awakened in the guest room by his cries. She waited to hear Allison's footsteps pass her closed door and for the crying to subside. All she heard, however, was Nico's continued cries, which were getting louder. Still she heard nothing from Allison. Camilla got out of bed and opened her door. The hallway was dark. Nico was still crying. Camilla went into his room. He was standing up in his crib, sobbing, his wet cheeks illuminated by the room's nightlight. "Mommy, up," he wailed, reaching out his hands to her. Camilla began to lift him up, whispering assurances that he would be all right, she was there now, when suddenly, Allison was there also.

"What are you doing?" she spat at Camilla, immediately snatching Nico out of Camilla's arms. "It's my night. You're not supposed to do this. You can't touch him on *my nights*. You're the one who wanted this." Then, she turned her back on Camilla, whisking Nico away to the master bedroom. Stunned and hurt, Camilla retreated to the guest room. She tossed on the bed for the rest of the night, unable to sleep.

In the morning over breakfast she asked Allison if they could talk about the ground rules for the schedule.

"I mean, it's senseless for one of us, no matter what night it is, to hear him—I don't know maybe one of us is so exhausted we won't hear him—and not do anything about it. It doesn't seem fair to him," she told Allison.

Allison stood up, collecting her plate of toasted raisin bread and her coffee cup. "It was your idea to do this, remember?" she snapped. "What's *senseless* is if you create a schedule and then don't stick to it. You said you needed to sleep. You won't sleep if you jump up every time he lets out a whimper. I was on my way when you picked him up. I'm only trying to help you get some sleep, which you said you needed. You did say that, right?" Allison stared at her for a minute and then walked over to the sink, carrying her dishes. She faced Camilla again. "It's pretty simple. Don't go to him. Don't touch him. Don't pick him up. End of story."

From then on, whenever it was Allison's night and Nico began to cry, Camilla was too afraid to go to him no matter how long it took Allison to get to him from the master bedroom. Some nights, especially after Allison had had a grueling day at the hospital, Nico's crying seemed to have no end, failing to wake Allison up. On those nights, Camilla leaned against the other side of her door, softly crying, her heart aching as Nico sobbed. She knew there was something wrong with what was happening, but she was too afraid, and also confused by Allison's argument that she was just being protective of Camilla's sleep, to do anything about it other than continue to suffer alone in the guest room.

During those months, treehouses were the last thing on Camilla's mind. By the time Nico turned two, Camilla had left, the treehouse never built.

Two years later, here she was, building that treehouse in the yard she was no longer allowed in, for the four-year-old son she was no longer able to see. Her relationship with Allison might be dead, but the mother in her was still very much alive and kicking.

❧❧❧❧

Whether Camilla was still Nico's mother became a topic of debate that they argued about in the months after Camilla left.

"The day you walked out that door and left us was the day you were no longer his mother," Allison texted her two months after she left. "Come back and you can be. Come back and you can see him."

Camilla texted back, "I left you. Never him." What kind of mother would she have been to stay and support a daily atmosphere of combat for her son to witness? Allison didn't agree, and nor did others.

"Is he in your life now?" Linda, a professor and friend at Tolland College where Camilla taught, asked. Or at least Camilla thought she had been her friend.

"No, he is not," Linda plowed on. Linda was only a few years older than Camilla, but seemed much older. She had the habit of not only wearing a different colored scarf that matched her jewelry every day, but also obsessively unraveling the scarf only to rewind it again around her neck like a snake any time she talked. She began to do that now. Camilla usually had to restrain herself from grabbing Linda's hands and reassuring her that there was nothing to be nervous about, that the scarf was fine. Now, she had the urge to strangle Linda with that lovely turquoise silk scarf of hers that matched Linda's Native American bracelets, necklace, earrings, and rings.

"You knew when you left she'd never let you see him unless you came back, didn't you?" Linda paused, and then added before a stunned Camilla had a chance to answer, "Yes you did. You knew that and you left anyway. Leaving is never without its consequences."

But, Camilla didn't know how anything would pan out when she left Allison except that she couldn't fight anymore and that she didn't want her son—yes, her son—to see that any longer. Everything else was a mystery to her. In those early days after she'd left, Camilla had felt heartbroken, yes, but also a sense of relief, of weightlessness, of safety. She read about Keats's idea of negative capability, or our ability to simultaneously acknowledge the unpredictable nature of events and yet conduct ourselves with confidence and happiness. Keats knew that sometimes life's big questions couldn't be resolved, that all you can do is go on. Camilla believed that she only had to go on and Allison would eventually see that Nico needed Camilla in his life again as much as he needed Allison. That they'd set up a weekly visitation schedule. That Camilla's love for Nico had never wavered. That she had sacrificed everything so that Nico would be saved from witnessing the escalating fighting between them.

Yet here was Linda lecturing Camilla on consequences and what she knew.

"Fuck Linda and her premeditated consequences," Taylor consoled her that night over another dinner of greasy burgers and far too many drinks at Bukowski's. "None of us know what's going to happen. All you have to do is show up every day of your life. Make a plan for that day, and that day only. If it works, bravo. If it doesn't, well, you've only screwed up one day. Bravo again. Nothing's in our control if you think about it. All we can do is deal with the day in front of us."

Camilla pushed down on her hamburger bun with her index finger until a small pothole formed. The white crushed dough reminded her of a soft, small belly. She stopped pushing.

"But what if I can't get past this?" she asked, her voice shaking because she wanted to cry, she needed to cry, but she couldn't cry anymore. Still, the pressure was there, a tea kettle with the spout cemented over with a wad of gum that swelled and threatened to shoot loose as the months went by.

"What if I can't stop missing him? I can't go on like this. Look at me. Two years and I'm still..." She didn't finish the sentence. Instead she took out her penknife but before she could open it, Taylor was shaking her head and ordering her to put it away.

"One day you're going to get us thrown out of here." Taylor paused. Reaching into her sunny yellow messenger bag, she pulled out a small wooden box no bigger than a postcard and placed it between them standing it on its end. "Check it out. I'm doing a series."

Camilla was hardly in the mood. Here she was destroyed by missing Nico so much, and it was just so typical of Taylor to turn the conversation to her and her precious art.

"Go on. You know you're curious," Taylor said, smiling.

When Camilla lowered it so she could open the lid, Taylor laughed. "Hold it up, silly. It doesn't open. There's a spyhole to look through."

Taylor's laughing rankled her more. Still, she did as Taylor wanted and put the spyhole up to her eye. Camilla knew she was expected to look and give off exclamations of surprise and wonder over the sheer brilliance of it all as Taylor always demanded whenever she showed her whatever new object she was working on. Camilla might be attached too much to people, Taylor might be right to call her Earlobe whenever she got too fixated, but Taylor was equally attached to *things*. For all of her spouting Buddhism and not being attached to anything, Taylor didn't follow her own advice. Camilla couldn't muster it up now to cover her mouth in mock awe now and follow through with her end of this dance. She was stung by Taylor's ability to move on whenever Camilla brought up that she still wasn't over the pain of losing Nico. Taylor had never been a mother. She'd never understand.

Camilla squinted.

The inside was painted the color of army camouflage fatigues. Little rubber army men played out a battle scene. In the center was a nurse figurine with a tiny white cotton bandana covering her eyes.

"It's called 'See No Evil.'"

Still smarting, Camilla couldn't stop herself. She told Taylor, "More like, 'See No Subtlety.'" She put the box down on the table and looked away, sipped her beer.

Silently, Taylor tucked the box back inside her bag and turned back to Camilla. "Look, if you can't go on, I'd say that qualifies as DEFCON 1," Taylor said, as if they hadn't left off the conversation.

She lit a cigarette first for Camilla and then for herself. "Here," she said. "You won't disfigure the furniture with this." She took a long drag, eyeing Camilla, and blew out a lungful of smoke.

"Defon one. And that would mean what, exactly?" Camilla asked, pushing her uneaten plate away. She was pleased that they were talking about her problems again, but she didn't want to get mired down in Taylor's funny military quips and lose sight of how desperate she really had been feeling lately. It had started to feel like the more time passed, the more she imagined holding Nico in her arms again, or walking him to his pre-school, past a retired crossing guard who held up traffic for them on the street. He was the last thing she thought of before going to sleep at night and the first thing she thought of when she awakened. Not that she was getting much sleep. Her sleep was often fitful and on the surface of being disrupted. Sometimes when she woke, she was riddled with the question of whether she had made the right decision to leave. Not because she missed Allison. She didn't; she was afraid of her. She missed *him*. She ached to be with him again. Time heals all wounds was a lie. Sometimes time only resulted in the wound getting infected.

Taylor waved her cigarette in the air, and, shaking her head, told her, "DEF-*CON* 1. The things you don't know. You better find Nana Taylor when the bomb goes off is all I can say."

"*Taylor.*"

Taylor leaned in as if she was about to unveil a hush hush secret on WikiLeaks.

"DEFCON 5 is your everyday normal day. Just the ordinary threats. DEFCON 1, we go on the offense."

"Jesus." Camilla fell back against the wooden booth.

"You need to have a backup plan," Taylor said, exhaling another plume of smoke. "You have to be ready. If you can't go on like this, you—we—need to do something.

Camilla raised her eyebrows at this. "What are you—"

Taylor ground her cigarette out as if it were the enemy and reached for the check.

"We do something so unexpected she won't know what hit her or how to react. Something for *him*." Taylor held up the drinks check. "I got this. You have enough problems to deal with."

Before they arrived at Taylor's apartment in Boston they had hatched the plan to build the treehouse.

⁂

By the time Camilla climbed up to the fourth rung on the ladder against the oak tree in the backyard at the old house, she realized it was tilting. She hadn't stuck its feet into the dirt deeply enough, and now its metal shoes were sliding on top of the soft pine needles. *Come on, get going*, she admonished herself. *You only have a week.* She was counting on Allison sticking to her annual one-week Fourth of July vacation with "the team" in Wellfleet, something Camilla was forced to be part of and had suffered through almost every year. After a year's break when Nico was born, "the team" resurfaced in Allison's life and the group vacation was back on. The irony was not lost on her that the obligatory week away was now the only thing making her plan possible.

Climbing down, she grabbed hold of the ladder and pounded it down more securely. The vibration hit her right middle finger, setting off a cascade of pain like she'd closed a car door on it. She'd had a bad accident when she was four years old while carrying some milk bottles and nearly lost that finger. Now, she instinctively did what she always did when she caught it wrong: she stuck it in her mouth and sucked where the heaviest rope ring of stitches still were visible.

"Ooh boy, that hurts," she heard a voice behind her. "You whacked yourself good."

The next-door neighbor, Sam Peck, was standing there, sweaty and red-faced in his too-tight bicycle shorts and wife beater, neither of which, Camilla thought, he had the body or the personality for.

"Imagine," Allison used to say, shaking her head, whenever they saw Sam walking around in his adjacent backyard in those bicycle shorts that now had the appearance of sausage wrappings. "That man stood in front of the mirror this morning and said, 'Damn, I look good.'"

This was when Allison could still make Camilla laugh, which she did, often.

Camilla, in her head (and to Allison in those better days) called him Pecksniff, the bogus surveyor and architect in Dickens's *Martin Chuzzlewit*, who actually never designed or built anything, but interjected his opinions about houses whenever he could. From the day Allison and Camilla had moved into their Victorian house, Pecksniff the neighbor was quick to offer all kinds of advice on their home, secure in the knowledge that he had lived next door for twenty years of owners coming and going. He was fond of saying, "I'll unlast you all." The first time he said it Camilla thought she'd misheard him. But no, "Unlast" it was, every time he said it, which was frequently.

"You want to use an oil-based paint on those shingles," he'd told her once when she'd run into him on an otherwise empty path in the nearby woods.

"That's a peony tree, you got there, not a bush. A peony *tree*." This tidbit he offered while standing on his tiptoes and spying over their six-foot fence as Camilla watered their back gardens.

Another day, he insisted on joining her as she was gardening out on their adjoining side property. There was no fence there, only their two gardens running right up to the imaginary property line, like East and West Germany. Pecksniff sat down right on that line, bicycle shorts on and a beer bottle dangling from his hand, as he advised her with a knowing smile, "You know that stove you got in there is an original 1920 O'Keefe. You ever want to get rid of it, I'd be glad to take it off your hands. Not a problem."

Pecksniff rubbed his buzz cut then and exhaled loudly, as if the idea of the physical labor *that* would entail could only be expressed through sounds. Camilla thought of a favorite saying by the Greek philosopher Theophrastus: "In the proffered services of the busybody there is much of the affectation of kind-heartedness, and little efficient aid."

The stove was a 1947 Garland—not a 1920 O'Keefe—whose pilot lights were constantly on the fritz, resulting in a perpetual whiff of gas in their kitchen. Allison and Camilla replaced it with a Wolf and gave the Garland to the very appreciative deliveryman and his son.

Now, here was Pecksniff sniffing around in what was once her backyard when all she wanted was to go unnoticed for the week of treehouse building. How long he had been standing there she didn't know.

"Wacha doing?" he asked, snapping the waistband of his cycle shorts. Before she could answer, he went on, "You know that tree is prone to gypsy moths. Might not be a good idea to build anything on it." He gestured to her wood pile and tools.

"Winter moths," Camilla said under her breath as she began to climb the ladder with one of the two-by-fours dragging after her. "And we sprayed for them."

"What's that?" Pecksniff asked. He lifted the tail end of the two-by-four, which almost threw her off the ladder.

"Don't do that!" Camilla yelled down at him.

"Geez! I was only trying to help," Pecksniff snapped, but he let go of his end. He started to climb up behind her.

"Please don't come up here!" she said quickly as she slid the two-by-four far out across a couple of the thickest tree limbs. She began to climb down the ladder, forcing him to do the same.

"Look, I appreciate your help but I really don't need it and I just want to do this myself," Camilla said when they both were back on solid ground.

Pecksniff rubbed his buzz cut again. "We haven't seen you around for a while." He stared at her. Besides his penchant for too-tight bicycle shorts, Pecksniff's other constant characteristic was his Pug-like eyes, with their ability to always seem as if they were teary or soulful.

"Oh please," Allison had said when Camilla mentioned that to her after they'd first met Pecksniff and his wife, a woman who looked astonishingly like the Saturday Night Live androgynous character Pat. "His eyes are not *soulful*. They're goopy. You always romanticize everything. He looks like he has pink eye."

Those goopy eyes were now fixed on Camilla, waiting for an answer. Instead she walked over to the pile and pulled around her waist the stiff carpenter's work belt she'd bought along with everything else the night before at Home Depot. She could feel Pecksniff's goopy eyes on her as she buckled the belt and filled it with lag screws, the drill, and a ratchet set. She could feel them as she pulled out another two-by-four. She began to climb back up the ladder. *Go away*, she thought.

"I get it, Milly. You don't want to talk about your problems," Pecksniff called up as she slid the wood onto the same tree limbs but six feet away from the first two-by-four, snuggled against the trunk itself.

"Hey, Al knows you're here, right?" he suddenly asked.

The only thing that saved her then from panicking and falling out of the tree was the absurdity of him calling Allison "Al." Al, as if he and she were on such intimate terms. No one would have the balls to call her Al. Camilla started to laugh. If "Al" *had* been there, she would've shot him one of her Godfather smiles and then sliced up his sausage legs, cooked them up on a spit, and sold them around the corner at the town park as kebabs, burnt and all.

⚜ ⚜ ⚜ ⚜

Camilla knew that Pecksniff could hear the familiar screeching sound of a lag screw being stripped as she leaned as hard as she could into the power drill. But she refused to give up in front of him.

He hadn't left. He'd sat down on the ground, his chubby legs awkwardly crossed, his palms on the ground so that he could lean back and watch her. For fifteen minutes she'd been trying to drill one of the screws through the two-by-four into the tree trunk.

The screw had gone halfway in before hitting what felt like a cement wall. The problem was she couldn't get enough purchase on it. She was straddling a tree limb. She needed a better angle. She cursed Taylor for not showing up when she had promised she would.

"Look, I'll come later, I promise," Taylor had said that morning on the phone, her voice slurry with lack of sleep or an abundance of alcohol—or both. It was six o'clock in the morning and Taylor had just gotten home from some party after a public art exhibition reception at Boston's Institute of Contemporary Art.

"Just once I wish you had follow-through," Camilla complained, and hung up the phone.

"Damn it," she muttered now. All she was doing was stripping the screw. The drill bit and screw were so hot she couldn't touch them. She tried to reverse them out, but they remained stuck.

"Those oaks are tougher than you think," Pecksniff called up, laughing.

"That isn't helping," Camilla blurted out. She couldn't stop herself. *Don't engage, don't engage,* she reminded herself.

"Wait a minute," Pecksniff said, and before she could stop him, he was scrambling up the ladder again.

"I don't need—"

"Yeah, yeah, give it here." When she didn't, he quickly lifted the drill out of her hands, and shoving himself between her and the tree, almost upset her delicate balance, forcing her to move back on the limb.

"Watch it!"

"Yep, that's the heartwood you're stuck in," Pecksniff told her.

He put his face so close to the screw that his nose was touching the bark. "You know, it's really the klingon in the tree's core that makes it so strong. You can practically smell the stuff. Nature's own best glue," he added and chuckled at his own joke.

"*Lignin*," Camilla muttered.

Pecksniff looked over his shoulder at her. "What was that?"

"I think you smell the screw," she lied, rather than fill him in on Tree Infrastructure 101. "Can you get it to go in?"

The drill buzzed loudly and the screw screeched against the hardwood's center as Pecksniff put his full weight into it. Then there was silence.

"Well, one down," he said, and looking back at her on the limb, smiled. "Hand me another screw will ya?"

Reluctantly, Camilla did. She had wanted to build the treehouse herself, or at the most with Taylor's help. That seemed fitting as they'd both hatched the plan for it. It was to be a gift for Nico, yes, but she also looked at it as penance for her leaving. Although Doris, her therapist, could tell her during every therapy session that she had not had any other choice but to leave, still Camilla wondered if that was something she told herself to feel better, to stop feeling so guilty. If Pecksniff helped, then the whole idea became a community project, an it-takes-a-village show of togetherness and love. Then where was the act of contrition? Where was the absolution? What chance then could she have to hear *Et ego te absolvo a peccatis tuis*? The Greeks believed that only the Gods could absolve someone of their guilt from a heinous act. They required the sinner to perform some act that would prove their worth. Heracles had ten labors before he was set free from the Furies for killing his wife and children. When two of the labors were disqualified, two more were added, including going down into Hell.

Camilla had done the worst thing you can do as a mother: she had left her child. What would her absolution be? All she had was this treehouse.

I've had it too damn easy, she thought as the drill started up again. *I only have to build this little treehouse, and I can't even do that on my own.* Her feet swung a little in the breeze as she sat on her tree limb, watching Pecksniff do the hard work. She imagined Nico swinging his feet as he sat on the edge of the treehouse's floor, not a care in the world, happy to be in his little home, his sanctuary. Built by his *other* mother.

She tapped Pecksniff on the shoulder. The drill stopped and Pecksniff turned to look at her. She held out her hand.

"I have to do it," she said.

"But—"

She moved her hand closer to the drill, shaking her head.

"I have to do it," she repeated, her eyes filling. She shook her head again and stared down into the garden. She added, "Please," her hand reaching blindly out in the air.

"Okay," Pecksniff said reluctantly, handing her the drill. Still, Camilla wouldn't look at him as her fingers closed around the drill. "But, if you need anything, just holler," he added. "Anything at all. I'm here."

As he clambered down the ladder, Camilla thought of Oscar Wilde saying, "It is the confession, not the priest, which gives us absolution." She watched as Pecksniff lumbered away. But, right before he went through the gate, he suddenly turned, gave her a tight-lipped smile, and waved. It was a barely there, short wave. The kind of wave you give to someone you're going to miss, the sadness, the weight of it, preventing any kind of a flourish. You're on the pier and the ferry taking your friend away is chugging slowly backward, the distance between you immutable, growing. Good-bye.

Benjamin

Camilla had almost finished nailing down part of the plywood flooring on to the two-by-fours when she heard a small voice from below somewhere nearby.

"Hello?" the voice said. She immediately could hear the nervousness in the voice, the almost pleading quality of it.

"Hello?" it said again. "Daddy?"

It was Benjamin, the eight-year-old from the house that was behind where Camilla was perched in the tree. Benjamin had been born shortly after Allison and Camilla had moved in, and when Nico was born Camilla had imagined the two boys would grow up together, that the older Benjamin would look out for Nico his entire life, like a big brother. She imagined them playing with trucks and then riding bicycles together. Being on the same soccer teams after school. Forming a secret club in the treehouse she was building now.

"Hello," Benjamin called out again, louder. "Daddy?"

Camilla heard him bang on his back door.

"Daddy!"

Camilla had the urge to call to him, or to climb

down and see what the problem was. But she wasn't there to fix anyone else's problems, she reminded herself. She was there for one purpose. One thing only. To finish building a treehouse. She began to hammer the plywood again. She slid another plywood piece next to it, completing half of the floor. She began to hammer nail after nail.

"Milly," Benjamin's voice wafted to her, close by. Very close by. When Camilla turned her head she saw that Benjamin was almost at the top of the ladder, clutching the rung, white-knuckled, for dear life. He was a beautiful child who looked like he belonged in a commercial where a throng of smartly clothed kids are laughing as they eat candied apples on hay bales. Tall and lanky, he looked older than his eight years. From a distance, his lips were a beautiful ruby red. His blond hair was close to whiteness, especially in the summer. Once, Camilla had made the mistake of calling him a little tow-head and for weeks afterward, Benjy had been upset, repetitively asking her whether she meant his big toe or his small toe. She tried to explain that calling him a tow-head had to do with the color of flax, that the word "tow" was from the Old English for spinning, which only made him cry more.

"Oh, for Pete's sakes," Allison said. "He's five. He doesn't know what flax is." Squatting down so that her eyes were level with Benji's, she said, "It's a color, honey. It's almost white. You know like sugar. Camilla's just saying your blond hair is so light it's almost white."

His height and beauty had done their share of surprising adults when they approached and instead were greeted by a boy who spoke much too loudly and repetitively for his age. Up close you realized, too, that his red lips weren't a painter's dream. They were severely chapped from constant, uncontrollable drooling. Now his face was smeared with dirt and what Camilla could see were tear tracks.

"I'm locked out," he said too loudly, overcompensating for the trembling that Camilla could hear in his voice.

"Don't move," Camilla said. She crawled over to him. "Here, take my hand."

But Benjamin shook his head, holding on tighter to the top rung. His bottom lip quivered.

"Benjamin, take my hand. It's okay. Come see what I've done."

When he still resolutely wouldn't budge, she said softly, "It's a treehouse for you and for Nico. Don't you want to see it?"

In spite of not liking anyone to touch him, Benjamin took her hand and allowed himself to be pulled the rest of the way onto the platform. He sat next to Camilla, practically in her lap, both of his hands wrapped around Camilla's forearm like a monkey bar on the school playground. Camilla watched as he slowly looked around, first at what she'd built so far, and then down toward his own house.

"Wow. You can see everything from up here. There's my house, Milly," he said, and, loosening one of his hands, pointed. "There's my house," he repeated. His other hand dropped off her.

"What happened? Where's your dad?" Camilla asked.

Benjamin shrugged, and then jerked as if he'd almost lost his balance by doing so. "Whoa!" he cried.

"You're okay, you're okay," Camilla said, briefly touching him on his shoulder. "Where's your dad?"

"Nico will love this treehouse. I love this treehouse. This is our treehouse. This is our treehouse, Milly," Benjamin shouted. "This is our treehouse, Milly!"

"Yes, this is your treehouse, Benjy," Camilla said back rotely. Unless she acknowledged what he was saying, he would repeat the same sentence over and over for twenty-four hours or until he became hoarse. Within a year after he was born he'd been diagnosed as autistic.

"He's on the spectrum. Caroline isn't taking it well," Malcolm, his father, had bluntly told Camilla and Allison a few weeks after they'd received the bad news. Caroline, Benjamin's mother, distraught and her hope depleted that whatever was making her boy different would go away as he got older, took to her bedroom where she spent much of her day staring out a window that looked out on an elementary school's playground, the "normal" children playing there a constant reminder of what her son would never do or be. It was something out of Dickens, Camilla had thought, calling her Miss Havisham in her head. The pale oval face of a woman watching all the children playing tag and seesawing and swinging.

The diagnosis had turned everything topsy-turvy for the Freemans, yes, but for Camilla as well. She thought how Benjamin, from the Hebrew meaning son of my right hand, was not to be the right hand of anyone, ever. He was not to be depended on to safeguard Nico or anyone else. When she heard about the diagnosis, Camilla saw the universe flipped upside down: a younger Nico would be taking care of Benjamin his whole life. They would never go to the same school, the one on the other side of Benjamin's yard. Nico would, but not Benjamin. They would play trucks together, but Camilla imagined that often that would end in tears as Benjamin always had to have a certain color truck, the specifications changing daily, bewildering Nico, who tried his best to offer the right truck before Benjamin would start his chanting: bluetruck, bluetruck, bluetruck, his volume pitching inexorably into a scream.

Would they really use the treehouse together? she thought now. Camilla was shocked that Benjamin had had the courage to climb the ladder at all, yet alone to the top. He was a timid boy, his weakness a glowing aura, his eyes never quite connecting with you, with his surroundings. Or at least that's what you thought at first before you realized the opposite was true: he took in everything. He took in so much he had to avert his eyes to provide some respite from the colors, from the movement, from life's cacophony. It was all too much.

Perhaps Camilla was wrong and Nico and Benjamin would play together in the treehouse. They'd develop a secret language up there. It'd be their sanctuary together. Their safe place from their families. From the world. *As long as Allison allows it*, Camilla thought bitterly as she lightly touched Benjamin's shoulder again.

Benjamin looked at her now, and as if guessing what she was thinking, gave Camilla a sly smile. "Daddy's music is too loud," he said. "Too loud." He covered his ears and laughed.

Camilla laughed, too. She placed her hands over his on his ears.

"Is this better?" she asked, smiling.

Benjamin nodded, but he slid his hands out from under hers.

"How about we go down the ladder together and I talk to your dad?" Camilla said.

He shook his head.

"Where is Nico? I want Nico."

Camilla sighed. "Nico's away for a few days, honey. He went to the beach. He'll be back on Sunday."

He shook his head again. "I want Nico. Nico Nico Nico Nico." He picked at a scab on his knee, flicking at it each time he said, "Nico."

When he went all OCD, as Allison used to call it, Camilla struggled with not shouting, "Stop. Stop talking. Just stop!" She struggled with covering her own ears, as Benjamin had done while talking about his father's playing music too loudly. She struggled with matching the screaming boy in front of her with the boy that was also an artistic genius at eight years old. He'd always been attracted to collecting miniature dolls—he called them Little Person 1, 2, 3, all the way to 100. No matter how many there were in his stable he always knew their numbers. He never wavered, or scrunched up his face like an old person trying to remember the details. He knew. He set them up in scenes of families in strife, around tiny Formica kitchen tables or on French sofas in front of fake fireplaces: Little Person 1 choking Little Person 2 as she reached for a bottle of milk. Little Person 45 pushing down Little Person 21 so that her face almost touched the plastic fire flames in the fireplace. He touched them lightly, moving them this way and that, perfecting the scene in ways he alone saw. Then, when everything was acceptable, he took out an artist pad and a box that once had housed Cuban cigars and now held perfectly sharpened colored pencils, each point an exact replica of the others, and he would draw the scene, not stopping until it was done.

It was Allison who discovered and then nurtured this talent of Benjamin's. One day when he was three years old, his father talked Camilla into watching him for two hours while he did the grocery shopping.

"Please," Malcolm pleaded, running his large hands over his bald shaved head as if he'd forgotten with all the chaos in his life that he had no hair. "He'll be good. Won't you, Benjy?"

Benjy, crouching by the screen door, had looked up from where he was trying to place the wire threads exactly so. Then he looked back to the screen, his bottom lip folded into his teeth, his front teeth morphing into an unattractive overbite.

Allison was upstairs in her study, trying to finish follow-up calls to her patients. Camilla hesitated, and in that moment Malcolm quickly uttered a "thank you so much" and ran out the front door so as not to disturb his son.

Benjamin hadn't been good. Not at all. Ten minutes after his father left, Benjy, frustrated that the back door was uncooperative to his persistent alignment, began to wail, and, throwing himself face down, kicked his sneakers and pelted the floor with his fists. In no time, Allison was there next to Camilla, asking what all the noise was about. Somehow they got him sitting up at the kitchen table where he fixated on a plastic pouch with Allison's highlighters, a variety of colors that she used to indicate different comments on her residents' patients notes.

"Rainbow rainbow rainbow," Benjy chanted, forgetting about the screen door.

"Okay, Picasso, they're all yours," Allison said, smiling. She brought over one of her yellow legal pads and placed it in front of him. "Go for it."

Benjy stared at the highlighters with awe and then straight into Allison's eyes. It made Camilla's heart pinch and she almost clapped her hands, but she knew that would ruin the moment—whatever this moment was. So, she said nothing, showed nothing. Later that night, as they were getting into bed, Allison suggested that Camilla might be more encouraging of Benjy.

"Imagine growing up in that house? It would make me autistic, for god's sake," she said. "Art will save that kid, trust me. If he's saved at all. God, I hope our baby won't be like that."

Camilla worried secretly about that, too. When they had been approached by their OB/GYN with the question of whether they wanted an amnio procedure to determine whether Nico the fetus was destined for a life like Benjamin, Camilla had tried to persuade Allison to do it despite the risk of the procedure itself injuring him.

"And what if they tell us something is wrong with him? What then?" Allison asked her.

"We'll have options," Camilla said softly, wary of where the conversation was headed.

Allison's face hardened. "Oh, I get it. You'll want to get rid of him if the news isn't exactly what you want, is that it?" Allison said, her voice growing louder. Then she shouted "Baby Killer" at Camilla and stormed upstairs.

Allison had been right about Benjamin, though. Art had saved him the past five years. No matter how out of control Benjamin became, if you put a pen or a brush and some paints in front of him he became as quiet as a monk, studiously recreating the pots and pans hanging overhead or the refrigerator or the spice rack on the wall.

And Nico wasn't like Benjy at all. Nico could stare into your eyes until you looked away.

"He's an old soul," strangers told her in grocery store lines, at the playground, and around the neighborhood when Camilla walked Nico in a stroller hoping the motion would put him to sleep, his eyes wide open, a smile on his face as he took in everything like one big data dump.

"We have some new crayons in the house, do you want to see them?" Camilla lied now to divert Benjamin in the tree.

He immediately moved toward the ladder.

"Hey, not so fast," Camilla said and grabbed his belt to make him stop.

"I have to go down first, buddy," she told him.

They went down slowly, Camilla pausing on each rung to make sure his feet landed safely first before she moved another notch below him. She imagined doing this for Nico. No, she would never be able to do this for Nico. She would never sit in the treehouse with Nico and then when it was time for them to go into supper, she would never say to him, "Wait. I have to go down first, buddy." She could say it for her neighbor's—her ex-neighbor's—child but never for her own. She would never know whether Nico liked the treehouse, or who he played with up there. She would never know if he would even see the treehouse. Perhaps he and Allison would return home in the dark and he would've fallen asleep in the car, and Allison would carry him straight to bed. Perhaps as Allison turns to leave his room, in her peripheral vision she sees the treehouse in the moonlight and for a moment she thinks she is seeing things. Perhaps she questions for a second that she's in the right house. Realizing what it is, she races down the stairs, grabs up a toolbox, and proceeds to take the whole thing down, efficiently, quietly, like a mudslide silently makes everything disappear as if it never existed: plants, trees, houses. It will be gone by the morning, before Nico wakes up. The only sign of it the small holes in the tree branches where it had been nailed in.

Camilla realized with a pang that she'd never know if this was how it would play out. When she left the house for good, she left the knowing. She gave herself up to the unknowable. The darkness. She'd chosen blindness.

Pausing on a ladder rung, overcome with sadness, she hugged Benjamin's tiny legs, stopping him from going farther.

"Tickling," he said, quietly. Just the once. Tickling. And then he giggled. The feathery laugh of a young boy. It almost made Camilla sob, but she caught herself, and, forcing herself to let go of the boy's soft legs, she continued down the ladder.

When they reached the bottom, she squatted down to his eye level. She always had to fight the urge to wipe his mouth for him, to soothe his rough lips with Chapstick or Vaseline. His eyes settled on something over her shoulder. A bird? A tulip? Pine needles on the ground? Did it really matter? He was a beautiful boy looking at everything that was alive in this yard, this world.

"Hey, buddy," Camilla said. "I just remembered I don't have keys to get into the house. Let's go see if your dad has them, okay?"

"Keys keys keys," Benjamin shouted and took off like a shot for his house. "Hurry, Milly. Milly, hurry!"

As she walked around the fence dividing their properties, he was already banging on his back door and there was Malcolm, his father, letting him in, with a look of bewilderment on his face when he saw Camilla standing in his driveway, her tool belt jauntily resting on her hip, her face trying to settle against the tug of crying.

Malcolm

"So, you're back," Malcolm said as he walked toward Camilla in the driveway. Benjy had disappeared into the house. Malcolm said it as if it were a statement of fact, not a question, not something that was hard to believe. He said it like it was inevitable, only a matter of time.

For a minute, she thought how easy it would be to slip back into the neighborhood, to return to her old life of chatting with the neighbors in her customary attempts to soften any bad perceptions they had of her and Allison. Sometimes their fights had gotten out of control. Right before she finally left, during an escalating argument in the garden, Camilla had run into the house and had locked the back door behind her so that she could keep Allison out for a few minutes. Whenever she tried to escape from Allison within the house during a battle, Allison often pursued her into one of the bedrooms or bathrooms, continuing to badger her until she wore Camilla down into apology and concession. This time they were outside. Stymied by the locked door, Allison put her fist through the glass, reached through the remaining jagged glass, unlocked the door, and stormed in, enraged by Camilla locking her out of "her own home."

"Don't you ever do that again!" Allison shouted at her, shaking from anger. "Are you insane? What the hell is wrong with you?"

Camilla froze on the spot by the kitchen counter. Seeing anyone smash a glass door was frightening enough; living with that person and knowing that she depended on her hands for her livelihood and, losing all reason, went ahead and did it anyway, was terrifying to her.

Camilla still carried the shame that the neighbors must have heard something during that fight, and others. She looked away from Malcolm, toward the crab apple tree in his side yard. Before Benjamin had been born, Malcolm used to complain to them about the mess it left behind: the crushed, impossible-to-rake-up pink flowers in October followed by the rotting, brown, mushy, cherry-sized fruit on the ground in November. Behind his back, Allison called him Malcontent instead of Malcolm. This day the tree was in bloom, the delicate pink flowers sending out a sweet smell even as the dreaded midget apples were appearing. Camilla could smell Malcolm's cologne, too: a musky, bourbon-like scent.

"Camilla?" Malcolm said, his look of bewilderment changing into one of concern when she didn't answer him.

"Um, no," Camilla said, turning back to him. "Just here to build Nico a treehouse."

"In this heat," Malcolm said. Again, not so much a question as a confirmation. Like it was the most normal thing in the world for her to do. Malcolm was one of those people whose career acutely matched his personality. He was a Clinical Manager at a Boston hospital, paid to be unflappable when multiple deadlines and competing demands from you-can't-say-no-to-me physicians came crash-carting in. He was paid to ignore the chaos around him and get the thing—whatever the thing was—done. And under budget. Camilla thought his name had been perfectly chosen for him by his parents: in Shakespeare's *Macbeth*, Malcolm III was one of the sons of King Duncan and his nickname was Canmore or Big Head. Malcolm the neighbor had such a head: blocky, like something carved out of the side of a mountain, the top of it a boulder of shaved baldness. His body was stocky, too. A Rock 'Em Sock 'Em Robot toy from the sixties. He wasn't exactly good-looking, but Camilla could see how the hospital nurses would seek him out when they needed a bit of ballast, a buoy, something to steady their stressed nerves. Camilla watched him run his hand over his round pate, the same movement he had done when he'd come over to their house that night and told them that his new son was "on the spectrum." She wondered if it was a sign that he was nervous.

"A treehouse? That's an undertaking," Malcolm said to her. "I see you're all geared up for it." He pointed at her tool belt.

"How's Caroline?" Camilla asked.

"The same," Malcolm said, his hand rubbing the back of his neck now. The back of his neck was covered in a downy fur, as was his back, which Camilla knew from once seeing him mowing the lawn without a shirt on. It was obvious he was a hairy man and yet he shaved his head. Camilla had always wondered why. To stay cool? But he did it in the winter, too, preferring to wear one of those hats with the faux fur earflaps as he shoveled or shoved the snowblower up and down his rather long driveway that separated their houses with the fence. Was it an attempt to be hip? His penchant for Hawaiian shirts argued against that. Besides, Camilla had thought, he'd be much more attractive if he did let his hair grow. If his neck and back was any sign of how thick his hair would be, he should let it grow. Maybe he was one of those men cursed with a carpet of hair covering every inch of his body but his head.

"I have the week off," Malcolm was saying. "Usually, we go to Yarmouth, you know?"

Camilla nodded. She remembered that his parents owned a house there, and Malcolm, Caroline, and Benjy would go every year to get away from the madness of another Boston Fourth.

"But you're not—"

"No, not this year," Malcolm cut her off, shaking his head. "She thinks my parents hover too much." As soon as he said it, his neck turned pink. "It's going to be super hot this week. Tough week to be building anything, yet alone an entire house. Someone helping you?"

"It's only a treehouse, Malcolm," Camilla said, but she was thrown slightly by the news about the hot temperatures. She thought the weatherman had said warmish weather, not hot. How hot was "super hot"?

"Once you build it, you know that Benjy's going to want one, too."

"I'm sorry," Camilla said automatically. She also automatically heard Taylor's voice saying, "Stop apologizing for things you're not responsible for. Jesus, while you're at it why don't you say you're sorry for China's occupation of Tibet, or global warming?"

Taylor was right. She did need to stop apologizing, to stop feeling so guilty for everything. Doris said it was all part of being a "fixer." Camilla had two modes of going through the world: either fixing the problems of the world or apologizing for them when she couldn't. It was a survival holdover from the years she'd spent with Allison. Taylor said she should have her own reality TV show called *The Apologetic Chef* because every time Camilla served someone a dish she'd cooked she'd say, "This didn't turn out as good as it usually does, I'm sorry," or "I'm sorry, you probably don't want to even taste this."

Malcolm shrugged. "He'll probably be playing with Nico every day in this one and won't need his own, right?" Camilla debated if he was trying to be sarcastic. She didn't know what the right answer was. She was simply here to build the treehouse. Past that, she had no jurisdiction, no leverage over whether Benjy would be allowed in the treehouse or not. She wondered how long it had been since Malcolm or Benjy had been invited over by Allison. How long it had been since Allison had called out hello or waved to Malcolm, or had been in the backyard, or their driveway as Camilla was now?

"She doesn't let Benjy come over anymore," Malcolm said, as if reading her mind. "She put a stop to that a week or so after I saw you leave."

Camilla looked away. He'd *seen*. She felt her neck getting hot, and knew it was a lot redder than Malcolm's had been. Then, she was immediately back there in the house on the day she finally left.

※※※※

It was a Saturday. They'd eaten breakfast. Scrambled eggs, sausage, toast. Nico was in his high chair at the kitchen table with them. He was two years old. He held his sausage stub in his fist and waved it in the air like a wand, touching Camilla's elbow with it as if casting a spell. "Abacabra froggy," he called out. Camilla and Allison laughed at that.

"Eat," Allison told him, pointing at his scrambled eggs.

Nico shook his head. Instead he shoved the sausage in his mouth. He knew it was too big of a piece. His mouth could barely chew it, and chunks immediately began falling to the table.

"Hey mister wizard, you're losing it," Camilla said, smiling.

Allison didn't find it funny. "What are you teaching him when I'm at work?"

Nico tried to say, "Mister, mister," but the sausage mess jammed him up. He started to laugh and then coughed, spraying a few of the mashed bits.

"He's eating, isn't he?" Camilla told her, laughing only because he was.

Tired of the huge wad, Nico spit it out onto his plastic Thomas the Train plate.

"Great, just great," Allison said, her voice becoming low and mean. Standing up, she grabbed his plate and whisked it away to the sink. "I don't have time to clean it all up."

Picking up the rest of the plates, Camilla joined her at the sink. "It's okay. I'll do it. He ate most of it."

Allison faced her. She sighed. "I know. I just have this deadline. We're trying to get a manuscript out by Monday."

"I'll clean up. Go. Do your paper."

Allison frowned. "I really don't want to go in. There's only a few edits."

"So, finish it here."

Finally, Allison smiled. "Yeah, right. You know that'll be impossible. I'll want to be with him." She beamed at Nico in his high chair. He was busy turning his sippy cup upside down on the kitchen table and then righting it again.

"I'll take him food shopping," Camilla told her. "We need some things anyway."

"Okay," Allison said reluctantly. "Come back fast though, okay?"

Camilla laughed. "That kind of defeats the purpose, doesn't it?"

"Stop giving me a hard time," Allison snapped, and then immediately added, "I'm sorry. I don't mean to be a bitch."

Camilla almost told her, "Then don't be," but thinking better of it, said instead, "We won't be long."

She intended on driving straight to the nearest Whole Foods Market, but when they got there the parking lot was the typical Saturday morning stress-mess with too many cars and no spaces left. So, she jumped back on Fresh Pond Parkway, thinking she'd try another one that was twenty minutes away. Nico amused himself in his car seat in the back, playing with his Sprout Cubby tablet. The morning had been on the verge of plummeting into another spin out. Camilla was consoled now, though, by hearing the squeaky chirps of Chica, Sprout television's cartoon chicken, every time Nico matched the screen's animal playing cards correctly. Nico loved Chica. The chunky chicken let loose with her high-pitched peeps whenever she got excited, which would send Nico into fits of giggling.

Camilla's cell phone rang. It was Taylor.

"Hi, stranger." When Camilla filled her in, Taylor told her, "I'll come meet you. We can get coffee."

Camilla hesitated, but then she told her yes. It had been weeks since they'd even talked on the phone. The last time they'd seen each other was four months before when Camilla had run into her one night at Toys "R" Us. Allison had stayed home to put Nico to bed and sent Camilla out with a list of toddler educational DVDs to buy, although Nico wasn't two yet then. Taylor was there to buy a squadron of rubber toy soldiers and an army tank. They talked for ten minutes, but Camilla began to get antsy. She needed to get home. Allison would be wondering where she was.

"Jesus, she's got you on a short leash," Taylor complained. "Look at you. Are you okay?"

Camilla took a step back, and then another. "I'm fine. Just busy. I have to go." She turned on her heels.

Taylor called after her. "I'm worried about you. Call me."

When she got home, Nico was asleep in his upstairs bedroom. Allison was at the kitchen table, paying bills.

"I got all of them," Camilla told her, taking the DVDs out of the bag and placing them on the table as if to prove it.

"Did you?" Allison closed her checkbook and stood up. "There must've been quite a line," she said quietly, not looking at Camilla. She shuffled the stamped envelopes into a stack. "Well, I'm tired. I'm going to bed." She picked up the stack of paid bills and went upstairs.

It was only eight thirty. Although Camilla knew she shouldn't, she felt guilty as if she had done something. Something with Taylor that she should be ashamed of. Should she go after Allison and tell her about running into Taylor? Or would Allison accuse her of lying, of coming up with a story about their meeting being totally unplanned? Camilla began to tremble out of nervousness. She couldn't take another episode. Nico was asleep. As innocent as her running into Taylor was, better not to say anything. It was the only way they would have a peaceful night. Still, when Camilla slid into bed next to Allison, somehow she felt so much like a criminal that once she knew Allison was asleep, she slipped back out of the bed and stayed the rest of the night in the guest room.

Now, when she hung up from Taylor on the way to Whole Foods, she felt that same pinch of remorse, as if she had agreed to meet Taylor at a hotel. It was ridiculous. But, Nico was two years old now. He was talking. He was observant, fixating on strangers whenever they went to the supermarket, or to the park. What if when they got home he said something that would let on to Allison that Camilla had had coffee with Taylor? She felt the tremor start up in her fingers gripping the steering wheel. Her stomach clenched. She began to chastise herself for giving in to Taylor. She should've told her no. But then, Chica squeaked and Nico laughed, happy that he matched another two cards correctly. Camilla shook her head. She couldn't believe she'd almost been turning her toddler into a spy of sorts. *It's just coffee. I should be allowed to have coffee.* Allowed. How had her life become this?

Taylor was waiting for her at the supermarket's entrance when Camilla walked up, holding Nico's hand.

"Jesus, he's so big!" Taylor said, immediately squatting down to Nico's eye level on the sidewalk. "Hey, buddy. I'm Taylor."

Camilla started to walk away with him toward

the entrance. "Sorry, I don't have much time," she called over her shoulder to Taylor.

"Okay, Commander." Taylor quickstepped next to her as they made their way to the coffee bar inside the store. Camilla was dismayed to see there was a line of customers. Waiting, Taylor again squatted down to be at Nico's level. She asked him how old he was, and, pointing at the baked goods case, asked what his favorite cookie was. She wasn't like other adults who talked in a baby voice to kids or who asked questions but then didn't listen to the answers. As Taylor pointed to each of the cookies in the case, she waited for him to say whether he liked it or not before moving on to the next one. When she pointed to an oatmeal raisin cookie and Nico held his nose, Taylor told him, "Well, we're absolutely not getting a stinky oatmeal raisin cookie like that, are we?" Smiling when she spoke to him, Taylor told him that chocolate chip was her absolute favorite cookie too and they definitely needed to get two cookies. Grinning, Nico reached out to hold Taylor's hand. Camilla felt sick to her stomach. *Don't. Don't make him remember you*, she thought. When Taylor tried to engage Nico in a game of peek-a-boo, Camilla picked him up, claiming the line was moving. She was so nervous. She shouldn't have answered the phone. Nico would remember all of this and say something when they got home. Camilla was sure of it. She was just about to call the whole thing off when the cashier asked for their order.

Waiting for their drinks, Taylor began to tell Camilla a story, but Camilla was too nervous and preoccupied. She only half-listened to Taylor telling her about some woman that had gotten one of the South End warehouses to stage pop-up art exhibits.

Their two lattes and the bag of cookies finally appeared on the counter.

"Look, I'm sorry, this took too long," Camilla told Taylor, grabbing her coffee. "We have to go."

Taylor handed Nico his cookie. "Are you kidding?"

"I'll call you. I promise."

"Have I done something?"

Camilla shook her head, backing away as she held Nico in her arms. He swiveled his head around, the better to see Taylor. "No, Mommy," he said. He held his cookie out to Taylor as if he was trying to make amends for their sudden departure.

"I'll call you," Camilla said to Taylor. She turned before Taylor could say anything else and went quickly toward the grocery cart corrals at the front of the store. When Taylor started to follow her, Camilla told her, "Please. Don't. I need to go." After that, she threw the latte out and rushed through the shopping, speeding the cart up and down the aisles with Nico in the seat, pitching the items that Allison had put on the list into the cart as fast as she could. Luckily, Nico was fixated on eating his cookie. By the time she'd paid and they were in the parking lot, her heart was racing. She quickly buckled Nico in, his hand still grasping part of the cookie. She drove home as fast as she could.

Still, it wasn't fast enough. Allison was sitting outside on the front steps of the house, her phone next to her ear.

"I was just calling you," she said as Camilla got out of the car. She walked down to meet them, a tight smile on her face.

"You were?" Camilla tried to keep her voice level as she went around the car to get Nico.

"I got him," Allison said. "You get the bags." She

opened the door closest to Nico. "Where were you?"

Camilla popped the SUV's hatch. "What? Oh, Alewife was packed so we went to Central." Grabbing the three grocery bags, she followed Allison, who was carrying Nico, up the steps. Nico was finishing off his cookie, his lips and cheeks smeared with chocolate visible over Allison's shoulder.

"He hasn't had his lunch yet," Allison said grimly as she went through the front door. "Where'd you get it?"

Camilla placed the groceries on the kitchen counter. "What?" She began to put away the milk and mayonnaise and eggs.

"Why do you keep saying 'what'?" Allison took the last chunk of cookie out of Nico's fist. "Where'd you get *this*?"

"No, Mommy."

Camilla focused on pyramiding several apples in a bowl on the counter. Allison walked Nico over to the sink. She turned the water on. "You're a mess. Mommy needs to clean you up."

He shook his head. "Cookie!"

"Later," Allison told him, stifling any protest by scrubbing his face with a washcloth. "You can watch Barney, okay, honey?" Nico smiled and clapped his hands. He loved the purple dinosaur. Camilla breathed a sigh of relief. Normally, Allison used TV as a last resort for him, unless it was to watch an educational DVD. Barney was, according to Allison, the show for kids who rode the short bus. She rarely agreed to his watching it.

Camilla finished putting the food away while Allison dried Nico's face and settled him in the family room off the kitchen in front of the television. Camilla was about to go upstairs when Allison came back into the kitchen.

"So, where were you?"

Camilla froze in the entryway. She'd been wrong. They weren't going to move on from this. Not at all. It hit her in her bones that something bad was about to happen. She stared at the tile floor. She felt as if she was already leaving the room, though she could see her boots firmly standing there.

"Please, Allison," she said quietly, staring at her feet.

"Where were you? It's a simple question."

"I thought you wanted to work on your pap—"

"Where. Were. You."

Camilla looked up. "Please don't be mad." But Allison's face was already hard. Her fists were clenched at her sides, rammed against her jeans.

"We ran into Taylor," Camilla said in a rush. There. It was done. It was out in the ether, floating and smothering that room, like one of Taylor's stories about the canisters of Agent Orange blanketing Vietnam.

"I see." Allison glared at her.

"Allison, please. Don't make this into a bigger—"

"So, Taylor, who doesn't have a pot to piss in, came all the way over to shop at the most expensive—"

"Whatever it is you're thinking—"

Allison took a step toward her. She stabbed at the air with her hand. "I don't think. I *know*. You planned to see her and didn't want to tell me. So instead you lied. All that crap about giving me time to work on my paper. What else are you lying about?"

"She called me, I swear, when we were driving there."

Allison took another step toward Camilla. "Guess

what? I don't believe you." Her voice bordered on a hiss as she closed in. Camilla took a step back, afraid that Allison was going to come at her, but instead, Allison turned and walked quickly away toward the family room. Camilla felt a momentary sense of relief. Thank God. She'd been wrong. It was over.

Then Allison came back.

She was carrying Nico, who clutched his favorite fleece blanket to his chest, his face a horrible mixture of fear and whether he should yell about being snatched away from Barney.

"All you do is evade and lie to us!" Allison said, her voice rising as she walked straight toward Camilla. "You don't want us! You don't want a family! Go! Go and be with Taylor!"

Camilla turned and ran up the steps leading upstairs. She had to get away. She didn't want Nico to see any more of it. If she could get away, she could close a door between them and Allison would have to eventually calm down.

She almost made it to their bedroom when she realized that Allison was close behind her with Nico still in her arms. She'd run after her. Camilla stopped. Whimpering, Nico was plucking nervously at the fuzzy fleece.

"Please, you're scaring him," Camilla begged.

Too enraged to get a hold of herself, Allison snatched the blanket out of Nico's hands and shoved Camilla hard with it. Camilla fell back against the hallway wall, the fleece sticking for a moment from the impact against her chest before it fell to the floor. Nico wailed, ducking his head into Allison's shoulder. Stunned, Camilla began to cry.

"Stop it!" she cried, pushing off the wall.

"Look what you've done!" Allison yelled. She caressed Nico's cheek, telling him it would be all right. Then, she bent over to retrieve the blanket. When she did, Camilla darted past her, running back down the stairs. She didn't stop to think for a second about what she was doing. She grabbed her car keys from the hall table and threw the front door open. She was out on the front steps. Then, she was sprinting toward her car on the street. She was in the car, starting the engine. Her whole body shook—*hurry, hurry, before she gets here*—her fingers tightly gripped the stick shift and her feet began pressing the gas and the clutch pedals and then...

She was free.

≈≈≈≈

"How many years of torture can you take?" Taylor told her when Camilla showed up at Taylor's apartment ninety minutes later. "Waterboarding would've been fucking easier." She hugged Camilla and brought her inside.

Camilla slumped down on Taylor's couch. She'd finally stopped crying after sitting in her car outside of Taylor's home for close to an hour. She was exhausted, still shaky. She sniffed hard. Taylor sat down close to her.

"She could do whatever she wanted to me. Not *him*," Camilla told Taylor. She was staring at the tiled floor. "I won't have him—" She broke off and began to cry again. "He was so upset. She took his blanket and then..." Camilla tried, but couldn't finish the sentence. They sat for a moment in silence. Finally, Camilla looked up at Taylor. "It's over. I'm not going back."

"You've taken yourself out of the equation, Mills," Taylor said, kindly. "Thank God." She lightly knocked Camilla's thigh. "The war's over. Maybe now he'll have some peace."

≈≈≈≈

Camilla breathed in the scent of the crab apple blossoms in Malcolm's yard. How much had he heard or seen that day? She imagined him turning away from his bedroom window, after she'd driven away, and quietly going into his son's bedroom where he slipped in next to his son on his twin bed covered with superheroes so that he could breathe in Benjy's smell, taking comfort in the quiet of his own home, as crazy as that was with a wife who no longer left her dark room filled with grief.

"I'm sorry," Malcolm said quietly to her now. "I don't mean to embarrass you. It's not your fault. She never really liked Benjy."

Camilla looked at him. "No, she did, she gave him all those art supplies—"

Malcolm held up his hand. "It's okay, Milly. You don't have to make excuses for her. It is what it is. I know that she gave Benjy that. And I'll always be grateful to her for it. She should have given as much to you." He smiled wryly then, and Camilla could see why he was so successful at the hospital.

"He was locked out, you know," Camilla said. "Benjamin. He was locked out. I turned around and found him next to me up there on top of the ladder." Camilla pointed up to the platform she had made.

Malcolm smiled again. "Is that what he told you? It wasn't locked. He must've seen you and wanted you to notice him. He's into playacting these days. Last week he told everyone he was invisible. You know how kids are."

Malcolm looked back at his house, a pink blotch suddenly forming on his neck again. "Sorry. I should go see what he's up to. It was really good to see you, Milly."

He started to walk away, but when he was almost at his screen door he turned back.

"You know, for all her faults, for everything she did to you, Nico's a great kid, so maybe she's not all bad." He hesitated and smiled again. "But of course there's another option, too." Then he turned and opened the screen door, and disappeared.

Camilla was left wondering what the other option was. Was he referring to the nature versus nurture debate meaning Nico was simply born good? Or was he talking about an influence Camilla might have had on him, that although she had only been with him two of his four years, she'd left an imprint on him every bit as powerful as a strand of DNA.

Then she heard the familiar sound of a car with a bad muffler drive up and park, a door slam shut, and Taylor's familiar voice calling out, "Is the lady of the house home?"

Taylor

"Hey, you," Taylor said as Camilla returned through her gate. Taylor was standing at the base of the ladder, looking up into the tree, checking out the underside of the treehouse's partially built platform. Her brown ringlets glistened in the sun, still wet from her shower. Despite what Camilla knew had to have been a very late night, Taylor looked as beautiful as ever. Lack of sleep only deepened her wide cheekbones and softened her blue eyes to a pale grey. An internationally known photographer had included many shots of Taylor in Taschen-produced books of the cool kids at clubs and after-parties. Taylor always stood out as the center of the still life. Your eyes went directly to her in every photo.

Her brown curls naturally had that soft, unkempt look that usually was only achievable by most women after an hour of perfect tweaking and tugging and the applying of expensive hair product. Her lithe body was draped always in brightly colored, sexy cotton or linen that made you imagine hot days in tropical towns.

That hadn't always been the case, though. Previously, Taylor had always dressed, like Camilla, from head to toe in black: black, scuffed combat boots; black tight jeans; black studded belt; black hoodie with a black tee underneath. She started to dress in the Copacabana colors after she and a girl she picked up at a club had ended their one-night stand by driving to Logan Airport and scoring standby seats on an early morning flight to South Beach, Miami for the weekend. When Taylor returned, her black garb was transformed into a rainbow of linen and silk cotton. She declared that punk was passé. She took to wearing several necklaces with medallions bearing the Buddha, ohm, yin and yang signs, and elephants, and a mala bead necklace wrapped several times around her wrist. Her black, beaten-up messenger bag was replaced with one the color of grapefruit. Camilla couldn't quite buy the sudden reversal, from dark to light. She kept expecting the old Taylor to re-emerge. After all, it's only a matter of time before the born-again prisoner reverts to the familiar practice of hot-wiring cars.

Camilla could never understand why Taylor had been attracted to her when they'd first met and hooked up. It'd only lasted three months, and really, they'd only spent Friday nights together. What did that add up to? Twelve nights? Or maybe only ten, as Camilla remembered there were some Fridays when she didn't hear from Taylor despite Camilla leaving her several messages.

"Your leaving me five messages won't get me to call back any sooner, Earlobe," Taylor had told her once. "If I'm painting, I'm painting. I'll call you as soon as I can."

Camilla always suspected that Taylor hadn't been painting, though. She'd been busy with something else. Or *someone* else. Whenever she looked at the one photograph of the two of them, taken by one of Taylor's exes at another ex's party, that Taylor had framed and placed on one of her bordering-on-hoarder overflowing bookcases, Camilla stared down the photo, forcing it to tell her the truth of why Taylor had ever wanted to go to bed with her. There was Taylor, caught mid-gesture or mid-word but always looking beautiful as if she purposely posed that way to get you interested in finding out what she was saying in that moment. And then there was Camilla, her dark brown bob and straight-across-the-brow bangs giving her the appearance of a flapper, but the happy-go-lucky semblance was marred by Camilla's angular face and her thin smile. She had Taylor's preferred body type—small, boyish even—but she didn't wear the see-through, sexy shirts over camisoles and tight jeans that Taylor looked for. Camilla preferred to dress as nondescript as possible, like Taylor used to, the better to go unnoticed, invisible. Androgynous black T-shirts with black jeans. "You could be on a SWAT team," Taylor once told her.

"About time you showed up," Camilla told Taylor now, trying to sound as put out as possible by Taylor's late arrival. Then again, if she had shown up any earlier, Camilla would have missed seeing Benjy probably, and then Malcolm as well. Benjy never would have climbed up if Taylor had been there. Camilla thought about what seeing both of them meant, what the deeper meaning was, what the lesson was that she was supposed to learn from it. "Sometimes rain is just rain" was something her therapist, Doris, would say whenever Camilla overanalyzed something. Camilla broke the thought. The truth was she was happy that Taylor had shown up at all. It was difficult to pin Taylor down, to get her to commit to anything, let alone something requiring working in the hot sun at a house she was not able to visit for years. Instead Taylor would call you on her way to Bukowski's with a "What are you doing right now because whatever it is it pales in comparison to what awaits us?" And inevitably you'd drop whatever it was that you were doing and get to Bukowski's as soon as you could. Because when it came down to it, Taylor was right: whatever it was you were doing was never as fun, as unexpected, as alive, as being with Taylor. Perhaps Allison had been getting at something when in her paranoid manic states she would accuse Camilla of wanting to be back with Taylor.

The flip side of Taylor's attractive adventurous spirit was the core of her: her constant inability to be happy—even satisfied—with what she had, whether it was her art, a job, or a girlfriend. Taylor's love life was a revolving door of women. Sitting at Bukowski's with

Taylor included a good amount of watching Taylor eye every other woman in the place before she would, *could*, settle down, and actually look at and talk with Camilla. *Fun does not equal faithful*, Camilla often reminded herself after another safe, raucous night with Taylor at Bukowski's.

Being faithful had kept her all those years with Allison. For years, knowing that Allison wanted her and her alone had given her a security she had never known during the three months that she and Taylor had been lovers. Allison didn't so much as look at another woman during the thirteen years they were together. But somewhere along the line, that faithfulness had escalated into an obsession that felt like Allison was strangling Camilla, like one of those sex scenes in which the aggressor strangles her lover, then releases her hold in a momentary relief of pressure, then strangles, then releases, until both reach some sort of racing-to-death climax.

"You ever leave me, and I'll be the one with her hands clamped around your ankles as you try to get away," Allison had told her on more than one occasion after a fight. The image still haunted Camilla years later.

"You're not going to be all pissy, are you?" Taylor asked her now, one of her pink high-tops resting on a ladder rung. She began to climb up the ladder. "I mean, this was my idea, if you can tell the firing squad to stand down."

In spite of herself, Camilla smiled.

When they were both standing on the half of the flooring that was finished, Taylor saluted Camilla and clicked her rubber heels together.

Camilla laughed. "Okay, you made your point."

Taylor glanced around. "Wow, you've almost finished it."

Camilla laughed again. "We have to finish the bracing so we can nail down the rest of the floor today."

"Those are words I never expected to come out of your mouth," Taylor said, smiling. "Hey, check it out." She reached into the bag slung on her shoulder and pulled out a GI Joe. She wagged him back and forth toward Camilla as if she wanted Camilla to take him.

"Wow," Camilla said, sarcastically. The action figure's red-orange plastic hair clashed with his army fatigues.

"This is an original from 1964! Look at the scar on his cheek! That's the way you know it's an original. And look." She held out his tiny right hand toward Camilla. "They made a mistake on the originals and put the right thumbnail on the wrong side of the thumb. You can't find these anymore."

Camilla scoffed. "Except on eBay."

Taylor shoved the doll back in her bag. "I was going to tell you about the box I'm building for him, but forget it."

Immediately, Camilla felt bad for not being more enthusiastic. The truth was she liked to think that she was Taylor's main go-to person for feedback on her art. Or was she?

"Look. There's just a lot to do here," she told Taylor, her voice harsher than she wanted it to come out. She was disconcerted from her worrying whether Taylor asked only her or other women for their opinions. She waved her hand around the platform for effect.

"Let's go then," Taylor said. "We don't want to face she-who-shall-not-be-named before Nico's home away from home is finished," Taylor added. Camilla caught the meanness of it, but let it go. If they didn't stop picking at each other, the day would be ruined entirely.

"What do we do next?" Taylor asked, dropping the bag on to the platform as if what was inside was no longer precious to her.

Camilla pointed back down toward the ground. "First we build."

They worked silently, building a couple of V braces out of two-by-fours. Then, they climbed the ladder, Camilla going first, with Taylor right behind her, the both of them holding up the new brace. When Camilla's head reached the platform, she stopped.

Over her shoulder she told Taylor, "The top goes against the platform. Hold it steady so I can nail it. Steady, damn it."

"It is," Taylor mumbled under the strain of holding the V by herself. "Stop talking and hammer the fucking thing."

Taylor was right. The brace hadn't moved at all. Camilla had pretended it had because Taylor's hot breath on her neck, her small shoulders pressed against Camilla's back—was she on the same rung as Camilla?—were making her dizzy. Camilla quickly pounded in two nails, one for each of the ends, onto the platform's base.

"Done," she said, immediately regretting it as Taylor let go of the base of the V and shifted to go back down the ladder.

"What are you doing?" Camilla said fast. Taylor stopped below her. Looked up. Camilla told her, "I need you to hold the bottom against the tree so I can hammer that in, Einstein."

As soon as it came out of her mouth, she leaned her forehead against the ladder rung so that she wouldn't have to see Taylor's astonished face. She hadn't meant to say it. Einstein was what the kids at her elementary school had called Taylor after she had been left back a grade. Taylor had confided this to Camilla when they'd been girlfriends, one night in bed, with the lights off, their arms wrapped around each other, telling the other their deepest shames. Camilla hadn't meant to say it, but now it was there in the air around them, a cloud swallowing them whole before a torrential downpour. Why had she said it? To get back at Taylor...for what? Still being able to make Camilla physically attracted to her? For standing too close to her? For being oblivious of her power over Camilla and all the women in the world? For so nonchalantly deciding to simply go back down the ladder, without a thought or attraction of her own for Camilla? Taylor, though, had been the most supportive during the past two years when Camilla had struggled every minute to get through every day. Not once had she said anything about Camilla living with her rent-free for the first five months. Not once had she suggested that Camilla was wrong for leaving Nico.

"I'm sorry. That was awful," Camilla said. She looked over her shoulder down at Taylor. "I don't know why I said that."

"Bullshit," Taylor said quietly, but then she reached up and grabbed the back of Camilla's ankle, pretending like she was going to throw her off the ladder. "Die, bitch, die," Taylor yelled, but she was laughing and at once the awful cloud moved away.

"I'm really so sorry, Tay," Camilla said, but Taylor waved her off, her hand lifting from Camilla's ankle that still felt warm.

"Don't make a bigger deal out of it," Taylor said seriously. "I don't have the energy to console *you* now."

Camilla felt the slap of it. The problem was they knew each other too well. Knew what moves to make to keep the dance going between them. How to hide those moves when they stepped on each other's toes just enough so the audience wouldn't see, but they themselves would feel the here-then-gone-pain of it. Taylor was the only person to have ever called her on duplicating the very behavior that she hated in Allison: the manipulating of the other person into a fight to force them to feel sorry, so sorry they'd end up consoling the person who had started the fight in the first place. Allison was a master at it, turning Camilla around any time Camilla tried to tell Allison that she was upset about something Allison had done. Camilla ended up being the one to say "I'm sorry" every time.

"You know, you're starting to do that, too," Taylor had told Camilla one night months before. "It's like I can't even tell you something you did that bugged me without it ending with me apologizing and handing a box of tissues to you."

"Can you hold the bottom so I can finish this one?" Camilla now asked meekly. How did they get to this awful place so quickly? Taylor had been there less than an hour.

Taylor waved away a yellow jacket that buzzed by her head. "I know you're stressed and everything," she told Camilla. "Who wouldn't be in this situation? I mean, I'm scared and she never went Cujo on me ever, but—"

"Can you please?" Camilla pointed to the bottom of the brace with the hammer. She forced herself to smile. They were not going to get into that now. Not here, where Malcolm might hear them, or worse yet, Benjy, who might for days afterward race around his house from room to room shouting, "Allison Cujo! Allison Cujo! BAD DOG! BAD DOG!"

Thankfully, Taylor smiled and said, "Your wish is my command, Mills." That broke the tension. Climbing back to Camilla, she nestled into her monkey-on-the-back spot. She lifted the brace from Camilla's left hand. As she reached out to place the V's bottom against the tree trunk, she leaned more into Camilla, her breath now in Camilla's ear.

"Concentrate now, Mills," she whispered huskily into Camilla's ear. Camilla gripped the hammer tighter and, pulling out a lag bolt and a washer, placed both against the overlapping wood, and whacked the hell out of it. The wind picked up. Camilla heard the platform shift above with the wind, which was exactly what she wanted it to do and why she had created small slots where the platform was bolted to the tree. The slots around the bolts allowed the tree to sway in the wind, to be flexible no matter what wind greeted it. The treehouse would move with the wind, rather than ripping from the tree and falling to the ground. Camilla leaned her forehead against the ladder's cool metal rung in front of her, and found herself wishing that she could have been built with lag screws and four-inch slots, a bionic woman who moved with the punches of life, who might shift or tilt or lean, but who would never go down for the count.

"One down, one more to go," Taylor said behind her, and started to climb down.

❧ ❧ ❧ ❧

Camilla had thought that the worst part was leaving Nico that day after the awful fight, but it wasn't. The worst was yet to come. During the days that followed, Camilla had to deal with the devastating heartbreak of knowing she would not be living with him full-time anymore. There was also the relentless barrage of phone messages, emails, and text messages from Allison. Most of them were angry diatribes of everything Camilla failed at: relationships, parenting, having a real career. Sometimes, though, they'd start out with a plea for Camilla's return, only to slide into rants about every psychological effect Camilla's leaving would reap for Nico. One text read: *You do realize you're depriving him of a brother or sister.* It was accompanied by a photograph of the birth announcement for the second child of one of Allison's colleagues.

Five months after Camilla left she purchased a condo in Cambridge and moved out of Taylor's. Then the boxes started to be delivered. They were full of anything that Camilla had bought for Nico after he was born: a small blow-up swimming pool with an electric pump, a child's sun tent for the beach, toy trucks, books.

It seemed like every week when Camilla would come home after teaching there would be another box on her front porch. For months, Camilla simply carried the boxes into her new home and, climbing straight into the attic, placed the new box on top of the others that had arrived before. She didn't look in the boxes; she was afraid that she would find something she wasn't yet ready to see.

"Oh, fuck me," Taylor said to her on the phone one night after Camilla had received five boxes all at once. It was after midnight. Camilla had been sitting on her kitchen floor for the past hour, wondering how many more boxes she'd receive and what she would do when the attic was filled with them. Where would she put any boxes after that? Taylor was the only other person she knew who was an insomniac like her. The only person who would be awake. The only person she could confide in about the boxes. Her albatrosses. The cement blocks tied to her ankles in a bottomless lake.

"Just refuse delivery. Send them the fuck back, Mills," Taylor told her.

"I can't. She'll see that as engaging with her."

"Throw them the fuck out, then." Camilla heard Taylor strike a match and the sound of her taking a deep drag on a cigarette. Camilla wished she had a cigarette, too. She still bummed them off Taylor now. Why didn't she buy her own?

"I can't," she said. "I can't without knowing what's in them."

"Then I'll do it," Taylor said. "We need to keep your A.O. clean."

"My ay-oh?"

"Your area of operation."

"No, I have to do it," Camilla said. Sitting on her kitchen floor, she cradled the phone in her neck and hugged her knees with both arms.

She did it a few months later. On a warm, sunny morning in June, she finished her cappuccino at her kitchen counter and walked into the guest room, pulled the hidden ladder down from the ceiling, climbed up, and began to methodically go through each box. Several held photographs of Nico as he'd aged during that year that she hadn't seen him. Sitting in the attic's heat, Camilla started to sweat. She couldn't decide whether it was another way for Allison to punish her, or a ploy to entice Camilla to return. She lightly ran two fingers down each of the photographs, taking in his still curly long dark hair and brown eyes, her fingers grazing across the clothes that with each passing month she no longer recognized, and his increasingly posed smile. She scrutinized that smile, looking for signs of sadness masked by a false bravado, evidence that her leaving had scarred him. Her chest tightened with each photograph, but she willed herself not to cry, telling herself that she had no right to do so. *Look. Look*, her mind told her. *This is not yours anymore. You made a choice. You don't deserve the relief of tears.*

But then she opened a box and there was the small tent she'd bought to lay Nico down in for a nap on the beach. The tent and its poles were tucked away in its light blue carrying sack. Camilla picked it up out of the box. She heard sand falling inside. Immediately, she let out a sob. Allison hadn't cleaned it before sending it off to her. Had she used it in the year since Camilla had left? Or was the leftover sand from their last family trip to the Cape together? Had Allison left the sand in there as a stab, a reminder to Camilla of their beach trips together as a family? Of that last time at Race Point in Provincetown, their last family vacation together, when Camilla had wiggled into the tent herself so that she could lie next to the sleeping Nico? Or had Allison simply packed up the box as quickly as possible as it was so painful for her also? Crying, Camilla tipped the sack this way and that, hearing the sand in the hourglass shift from top to bottom and then back again. Finally, the stifling attic heat became unbearable. Camilla repacked all the boxes, and after climbing down the ladder and letting go of the ceiling door string, she heard the overhead door lock into place.

In the end, she ended up giving many of the boxed items to a friend from graduate school. After several dead-end relationships with men, the woman had decided to go through IVF on her own. That's how much she had wanted a child. Although she had a good paying job at a well-known medical journal, she was a single mother and was happy to accept hand-me-downs for Adam, her son. She greeted Camilla at her apartment's front door with Adam in her arms and a thin smile on her face that threatened to slide from happiness to pity. Camilla placed the inflatable toddler pool and the pump on the living room floor.

"Uh-oh. Uh-oh," said Adam, his mouth forming the words slowly.

"Sorry," her friend said. "It's one of the few words he knows. That and 'Up, Mommy.'"

When Camilla handed her the beach tent, the sound of sand falling against the nylon silenced all three of them.

"Uhhh—" said Adam.

꙳ ꙳ ꙳ ꙳

The second treehouse brace went faster than the first one. They worked in sync now, knowing what they had to do, the impending darkness urging them on. Camilla secured the fasteners quickly, especially when Taylor again leaned against her to hold up the bottom of the final brace so that Camilla could drive the bolt through into the tree.

"Let's take a break," Camilla said as soon as she hit the lag screw the last time. Taylor was still up against her. Camilla swiveled her body as if to start going down the ladder sideways, shifting Taylor off from against her back, forcing Taylor to begin the descent.

"Okay, okay," said Taylor. "What's the rush, Speedy Gonzalez?"

But when they got to the ground, Camilla immediately went over to the pile of plywood, grabbed a piece, and started to carry it toward the ladder.

"I thought we were taking a break?" Taylor said.

"I want to finish getting the floor on first."

"What's wrong?"

Camilla stopped on the second rung, one hand holding the ladder, the other gripping the top of the plywood panel.

"Nothing. There's not a lot of time to do this," she told Taylor with her back still to her. Then she began to slowly go up the ladder. "Are you helping or not?" she called over her shoulder.

"Not until you tell me what's wrong." Taylor stayed on the ground, her arms folded across her chest.

When Camilla got to the top of the ladder, she slid the plywood onto the framing. She looked down at Taylor.

"This isn't easy for me, you know," Camilla said. Her voice sounded false. Whiny. "I mean, any minute, she might decide to come home early, you know, like she always does and..." She couldn't finish the sentence. She knew that wasn't really why it was hard. Allison and Nico had left that morning. They wouldn't be back so soon. As neurotic as Allison was about something happening to the house—a break-in, a flood, an act of God—she'd never want to return the same day they left for vacation.

"I'm sorry," Taylor said, backing off from it. She began to climb up the ladder. "Let's get this done, then."

Camilla felt awful for misleading Taylor. She shook her head. "Don't apologize."

Taylor stood next to her on the section of floor that had already been done. She wrapped her arms around Camilla, hugging her tightly.

"I'm sorry," she said into Camilla's ear.

At first, Camilla tensed within the hug, only to give in to it. As she did, she thought of Allison. *So this is how it feels to manipulate someone*, Camilla thought. She wondered if Taylor knew what she was thinking, how much Taylor wasn't letting on that she knew. Feeling Taylor's hands on the small of her back, she hated that she liked feeling them there again. Part of her was also surprised that it was something that she'd wanted so much. After so many years, she couldn't believe it. What was the half-life of relationships that had ended? When would the electrical charge finally blink out and die?

Maybe it had nothing to do with Taylor, Camilla reasoned. Maybe it had everything to do with her being at her old home, in the backyard where she had so painstakingly gardened. The backyard to which she used to escape when being within the physical confines of their home with Allison had been too much for her. In the backyard where she was now building something for Nico. The hug was a bit of solace, nothing more. Or maybe it was because she hadn't been touched in two years. Hadn't been hugged except by friends. But Taylor was her friend—she couldn't be anything more than that. Camilla remembered in one fell swoop the three months she'd been sleeping with Taylor. The ogling other girls right in front of Camilla at bars, parties, or on Commercial Street in Provincetown where a parade of visiting lesbians sauntered past Camilla and Taylor as they sat on a bench in front of Spiritus Pizza. The many nights when Taylor would be unavailable, finishing up some new painting or installation piece. The time Camilla found a pair of underwear folded neatly in one of Taylor's books like a bookmark. The underwear hadn't been clean. These images coalesced like the CliffsNotes versions of the books on Camilla's assigned reading list that her students read so that they could get the gist, the bottom line of the book rather than any of its nuances or allusions, or understand them very deeply. No, she couldn't be with Taylor again. That was her bottom line.

Camilla gently pushed Taylor away. "Thanks. We should really finish this, okay? Can you bring up the last one?"

Taylor smiled and clicked her heels again, without the salute this time.

When she came back up the ladder with the last plywood panel, Taylor said, "You wouldn't believe who I ran into last night at the ICA thing." She dropped the panel onto the finished portion, and then knelt, sliding the wood over the final empty rectangle of the floor.

"Hand me some nails," she told Camilla, and, without looking, held an open hand back for them. "Patty."

"Patty?" Camilla poured a bunch of nails into Taylor's palm.

"Yup. Patty from the bar?" One by one, Taylor began to hammer in the nails.

"Patty from the bar." Camilla tried unsuccessfully to keep the derision out of her tone. She remained standing behind Taylor, watching her shoulder flex with the up and down hammer movement.

Taylor stopped hammering. With a nail between her lips she looked at Camilla over her shoulder. "Yes. Patty from the bar." She spoke with the nail still in her mouth. It looked sexy when she did it. Like it was a cigarette. "The one you said was hot, remember?"

"Did you go home with her?" It was hopeless. Camilla knew she was being ridiculous. Was she jealous? Why had she asked Taylor to help her anyway?

Taylor smiled. "What do you think?

"That's great, Tay, just great."

Taylor went back to hammering the nails in. "Don't you want to know what happened?" she asked over the sound of the last nail being whacked to death.

"I think I can guess."

Camilla picked up her own hammer and shoved it into an empty slot on the stiff tool belt around her waist. She fiddled with the screwdrivers and pliers in their slots.

Taylor was sitting on her ass now, watching her. "The imagination is a beautiful thing, isn't it?" She started to laugh. She shook her head. "Mills, you are one weird chick, you know that? So how 'bout you tell me what you think happened, and I'll tell you what really happened?"

"I'm not playing this game," Camilla said, moving toward the ladder. "We're done. You can go home now."

"Oh, come on. Don't be pissed."

Down on the ground, Camilla started to cover the piles of wood with the tarp she'd brought. When Taylor came down with her bag slung over her shoulder and across her chest, she picked up a corner of the tarp to straighten it out, but it only pulled off the part of the tarp that was covering the wood on Camilla's side, leaving it exposed. It was as if Taylor was purposely trying to make the wood vulnerable if it rained that night.

"I got it," Camilla said, tugging the tarp back.

"Let's go grab drinks at B's," Taylor said, letting go of her corner. She wiped her mouth. "I'm thirsty."

"Not tonight. I need to get some rest. I'm going to come back here early tomorrow."

"Oh, come on. How early?"

"Don't worry about it. I'll be fine. You don't have to come back."

"That's not what I meant."

"I don't want to go, Taylor."

"Why?"

"Is Patty working tonight?"

"I have no idea."

"I bet."

Taylor held up her hands. "Okay, I surrender." She walked away toward the gate. "When you get over your little PMS snit or whatever it is, you know where to find me, *Earlobe*."

"Thank you," Camilla called weakly after her. Taylor walked through the gate. She raised a hand with her back still toward her. Camilla shouted, "For the help. Thanks for the help."

The gate closed. Camilla stared at it while she heard Taylor's car start up and then depart. She looked up at the treehouse. At the darkening sky overhead. Around the yard. She was alone again.

She took off the tool belt, hung it over her shoulder, and walked through the gate to her car.

Day Two

Wallace

The next morning, Camilla overslept. She had never been an early riser, but she'd thought that setting her cell's snooze alarm to go off every fifteen minutes starting at six thirty would get her up and out. Exhausted, she kept swiping the alarm notifications off and falling back to sleep. Tim, the downstairs neighbor, succeeded where her cell failed. His banging on her condo door did the trick.

"Really? Didn't you hear it?" he said grumpily to her when she opened her door. He was standing on the landing in blue and grey striped pajamas. He looked like an escaped convict with his Caesar haircut that was popular with all the gay guys now with its crew cut on the sides and back and longer hair in the shape of a mini bowl on top. On his feet were puffy slippers made to look like moose heads, antlers and all. Camilla tried not to stare at them. He was supposedly a writer from a reality TV show involving trailer park people, but when Camilla told Taylor, who watched the show, Taylor swore his name never appeared in the credits.

"Sorry," Camilla mumbled, still half-asleep, tugging at the bottom of her T-shirt over her underwear. Her arm hurt as if she'd been lifting weights at a gym all night. She rubbed her upper arm, grimacing a little.

"Late night?" Tim asked.

Camilla nodded. Tim would forgive her a late night of partying. He would never understand that she was exhausted solely from the emotional and physical drain of beginning to build the treehouse. He didn't know about Nico. He thought of Camilla as a brokenhearted woman whose girlfriend had left her after a lifetime of coupledom. Camilla hadn't exactly told him that, but she didn't correct him when he went down the wrong path after she'd simply told him one day that she was recovering from a long-term relationship.

"I've been there, girlfriend," he'd said, nodding his head in solidarity. "Fuck them. They don't know what they're missing." Camilla knew then that Tim had been left by his boyfriend. It was confirmed when she spent the next two hours listening to every sordid detail of what seemed at first to be a ten-year relationship fueled and killed by meth overuse.

"It wasn't all *Breaking Bad*," Tim said sheepishly. "It's not like we cooked or anything."

But in the months that followed, whenever she ran into Tim on the interior stairs they shared or outside on the porch as they came and went to their cars parked on Longfellow Street, he would say something that would have Camilla questioning whether it was all a made-up story, that in fact he'd never done meth, or any drug for that matter. Like how he kept telling her, "We'd been like over the moon all the time" instead of "on the moon," which Camilla knew from internet research was the right phrase for saying you were high on meth. The phrase had sounded off to her, and it bugged her enough that she sought out a website of meth terms. Then there was the time he told her that he and his boyfriend had run out of their supply and had spent all weekend chasing the ghost. That same website said that "chasing the ghost" was when you fire up the stem of the glass to bring down residue to re-smoke it. Or how he always said "baggie whore" instead of "bag whore."

"What are you now? Popeye Doyle?" Taylor told her when Camilla reported all of this to her. "Over the moon...on the moon. So what? The man fucks up his prepositions."

"Idioms mean something to the drug culture," Camilla said, stubbornly. "They're a telltale sign—"

"Shouldn't you have said, 'Idioms mean something *in* the drug culture'?" Taylor asked, smiling.

Nevertheless, Tim was, Camilla concluded, like those white, suburban, trust-fund boys who play hardcore rap music as loudly as possible in their Lexuses on the way to their tennis club.

Now, Tim stood outside her door, moving the left moose head across the right moose head and sliding it back and forth. Strangely, there was something faintly erotic about it.

"Where'd you go?" he asked her, suddenly awake and perky with the idea that he could live vicariously through her. He'd confided previously that he was a daily attendee of "The Program." He still had a taste, though, for the drama of the party life, often criticizing Camilla for "not living large."

She shook her head. Sometimes not giving Tim any details was the easiest way out. He'd fill in with his own imagination what she couldn't provide.

Tim smiled and cocked a finger gun at her. "I gotcha. One of those, huh?"

He didn't wait for Camilla to respond. He went on, blessedly filling in the gaps. "Late night. You left

B's, went to some dyke's apartment, smoked—no, wait—you did E! Then...you, what? Wait, don't tell me. You go down to the Charles to watch the sunrise?"

Again, he didn't wait for a response. Instead he cocked and shot his finger gun at her again.

"Yessss, girlfriend. Snap. I feel you. That's exactly what you did. I can see it in your eyes. Your jaw giving you a workout? All grinding and shit?" At this he clapped his hands together loudly. "Shit, I miss those days. All right then. Go back to bed. Just make sure your alarm is off, okay? That owl call or whatever you have it on is 911 material. You feel me?"

As soon as she closed her door, Camilla raced up the steps. It was already eight o'clock. She had lost another thirty minutes standing there and talking to that wannabe meth head.

ﾍ﹏ﾍ﹏ﾍ﹏ﾍ

It hadn't rained the night before. The tarp was dry and already hot from the sun beating down. Camilla marveled that the treehouse floor and the braces were still poised overhead, waiting for her. No act of God had taken them down in the night. Allison hadn't returned home to wreak havoc on it. They were still there.

She made several trips up the ladder to the platform carrying the remaining two-by-fours. After she was finished, her arms ached even more. It was only Day Two and already she was so sore she didn't know how she'd bring up the rest of the plywood for the walls, let alone the bags of shingles for the siding. Then there was still the roof to do. Maybe she could leave off the roof. No, that would be cheating. Allison would see in a second that she had failed again. "It's called a tree*house*, not a tree *platform*," Camilla could hear Allison's voice say.

She groaned when she picked up two of the two-by-fours and nailed them together. Just the vibration of the hammer on the steel made her forearm hurt. Nothing to do but suck it up, she told herself. She laughed. The classics professor turned carpenter. Even her language was deteriorating.

She carried the two joined pieces to one of the platform corners and attached them to the side of the frame using her drill. Four feet high, the new corner post came up to her chest. She imagined being there with Nico and him standing there, his back against the post as she drew a line on the wood next to the top of his head. And each year after that they'd do it again. Line after line after line. The image gave her a burst of hope and energy. She quickly went back to the two-by-fours and pulled out a couple more.

The next two hours she spent finishing the posts at the other three corners, and nailing railings at the top of the posts from corner to corner. She began nailing the plywood to the sides of the platform. Nearest the ladder, the plans she had printed off the internet called for a doorway, so she made certain to use the shortest piece of plywood on that side. She had two sheets of plywood on and was crouching down to hammer nails into their bottoms when she heard the squeak of the gate. The sound froze her. She automatically stayed where she was, but crouched down. She held her breath. Was it Allison? Had she come back early? Maybe it was Benjy. No, he would already be shouting her name. Finally, she heard a voice.

"Milly?" a man's voice called out. "You up there?"

It was a voice at once familiar to Camilla and yet, not. "Milly?"

She couldn't identify who it was. *Think, think.* Then, she heard the sound of hard soles on the metal ladder rungs.

She stood up.

Wallace. It was Wallace Fields from her college department. He'd recently become Chair. The college was hell-bent now on bringing education into the technological stratosphere, as the Provost referred to it incessantly, and Wallace was the only one in the Classics Department that had taught a class remotely related to that. *Socializing Sophocles, Twittering Tibullus* was one of his courses. *New Media in the Classical Age* another.

"Tibullus wouldn't Twitter if his life depended on it," Camilla griped to Taylor one night at the bar. "He was an elegiac poet, for God's sakes. None of his poems would fit in a hundred and forty characters."

"Please," Taylor said, holding up her hand. "If you're going to go all Grecian Formula 44 on me, I'm going to need a bottle of Ouzo."

Now, here was Wallace in his seersucker suit and his trademark shiny red bow tie that matched the shiny red socks that poked out from his skinny wingtips every time he lifted his feet to go up another rung. He was carrying a large envelope against his breast as if it was precious cargo. He was a man in his forties, with a memorable appearance—*that* Camilla had to give him—with his startling red hair that looked like a helmet of one-inch porcupine quills all around his head, and his goatee that told all the students: I may be older than you, but I still know style when I see it.

"Wallace, what are you doing here?" The only one at Tolland whom she'd told about moving out was

Linda, who detested Wallace.

Wallace reached the platform, his skeletal body casting a long, ghostly shadow on the plywood. He looked around. "This is really something. Are you building this?" He was smiling broadly as he took in the view from every direction as if he were on a hill in Tuscany. You couldn't trust anything that came out of Wallace's mouth; every compliment had a motive behind it. Camilla had nicknamed him Heep in her head after the obsequious villain, Uriah Heep, in *David Copperfield*. Wallace even began many of his discussions with, "In my opinion," mirroring Heep's constantly stating "in my 'umble opinion" whenever he was going to lower the boom with another act of deviousness.

"Wallace, how did you—"

"I took a chance you hadn't gone away for the Fourth. Forgive my presumption, but I thought you'd want Nico to watch the fireworks. In my opinion, most parents around here do." He took out a pressed snowy white handkerchief from his inside breast pocket and dabbed at his forehead. Camilla could never figure out if Wallace's gestures were manly or feminine. Posed, like a dandy's, or a consequence of an upper-class childhood. She realized that the department must still have her address listed wrong. She'd changed it with Human Resources and payroll, but had forgotten to update the department secretary. It never failed to surprise her how disconnected communication was between administration and the college's academic departments.

"Anyway, I wanted to talk to you about this." He showed her the large envelope in his hand. "Is this safe to walk on?" He motioned the floor between them.

"That's not a comment about your building skills, which I am very sure are superlative." He smiled again, this time more uneasily.

"Wait," Camilla said, holding up a hand. She slid the hammer in her hand back into the tool belt slot and walked over to him. "What is that?"

"How is your wonderful family?" Wallace asked. He cocked his head. The gesture was a favorite of faculty. Camilla used it herself when she asked a student why his paper wasn't turned in. It could either be interpreted as being suspicious of the answer or very interested in hearing it.

"Fine, fine," Camilla mumbled. "What's in the envelope?" She asked him this again to stem the tide of embarrassment that was threatening to engulf her and wash away any of her normal filters. Since she left Allison, she always was nervous that people knew more than they let on. This thought would be followed by incapacitating shame and guilt. If she didn't stop it, she'd end up regurgitating the whole sorry business to Wallace. Within minutes of his leaving it would be gossip, zooming around every hall of her college, not simply confined to her own department. And what would they then do with this information? Judge her. She could hear all the whispers, the catty remarks now. She left her own child. Who does that? Drug addicts and alcoholics. Prostitutes. Women who were losing in the game of life. They'd spun the wheel of fortune too hard. They'd gotten cocky. The wheel had flipped off its axis and rolled away down a hill, its revolution gaining momentum away from them, leaving them high and dry and prime meat for death. They'd abandoned their children to save themselves. They would see Camilla as no different.

Wallace was talking. Saying something about how the Amazons were master carpenters. "Everyone talks about their fighting prowess, but in my opinion they did much, much more than simple sword jousting."

Camilla almost laughed. She would've laughed at any other time, but she was irritated that he was there. Why *was* he there?

"Jousting uses lances," she said, trying to get back into the conversation.

Wallace looked at her. "It was a figure of speech."

"Well, not real—"

Wallace handed her the envelope. "One of your students has filed a complaint against you. I thought it would be best if I hand deliver this to you myself, rather than email it to you."

"What? Who?" Camilla noticed the large CONFIDENTIAL in red across the front as if he were a CIA operative. She turned it over and began to break the gummy seal on it.

"Cindy Hunter." Wallace gravely announced the name as if it was attached to someone important that Camilla should know.

Camilla looked at him, helpless. For a moment, she couldn't place the name with a face. Teaching three classes of thirty students every semester for ten years at Tolland College, which had eight thousand undergrads, had morphed all the names into one big bowl of swirling Bingo numbers. At each number announcement, you had to scan your cards aligned closely on the table and myopically try to find the matching square, all the while your two fingers are jiggling the magic marker between them. *Cindy Hunter. Did I have a Cindy Hunter?*

"Claims the incident happened almost two years ago. Her sophomore year," Wallace continued. "Sexual harassment. Know anything about this?"

The normally loquacious Wallace was suddenly speaking in rapid-fire sentences, as if he was a cop interrogating a prime suspect. The compliments were gone now. He was on a mission.

"I don't even know who you're talking about," Camilla said, sliding the papers out. They were clipped together and she scanned them quickly, trying to find the reality of it as her mind was still trying to remember who Cindy Hunter was. She was certain there had been a mistake. Somehow either Wallace or this girl had erroneously attached her name to whatever it was that happened.

"It's the shock, I am sure, dear. Look at the last page. Her photo is there."

Camilla hardly heard what he was saying. Instead, she had finally found the part she had been looking for: the girl's complaint.

When I received my essay on The Upanishads and Herman Hesse back from Professor Thompson, there was a note from her telling me she wanted to meet me the following day, October 2, 2014, at 9:00 PM in her office. She didn't say what the meeting was about. It was weird that she wanted to meet me so late at night. The next night, when I walked into her office, she tapped me on my arm and told me to sit down in the chair next to her desk. She said something about the word upanishad *being Sanskrit for "sitting down near." That they believed you had to sit next to the teacher to learn. Then she closed the door to the office. I sat down. I was very nervous as I'd never met with another professor behind closed doors or so late at night. I pulled out my paper from my knapsack and put it on the desk between us and asked her what she wanted to speak with me about. She claimed the paper was excellent. She began to point out various sentences in the paper that she said worked. Her left hand pointed to one sentence and when I placed my hand there to shift the page to an angle where I could read it, her hand touched mine. Then she removed her hand and smiled. Like it was an accident. I didn't know what to do. I was so nervous. I asked her what my grade was and whether there were any changes I needed to make in the paper. She told me, "That depends." I felt my face get flushed then. I didn't know what to say and I was very flustered. Something didn't seem right. Then she laughed again and told me I would get an A. She put her hand on top of mine and said that I was her best student and that we should meet at this same time the following night so that she could teach me about a few other topics related to the Upanishads that would help me on my project. She said she only did this with her very best students. She was so nice when she said it, smiling the whole time, that I thought maybe I had misread what had happened. I agreed to meet with her because I thought it would improve my grade.*

I moved my hand from underneath hers and placed it in my lap and she laughed and apologized, saying she was so caught up in what we were reading she hadn't realized her hand was on mine. Then my essay somehow fell off the desk near my feet and when she bent over to pick it up she touched my naked ankle by the top of my sneaker. When she sat back up in her chair, she told me that she was sorry, she was not herself. She and her girlfriend, Allison I think she said her name was, were having problems. That she had moved out. It was crazy. I had no idea that Professor Thompson was gay. She told me they had been together for a long time. That

*they had split up. I told her I was sorry because I didn't
know what to say. She just laughed and said, "Oh, right."
Then she laughed again and she began to unbutton her
cardigan. She was only wearing a bra underneath.*

Camilla angrily crumpled up the pages. "This is
bullshit," she said loudly. "I don't even wear cardigans.
She's crazy. Why did she wait so long? She's obviously
lying. I can't read any more of this."

Wallace took the pages out of her hands and
smoothed the crumpled ones. He handed them back
to her. "She claims she was worried that there'd be
reprisals. She's graduating this coming year, says she's
never gotten over it, and doesn't want this to happen to
anyone else. Please finish reading. Then we'll sit down
in the house and have a nice chat about it. Your house
is so beautiful. Do I detect you to be a Bloomsburian
at heart?" He motioned to the Victorian house below.
"You're so fortunate to be able to afford such beauty
on a faculty salary. But then, you have your doctor.
While I am, as we say, *sui generis.*"

Camilla started. Sit down in the house? She
couldn't *get* into the house. *Focus on this, not that,* she
told herself. Her breaths were coming fast, as if she'd
just gone up and down the treehouse ladder several
times carrying a donkey laden with all the Sanskrit
books ever written. She couldn't even correct him on
the "sui generis." He'd meant *sans* generis: without the
same kind. Instead he'd said the Latin phrase for *of its
own kind.*

"Shall I help?" Wallace said. "Would you like me
to read it aloud? Happy to help."

"No, I'm fine," Camilla said and focused on the
pages in her hands.

Professor Thompson turned on some jazz music on her computer. She told me I was beautiful. Then she made me touch her breasts and she rubbed mine. I felt like I'd faint. I didn't know what to do. The whole time she was telling me about grades being so subjective that sometimes A-students ended up failing courses for what she called "simple infractions." She pinched my nipple and said, "But you're not a bad girl, are you?" I don't know how much time passed. It seemed like I'd been trapped in there for hours. After a while she finally moved my hands from her breasts. She began to button up her cardigan. She told me to button my shirt, that it was late, and I needed to go. She didn't even say good-bye. That was the last time I met with her. When I got my grades I saw that she had given me a C+. She'd promised me that I would get an A.

Camilla looked up at Wallace. He was sweating now from the afternoon heat. His cologne smelled old. Whatever brand it was, the hot temperature was metamorphosing it into something ancient smelling like the *Dead Sea Scrolls*, or like the sulfur smell you get for two days after eating garlic. Wallace dabbed at his forehead. His handkerchief came away slightly coffee colored, like papyrus.

Camilla flipped past the signature page attesting that all the above was true to the last page and stared at the photo.

She recognized the girl. She had been her student. She had met with her, but only once. Camilla had a foggy memory of the girl showing up at the end of her office hours to talk about why she had received a C+ on the paper she had mentioned in her harassment claim.

Only the once. The girl, who had been very verbal in class, her hand shooting up for every question Camilla lobbed out to the class, had stopped participating after that one conference. Most of the time then she'd slouched in her chair, reluctantly answering only when Camilla called on her, trying to draw her back in.

"Okay, she was my student," she told Wallace. "But I only met with her once."

"Are you and Allison having problems?" he asked suddenly.

Camilla startled. "Listen, this is bullshit. It's a pack of lies. She was mad, *is* mad, that I gave her a C+. Which she totally deserved."

Wallace glanced toward Malcolm's house. Camilla noticed Benjy riding up and down his driveway, all the while loudly saying, "I'm a fast bike rider. I'm fast. I'm the fastest bike rider in the universe." How long had he been doing that?

"Let's sit down inside, shall we, and you can tell me your side," Wallace said softly. "In my opinion, it's best to tread lightly with these things."

"I can't. We can't," Camilla corrected herself. She watched Benjy. Better that than look at Wallace who, it was clear, was on a truth-finding mission. When Wallace didn't say anything, though, she looked back at him.

Wallace raised his left eyebrow. Again, Camilla wondered if he was a dandy or whether he was secretly independently wealthy, from old money, accustomed to using such gestures to politely imply derision or disbelief.

"Oh?" he murmured.

"They're at the beach for the day. I stupidly forgot my keys inside before she left with Nico."

"Ah," Wallace said. Camilla knew immediately he didn't believe her for a second. "Well, then," he said, looking around. "This will have to do. It is a lovely view, Camilla." His smile disappeared. "Tell me everything that you know about this student and any interaction, *any* interaction, you had with her." He paused, collected himself again. "If you want to, that is. It would be best, I think. Not that I am telling you what to do." Without waiting for her answer, he took out a gleaming gold fountain pen and small writing book from his breast pocket. Camilla had an image of the sixties game show *Let's Make a Deal* in which audience contestants must pull out boiled eggs or decks of cards or cave dolls with purple crazy hair from their pockets.

"Might I suggest, if I may, that you start at the beginning?" he murmured, taking the top off the fountain pen and clicking it tightly on its bottom. "In my opinion, that is usually best."

༄ ༄ ༄ ༄

There wasn't much to tell. An hour later Wallace was gone, the few details locked in his breast pocket for eventual transcription into the department's formal files. Copies would be sent, he told Camilla, to the Dean of the College, the Provost, the Vice President of Human Resources, and to the new position of Student Harassment Liaison, recently filled by an alumnus that had been one of Camilla's former A-students.

"Well, we can thank God for that," Wallace had said when she informed him about the model student.

"Wallace, I did not do this. I don't need one of my former students to prove that. Cindy is obviously mentally deranged."

Wallace huffed a bit. "Better to call her 'the student.' Shows distance. And you may want to stay away from the amateur psychological assessments. In my opinion. If I may say so."

"I'm never on campus that late," she said weakly. "What do you mean, stay away from?"

"Unfortunately, there'll be an inquisition of course."

Camilla felt her heart beat faster. "An inquisition?"

"I am sorry. I meant an investigation. Once a classics professor, always a classics professor, I guess." Wallace gave her a thin smile. "I am sure it's going to be okay if we stick to what you just told me. Besides, I can't really see you liking jazz."

He laughed half-heartedly. His little joke was supposed to make Camilla feel better, but it fell flat. All it did was make it seem more likely that Wallace was wondering if something *had* happened between her and "the student." Maybe not everything that "the student" had described, but perhaps some of it. Camilla didn't like the "stick to what you just told me," either. As if she had fabricated her side of the story and should not sway from it.

"I must go," he told her. "My goodness, it's hot up here. Nico is going to love this, right? He's not walking yet, is he?"

Wallace didn't have children. He had no capacity for remembering how old faculty children were, nor at what stage eating, walking, and talking occurred. In Wallace's world, kids were either slurping at baby bottles or fully grown up and speaking five languages. There was no messy chrysalis involved. One day they all were simply butterflies.

After he left, Camilla slumped down on the

platform, crossing her legs and cradling her head in her hands. No matter whether she stuck to what she had told him or not, this was not going to go away in the weeks to come without a shit storm. She wondered if she would need a lawyer. She thought of Allison. How if she and Allison were still together she wouldn't need a lawyer because Allison would tear "the student" apart before the Provost, the Dean, and her prior model student. The girl would end up in a mental hospital from the verbal beating Allison would give her.

"Shit," Camilla said aloud. Then, despite Wallace's advice on keeping her distance and letting the investigation run its course, Camilla wondered how the hell Cindy knew about Allison. What's more, how the hell did Cindy know that she and Allison were no longer together?

≈≈≈≈

It didn't take her long to find out. Or rather, for Taylor to find out, or at least discover some of the story. Five minutes after Wallace left, Camilla was on the phone with her. Sitting on the treehouse platform with her back against one of the posts, she filled her in. "I mean, who waits for almost two years? There should be some kind of statute of limitations to prevent these nuts—"

"Actually, it's not unusual for sexual harassment victims to take a long time to come forward."

Camilla could hear the familiar fake typewriter clicking of Taylor's cell phone.

"Oh, now you're a social worker? Are you texting someone?" she asked, angrily. "How are you typing and talking to me at the same time?"

"No, I'm not texting someone. I'm looking up this whack job student of yours. And really, when are you going to get out of the dark ages you've been living in? I have my Bluetooth on, silly."

The sound of her typing stopped.

"Well?" said Camilla.

"So nada on your little fantasist. Whoa."

"What? What whoa?"

"I just Googled you on a lark. Shit, girl. You have over three hundred cites under your name."

"Camilla Thompson isn't an unusual name, dumbass."

"Dumbass, huh? I'm the one you called to help you, remember."

"Sorry."

"What I was going to say was…" Taylor's voice trailed off.

"Taylor? Taylor?"

"I'm here. Sorry. Shit. I just pulled up a photo of you and she-who-shall-not-be-named. You both have champagne glasses in your hand—"

"Taylor, concentrate, all right? I'm not interest—"

"Jesus, will you shut up a minute? You're wearing a *cardigan*. Didn't you tell Wallace—"

"What? I haven't. Oh shit. That was that stupid anniversary party for that awful Republican physician she works with and his wife. Remember I told you how they live in this horrible McMansion and you'd think with all the money they made they would have jacked up the heat, but no, it was like Siberia in there, and I was cold and Allison lent me a sweater she had in the car."

"That's one mystery solved," Taylor said.

"This isn't some kind of game, Taylor. Fuck,"

Camilla wailed. "Wallace will never believe me."

The phone was silent. Then Taylor said, "Look. Give me tonight to dig a little deeper. I know that little shit isn't as smart as she wants to come across. Upanishads. More like, up my ass. Please. The dialogue she gave you is like a bad B movie starring Barbara Stanwyck. That girl is just a bad pulp dyke wannabe."

Camilla didn't say anything. She was still stuck on knowing that there were photos of her and Allison floating around on the internet, ripe for any nut case, Allison included, to copy and use as they wished. Camilla had never Googled herself. That went hand in glove with looking in the mirror too often, something her mother had told her she must never do. "Ego is what makes us look in the mirror," her mother would say. "And ego is nothing to look at, trust me." Her mother, though, didn't follow her own advice; checking her reflection and fixing her lipstick was as routine as smoothing down her skirt when she stood up from sitting in a chair.

Camilla thought also of the time that Allison had scolded her for being "too thick" with her students. This was after Camilla had brought in pizza for the last day of class.

"It'll bite you in the end," Allison had said. Camilla almost commented on the word choice around an innocent pizza party, but she knew from the serious look Allison was giving her that those would be fighting words, so she kept her mouth shut.

At the time, Camilla had chalked Allison's comments up to her increasing obsession concerning Camilla. Any time Camilla spoke about enjoying her time with anyone, Allison was quick to point out a possible bad personality trait in the person or a consequence of hanging out with them. But now, she wondered if Allison had been right: that Camilla had opened herself up to the Cindy Hunters of the world; that she had, in effect, only herself to blame for what Cindy Hunter had done. Cradling her cell in her neck, she was surprised to find herself tearing up. Once again, Allison was making her feel as if she was to blame for everything. They hadn't lived with each other in two years and still Camilla slid into beating herself up at the earliest opportunity.

"Mills, you there?" Taylor's voice came out of the phone.

Camilla sniffed hard. "Yup. Just thinking."

"Well, don't. Give me some time. There's something bad going on here—"

"You got that right."

"No, I mean, something we don't see or know yet. Meet me at the bar at nine tonight, okay? I'm sure I can find out more by then."

When she hung up, Camilla stood up from the platform, shaky from everything that had happened that day. It was close to five o'clock. She hadn't accomplished what she had needed to do to stay on track. She should finish all the siding, including the shingles. That was what she was supposed to do according to her building schedule. She should stay where she was until she had to meet Taylor at the bar.

She cupped her forehead underneath her bangs, feeling the sensation of her sweat wetting her hand. The familiar gesture calmed her nerves and her thoughts, as if it was a mother's cool hand feeling her child's forehead for signs of a fever. A cool breeze filtered through the warmth.

How much more would the gods dump on her?

                  Randi Triant

Camilla hated when she'd overhear the priests-turned-professors at her college talking about the troubles of some student, ending with that old sawhorse: God only gives us troubles we can shoulder. That made no sense to her. So, if you're weak and can't take on any speck of illness or tragedy or death, you scooted through life scot-free, easily serpentining around them on the obstacle course of life? After going through all those years of fighting with Allison and then suffering the loss of spending any time with her son, Camilla had had enough. She understood these were all choices that she made. She understood that the gods—whoever they were—had nothing to do with what had happened. But surely they saw how burdened she was. Surely they saw her trying to rectify, trying to offer the penance of building a treehouse in ninety-degree weather when she could be reading a bestselling thriller at Cranes Beach, with some kind of ice-cold vodka punch in a plastic cup parked in a cozy holder on her chair. Surely the gods saw that Cindy Hunter should be stopped by an act of God. Deep down, though, Camilla knew there would be no act of God. That if Cindy Hunter was to be stopped, it would have to be done by her and Taylor. She realized that all her hopes were pinned on Taylor's online virtuosity. Taylor had to ferret out the connection, the answer to everything.

Slowly, Camilla bent over and picked up the hammer from the plywood floor. Sliding it back into her tool belt, she descended the ladder to begin the exhausting process of hauling up the heavy packages of shingles.

Later that night, two beers in and tucked into a corner wooden booth, Camilla felt more hopeful, though her body was a mess, every muscle strained or stiff with pain. She'd only finished part of shingling the treehouse's sides before it was so dark she'd hit her fingers twice, hard, with the hammer. At first, while packing up, she was riddled with a sense of failure, and then guilt. She'd never finish it in time. Why hadn't she bought a propane lamp at the hardware store, or one of those headlamps that were so popular now at outdoor sports stores, so that she could work through the night? Maybe she wasn't truly committed to finishing it. The treehouse took on the shape of her relationship with Allison: unfinished, broken down, a symbol of everything wrong in the world. If she'd been serious about this, she would've gotten a lamp, planned her time better, demanded that Wallace leave before he'd been able to mention Cindy Hunter. She would've done something, anything, to stay on schedule.

But, now, at the bar, watching Taylor across the table as she tapped furiously on her MacBook Pro, Camilla felt a calmness that she hadn't felt since she and Taylor had hatched the treehouse idea. She would finish it. She was only slightly behind. She could make up the lost time tomorrow. Besides, shining a beacon of light as she worked late into the night would surely have had some neighbor—Pecksniff or someone from up the street that she'd never met—coming over to investigate, or worse, calling the cops. Yes, the miner's headlamp would have been a bad idea. Maybe Taylor would help her all day tomorrow.

As if Taylor knew what she was thinking, she looked up, her fingers stopping in mid-air over the keyboard. Taylor gulped her beer and set her half-empty glass down. She reached into her bag, unwrapped a piece of black velvet material from around a package, and slid a new box that was a foot high and four inches wide across the carved-up table. It looked like a miniature coffin with a small hole in the shape of an eye near the top.

"Stop staring at me and let me work. Amuse yourself," Taylor told her and then, looking back down, began to furiously tap the keyboard again.

Reluctantly picking up the coffin, in spite of her really not wanting to do so because she was afraid that would by itself bring some bad mojo into their lives, Camilla placed the box as near to her face as she could without actually touching it. To touch it surely would end up in someone's death. Inside was the GI Joe from the day before, but now he was half-dressed in tattered and bloody mummy wrappings the color of weak tea, his camouflaged fatigues poking through, his head and one eye covered in what looked like a blood-soaked head bandage and his scar somehow leaking a liquid the color of mercurochrome. Camilla inadvertently let out a gasp as she realized that he was lying on top of a floor covered with tiny plastic baby girl dolls that were dressed as geishas, their faces powdered a deathly white, their lips and cheeks a startling red, their bodies covered in beautiful purple, aquamarine, and pink satin.

"Finally," Taylor said, and Camilla lowered the coffin, thinking she had heard the gasp.

"It's amaz—"

"So, here's the thing," Taylor interrupted her, still staring at her computer screen. Camilla felt her mind swirl and plunge into a drain hole. The thing? So, there's a *thing*.

"Wallace said there would be an investigation, right?" Taylor asked.

Camilla nodded. She pushed the coffin box toward Taylor, who nonchalantly picked it up and, covering it up again in the black velvet, slid it back into her bag.

"That means that either the pulp dyke wannabe or her Dean requested it. Look." Taylor turned her laptop so that Camilla could read the screen. "This is Tolland's policy of all harassment claims. Wallace said there'd be an investigation, which means that someone asked for that. Someone has to request a hearing. When did Wallace say he got told about it?"

Camilla shrugged, immediately feeling shooting pains go up her shoulders and neck. She winced.

"Stop being a wuss," Taylor told her. She pointed to the screen. "You have fourteen days to get your shit together before your ass is hauled before this committee and they bomb the shit out of you."

"Shit," Camilla said, reading but not reading Tolland's harassment policy in front of her. The word "harassment" seemed to be mentioned every other word.

Taylor turned the screen back around, her eyes narrowing. She began typing again.

"Don't worry so much," said Taylor. "Bingo. Look what I found." She let loose a few more keystrokes and started to turn the screen back, but then said, "Scoot over, I'm sick of playing spin the laptop." As tense as Camilla was, Taylor's phrasing still sent a shot through her that was not painful. She moved over just in time as Taylor slammed into her side.

"Christ. A little more room would be nice," Taylor told her. "Okay, look at this. I found this on our girl. Looks like she's pre-med."

Camilla read what appeared to be an article from Tolland's student magazine. She didn't read the magazine. The one time she had, she'd found the articles dull, centering on a few of the self-promoting students or a faculty member who always looked uneasy in the accompanying photograph. Camilla's mailbox at school would become jammed with the monthly glossy until one of the secretaries would empty it out so that her real mail could be slid in. The article was a year old and reported on undergraduates who were pursuing different pre-med avenues. Cindy Hunter had been interviewed as an example of a pre-med, Humanities major. "The Humanities teaches us how to be critical thinkers," Hunter was quoted as saying. "It teaches us how to take in everything being thrown at us and cut through to what's important. Whether we're diagnosing the human experience in great literature or triaging in the emergency room, it's all the same thing."

"Okay, so she's good at analogies," Camilla said, looking at the screen as she scrolled fast down the article. "She's a liar."

"Think," Taylor said.

Camilla leaned back against the booth's rounded back.

Taylor finished her beer. "She's pre-med." She smiled knowingly. Camilla started to feel pissed off. She hated when Taylor would act like she held the secret to a universe that Camilla couldn't come close to comprehending.

"And?" Camilla said. She picked up her beer to finish it as well. At least she could keep up with Taylor on that front. But Taylor put her hand on top of the glass just as it was about to reach Camilla's lips and lowered the glass.

"She's. Pre. Med," she said, enunciating each word.

"And again...and?" Camilla looked down at Taylor's hand. It was covered in gesso and paint, as it always was. When they'd been lovers Camilla had loved lifting Taylor's hand up from her stomach and studying all the swatches and dabs that formed an abstract painting. An abstract painting that Camilla tried to decipher the meaning of, but was never able to.

Taylor dropped her hand. Camilla felt it as a rejection, as if Taylor had been holding her hand, not the beer glass.

"Fine," Taylor said. "I'll spell it out for you, Professor. Tolland has a requirement that the students do an internship every year, right?"

Camilla slowly drank the rest of her beer.

"And who do we know that works for a hospital?" Taylor added. "You do the math."

"No," Camilla said, putting the empty glass down. "You don't think—"

"I don't think. I *know*. In my bones."

Taylor held up two fingers to a waifish Audrey Hepburn waitress who had been taking the order of a table nearby, but abruptly broke it off and went straight to the bar end where Camilla heard her ordering two beers. The girl was dressed in tight jeans and high-tops. A black bra could be easily seen through her light pink gossamer shirt.

"How do you do that?" Camilla asked Taylor. The truth was she really didn't care how Taylor got such immediate attention she did from a minimum-wage, minimum-age waitress. She just wanted a diversion. Camilla was rattled. She thought about asking to see the coffin, not because she wanted to see it again—it was horrible to look at—but she was more afraid of where the conversation was going. She slipped her penknife out and began to carve underneath the table, one line next to another like you do when you're drawing tick marks to five and the fifth mark is a slash across the four preceding ticks. The idea of Allison somehow connecting with Cindy Hunter through an innocent internship and using that to get revenge on Camilla was too much to think about. Was Allison so angry that she would set out to end Camilla's career? It couldn't be possible. The Allison Camilla knew, the one she had loved all those years, understood and was very protective of their professional lives. How could she do such a thing? She couldn't. It wasn't possible. She would never.

But, maybe she had. Camilla thought of all the critical comments Allison had made about Camilla's job. Always during their fights. How it was a breeze compared to what she had to deal with in the surgeon shark pool. That's what she had called it: the shark pool. How dealing with students was nothing compared to the shark pool. How Camilla had the summers "off," although Camilla had tried to point out her summers were spent reading new texts for possible inclusion in a future semester, or re-writing her syllabus and curriculum to add some new field of inquiry, or struggling with another essay of her own to stave off the publish-or-perish guillotine. Had Allison ever paid her teaching at Tolland one compliment? Camilla tried to remember any now, and couldn't.

Audrey Hepburn slid two glasses, sweating from their cold beer, across the table. A business card was stuck on the side to the wetness on the one she placed in front of Taylor.

"Call me," the waitress told Taylor and then, leaning across the table, she said into Camilla's ear, "What did that table ever do to you?" Before Camilla formed a comeback, the girl had turned away.

"Really? Bar waitresses have business cards now?" Camilla said when the girl was out of earshot. She hadn't liked that the girl had caught her *in flagrante* defacing the furniture. She meant to say the "really" with an edge of sophistication, but it came out sounding whiny and uptight. She looked away, trying to find where Audrey Hepburn was and what she was doing. She'd gone back to the table that had been trying to order their drinks before Taylor had waved her two fingers in that direction. None of the four men seemed to be giving the waitress a hard time about it, either. In fact, one of them was saying he was sorry, but could she repeat the beer list one more time. Camilla was disgusted. She didn't stand a chance in a world like this. She wanted to pull the guy up by the back of his T-shirt collar and yell at him, "She should be apologizing to you!"

Taylor laughed, shaking her head, peeled the business card off, and slipped it in the breast pocket of her jean jacket. "There's a first for everything," she said. "Anyway, why do you find it so hard to believe that she-who-shall-not-be-named would have the balls to do it?"

Camilla lifted her eyes from Taylor's breast pocket.

"The balls, as you so eloquently put it, have nothing to do with it. I just don't believe she'd cross the line like that. What you're telling me is...what? Somehow Allison sought Hunter out for an internship slot because then she…what? Knew that Hunter was mentally off and would be easily persuaded? To what? Set me up for a harassment suit? There's too many far-fetched steps."

Taylor lit up a cigarette. "What if it's simpler than that?" When Camilla started to interrupt her, she raised a hand, her fingers laced around a cigarette. "No, listen. What if Cindy Hunter had a thing for you? No, listen. Just wait till I'm finished. What if she found that same photo of you that I did—the one with you and she-who-shall-not-be-named and—"

"Could you please stop calling her that?"

Smoke streamed out of Taylor's nose. "Okay. Allison. There. Happy? What if Hunter sees the photo's caption and sees that Allison works at the hospital—"

Camilla groaned and rested her head in her hands.

"Just shut up a minute," Taylor said. "What if Hunter finds all that out, applies for an internship, gets it, and—"

"And what? Meets Allison? So what? How does Allison then start brainwashing her with the whole harassment angle? You've been reading too many Highsmith novels."

Taylor took a long drag. "Look. I don't know how it all fits together, but it does. At least it's something. We need to start digging now. And I promise you something will turn up about it. We will find something. It's weird that there isn't one photo of the wannabe anywhere on the web. And by the way, *The Talented Mr. Ripley* was totally underrated. The book and the movie." She paused, and took a sip of her beer. "We *will* find something. I promise you."

But instead of assuring Camilla, this promise only

made her more anxious. She had enough to deal with building the treehouse. The treehouse. How would she ever have the focus she needed now to finish it? She'd already found out enough about her life. How, when it came down to it, her life for the past fifteen years had been built on one of those sinkholes in Florida that the news reported on every night. No, better not to find out more. No good would come of that, Camilla was sure. Knowledge was power, but it also brought consequences. She should remember to tell Linda that at the next faculty meeting. Undoubtedly that would cause a flurry of scarf winding and rewinding.

"By the way," Taylor said. "You did exactly what I want everyone to do when they see Joe at my exhibit. One large gasp for mankind, one giant step for peace." Then she stood to go to the bathroom.

Day Three

July 4th

Audrey

The next morning, Camilla woke early. Her head was pounding and her mouth was dry. Why had she stayed so late at the bar with Taylor? She started down the dead-end road of recrimination, judging herself again on whether she was really, truly serious about building the treehouse or was it another example that, as Allison had accused in a text, Camilla didn't have it in her to commit to anything. That she was missing some critical emotional DNA strand. Rubbing her forehead as if to erase the thought, she forced herself to get out of bed.

She made a cappuccino in a small bowl and went onto the deck. She sat at the only furniture out there other than a few straggly plants: a rusted metal café table and two metal chairs for which she'd overpaid at a pricey Asian furniture shop near Taylor's condo in Boston's South End. The air was humid, heavy with moisture, which always caused her to have a headache. It was a question of the weather, that's all, she thought. Not a result of some deep-seated inability to commit. None of the backyard's oak tree's leaves were moving. It felt as if the tree was waiting for something to happen, someone to say get on with it, and the leaves would come alive just like that. Sounds from the park around the corner wafted over to Camilla: children playing baseball, their parents shouting encouragements to them, the crack of a metal bat hitting a hard ball, then the uproar of shouting again.

At first, Camilla had hated and dreaded those sounds after she'd moved in. Every crack, every shout reminded her of Nico. Would he be a baseball player or not? How many games would he play in that she'd never see? Who would teach him how to play? Allison wouldn't be able to. Camilla had been the athlete between them. When she was six, her brother had kept her on their front lawn with a mitt and a ball until she, as he told her, stopped throwing *like a girl*. Sipping her coffee, she shook her head when she thought of Nico, choosing to think instead of her brother and how patient he had been with her.

She heard the sounds of claws on metal from a squirrel racing toward her along the side house gutter. She turned in her chair, the chair's feet scraping against the wood deck. Startled, the squirrel stopped dead in its tracks. It was a scrawny thing with a thin, long snout. He was always using her deck as a launching pad into the oak tree. From there, Cambridge was at his mercy as he jumped from branch to branch, tree to tree, and roof to roof. Camilla had nicknamed him Cosimo after the boy in Calvino's novel *The Baron in the Trees*, who decides after refusing to eat a dinner of snails prepared by a sadistic sister to climb up a tree and never come down again. From then on, Cosimo moves from tree to tree, watching humankind from afar.

Cosimo the squirrel looked at her and bounded back the way he had come, disappearing along the gutter, over the roofline at the front. There was another hollow ting of a metal bat hitting a ball in the park. Camilla drained her bowl. She tasted the sugar that had clumped on the bottom, its sweetness cut by a surprising sliver of sour from the espresso's acidic residue. Nothing was ever as it seemed. Wincing, Camilla carried the bowl to the back door and went in.

❧ ❧ ❧ ❧

Taylor showed up at the treehouse later that morning, with Audrey Hepburn in tow. Camilla was picking up another shingle when she heard the bad muffler on Taylor's ancient Volvo station wagon before she saw the car turn onto Longfellow and park near the side gate.

"Are you kidding me?" Camilla mumbled as she saw Audrey get out of the car, laughing from something Taylor had said. She was still dressed in her bar clothes from the night before: the see-through shirt covering the black bra, the tight jeans, the high-tops. At least she wasn't wearing any of Taylor's clothes.

"Hello to the house," Taylor called out as the two of them came through the gate.

Camilla stood looking down on them, a hammer in one hand and her other hand on her hip, resting on her stiff tool belt.

"I brought some help," Taylor said, looking up, her right hand cupping her forehead as a sun shield. Audrey Hepburn rested one hand on Taylor's shoulder, shielding her eyes with the other when she looked up.

Camilla tilted her head to the sun. "It's such a beautiful day, I'm sure you'd rather be spending it some other way," she called down. She hoped Taylor could hear the clipped tone she used and get the message.

"My father is a builder," Audrey called up. Camilla lowered her eyes to look at her. "I'd love to help. I used to help him until I started to work at the bar. Taylor told me all about—"

"Oh, Taylor did, did she?" Camilla stared down at Taylor.

Taylor laughed. She moved toward the ladder and started to climb. The girl followed her. Camilla had the urge to sail the top of the ladder off the platform.

"Don't get yourself wrapped around a wing nut, Mills," Taylor told her. Another one of Taylor's militarisms. It meant don't go all crazy, around and around. "I just told her you needed to finish building the treehouse this week. For a *friend*," she added as she stepped on to the platform. "Happy Fourth by the way. Wow, it's really almost finished. Well done, Mills."

No, Camilla thought. *You think complimenting me is going to make it all right that you showed up with her? Think again.*

"No, it isn't," she told Taylor impatiently. "Not even close."

"This is Audrey," Taylor said, and Camilla almost burst out laughing. Was that really the girl's name? Of course it was.

"So, do you want me to help you finish the shingles, or do something else?" Audrey asked. Reaching over, without asking, Audrey lifted the other, smaller, hammer from Camilla's tool belt resting on her right hip. The gesture was so intimate that Camilla was left speechless. Who was this girl?

Taylor simply smiled, like it was the most ordinary thing in the world. "Guess you're fresh out of hammers. Damn. What can I do, besides watch two beautiful girls?" she said, holding up her hands. "It's a hard job but somebody has to do it."

Audrey laughed. "How about you bring up the rest of the shingles, lazybones?"

Camilla was stunned when without saying anything, without a sarcastic reply or a clicking of her heels, Taylor gave Audrey a peck on her cheek and walked toward the ladder.

"What's your secret?" Camilla asked Audrey. She didn't expect an answer, really. She didn't ask it because she was interested or because she thought Audrey had a secret way of making Taylor do her bidding. She meant it sarcastically. She was surprised then when Audrey answered her with a serious face.

"Honestly? I'm good at it," Audrey said.

It was only when Audrey walked over to the pile of shingles, grabbed a plank and a handful of nails, and began to hammer on a plywood side, that Camilla realized Audrey had been talking about her building skills and not her ability to manipulate anyone at will.

                                             ঌঌ৯৯

Audrey *was* good at it. She did the shingles at three times the speed that Camilla could. Camilla thought she'd be a ditzy talker and she'd been wrong about that, too. Audrey hammered away, methodically covering every four inches with another cedar square, the only sound coming from her the thud of another nail being pounded in. Even Audrey's hammering was perfect: two shots and she moved on to the next nail. Camilla tried at first to compete, to keep up with Audrey's rhythm, but it was useless. She had to admit also that she admired how Audrey didn't call attention to herself, how she never made a comment about

Camilla's slowness or lack of building experience. After a few minutes, the two of them were wordlessly working on plywood panels next to each other as if they'd done that their entire lives. Camilla was reminded of how over the ages since the Medieval era this was how carpenters became close: in the silent work they did every day, in the simplicity of raising a hammer and moving on to the next shingle, breathing in each other's smells. She recognized Audrey's earthy smell as patchouli. That caught her off guard too. It was such a seventies scent.

After Taylor had brought up the rest of the shingles, she'd tried to engage Audrey, but Camilla could see that Audrey wasn't having it. Taylor had tried to encircle Audrey's waist from behind, folding her own body over Audrey's bent one as Audrey reached over the side of the plywood to hammer another shingle on. Her hammer raised, Audrey glanced over her shoulder, and said, "It's always funny till someone gets an eye poked out," and shook Taylor off.

"Okay, okay, Catie Carpenter," Taylor said, backing off and raising her hands in mock surrender. "I'll be over there if you change your mind."

Audrey hadn't changed her mind, though, and within a few minutes she was telling Taylor to bring up the two-by-fours to frame out the roof. After that, she suggested that Taylor bring them back some lunch from somewhere in town. Not daring to look up, Camilla heard it all, amazed. She kept her head down, focusing on aligning her shingles.

"I'll have a provolone and salami on a baguette with mustard and pickles," added Audrey, continuing her hammering. "Oh, and bologna. Ask them if they can add that in, too. And hot peppers."

Again, Camilla was surprised. She'd pictured Audrey in her see-through shirt and tight jeans as one of those girls who used their fingers to comb and peck through a mound of lettuce and maybe a few cucumbers, nimbly eating only a corner of the food before pushing it aside.

"They're probably going to be closed," Taylor said. "It *is* a holiday. Which reminds me. This here is costing you double, Mills. You know, holiday pay?"

Camilla laughed. "Jack's will be open. He never closes. All those customers wanting picnic lunches for the big bang."

Taylor stood there, staring at the two of them. Camilla began to feel she'd gone too far. What had gotten into her, ordering Taylor about?

Audrey stopped hammering and looked up. "Can you please get the lunch? Either that or I'll go and you can finish this." She held out her hammer toward Taylor.

Reluctantly, Taylor turned and walked toward the ladder. "Who put you in charge?" she muttered.

After Taylor left, Camilla and Audrey continued to work in silence, moving on to the last plywood panel together.

"Wait a sec," Audrey said, finally breaking the silence. Standing next to each other, Audrey slid her fingers into one of the pouches on Camilla's tool belt and unhooked the metal tape measure. Camilla felt that same frisson of intimacy that she had when Audrey had taken the hammer from her belt. She wondered why she didn't feel put upon, or that Audrey was too aggressive. She felt happy. Happy that Audrey wouldn't think twice about doing it. Happy that Audrey was so confident and relaxed around her. Camilla realized that she felt relaxed, too. Who *was* this girl?

Audrey measured out the length of the panel. Sliding her hand in her back jeans' pocket, she lifted out a stub pencil, along with a small notebook that fell on the platform by her feet. Camilla reached down and picked it up. It was no more than two inches, covered in a fine green paper with painted outlines of leaves in beautiful browns and oranges.

"I'm a writer," Audrey said, shrugging. She held out her hand. Reluctantly, Camilla gave the tiny notebook back. She wanted to see what was written inside. Audrey slid it back into her pocket.

"Oh?" Camilla said. "What do you write? I mean, are you a poet or a fic—"

"Memoir stuff mostly," Audrey said, looking away. Bending over again, she drew a line down the panel from top to bottom. "Okay, you should be able to fit in six shingles on your end and I'll do this end. We'll meet in the middle." She immediately began to lay the next shingle, her head down.

Camilla watched her for a moment and then said, "I actually went to school for creative writing. Well, as an undergrad. I thought I was going to write the Great American Novel." When Audrey didn't say anything, Camilla went on. "I only changed to literature when I went for my master's and doctorate. Ya got to pay the bills, you know." She laughed. She hated that she sounded so pretentious. So stupid. Her laugh had sounded a bit false also, like she was trying to show Audrey that she wasn't serious about being an academic. What did she mean anyway by saying that about paying the bills? She regretted that. Audrey would probably think of it as an insult, as if Camilla had been lecturing her: *Don't think you can make a*

*living from being a writer, because you can't. No one
can, except Danielle Steel or James Patterson.*

Audrey continued to nail up the shingles on her
end as if she hadn't heard a word Camilla had said.
Just when Camilla gave up on Audrey ever talking
again and had turned toward her own end of the panel,
Audrey said, "I had to drop out." Camilla faced her,
waiting for her to say more.

Straightening up, Audrey gave that shrug of hers
again. It moved her shirt slightly. There was a small
flash of stomach before the shirt covered it again.

"My dad. He wasn't very happy when he read
some of my work and saw that I was writing about
him."

Looking down, Audrey lightly tapped the
hammer against the railing on top of the panel. The
gesture reminded Camilla of someone scuffing the toe
of his shoe into the dirt, like a child about to confess
to something. *Oh no*, Camilla thought. *Please don't.
Don't ruin this.* The thing is, if someone confesses to
you, you're obligated to respond to the confession.
You can't simply leave it to hang in the air, ignored. It
will never disappear that way. You'll always remember
that awkward moment when you didn't say anything,
when you didn't console the person, or offer any kind
of affirmation. And what could Camilla say to any
confession from this girl whom she'd started to like for
her silence and ease? She didn't know her at all.

"He wasn't an evil man," Audrey continued. "But
he wasn't a good man either." She paused. "Who was
it who said evil is banal?" For once, Camilla stopped
herself from acting the professor. She didn't tell her
it was Hannah Arendt. Or that it was a reference to
the horrible Nazi, Eichmann, who ordered hundreds

of people to be killed in the gas chambers. Nor did she correct her by telling her that her father's deeds, no matter what they were, could possibly be anywhere near the evil of Eichmann.

"Anyway," Audrey went on. "After that he refused to pay for college unless I switched to accounting or something. I like working at the bar because I can write during the day. And as my favorite writing teacher used to tell me, 'It's all material, darling.'" Audrey smiled. Her teeth were smallish and white, and coupled with her blond pixie haircut, the smile made her look like a teenager. Something about that made Camilla relax again. And she liked how Audrey had circled back to the writing part of it. How she was taking the braver stance of confiding in Camilla about her dad, but not getting caught up in some exaggerated story of how she was scarred for life because of her relationship with him or, heaven forbid, starting to cry about it. Everything about Audrey was light. Her see-through shirt. Her small body. Her golden-boy hair. After so much dark drama in her own life, Camilla felt refreshed by this girl. Her ability to say something serious and then step back and laugh about it. Not to get mired in the muck. To say, I know life is rotten sometimes, but I'm going to use that rottenness and be happy. Camilla wished she could do that.

"It's for my son," Camilla found herself blurting out. "It's not for a friend, like Taylor said. I'm building it for my son. Who I cannot see anymore." She gestured to the house below. "I used to live here. They'll be back at the end of the week." Then she shrugged in poor imitation of Audrey, as if to say, *Ah well, what can you do?*

Audrey stared at her. "Well, then, we better get

going and finish it," she said and bent over the side with another shingle.

Camilla felt disappointed. She'd offered Audrey a string of vintage pearls and Audrey had thrown them into a jewelry box of costume pieces and cheap baubles and closed the lid. Camilla wanted something more from her, but she couldn't say what that was. At least Audrey hadn't tried to console her. At least there was that. That would've been awkward. *Oh well*, Camilla thought. *At least that's the end of it.* They'd return to their hammering and forget the rest of it—until she leaned over the plywood wall and, holding a nail in one hand and a shingle in the other, she felt what seemed to be a hand pressed between her shoulder blades. It was only for a second. So brief. So light. *You're not alone*, it said. Almost immediately, it was gone, Camilla couldn't feel it, and she wondered if it'd ever happened at all.

꒰ ꒱ ꒰ ꒱

They'd finished covering the last wall with the shingles when Taylor returned with their lunch. The walls came up to their shoulders.

As Taylor came up the ladder, she told them, "Y'all look like a couple of cows in a pen, getting ready for the slaughter." There was a large bag with their sandwiches in the crook of her left arm. Reaching into the bag, she pulled out a beer and held it out to Camilla.

"No, thanks. I have to finish the framing for the roof today," Camilla said, pointing to a bottle of water on the floor. "I'll take one of those sandwiches, though."

"All work and no play makes Milly a dull girl,"

Taylor told her. She held out the beer to Audrey, who also shook her head.

"I have a lethal weapon in my hands," Audrey said. She raised her hammer for effect.

"It's not a gun," Taylor said, irritated. She handed out the sandwiches. The three of them sat in a circle on the treehouse floor: Taylor with her legs straight out like a guy, Camilla with hers bent up close to her chest, the soles of her work boots flat on the platform, and Audrey in a pseudo lotus position. They ate their sandwiches in an uneasy silence. It seemed as if one of them would say something at any minute, but no one did.

A blue jay, followed by another, landed on the railing, squawked, and then they both flew off. Taylor drank her beer quickly—too quickly—and Camilla wondered if she was pissed that no one was following her lead anymore. Camilla heard the sounds of children on the elementary school's playground behind Benjamin's house. She thought of several things to ask Audrey, but each time she'd discard the thing as being stupid or not very interesting. Taylor, always so verbal and sure of herself, unrolled and then picked at her rollup of hummus as if she was getting rid of microscopic ants. Camilla saw Audrey wolf down her Italian bomb like a longshoreman and was again struck by the dissonance between her waifish appearance and how she acted. *No matter what happens*, Camilla thought, *I will remember this moment.* Not everything is as it seems. The treehouse was quickly showing her that.

Taylor leaned over toward her messenger bag. Foraging around in it, she pulled out an army Jeep toy. She set it down on the platform and then rolled it toward Audrey. It knocked into Audrey's knee. "What's this?" Audrey said, still chewing her sandwich. "A new piece?"

Taylor shrugged. "I'm trying to decide if I should use it or not."

"How much did you pay for it?" Camilla asked. She didn't want to talk about Taylor and her art. She wished she could figure out what to ask Audrey.

Taylor scowled. "Typical," she said. "I'll show you at the house, Audrey, what I was thinking." Reaching across, she retrieved the Jeep and slid it back into the bag. Camilla was pissed. She hated how Taylor could so easily get the upper hand yet again and dismiss her so entirely. Her and her art. So superior to everyone else. Or, at least to her.

Taylor picked at her rollup, removing slices of red onion. The sandwich looked like roadkill. She licked her index finger.

"So, I found a connection," she said casually. "You know, between the dyke wannabe and she-who-shall-not-be-named."

Camilla stopped chewing her mozzarella and tomato sandwich.

"You have something," Audrey said, and, leaning over, wiped a corner of Camilla's mouth with her index finger. She sucked on it. "Balsamic."

Camilla felt the treehouse shift. She looked down at what was left of her baguette, swallowing what was in her mouth.

"Don't you want to know what it is, Mills?" Taylor asked. "Or are you too busy?"

"Yes, of course I do," Camilla said, but she wasn't sure she really did. Especially in front of Audrey. When the Greeks stood before the oracles they had to be ready for anything. They had to accept what their future would be as it was foretold. It had been such a good morning, Camilla realized guiltily, until Taylor had come back.

"What are you talking about?" Audrey asked. She'd finished the rest of her meal and was scrunching up the deli wax paper, getting ready to stand up and start framing out the roof, which would end the lunch.

"Can't we talk about this later?" Camilla reached over and began to fold up Taylor's uneaten mess, along with the rest of her sandwich.

"I'll eat that, if you're not going to." Audrey slid out the other half of Camilla's baguette before she could close up the packet or say anything. With her other hand, she also grabbed Taylor's mess with its wrapping and shoved it into the empty paper bag. Then she took a bite out of the leftover mozzarella and tomato. Camilla had the urge to reach over and pretend that there was a drop of balsamic on Audrey's mouth that she could wipe away now. But Taylor was staring at her, not Audrey, and Camilla refocused her attention on her.

"Okay," Taylor said, slowly, staring at her. "But there's definitely a connection." She smiled her knowing smile.

"I need to finish this right now." Camilla waved her hand in a circle over her head. Her heart was pounding. She was torn between wanting Audrey to be gone so she could hear whatever it was that Taylor wanted to tell her, and wanting Taylor to be the one to leave so that she and Audrey could be alone and continue to work on the treehouse.

Taylor stood up. "We'll leave you to it then. We need to get back to watch the fireworks, and Audrey has to work later anyway."

Audrey didn't move from where she was sitting cross-legged on the treehouse floor. She thoughtfully chewed and then swallowed the last bite of Camilla's baguette. "I think I'll stay and help," she said casually, balling up the empty sandwich wrapper and chucking it into the paper bag. The wad landed with a soft thud.

Camilla sipped her water. She avoided looking at Taylor. She didn't know what was happening. They were in a play where the actors play a prank, switching parts midway through the first act, leaving the director and the audience to catch up to what was occurring in front of them. The whole thing could fall apart or become something extraordinary, something they'd never seen before. Taylor was probably as surprised as she was. Camilla felt an undercurrent threatening to take down the entire treehouse.

Taylor laughed, but it came out forced, like a short bark. "Okay," she said slowly again. "How are you going to get back?" She jiggled her car and house keys in front of Audrey's face.

Audrey gently pushed Taylor's hand away. "No worries," she said.

Taylor laughed sharply again. "Did you hear that, Mills?"

Camilla stood up. Audrey stood, too. It was as if a string tied them together now, mimicking each other's movements, like they were each other's marionettes.

"What?" Audrey said.

Taylor laughed. "Nothing. That's only Camilla's least favorite expression in the world. Tell her, Mills."

"Tell me what?" Audrey asked.

Camilla looked at Audrey. She *was* young. She looked like she was what Taylor's exes called jailbait: so underage you'd end up in prison if you had sex with her. What had Camilla been thinking? Taylor was always so good at making Camilla see the obvious. Not what she *wanted* to see, what she hoped for, but what was stark naked in front of her. It was only a matter of time before Audrey would utter a "Whatever" or a "Dude" or a "Check it out."

"No worries," Camilla said, trying to make her voice soft, but fairly certain that no matter what she said, it would change everything and the connection between them would fizzle and die. "It's like saying 'no problem.' Students say it all the time when I ask them to revise an assignment. Like they have a say in the matter."

"So, I'm your student now?" Audrey said. She raised one eyebrow and, sticking out her small hip, slid her hands into her back jeans pockets. "I'm thirty-five."

Taylor laughed harder. "Uh oh, now you've done it, Mills. She just ambushed you with the age card." She started to strut toward the ladder, enjoying her victory. "I'll call you later. Come on, Audrey."

"I can drive you home," Camilla mumbled quickly to Audrey and touched her wrist. Then she thought better of it and dropped her hand. "No problem," she added. She tried flashing Audrey a smile to show her that she could be light, too. Could make fun of herself. That she knew how to slough off life's unimportant things. She thought, though, that it probably came off as false, and further evidence of her pretentiousness.

Immediately, Taylor turned around. She shook her head, laughing that harsh laugh again. She clapped her hands once. "Wow. Okay, well, I'll see you at my house at eight tonight, Audrey." She said it nonchalantly, but Camilla could tell that she wasn't happy. For once Camilla was the mouse outfoxing the cat.

Taylor added, "Oh, and by the way, Mills? She-who-shall-not-be-named and the wannabe worked together on something called the Free From Hate Clinic. Some hospital thing where they give free health services to gay runaways. I thought you'd get a kick out of that. Ciao." She waved and then disappeared through the doorway down the ladder.

"I think she took that well, don't you?" Audrey said sarcastically as they listened to Taylor's car drive away. "What was all that about the Free From Hate Clinic?"

Camilla told her about Cindy Hunter and what Taylor had found out. She left out a lot of the details from Hunter's letter. Camilla realized that she felt the details would incriminate her, would somehow convince Audrey that perhaps there was some truth in the story. There were so many specific details in the letter. Camilla taught her students that writing was all in the details. Generalizations rang false and were unconvincing. Well, Hunter had been specific.

"It's absolute bullshit of course," she told Audrey when she was finished. The second it was out of her mouth Camilla wondered if *that* came across as unconvincing, too, that she was protesting too much.

"And you're building this treehouse," Audrey said. She looked intently at Camilla.

"I didn't know about this student until after—"

Audrey reached out and grabbed Camilla's shoulder. Camilla felt Audrey's pinky resting on her neck. She tried not to close her eyes and let the feeling wash over her. She tried to pay attention to what Audrey was saying, to ignore how that tiny finger seemed to be moving slightly against her neck. The rest of her fingers were gently tugging on her collarbone.

"I wasn't saying that your building this was some way for you to avoid what's going on. I was just saying that it's a lot. You know, building this basically by yourself. Dealing with this crazy student. Not being able to see your son. I was just saying that it's a lot," Audrey repeated.

For once, Camilla didn't correct someone who had used the word "just." Camilla had the urge to tell her what she told her literature students: "Just" is a minimizing word. Try to avoid it. She let it go and instead nodded. She played with the hammer in her hands in the small space between them, twirling its handle over its head again and again until Audrey's other hand stopped it mid-cycle and Camilla was forced to look straight at Audrey's face: the ends of her blond eyelashes that seemed silver tinted, her brown eyes and their wide-eyed shape and intensity reminding Camilla of her favorite childhood doll, Jerry Mahoney, who always looked so happy. The tiny bump in her nose, which undoubtedly had a story behind it, a story Camilla found herself wanting to know.

Somehow Camilla managed to say, "We should get started on the framing." That broke whatever spell had landed on the treehouse that afternoon. Camilla wondered if the spell was one of *eros*, erotic love, or of what the Greeks called *philia*, friendship. Most people thought there was only one kind of love spell you could cast over someone, but the Greeks thought there were two. One could land you in bed fucking the woman of your dreams. The other would get you no more than a shared ice cream cone.

Without a word, Audrey dropped her hands

from Camilla, walked over to a corner of the platform, and began to hammer in the first two-by-four for the roof. Camilla felt the small space between them widen and grow as big as the Colosseum. As if on cue, the sounds of firecrackers going off down the street started up, followed by the smell of burnt pencils, as if a war had begun.

Taylor

Camilla had meant to call Taylor that evening, but by the time she and Audrey had finished the frame for the roof and she'd dropped her off at Taylor's home and then driven back across the Charles to her own home in Cambridge and taken a much-needed shower, it was already nine o'clock. She knew Taylor would be with Audrey, waiting for the Boston fireworks to begin. Audrey had told her that much when she'd asked to be driven to Taylor's instead of her own home.

"I thought you had to work," Camilla had said sullenly.

If Audrey heard her tone, she chose to ignore it, saying only, "I do. My shift is at eleven."

Maybe Taylor's upstairs neighbors had invited them up to their rooftop terrace to watch the spectacle of flying dragons breathing out plumes of red sparkler fire, cascading waterfalls of white flashing lights, and exploding purple hydrangea-like balls high in the sky. Or maybe Taylor and Audrey had walked down Clarendon Street to the river to join the million tourists and residents jacked up for the show, waving their Star Wars light sabers and miniature American flags glued on chopsticks. Camilla dialed Taylor's cell phone anyway. Taylor didn't pick up.

In spite of having Audrey as a diversion that afternoon, Camilla's interest in knowing more about what Taylor had learned about the Free From Hate Project had grown with each passing hour. She couldn't believe that Taylor had been right; Allison and Cindy Hunter were connected in some way. She wasn't ready yet to believe in Taylor's hypothetical story that Allison had used Hunter in some kind of revenge plot, but still, Camilla was unnerved by them having *any* connection at all. When Taylor didn't answer her phone, Camilla decided to simply drive into Boston to the bar. Taylor would probably end up there after the fireworks were over. She told herself that, but in the back of her mind she knew Audrey would be there for sure.

As she drove through the Cambridge treelined streets, past the boutique stores in Huron Village selling expensive blown glass bowls and children's toys made in Germany, Camilla thought about Allison. She was not convinced at all that Allison would, could, be capable of such an underhanded scheme. Allison had always been so protective of their careers, much more protective than Camilla had been. When Camilla mentioned wanting to come out to the rest of her department several years back, Allison cautioned her against it, reminding her that Camilla was up for tenure within a few years.

"You don't want to hand them the ammunition as they lock and load," Allison told her. Camilla refrained from telling her that was something Taylor would say.

"Let them judge you only on what you've done professionally," Allison continued, "not what you do personally." She'd been right, too. The following year, a male professor and expert on Edgar Allan Poe was denied tenure in spite of his having published widely on Poe, including a critically acclaimed non-fiction book investigating who the "Reynolds" could have been that Poe reportedly called out repeatedly for as he was dying, delirious, in a Baltimore Hospital. The professor had made the mistake of bringing his boyfriend to Tolland's faculty holiday party. It turned out that on the faculty tenure committee was a horrible homophobe named Ferol Finch, who rarely taught anymore due to his heading up a research project dating thousands of papyrus bits and fragments, mostly in Greek, from the Roman and early Byzantine periods.

"Ferol lived up to his name," quipped Allison when Camilla reported the news. "His last name should be Rabid, not Finch."

"Ferol Finch needs to get fucked," said Camilla.

"Nice alliteration. Now, aren't you glad fickle Ferol Finch has been ferreted out before he could famously fuck up your future?" Allison smiled. "Pretty good, huh?"

Camilla wasn't in the mood for more of Allison's alliterative joking, although she was glad she'd heeded her advice. She sailed through the committee, receiving tenure the first time she tried.

Now, she wound her way through the back streets of Cambridge because both Storrow Drive and Memorial Drive were shut down for the crowds migrating toward the Charles River to see the fireworks. Crossing over the BU bridge, Camilla decided Taylor had to show her some hard evidence before she'd believe that Allison had anything to do with Cindy Hunter's accusation.

There were packs of people walking over the bridge, along with several bicyclists who acted as if they were driving eighteen-wheelers, taking up full lanes as they sped along. Camilla wondered how Audrey got to work every day from her Somerville apartment to the bar in Boston. She looked like someone who would ride her bike. Cambridge and Boston were such bicycle towns. The joke was that if it wasn't the cab drivers that got you in an accident, the bicyclists would. Half of them didn't wear helmets and the other half rode down the middle of the car lanes in spite of the cities pouring money into redesigning major streets to include side bicycle lanes. If Audrey did ride her bicycle, Camilla mused, she undoubtedly wore a helmet and stuck to the restricted lane. She imagined Audrey on one of those new fixed-gear bikes that also had a basket on the front with plastic flowers strung through the wire mesh.

She didn't really know Audrey at all, but she already had a vision of her as someone who was careful yet cool. Someone who was the leader of the pack of the neighborhood children, not a follower. Someone who looked out for the younger, weaker ones. The type of person Camilla always wanted to be as a kid, instead of the kid she was. The one who stood in the background. In the far corner. The watcher. Invisible. Someone like Audrey could bring Camilla out of her turtle shell, out of her endless thinking, and maybe she could give Audrey a sense of gravitas. She could show her that she could do anything she wanted to despite life's challenges.

With four bikers riding next to each other across the lanes, Camilla was forced to slow down to their speed as she came to the other side of the bridge. The stoplight at the bottom of the bridge turned red and she had to stop. It was ten o'clock. Camilla hoped that Taylor hadn't already left the bar with some girl. She realized then that she no longer thought of Taylor sticking around for Audrey. She already had her moving on to someone else. It was ridiculous. *She* was being ridiculous. *Audrey is too young for you*, she reminded herself. *Focus on getting to the bar so you can find out what Taylor knows.*

When the light turned green, she took a chance and made an illegal left turn onto Commonwealth Avenue. She drove as fast as she could, finally pulling into the garage next to the bar where the parking would cost her more than her bar bill for the night.

Inside, Taylor was sitting at the end of the packed bar. The Clash was blasting over the speaker system that London was calling. Audrey, who was filling in as bartender for the holiday, was tipping two bottles of tequila into margarita glasses. She glanced over and smiled as Camilla passed by. Camilla raised her hand but Audrey had already turned away and was digging ice out of the freezer with a scoop.

"No table?" Camilla shouted to Taylor when she finally reached her through the crowd. "I thought you had a standing reservation."

Taylor laughed and removed an empty beer bottle off the stool next to her, waving at the stool with a flourish. "Your chariot awaits." Taylor slid a beer over in front of the empty stool. Another beer was in front of her, with two shot glasses filled with an amber liquid. Sitting next to the open stool, two men covered in skull- and dragon-themed tattoos were halfway up a pyramid of full shot glasses.

Camilla sat down. "How'd you know I was coming?"

"Ah. That was easy. A," Taylor held up an unlit cigarette, "I know you and I knew you wouldn't be able to go to sleep tonight without finding out what I know. And B," Taylor pulled another cigarette out of her pack and held it up, "you called my cell phone eight times, Earlobe."

"Three. I called you only three times. And stop calling me that."

They were shouting at each other to be heard over the music, which had now switched to Foo Fighters. Something about their yelling at each other eased whatever tension could have been between them after the afternoon they'd spent. They both laughed. Taylor lit both cigarettes and handed one to Camilla. Camilla took a sip of her beer. It was cold and refreshing.

"Nah-uh, Earlobe," Taylor yelled. She motioned to the shot glasses. "You're going to need something stronger than that."

"Tell me." Camilla took a drag off her cigarette and blew out the smoke.

Taylor shook her head. "First we drink. Then I spill." She threw back her shot in one fluid motion, slamming the emptied glass down on the wood bar counter. The two tattooed men let out simultaneous cheers and downed their own shots in reply.

"Thank you, sir, may I have another?" Taylor shouted. She held up two fingers. Camilla looked down the bar. There was Audrey, her hand on her hip, watching them. A customer was yelling his drink order at her, but she ignored him, grabbing a bottle of tequila on her way toward Taylor and Camilla.

"Better drink that fast, sistah," Taylor said loudly in Camilla's ear. "You don't want her thinking you're a lightweight."

Camilla threw back the shot, the fire consuming her throat. She quickly swigged from her beer to cool it down so she wouldn't cough.

Without a word, Audrey filled their shot glasses. When she turned to go, Taylor grabbed her arm. "Aren't you forgetting something, sweetheart?"

Audrey shook Taylor's hand off, reached into her pocket, and threw a five-dollar bill onto the counter. "I didn't think you'd come," she told Camilla. "I thought you'd be too tired."

Her words took on a totally different meaning than intended to Camilla. She felt that same wave of electricity in her body again and she had the urge to say something risqué, like "I'm never too tired for that, honey." But it sounded in Camilla's head like something a drunken old geezer would say. Taylor could've pulled it off, but not her. If Taylor said it, Audrey would be climbing over the counter. Before Camilla could figure out what to say, Audrey had moved away, and was already leaning toward the shouting man, taking in his order, but still looking in Camilla's direction.

"You're disgusting," Camilla shouted at Taylor. She was so mad at herself she had to take it out on someone. How dare Taylor make a bet out of her? Like she was one of those greyhounds racing on speed after a plastic rabbit, their tongues lolling out in desire.

Taylor laughed, which irritated Camilla more. She tucked the money into the breast pocket of her watermelon-colored T-shirt and patted it. She didn't have to say the words but Camilla heard her loud and clear: *I own you and I own her.*

Camilla took a sip of her beer and then downed the second shot. "So? What did you find?"

Taylor took her time downing her shot and drinking some more beer. "Let's get out of here. Go to my house. We can't talk in here."

Camilla almost protested. She'd driven all the way there, put up with being the butt of a cruel joke, and now Taylor wanted to leave? Taylor was right, though. An old AC/DC rocker had taken control of the sound system and was rampaging through a collection of sound-barrier-shattering Metallica. Camilla stood and started to walk away, but glanced back and saw Taylor leave a twenty on the bar, and then pull out the five from her pocket and leave that, too.

🐚🐚🐚🐚

Taylor's one-bedroom garden apartment was in the South End. The apartment was an artist cave; everywhere you looked were art supplies: new and used tubes of oil paints, brushes, stacks of old magazines, pieces of frames, buckets of gesso, X-ACTO knives, bubble wrap, tables covered in paint, found rusty metal objects, and broken pieces of pastels. To sit down on the one couch or the one chair in the living room you had to deftly slide over whatever work in progress had been left there, taking care to show Taylor that whatever it was, you knew it was priceless, and you were gentleness personified as you shifted it a bit to free up an inch on the sitting surface.

"Here, I'll do that," Taylor would say. She'd move it exactly the way you would have: to the next pile, or by gingerly carrying it to another cluttered table surface. Somehow, though, as you watched her, you began to doubt whether you could have carried that clump of red painted paper clips attached to an army helmet as successfully. You saw that helmet going overboard from your cupped palms, the paper clips breaking, scattering across the tiled floor like a botched game of

Pick Up Sticks. A possible masterpiece destroyed by your clumsiness.

A corner of the floor in the living room was covered with thirty cans of spray paint. For a time, Taylor had gotten into tagging on the brick sides of abandoned warehouses in Fort Point, where artists sometimes squatted. As soon as those were renovated into million-dollar lofts as part of Boston's seaport restoration project, Taylor moved on to dog parks that were near her brownstone. Her big beef was dog owners who didn't leash their dogs when they brought them to the park even though there were separate gated areas where the dogs could legally roam free. One night, Taylor was almost knocked over by a loose cannon of a Labrador as she crossed the park carrying a chessboard on which she'd glued two battalions of lead soldiers. After that, she started spraying *Leash Your Dog!* in bright pink on as many handball walls, basketball courts, and park sidewalks as she could. Ever since Camilla and Taylor had split up, the cans of paint always sat in the living room. When she visited, Camilla worried about the possibility of fire.

"What, like on those reenactment TV shows that have some humorless asshole deliver a moral lesson at the end?" Taylor said. She deepened her voice. "Louise often smoked in her bed late at night. She paid the price. Will you?" She laughed. "Or were you thinking of some kind of spontaneous combustion?"

In spite of the clutter, whenever she visited they always sat on that couch. This time, however, Taylor surprised Camilla when they arrived separately in their cars at the apartment. Once inside, Taylor stopped Camilla from going toward the living room.

"Let's go in the bedroom."

It wasn't as if Camilla had never been in Taylor's bedroom before. Certainly she had when they had been lovers twenty years ago. And there had been a few times since, usually because Taylor wanted to show her something, like the new comforter she'd bought at Target, or she wanted Camilla to help her replace a few dead spotlights in the ceiling. There was always a specific reason.

Here she was, though, for no apparent reason. The novelty of it made her uncomfortable. She tried to focus on what was in the room. Taylor's unmade bed was on the floor. The double room-darkening shades taped to the only two windows in the room acted like a pliable headboard. Two metal bureaus stood sentry, and seemed more in keeping with a military base than an apartment in the hip South End—Camilla thought they might be hand-me-downs from Taylor's military parents. The floor-to-ceiling shelves on each side held hundreds of books, along with leaning postcards that Taylor had received from friends and lovers traveling the world, plastic iconic figurines of Disney characters and comic strip heroes like Batman and Robin, an assortment of metal boxes, and Taylor's lifelong collection of stuffed bats. The first time Camilla had seen the room, she'd asked Taylor about those bats.

"I mean, most people are afraid of bats. And they're ugly," she'd told Taylor.

Taylor had been fondling one of them in her hands. She hugged it like it was a Teddy Bear and kissed it on its head. "That's the whole vampire baggage thing. Bats don't go after people. They go after insects. Mosquitos. Gnats. I think they're beautiful. And they love the night."

Looking around now, Camilla realized that

nothing had been moved from its original place of twenty years before. She wondered if Taylor ever dusted, if she still saw all the objects and books when she entered the room every day, or whether all of it had become like a comforter on your bed: necessary but unnoticed. Camilla noticed that there was still the framed photograph of the two of them that had been taken when they were a couple for a minute, and that showed how different they'd always be: Taylor the bareback horse rider through life, and Camilla the one who always pulled on the reins.

"I like what you've done with the place," she said and sat down on the bottom of the bed.

"Cute. I'm getting beers."

In the few minutes Taylor was gone, Camilla had the urge to read the backs of some of the postcards, but she didn't dare. She thought a few of them looked newish. One was of a red balloon with the word "hope" on it. Another was a beautifully hand drawn illustration of Notre Dame. The room had a veneer of patchouli to it as if a bottle had spilled on one of the cluttered bureau tops and not been cleaned up right away. She wondered how long and how often in the last twenty-four hours Audrey had been there to leave her scent behind.

Before she could think about that more thoroughly, Taylor came back in with two bottles of beer. She gave one to Camilla and clinked the tops of them together. She sat down next to Camilla. She kicked off her sneakers and pulled her legs up into a semi-lotus position. One of her knees rested on top of Camilla's thigh. Camilla stared at the double knots on her own black Vans. She wondered if Taylor would ask her what had happened after she left her and Audrey at the treehouse.

"So," Camilla said.

"So," Taylor said. She gulped at her beer.

"Come on."

"Okay, this is the thing."

At once, Camilla had that same feeling of dread she'd had before. Yet another "thing" was about to be unloaded on her. Another discovered box in the attic filled with letters that proved your parents weren't your parents after all. You were adopted.

She'd ended up not adopting Nico before she'd left. She'd started the process, meeting with a family law attorney, filling out the numerous forms. But every time she was about to submit the paperwork, to start the wheels in motion, the train was derailed by another argument about something Camilla had done that proved to Allison that Camilla wasn't fit to be his mother. Like the time Allison pointed out that the socks Camilla had put on him were polyester and didn't she know that they were flammable?

"Of course I didn't know that. I just grabbed them from his sock drawer," Camilla told her. "Why were they in there if I'm not supposed to use them?"

"I have no idea," Allison snapped back. "They were probably a gift from one of your friends. The question is, don't you even look at what you're putting him in? You don't really care, do you? It's all let's-get-this-over-with, isn't it with you? I mean, you say you want to be his mother, but do you really?" After being repeatedly chastised for whatever she dressed him in, Camilla stopped deciding on her own. Every morning while Allison got ready for the hospital, Camilla asked her what outfit she should dress him in. Avoidance was the path of least resistance.

"Mills?" Taylor was saying to her now. "You with me? The Free From Hate Clinic has its own website. It's badly in need of a web master and the design sucks—"

"Taylor, *please*."

"Sorry. The project's director is she-who-shall… sorry, Allison. She's been the director as far as I can tell for the past year. Basically, it's a free clinic thing, you know, a bunch of doctors get together and decide to give away their medical services for free. Probably makes them feel better about all that money they rake in. Anyway, they target gay and lesbian runaways who obviously don't have health insurance. They're especially hyped up about the rising hate crimes, you know, bullying, getting beat up, that sort of thing. They have a small clinic set up in the hospital but also have this van that goes to hotspots, like Harvard Square or Downtown Crossing. You know, where you see those kids all strung out and shit. I have to admit, it's pretty cool."

"Taylor, for fuck's sake. What did you find out?"

"Okay, okay." Taylor took another drink of her beer. "They have a group of interns that do all their scut work. You know, filing, Xeroxing, taking temperatures, driving the van around. Okay, okay. I'm getting to it. Chill out. Hunter was, or is, still an intern at it. They don't give the dates for the internships, just a list of the intern names."

Taylor placed her hand on her knee that was resting still on Camilla's thigh and smiled. She sipped from the beer bottle in her other hand.

"That's it?" Camilla asked. "You already told me they worked on the project together."

Taylor smiled more broadly, and swigged her beer.

"Yes, but what we didn't know was that something happened last year that *The Globe* had an article about, which I found, thank you very much."

Taylor drank from her beer. "*The Globe* was doing one of those feel-good articles about giving back to the community and was highlighting the clinic, how it involved several residents from the medical schools–Harvard's, BU's. Okay, okay. Stop looking at me like that. Just listen. Take a lude. Jesus. One of the runaways who was treated in the van at Harvard Square told the reporter that a resident had said some hateful slurs about the runaway being a lesbian while the girl was being treated."

Camilla shook her head. "Wasn't there someone else in the van? Besides, what does this—"

Taylor's hand grabbed Camilla's thigh. "That's just it. I'm thinking there was someone there who witnessed it."

Camilla tried to ignore Taylor's hand. She scowled. "Oh please. You think it was Hunter."

Taylor drank from her beer again. "Yes. Look, the article said it wasn't like a full-on attack. The medical resident, a woman, just was stupid. She asked the kid stuff about why she dressed so masculine and wasn't she afraid of being attacked because of it. There was a whole big shit show after that about training the residents better, blah blah blah. Anyway, I think Hunter was either there or read about it in *The Globe,* and that got her thinking. You said she was mad about her grade. Maybe she also saw the photo of you and Allison at that hospital fundraiser, she got the internship, and found out about you and Allison."

Unfolding her legs, Taylor lay back on the bed, placing her feet on the floor and resting her head in the middle of the mattress. "Pretty good, huh?" she said to the ceiling.

Camilla had a flashback to when Allison had said the same thing after her alliteration performance. She looked down. The double knot on her right sneaker was unraveling. Putting her bottle on the floor, she leaned over and retied the lace so that it matched the left sneaker.

Taylor asked her, "You're not going to say anything?"

Did it match? The knot still looked slightly off, as if it would come undone with the slightest movement. Her heart was racing. She felt nauseous.

"Mills?" Camilla felt Taylor's hand on her back. It began to move in a tiny circle at the base of her spine, clockwise.

"It still doesn't prove anything," Camilla said quietly to the floor. She tried to ignore Taylor's fingers increasing their pressure.

"What'd you say?" Taylor's hand stopped its circular motion. Her fingers tugged at the back of Camilla's black T-shirt. "Come here, so I can hear you."

Camilla sighed. She knew that there was a possibility that she was wrong. Taylor might be right. It was too coincidental that Hunter was an intern at a clinic that Allison was director of. Camilla wanted to be out of that room, far, far away, but the thought of actually standing and walking out was too much to handle.

Taylor's fingers tugged again. Camilla finally leaned back, ending up right next to Taylor. Taylor's hand came up on Camilla's stomach. It didn't move; it just lay there as if they were doing some type of operatic exercise to strengthen Camilla's diaphragm, like they did that regularly.

"What'd you say?" Taylor asked quietly. Camilla could see out of the corner of her right eye that Taylor's face was turned toward hers. It was an inch away.

Instead of repeating it, Camilla was surprised to find that she was crying. It wasn't like the women in so many Greek stories that were described as sobbing from one tragedy or another. Upon hearing a chorus of female mourners, Theseus said, "Whose is the wailing, the beating of breasts, and the keening for the dead that I have heard?" Tears edged out of the corner of Camilla's eyes like they were being squeezed out, the last liquid of a lemon rung dry. They slowly made their way down the sides of her face, falling off her jaw, soaking into the comforter next to her neck.

Later, she'd wonder if it was the tears that pushed Taylor into kissing Camilla, or if Taylor had planned to seduce Camilla all along. If so, when had she planned it? Was it when Taylor had left the treehouse that afternoon empty-handed without Audrey? When she'd been waiting for Camilla to show up at the bar? When she'd ordered them the shots or made the bet with Audrey that Camilla would show? Or when they'd sat down on her bed and found themselves in the same room from the beginning of their relationship? Maybe Taylor had been planning this since the day she and Camilla had split up.

Camilla would never know the answer. It didn't matter. Not with everything else that she had to face.

≈≈≈≈

Camilla awoke in the dark, her lips tender and dry. There was the metallic thunking sound of someone closing the front gate under the brownstone's front steps, the gate you had to go through to get into Taylor's apartment. For a moment, Camilla was disoriented. Where was she? By the time she realized she was in Taylor's bed and Taylor was asleep next to her, it was too late. There was the sound of a key in the front door lock, the lock turning, and the front door to the apartment opening and quietly closing.

Shit. She closed her eyes, pretending to sleep. Maybe whoever it was would see the two bodies and would silently leave the house, understanding that they'd missed their chance. Their seat in the movies had been taken when they'd gotten up for the bathroom. Camilla knew they—she—wouldn't leave, though. She knew who it was. She was only fooling herself about that. When she decided to open her eyes and say something, Audrey was already slipping off her clothes and then crawling into bed on the other side of Camilla. Camilla didn't move. Didn't open her eyes. Audrey spooned her from behind. She let out a soft sigh, her mouth close to Camilla's back so that Camilla felt her lips touch with each breath. As soon as Camilla thought Audrey had fallen asleep and maybe now she could get up and leave without them waking, Taylor rolled over and grabbed the two of them, crushing Camilla in the middle.

"About time you got here," Taylor murmured. When Audrey shifted a hand from Camilla's stomach over to Taylor's hip and pulled her tighter toward Camilla, Taylor said, "We know you're not asleep, Mills."

"Bathroom," Camilla whispered into Audrey's ear. Audrey was in the middle, her head resting on Camilla's shoulder and her arm across Camilla's stomach. Taylor was on the other side of Audrey, splayed across the side of Audrey's chest and stomach. Audrey moved her head away, still asleep.

Camilla hadn't slept at all. Audrey and Taylor had fallen asleep simultaneously the way two lovers do who have been sleeping together for a while. In the bathroom, Camilla looked at the plastic pink Cinderella clock that was on the wall. Six o'clock. The sun would be coming up soon. When was it permissible to leave? The thought of going back into the bedroom made her feel nauseous. She sat down on the toilet and peed. She washed her hands with Taylor's lavender liquid soap. She thought of Taylor and Audrey picking up the same pump bottle and washing their hands with the sweet lavender. Did it smell differently on them? She thought so. One of Allison's colleagues would taste cat litter every time he ate cilantro. *Our chemistries do their own thing,* Camilla thought. *We really have no control over them.*

She pumped more of the soap into the palm of her hand and washed her face with it. The smell brought her right back to the scene from the night before: their three bodies entangled, alternating who was below, who was above, who was under. Over and out, as Taylor would say. The bedroom had been so dark that at first Camilla couldn't make out whether it was Taylor or Audrey pulling her toward them. Faces were lost when they moved away. Then, suddenly, there was Taylor, kissing her shoulder. Camilla's eyes adjusted, then the darkness swept in as Taylor moved away and neither she nor Audrey was visible.

"Where are you?" Camilla had whispered, although she couldn't have said whom she was asking, and then, Audrey was there, kissing her mouth. Camilla had wanted desperately to turn a light on, even a night-light, something to take away some of the darkness, but when she'd tried to sit up, Taylor had gently pushed her down again. And while there had been moments when it'd all seemed overwhelming, when she'd lost track of who she was kissing, or who had their fingers inside of her, or who she was putting her mouth on, or if she was spending equal time with each of them, it had been an orchestrated dance of sorts.

Who was she kidding? she thought, looking in the bathroom mirror as she dried her hands. It was like a car accident during which everything—the sounds of metal on metal and glass breaking, the awful sudden jolt that takes control of the steering wheel, the careening into other cars, the coffee cup and boom box flying past your head—everything happens in such slow motion that you can actually read the letters S-O-N-Y flashing past in its trajectory. You can't stop it as much as you want to. Then, the accelerating of time, and you are abruptly and finally stopped, thank god, and staring through a shattered front window into an abyss of steam and smoke. Just when you feel that nothing further can happen, that you made it through safe, another car spirals into yours, the driver momentarily distracted by a fly that has made its way against all odds through his open window, setting off another chain reaction. Audrey was that final careening car. Audrey. Who might have fallen asleep at the same time as Taylor, but ten minutes later she was up and ready for Round Two, this time with Camilla only.

"Shh," she'd whispered in Camilla's ear as she

moved down Camilla's stomach, her legs and then her hands splitting Camilla's legs wide as her mouth continued to move down. "Don't wake her," Audrey told her. Camilla was just about to stop her when Audrey's mouth found her.

Afterward, Camilla felt guilty. She shouldn't have listened to Audrey. She should've awakened Taylor. Maybe Audrey herself had been asleep, hadn't been fully aware of what she was doing. Camilla had heard that sleepwalkers could carry on whole conversations with other family members at a kitchen table for hours, and in the morning have no memory of it. There was that story of the sleepwalker who went to his neighbor's house, shot him with a rifle, and had no recollection of it when the screams of the neighbor's wife finally woke him up. Why hadn't she shoved or kicked Taylor awake? If she had been the one asleep, wouldn't she have wanted that? If she hadn't been awakened, wouldn't she be pissed? Jealous?

Staring at her reflection in the bathroom mirror, Camilla realized, though, that she didn't feel guilty. She was happy. This was what she'd wanted. If she was truthful, it was why she hadn't immediately gotten up when she'd heard Audrey's key in the door. Having Taylor in the mix was the bridge she needed to cross to find Audrey. Taylor preached the survival-of-the-fittest military sermon to Camilla all the time. Camilla felt perfectly at peace for doing what she'd done. She told herself that. Her reflection said otherwise. Her bob was matted with sweat, hers and the others'. Her skin was flu-ish pale. Her lips were raw. Her usual soft blue eyes were hard and dark, two black olives.

"You are *not* okay," she whispered, and her doppelgänger repeated the words back. She thought of Allison and Cindy Hunter. Of Taylor and Audrey. She imagined them as dots that were connected in a constellation. Not the Big or Small Dipper, one of the more complicated ones. One of the ones where you can't take it all in at once. Like Orion the Hunter. Or Andromeda. The ones with ancient stories behind them. You have to follow the trail to piece it all together. What would be the next dot? Where would the stars take her next? Then, she thought of the treehouse. She felt something shift. She closed her eyes and imagined the treehouse, fully actualized. It was there in the oak tree. Unshakeable. Built to last. For Nico. Forever. It was the only thing in her life that was solid.

When she went back to the bedroom, she picked up her clothes silently and left, closing the door without a sound behind her. Dressing quickly in the front hallway, within a few seconds she was out the front door, then the gate. Outside, she walked up the three brick steps to the sidewalk. It wasn't sunny, as she'd expected. It was raining, hard. There were puddles on the brick sidewalks. Gutters on the brownstones were ringing with the sounds of water gushing through. Within seconds, Camilla's clothes were drenched, despite her running as fast as she could to her car.

Day Four

Jack

Despite her lack of sleep, her hangover, and soggy clothing, Camilla drove straight to the treehouse from Taylor's. The storm was a summer one; the rain ceased abruptly as if the well had run dry, and then the sun unexpectedly peeked out from behind the fast-moving cloud cover.

When she arrived at the house, she had to wear her sunglasses to see. It had become a lovely summer morning. The air smelled fresh, the humid air of the day before now gone. Camilla changed in her tiny vehicle, into clothes that she'd stashed in the back of the car ages ago: an old pair of cutoffs and a ratty T-shirt from grad school sporting a drawing of Emily Dickinson. She had to wear her soaked sneakers, but that was the least of her problems. As she walked up the path to the backyard with her tool belt fastened around her waist, the raindrops on the bluestone became silvery with drying.

Bound and determined not to let the night before screw up the progress she had made on the treehouse with Audrey, Camilla lifted the folded ladder and re-situated it against the tree, banging the feet down with more than necessary force. Upstairs, in the open-air room, she tore off the bright blue tarp hiding the remaining piles of shingles, plywood, and nails, and laid it out to dry. Images of the night before, followed by berating thoughts, flooded her. *Don't think, just do,* she told herself, but she couldn't help thinking about it.

She knew it was going to eventually turn into a shit show between the three of them, if it hadn't already. After all, Audrey and Taylor were still together at Taylor's house, probably still in her bed. She'd been flattered when Taylor had tugged her down next to her on her bed. Comforted. And she'd needed comforting. Taylor could be relied on for that. Or could she? Camilla knew the answer to that: truthfully, no. Taylor was like those people who send the most extravagant flower arrangement to someone who has lost a close family member, but don't show up to the funeral. She wouldn't be there when life got really messy. She could be there to buy you round after round of drinks to help you forget your failed life, but the minute you started sobbing into your beer, she would disappear.

For the next three hours, Camilla worked steadily, on, installing plywood panels against the roof frame that she and Audrey had completed the day before. It was hard work for one person. Perched on the top railing along the treehouse's circumference and holding on to a part of the roof frame for balance, she had to lift a plywood panel from its resting place against the wall and throw it onto a spot on the pitched frame. Then with her left shoulder holding the panel in place so that it wouldn't slide down, she tried to quickly pound in the nail. The first nail for each panel was the hardest. One time she hammered it in only to realize that the panel was not straight on the frame. There was little chance of her being able to pull the nail out without her falling to the ground, so she left it and moved on to the next panel. Another time the hammer slipped through her hand before she could return it safely to the tool belt. She watched as it bounced off the railing she was standing on, then spun to the ground. Rather than jumping off from the railing and climbing down the ladder, she pulled out the second, smaller hammer that she'd leant Audrey the day before. She thought of Audrey gripping the same place on the hammer's handle. She aligned her fingers as she imagined Audrey did. She felt the warmth, the heft. Audrey's hammer. She wondered if she'd always see it as Audrey's hammer from now on. No matter what happened between them.

Objects transformed into something else when couples came together, and something else again when they broke up. During the three months she'd been with Taylor, Taylor had worn Camilla's favorite suede jacket more than she had. It became a joke between them: who could grab the coat first out of the closet and make a dash for the front door in Taylor's apartment. One time they'd wrestled each other down to the floor for it, snapping off a button in the process. Every time Taylor wore it Camilla saw her own arms wrapped tight around Taylor's body, not the suede fabric. After they split up, Camilla kept it, but ultimately thought of it as Taylor's, not hers. She rarely wore it now. It hung, with its one missing button, in her coat closet next to her other winter coats. Sometimes she wondered if she should have relented and just given the coat to Taylor. Camilla gripped the hammer tighter. She banged another nail in. Where was Audrey now? Still in bed with Taylor? Camilla cursed herself for not waking Audrey up and asking for her help again. It would've been so much easier if she had. They would've finished the panels in no time, working together. It would've laid to rest Camilla's questioning if Audrey did really have feelings for her, or if last night had happened as a lark, or worse yet, if it had happened because Audrey thought she would please Taylor that way.

Would a ménage à trois work for the three of them? As much as Camilla didn't think so, there was something attractive about it. Such arrangements littered the artist world throughout time. For decades, Clive Bell, the Bloomsbury art critic, had put up with the painter Duncan Grant being the occasional lover and true love of his wife, the painter Vanessa Bell. They shared Charleston Farm in Sussex together. Duncan and Vanessa even had a child together, a daughter, and Clive and Vanessa had two sons. Camilla struck the last nail in the bottom corner of the panel. But, Duncan was gay, and although he was Vanessa's lifelong partner, he caused her, Camilla believed, unquestionable heartache. And what of Clive? From what she'd read, Clive didn't get what he wanted either. It was unequal from the start. That's what happened with three people involved. Inequality followed by jealousy followed by accusations, followed by hurt.

No, Camilla couldn't handle that. Last night alone was riddling her with doubt and shredding her self-confidence into confetti. Yet, what if she could only have Audrey if Taylor was part of the package? What then? It was ridiculous. How could she be so attached to Audrey? *You don't know her at all*, she reminded herself. She was acting like she was in her twenties, not late forties. She was ridiculous. Here she was, building a treehouse for a child she had left, and thinking about fucking a girl she didn't know. She needed to get her priorities straight. It was one thing for Taylor to behave this way. Taylor was Peter Pan. She'd be picking up girls until she was eighty. Maybe then, too. *You made a choice. You left a crazy relationship. Now, you're going to start up another one?*

She jumped down from the railing so that she could take a break and have some water. Suddenly, she was so hot she thought she'd faint. She hadn't noticed how strong the sun was. The sky was bright blue through the uncovered gaps of the roof, the clouds swept away to New Hampshire, or maybe Maine, by now. You'd never have known there had been a torrential downpour three hours before. Standing in the doorway near the ladder, Camilla gulped water from her plastic bottle. The water was warm, but it soothed her dry throat. She felt like her mouth would never be moist again. An image of Audrey's tongue touching hers sent an ache down Camilla's legs. She was in trouble. She had to stop these images. No good would come of them. In spite of this, she wondered if Audrey would show up at the treehouse that day. At that, part of her questioned why Audrey hadn't shown up yet. The hamster wheel of self-doubt started up again.

When she went back to climb up on the railing, she raised another panel to its place much more slowly. Her muscles ached. She felt exhausted. Weighed down. Her mind was like one of the cardboard boxes Allison had shipped to her, splitting at the seams from overstuffing, from the framed photographs of the two of them, from every card that Camilla had ever given her, from all of the presents that Camilla had showered her with—the CDs, the books, the clothing, the thirteen years of shirts and sweaters and scarfs and socks, a porcelain jewelry box, the disco ball bought for Allison's seventies birthday party, the necklaces and earrings, and finally the gold and silver band that they bought each other in California—all of it threatening to burst forth on to the ground at any minute, showing everyone its dirty laundry.

❧❧❧❧

She needed to eat. It was two o'clock and she'd eaten nothing all day. She didn't want to stop until she finished the plywood—there were still the shingles, the door, the permanent rope ladder to attach. The heat and her lack of sleep were taking their toll. With each nail, her hammering had slowed. She needed to eat and get something more to drink. A headache was wreaking havoc at her temples.

She drove into Wilbur's center. She hoped that Audrey wouldn't show up at the treehouse while she was gone and think she wasn't there. *Audrey is not coming, you idiot*, she told herself, shifting the Mini into second gear as she came down a steep hill onto Fortune Ave, the main street running through Wilbur. She and Allison had moved from Boston to Wilbur when they bought the Victorian house. Camilla had loved the house as soon as the realtor brought them there. Wilbur, though, was another matter. Camilla felt cut off from Taylor and her other friends who lived in Boston.

"It's only twenty minutes away," their realtor argued, and gave Allison a sympathetic look that said she could not believe that Camilla was being so unreasonable. The realtor was tiny without her five-inch heels. She wore a seersucker pantsuit that Camilla swore she'd seen in the window at Brooks Brothers on Newbury Street on a small boy mannequin. Her hair was cut short like a boy's, too. Any gaydar emanating from her was trashed, however, by those stilettos and the heavy gold jewelry she had roped around her neck, by the pendants hanging from her ears, and the diamonds circling her fingers.

"Twenty minutes by *car* and not during rush hour," Camilla said to her. She wanted to say more—how they'd have to drive everywhere now, including into the center of Wilbur, which was three miles away; how there wasn't even a decent café to drive to for an espresso on a Sunday morning—but the realtor was already whisking Allison through the rest of the house, steering her by her elbow and pointing out various things she called "accoutrements," as if Allison was blind. The realtor insisted on using a fake French accent. Camilla had the urge to yell at her that the word meant *a uniform*. It had nothing to do with any architectural element. Instead, she stepped through the house into the hilly backyard. Seeing the peony trees with their white dinner-plate-sized flowers, she envisioned a romantic wildflower garden to complement the rambling house. A home where she could contemplate big Dickensian thoughts.

Closing her car door now and walking down Fortune Ave, Camilla was brought back to that feeling of isolation she'd felt the first time she'd been in the house. She walked quickly, with her head down, past the doggy day care where she and Allison used to bring their poodle, Buddy, before he'd died. She wanted to avoid seeing the two owners, lesbians who were married to each other, both of whom were named Donna. They weren't their people, but Camilla and Allison had admired them for having the wherewithal to make their business and personal partnerships work for over twenty years. Still, Camilla hoped to God she didn't run into them now. They'd lost touch after Buddy passed. Who knew if they knew that she'd left two years before? The thought of explaining everything exhausted Camilla more. Breakups were like the walking mono that ran rampant through Tolland last semester: surprising regardless of all the telltale lead-up signs, riddling students with fatigue. Inevitable.

She made it safely to the deli where she found herself ridiculously hoping that she wouldn't run into Jack, despite the fact he was always there. Camilla had once considered him her only friend in that isolating town. He didn't own the deli; his father did. But he was there, almost every day, ensuring his legacy by his presence. His father and he were not on the best of terms because Jack was gay. He had phenomenal customer service skills, though, that his father couldn't deny were the cause of the deli's success. Jack remembered every regular customer's name, birthday, spouse and children's names, and favorite cold cuts. He remembered that Ginny Larsen liked her salami thin and her husband liked it thick, and their wrapped-up, divided pound of meat reflected that to the ounce. He'd hold open the door for Mrs. Sadler so that she could maneuver her handicapped cart through easily, joking that she should obey the town's speed limit. He congratulated the Maury twins on their recent soccer games even though he knew they both were klutzes, repeatedly tripping over the ball and receiving multiple penalties for carelessly kicking their opponent's legs.

Camilla learned all this one late afternoon the week after they'd moved to Wilbur, when she slipped in for a carton of milk right before closing. Jack invited her to join him for a glass of wine, which turned into a bottle, in the deli's back room. After that, they'd meet for drinks and dinner once a week at an old-school Italian restaurant across the town line because Wilbur was a dry town. Camilla would make sure that Allison would be staying late at the hospital those nights.

"How's your bologna salesman?" Allison would ask her in bed on those nights. She'd fall asleep before Camilla answered, not worried that it would turn into something more for Camilla.

The truth was that Camilla didn't know why she wanted Jack as a friend over the years she lived in Wilbur. He wasn't cultured. One night he asked her who Picasso was. He hadn't been joking. He also was completely closeted.

"Oh, no darling. After hearing what my father had to say about it, I decided to bolt that door shut," he told her the first time they were sitting over steaming plates of chicken cacciatore. She only knew he was gay because he had come out to her, after he'd seen her in the deli one of those rare times she came in with Allison on a Saturday. He looked stereotypically straight with his broad face and nondescript hair. His clothes were boring and conventional. He wore the same thing every day: a pine-colored knit shirt tucked into a pair of khakis, with a pair of those horrible dock shoes that Camilla believed Republicans wore.

More than any of that, he was a gossip. This perturbed Camilla the most. At first, she'd laughed at all his stories about all his customers, people that Camilla didn't know personally, but came to know, or so she thought, through Jack. He was unmerciful in his physical descriptions of people. "Girl, I thought they found a cure for the pox," he told her when he described one of his customer's unfortunate skin problems. He was more scathing when it came to their tragedies.

"Oh, that one," he'd say, his voice becoming more flamboyant as the night wore on and the wine flowed. "His wife walked out on him. But can you blame her, darling? I mean if you look like a rhinoceros you end up sitting alone in a mud patty. Jesus, Mary. Have a little pride."

Yet, Camilla had accepted every invitation to dinner with him. She was adept at steering the conversation away from anything personal about her, other than her academic life. She had seen him gossiping enough not to confide anything about Allison to him. Not that she thought he'd repeat anything to Allison. Allison called him Camilla's IRS write-off. No, it was more that Camilla worried he'd repeat whatever she said to another customer. What other patrons might he have dinner plans with the other six nights every week? When he'd try to pry her for details about Allison, Camilla diverted him by asking another question about some other deli customer. "How's that woman who lives on Berry Ave holding up after her son's OD?" she'd ask, and Jack would be off and running. "I always thought she was his pusher," he'd whisper as the story built on speculation and bitchiness picked up steam. If Camilla worried that there'd come a day when she couldn't divert him so easily, she was mistaken. The dinners petered out anyway, as soon as Nico was born.

"I can't," she'd tell Jack when he called. "Duty calls."

"I think you mean, doody, darling," he'd say. When he hung up, Camilla imagined that he was right back on the phone telling another customer that she'd become a nursemaid and had joined the battalion of customers that he asked politely about their children.

She had become what he called, "one of the breeders."

Then, without telling Jack anything, she left Allison, moved back in with Taylor for a few months before she found her own place in Cambridge. She hadn't returned to the deli until now. She could've gone to the Stop & Shop for one of their stale pre-made sandwiches, but she stood a good chance of running into several of her neighbors there. Maybe Pecksniff. Besides, she told herself, Jack's was an epicurean dream when it came to its sandwich menu. Not your typical turkey on a squishy white roll with tomato, iceberg lettuce, and mayonnaise. It offered The Battle Hymn, a pounded flank steak marinated in barbecue sauce and smothered in creamed corn on a bulky roll. There was a meatball sub, infused with cilantro and layered with salsa, called The Mexican Revolution. The Nirvana pleased the vegetarians like Allison, with caramelized bananas and melted chocolate in a rollup. All of this was Jack's doing. This made him even more indispensable to his father, and reminded Camilla that there was more to Jack than his lack of culture and his carping tongue.

Now, as she walked down the street toward the deli, she wondered if she'd befriended him simply because he had been so different from Allison and her tightly wound world of saving lives. Those gossipy dinners had provided a relief of sorts to her, a chance to step out of her own unpredictable life into the truly bottomed-out lives of others. "Your life starts to look so much better next to the lives of the urban victims of this world," Jack used to say. It put Camilla in mind of all the brilliant writers like Truman Capote who balanced their days of serious pursuits with friendships with chinwaggers and gossip mavens. Eventually, though, Capote was shunned for telling all himself. As Camilla's fingers grabbed the handle of the deli's glass door, she hesitated for a moment. Why was she here? Was it a test to see if she'd be shunned, to face someone who would know that she had left her child, who may have been deeply hurt himself when she'd left without a word? Or to see if she'd been forgiven and he'd welcome her, maybe not with open arms, but welcome her all the same with the newest story of a life in a ditch? What *was* she doing there? *I'm hungry, that's all*, she angrily reminded herself, shaking her head free of the psychological cobweb.

"Well, look what the cat dragged in," Jack called over the counter as soon as Camilla entered the store and the bells over the door tinkled.

Camilla smiled gamely. The shop was empty, everyone away for the rest of the holiday week.

When she didn't say anything, he said, "Well, hi there, Jack. How are you?"

Camilla forced a laugh. "Hey."

"I'm fine, but you look terrible," he said.

He did look fine. Camilla noticed that he was wearing a black T-shirt under his white apron instead of his usual knit shirt, and it was tighter, showing a buffer body than she remembered: not leaner, but more muscular. His now salt-and-pepper hair was cropped into a tight buzz cut. She realized she had no idea how old he was. She had never asked. He had never said.

"You look good," she said.

"What can I get you, dear?" he asked, suddenly all business. "We have some new items since you were here last." He motioned up to the sandwich board. "Let's see. Two years ago, wasn't it?" Camilla tried to read the selections, the letters jumping before her on the sign like fleas. It was useless. She felt his eyes staring at her and all she could think was how bad a decision it had been to come back. She felt lightheaded, dizzy. She'd only fainted once in her life, when she'd been a kid and had closed a car door on her fingers. She didn't want to faint, not here.

"I'll have the Indian Giver," she said quickly, choosing one of the new items.

"Well, you *have* changed," Jack cooed at her. "Aren't you the daring one now." The comment stung. *He knows everything*, she thought. But how? Camilla walked the short distance to the cooler. She grabbed a neon green sports drink that promised to double her electrolytes. Surely, Allison hadn't confided in him on one of her rare trips into the deli. But now that Camilla wasn't there to do the deli runs, maybe Allison had to come in more frequently. Maybe she had weekly drinks and dinner with Jack now. In a way, Allison was more Jack's type: the slice-and-dice misanthrope. The idea was preposterous. Allison and the bologna salesman? She had to get a grip on her paranoia. She was off-kilter. This was all Taylor's fault. Why had she gone to Taylor's the night before? Worse, why had she stayed?

"Not really," she finally replied to Jack as she slid the drink onto the counter.

His head was down. He was intent on making her what appeared to be chicken chunks awash in some kind of red sauce that looked fiery, topped by a chutney and sprinkled with fennel seeds and jalapeno slivers on naan bread. *Good god.*

"I guess you like it hot now," Jack murmured as he wrapped up the sandwich. He handed it to her over the counter and slid over to the register. As he punched in the numbers he slipped back into his business mode.

"Ten fifty, dear. How's Nico? He must be what, five now? When's his birthday again?"

Camilla felt immediate relief. So, he didn't know. He didn't know anything. He was flip-flopping weirdly because he didn't know how to act with her.

"He's four, actually." She felt her heart rate speed up. It was as if she was lying even though she was telling the truth. Did she have a right to talk about Nico like that? She would never be in his life again, but she would always know his age. She would never forget his birthday.

She could feel her eyes tearing up. "Thanks for the sandwich," she told Jack, and turned to leave so that she could get out of there as fast as possible.

He stopped her with his words. "That's it?" She had to turn around.

"Um, yes, it's just for me." She wagged the bag at him as she sidled closer to the door. "Thanks."

He shook his head and looked away toward the back room. "What did I do?" he said quietly.

"What?" she asked, startled. "Nothing. I've just been busy." She stumbled as she went on. "It wasn't... isn't...you."

Jack laughed harshly, turning back to her. "That's what the last guy I dated told me."

Camilla forced herself to laugh. "Look, I've got to go," she told him, and before he could object, she opened the door.

"Don't be a stranger," he called after her.

As she started up her car, she thought she could get through anything now. Leaning her forehead against the steering wheel, she concentrated on slowing her breathing. She couldn't blame everything on her leaving Nico. Some things would have happened even if she had stayed. Her friendship with Jack might have gone on for a few more months, but if she was honest, she had been getting sick of the dinners, of the catty retelling of the tragic lives some people had, well before she'd left. Maybe she'd begun the friendship out of a need to avoid her own life for a few hours over a plate of cacio e pepe, but when she'd left that life she no longer needed that emergency escape pod.

It didn't matter who she ran into now. She was living her new life. The old one sloughed away like skin removed at a fancy spa. Most people wouldn't know anything about her past. They wouldn't see her as the woman who had left a long-term relationship. As the woman who had left her son. As the woman who had slept with two women the night before. She wasn't anything like Hester Prynne wearing her scarlet letter for all to ridicule. They'd simply see her as she was: a tired, middle-aged woman who could stand a good meal, a hot shower, and better clothes.

When she got back to the treehouse, she bounded up the steps carrying the small white paper bag that already was showing red stains. The Indian Giver was mouth-on-fire hot. Burning coals might have been cooler to eat. Each bite seemed to make her feel more energized, to sit up straighter, as if it were a rite of passage. Camilla ate every bit of it. When she was finished, she licked her fingers and drank most of the sports drink. She stood up. A hot breeze passed over her. She tucked the sides of her bob behind her ears, picked up the tool belt, and went straight to the panel that still hung helter-skelter because of its one misplaced nail. It was the last panel to finish before she could start the roof shingles. Without worrying that she'd fall off the narrow railing, Camilla leaned against the roof and attacked the nail, shimmying the hammer's claw under the nail head and prying upward. That nail was a splinter in a palm, stubbornly refusing to come out no matter how you went at it with your tweezers and sewing needle.

But she refused to give up. The hammer slipped. Camilla almost fell. She tried again. Hugging the next panel, she attacked the nail again. Slowly, it began to lift. When it finally came out, and she nailed the board in right, she felt triumphant, as if she were the last gladiator standing.

Linda

Camilla had hoped to start on the roof shingles before she left. Within the hour, though, another summer storm was barreling through, this one more fierce than the one in the morning. She was ripping open one of the bags of shingles inside the treehouse when she heard thunderclaps coming from the west. It sounded like a drum corps parade coming closer and closer. Lightning crackled overhead; streaks of white dazzled the sky awfully close to the oak tree.

Standing in the treehouse doorway, Camilla looked out past the houses and heard shouting at the same time as she saw a wall of rain moving rapidly toward her from the west. The shouting was from the park around the corner across the street from the elementary school, the park that she and Nico used to play in. The rain was causing havoc among all the families barbecuing and pushing their kids in the swings. The waterfall hit her and the treehouse, which shifted from the force of the driving rain but stayed stable.

She took shelter farther inside the treehouse. She sat down. She listened to the water pelting the roof. Hail. Would the plywood withstand the storm? What would she do if the panels started to be ripped off, or even fly away altogether? The seams between them had started to drip water onto the floor. What if the entire treehouse tumbled to the ground, unmoored from its bracing? Would she start over? Was there time to start over? Would she have the energy for that? How committed was she? Camilla hugged herself as if she needed to feel something solid so that she wouldn't be swept away with her thoughts amid the downpour.

The hail was a thousand necklace beads crashing on the roof. Rain was angling through the open doorway of the treehouse, wetting the plywood floor. A rivulet inched its way down toward the other side, where she was hunched over. Taylor and Audrey were probably still in bed. Audrey probably called in sick. Camilla remembered staying in bed for days with Taylor in the beginning of their relationship, only getting out of bed when it was absolutely necessary, to go to the bathroom, or to get a drink or to order a pizza. But her thoughts were interrupted by a woman's voice calling as if from another memory. You-hoo, it said. You-hoo. The voice was high-pitched, loud, and suddenly she realized it was fighting with the rain to be heard. A real voice. "You-hoo!"

Camilla crawled toward the door. Who the hell was out in this? She peered over the edge. A large umbrella depicting a blue sky and clouds hid whoever was holding its handle underneath. The sight was disconcerting. As the rain and hail hit the umbrella's blue sky it was as if the whole world was topsy-turvy. The umbrella tilted, swayed with the wind. Whoever was holding it was in danger of losing it at any moment.

"What are you doing up there?" the woman shouted. She was wearing a trench coat that covered down to her ankles. A turquoise-colored scarf peeked out of the coat. Hail the size of dimes pinged off the bluestone path and the umbrella.

It was Linda from the college.

"What are you doing here?" Camilla shouted down.

"I'm getting drenched," Linda yelled up. "Come down!" She disappeared through the side gate. Camilla heard a car door close.

There was nothing to do but join her. A thunderclap sounded. The hail picked up its speed. Camilla covered the floor with the tarp and set off down the ladder. She ran to the car, soaked. Second time today, she thought. She hoped she wouldn't get sick. She was upset that Linda had come. That she had demanded that Camilla come down. What did she want? Why couldn't people simply leave her alone?

When Camilla shut the passenger door behind her in the small Toyota, Linda was already unraveling her scarf. The car was steamy; the heat was turned on.

"Jesus, Linda, we're going to die in here. It's July."

Linda turned down the knob, although she didn't put it to the off position. She re-wound her scarf around her neck. "What are you doing in this rain, Camilla? Are you nuts?"

"What are *you* doing? Why are you here?"

Linda looked in her rearview mirror and dabbed at her lipstick with her index finger. "My hair is positively ruined. Dammit. I just came from the salon. And I have a dinner engagement tonight." She did a quick bouncing motion at the bottom of her shoulder-length hair. She was a blonde, or at least she had been. Sometimes Camilla had seen a strip of grey appear separated by her part when Linda didn't book an appointment with her hair colorist on time.

"The question is..." She faced Camilla. "The question is, what are *you* doing here." She paused. "I ran into Wallace in the elevator. That man. I'd hoped to just slip in and start quietly working on my fall syllabus, but no, there he was, telling me all about how you had some cockamamie idea to build a treehouse by yourself. I told him he must be on drugs. I always suspected he smoked a little weed with his students. You know how he always tries to make out like he's hipper than the rest of us?" She tucked the end of her scarf back in by her neck and patted it. "Well, no, he said, 'I'm not on drugs,'" Linda went on. "But that *you* must be as he'd stopped by to visit you and there you were, up a tree like one of the lost boys, hammering away."

She leaned over, peering out through the front windshield as if she was picturing Camilla in the treehouse, banging away. Then, she sat up and turned back to her.

"Since when, by the way, are you and Wallace so chummy? You've only invited me here once and that was when you first moved in, remember, for that awfully tedious housewarming party? I mean, how many toasters and blenders can you use? Anyway, there was Wallace with his astounding news, don't look at me like that, it *was* astounding my dear and I don't use that word lightly. He said that Allison and Nico had left for the day and you had stayed behind to play carpenter. Well, then I knew that you had gone off the deep end. He had no clue that you were no longer living here—"

"Did you tell him?" Camilla said sharply.

Linda tugged on her scarf. "Of course not! What do you take me for? Listen, my dear, I might be blunt, I might tell you things you don't want to hear, but I am not a snitch or a gossip. I did not tell him a thing. I've never trusted that man. He lays the compliments on thick and you just know he's looking for some way to use you to get someplace else. He said that he knew we were friends and he wondered if I knew why you were building that treehouse at this time in your life. Like it was part of some religious conversion on your part and you were Michelangelo painting the Sistine Chapel. The next thing you know you'll be a Catholic. The man loves the sound of his own voice. I lied and insisted that I hardly knew you at all. That we were colleagues who sometimes found ourselves at the Xerox machine at the same time. He said, 'I'm a stranger in a strange land, right?' I stared at him as if he was the one who should be checking himself into McLean's for a thirty-day stay. He said, 'Carson McCullers. I think it rivals *The Great Gatsby* for best American novel, don't you?' He practically licked his lips from the thought that he and I were *bonding*. Why is it that buffoon cannot remember that I teach a course on *Mary McCarthy*, not Carson McCullers? I mean, how can anyone confuse *The Heart is a Lonely Hunter* with *The Group*? You'd have to be an imbecile. Finally, I escaped from him. I still cannot believe they have made that odious man Chair. I turned right around and got back in the elevator. I told him I'd forgotten something in my car. He's probably circling like a vulture outside my office at this very moment."

Camilla listened despite her mounting anxiety.

It didn't help that by then Linda had gone through her scarf cycle five times. Each time Camilla worried she would tie it too tight, like a noose.

Linda sighed. "I need a drink." She appraised Camilla. "Where's the closest bar? Some place we won't run into anyone we know." Camilla didn't know if she wanted to avoid having anyone see her with Camilla looking like a homeless person, or whether she was being protective of her.

"This is a dry town, Linda. We'll have to drive to Jasper. The next town over."

Linda snorted. "No wonder you left." She turned the key in the ignition and they set off.

❧❧❧❧

They ended up at McGeary's, where a bartender with a face the color of cold ashes was arguing with a fifty-ish drunken woman with short pigtails, who was sitting at the bar.

"I know what I saw," the bartender said.

"I'm telling you. I'm not a slut. I was just real nice to him," the woman said.

"Charming," said Linda as they made their way to a table that had a few peanut shell husks on it. The other tables were spotted with dirty glasses or leftover newspapers. The place smelled rancid and stuffy, as if from a moldy floor mopping, or like it had been closed down for a while for health reasons and then reopened prematurely. For all of the bar's emptiness, there was a waitress, her long grey hair held back with a sparkly plastic hairband. She arrived at the table before they sat down. She wore a plastic nametag that said, "I'm just the plumber."

"A double martini," Linda said. The waitress stared at her. "Okay, then a double Scotch. You do have *that*, don't you?"

The waitress glanced at Camilla. "The same," Camilla said. She was nervous. She didn't like to drink hard liquor before five and here it was only three. She needed something strong, though. She was sure of that. This wasn't a social visit. The waitress left to go get the drinks. When Linda started her usual scarf routine, Camilla said, "Can you stop doing that, please?"

Linda's fingers came to a rest. She shifted her hands to her lap. "Nervous habit," she said, smiling tightly.

"What are we doing here, Linda?" Camilla asked. "Why did you come?"

The waitress came with their drinks.

"Fifteen," she said, holding out her hand.

"Can we start a bar tab?" Linda said.

The waitress shook her head. "We don't do credit here."

"Oh for God's sakes." Linda shook her head when Camilla went to pull out money from her cutoffs. She counted out the exact amount from her purse. When the waitress saw there wasn't a tip in it, Linda said, "Didn't you just say no credit? How do I know how good the service is here? You might disappear, never to be heard from again." The waitress shook her head, and went back to her perch on a stool at the end of the bar, her back to them a clear sign that they would be ignored for the rest of eternity.

"I'm here because something is wrong. *Very* wrong," Linda whispered to Camilla. She leaned across the table, and then, apparently thinking better of it, settled back in her chair. "Why else would I be standing in the rain calling up to my friend who apparently has decided to leave academia for the fabulous world of pitch and beam."

Camilla laughed despite her anxiousness. "It's called post and beam."

Linda waved her hand at her, irritated. "The important thing is *why*? You should be writing another article over this break."

Camilla swallowed her Scotch. She was happy for the warming liquid snaking down her throat. Her clothes were still damp. She heard the rain slapping against the bar's front bay window. A chill made her shudder. She took another sip. Linda watched her, sipping her drink as if she were eyeing up a competition.

"Well?" Linda finally said.

"I missed him." Camilla shrugged. Took another sip. Placed the glass down and ran her fingers along the top of the glass. The bartender must've gotten tired of arguing with pigtails because suddenly there was a crackle and then the sound system spewed a folk rock song. Camilla wondered if it was The Lumineers? Mumford and Sons? She could never keep the new bands straight. One of her students last semester had made fun of her saying, "That's like someone your age confusing Led Zeppelin with the Rolling Stones." Before Camilla could lie and tell him that analogy was a little before her time, the student had already walked away.

"So, miss him," Linda said simply.

"I promised I would build it."

Linda shrugged. "To who? Her?"

Camilla shook her head. "To him. To me. I don't know. I guess, yes, to him." When Linda's eyebrow shot up Camilla quickly said, "Okay, not *to* him, but in spirit."

"And then what? Everything is all better?"

Camilla bristled. "I'm not a child who has a cut on her knee!"

Linda drank her drink, eyeing Camilla over the rim. She lowered it to the table. Looking at the amber liquid as if she were reading tea leaves, she said, "I lost a child."

"What?" Camilla said, her glass in mid-air.

"Ten years ago. Before you knew me. She was five. Leukemia." Linda went for her scarf with her right hand. Her other hand came up fast and grabbed the plucking one, held it tight, against the scarf, against her throat. "Not a day goes by that I don't think of her. Think of all the things I want to do for her. That I *can't* do for her. Not anymore."

Camilla felt like she couldn't breathe.

Linda shook her head. One hand was lightly patting the other against her throat, as if she was keeping beat to the song that was playing. "This dear friend of mine told me once that grief is like an heirloom ring you inherit. You get up, slide it on your finger every morning, see it occasionally throughout the day, and if you're lucky it reminds you of good things about the person, why you loved them so, and then, before you go to sleep, you take it off and put it back in the jewelry box for safekeeping. The next day you do it all again."

She finished her drink. When she replaced her glass again on the table, she reached out and grabbed Camilla's hand, surprising her.

"I'm sorry I gave you such a hard time when you told me you were angry that she wouldn't let you see your son again after you left. That was my own stuff."

Her eyes were wet. She gripped Camilla's hand

tighter. "You know what I hate? I hate when people ask me if I have any children." Linda's voice broke. "I mean, what do you say? If we say no, it's like we're not acknowledging them, like we've turned our backs on them, and not still loving them. If we say yes, then there are more questions, the story to be told. I hate that," she said, crying lightly. "Don't you?" Her fist, still holding Camilla's, tapped both of them against the table.

Camilla began to cry then, too. For a second she was embarrassed that they were making such a spectacle of themselves in that awful bar, and then, surprisingly, she didn't care.

"Fuck them," Linda whispered as if reading her mind, still tapping their enclosed hands against the table. "We know how great our love was for them. We know."

They sat for a moment like that, staring at each other, leaning across the table, their melded fists tapping the table. "Let's get out of this horrible place," Linda said finally. She released Camilla's sweaty hand. They both stood up.

When they were almost at the door, Camilla tugged on Linda's trench coat sleeve and asked, "What was her name?"

Linda stopped. "What? Oh. Lily," Linda said and laughed harshly. Her face got sad. "It was the worst name I could've chosen in hindsight. The only things lilies are good for are funerals."

Outside, the rain was letting up. Camilla was done for the day. She wouldn't go back and start on the roof shingles. She didn't care if the sun came out and dried everything up and she could get another three hours in. She'd been through enough.

Back in the car, Linda hesitated before turning over the ignition. "Finish your treehouse, Milly. Finish the bloody thing and then get in your car and drive like hell back into your life. Your *real* life." As if in answer, the Toyota's engine fired up and they began to move.

Camilla

Camilla didn't want to see Audrey or Taylor that night. She wanted a warm shower and her own bed after Linda had dropped her off at the treehouse and she'd driven home. It was only five o'clock. She didn't want dinner, either. The Indian Giver was still lodged, perhaps permanently, in her stomach. From time to time an acidic taste revisited her throat and mouth.

In the shower, she turned the hot water on as far as it could go. She washed her entire body and shaved her legs and underarms twice. She remembered that scene in *Silkwood*, where Meryl Streep stands in her shower at home, violently scrubbing herself to remove any vestige of the plutonium poisoning she ingested in the factory. No matter how hard she scrubbed, she couldn't get rid of the sick feeling that she'd been contaminated. Camilla didn't want to think about Linda or her child. She didn't want to think about all the mothers in the world who had lost their children. Many to disease or accident, sure, but for other things, too. Others, like herself, who had lost them to their partners for one reason or another. Addiction. Mental illness. Neglect. Divorce. She didn't want to think of the women who had lost them to women they no longer loved. Who made it impossible to stay. The mothers who by leaving were trying to do the right thing for the kids. The mothers who somehow were left with the feeling that it was the worst thing they could have done.

Camilla didn't want to think of these things. Maybe she had always kept Linda at arms' length all the years that they had worked together for that reason. Her gut had been trying to tell her something. Linda came to Camilla bearing Pandora's Box. Open it and suffer the consequences. The box had been opened. Deceit, blame, and trickery let loose from the jar that Pandora had uncorked.

In her steamy bathroom, Camilla poured herself a large dose of NyQuil, downing it in one gulp. Wiping clean a curving band on the mirror, she saw a naked woman, streaked with water rivulets, a nymph from a Greek myth, her pale face smudged with what was left of her mascara. No, not a nymph. The face looked ready for battle. She'd been transformed into one of the keres, female death spirits. Hesiod described them as "grim-eyed, fierce, bloody, terrifying."

But, hope had remained in Pandora's jar, Camilla remembered, never to be released. Humanities scholars had debated for decades if that should be interpreted as a benefit for humanity, giving comfort to anyone riddled with illness or the loss of a loved one. Hope still lived in the bottom of that jar. *Don't give up*, it shouted. Others argued it was another cruel joke of the gods, keeping the one thing from us that could help us avoid feeling depressed by our fate. Camilla had been hopeful that Allison would change, that the generous and loving Allison would send the angry and hard Allison away forever. She'd been hopeful when she'd originally created the treehouse plan years before when she'd been living with Allison and Nico. That hope had been reborn when she and Taylor resuscitated the plan, and began to build it. But what had such hope done for her, really? Had it changed Allison? Had it stopped her from leaving Nico? Had it returned Nico back to her? That, ultimately, was why she was building the treehouse, wasn't it? Deep down, she hoped that when Allison saw it, Allison would realize that she'd made a mistake. That Nico still needed Camilla in his life. That Camilla still loved Nico. Had never stopped loving Nico. If she were asked this minute whether she had any children, Camilla would answer. Would roar. Would raise a fist in the air. Yes. *Yes, I have a son.*

But, hope wasn't enough. It wasn't real. It wouldn't save her. Or Nico. Allison would always be Allison. Hope would probably, when it came down to it, only deceive her further. *Apate*, Deceit, had been one of the first of the evil spirits to fly the coop as fast and far as it could get away from Pandora. *Apate*. Daughter of *Nyx*, Night, and *Erebos*, Darkness. "I see you," Camilla whispered to her mirror image. "I see you. I won't be fooled. I won't be deceived." She'd build the treehouse. But after that, she wasn't counting on a life of bubbles and clover.

☙☙☙☙

Although the box for the cold medicine promised an uninterrupted deep sleep, Camilla's heart rate was speedy after toweling herself off. She tried to lie down on her bed. The comforter made her hot. She kicked it off. Then, she was cold. There were too many pillows. She threw one of them on to the floor. Her ankles itched from mosquito bites she'd gotten earlier that morning after the first rainstorm at the treehouse had stopped and the air was saturated with their buzzing.

When one of her toenails scraped against her other ankle, she got up and went to the bathroom to get a nail clipper. She avoided looking at herself in the mirror, at the mascara smudges that resembled a soldier's jungle makeup. The thought of exerting energy to wipe away the dark mess was too much. She sat down on top of her comforter heap on the bedroom floor, her back against the bed. Clipping her nails only set her on edge more. Her cell phone rang, startling her so much she cut the nail painfully short. *Shit.*

"Why aren't you here?" It was Taylor. She sounded drunk: too loud, too aggressive. Background bar noises were a scrim over her voice: people yelling and laughing, someone nearby repeating that they needed three drafts, someone else shouting over and over "you're a fucking asshole that's why," and a song by The Pretenders fighting to be heard.

"I can't hear you," Camilla said, although she could.

"Bullshit. Get your ass over here, Mills." Taylor started to laugh. "In your dreams."

"What?"

"Nothing. I wasn't talking to you. Just get your ass here."

"I'm already in bed—"

"Audrey wants you here."

"Tay—" But the line went dead.

Nestled on the comforter, Camilla held her mobile in her hands, passing it from one palm to the other like a hot potato. The nail clipper was on the comforter. It reflected a line of sunshine streaming in from her bedroom window. The spot was ice-white on the metal clippers. It was six thirty. What was she going to do, sit here all night and watch that spot grow smaller and smaller? She could be at the bar by seven and be back home before she knew it. It might not even be dark yet. She felt the tug of Audrey's hands on her hips from the night before. She got up and threw apart the folding doors to her clothes closet. Open sesame.

༄ ༄ ༄ ༄

When Camilla entered the bar, the loudness of all the competing sounds from the packed crowd was deafening. The Metallica junkie DJ was back. The sound system was cranked so high that the speakers rasped and crackled, making James Hetfield's voice barely recognizable. She threaded her way through clique after clique of drunken tattooed people, searching for Taylor. It was suffocatingly hot with all the people jammed in. Camilla wished she hadn't worn her suede coat. What was the point? To show Taylor that she could? Or to show Audrey she could be cool? She was sweating. Her black T-shirt would show large spots as soon as she removed the coat. Her skinny jeans and her combat boots weren't helping. Someone grabbed her sleeve. Camilla turned. Audrey was there, holding an empty round tray between them like a Greek shield. She was wearing a small white T-shirt with a black-and-white photo of the eighties girl group The Runaways on it, a black velvet miniskirt with a studded belt through its loops, and her black high tops. Her bare skin everywhere brought Camilla back to Taylor's bedroom.

"She shouldn't have called you," Audrey shouted in her ear. The metal tray pressed against Camilla's abdomen.

Camilla pulled her face away. "Did she leave?"

Audrey shook her head. Leaned in again at Camilla's neck. "She shouldn't have called you. I gotta go."

Camilla watched as Audrey tackled a nearby table, letting one of the women yell in her ear what all seven of the people wanted. Or at least the woman tried to. The rest of the table kept shouting out what they wanted.

Camilla found Taylor on the same stool as the night before. It was like something out of that movie *Groundhog Day* where the same thing happens over and over. Would the three of them repeat it all? Go to Taylor's. Get into bed. What if they did? Would Camilla do that again?

Taylor was dressed in a pair of white jeans and a fitted white western shirt with metal snaps on two pockets across her chest. Leaning fully over the bar, she stood up with her flip-flops planted on the stool's side metal rungs. She was talking excitedly into the bartender's ear, who was leaning over toward Taylor, both forearms squarely on the bar. Maggie had been one of what Taylor called her detox flings: twenty-eight days and it was over. Like all of Taylor's exes, they'd remained friends. It was Maggie who allowed Taylor to smoke in the bar, although even she drew limits when the bar was so packed.

Camilla was surprised to see there was an empty stool next to Taylor. When she got closer, Taylor glanced sideways and, throwing an arm around Camilla's shoulders, forced Camilla to bend into an uncomfortable position over the bar top as well, as if she was going to make her kiss it. Taylor gripped her shoulder. Then, she slid down onto her stool, releasing her clutch. Camilla felt immediate relief, no longer in that horrible bent-over position. But then Taylor's hand gently grabbed the side of Camilla's head and brought it closer to hers. They were allies again. Secrets could be shared in this position. The switch-up confused Camilla, kept her off-balance. Taylor was drunk. Camilla didn't like the roughhousing, though. It reminded her too much of Taylor's antics of the night before.

Before Taylor had passed out in the bed, she'd been the instigator and the director, subtly pushing either Camilla or Audrey where she wanted them to go. For a few minutes it was a silent film, which Camilla liked. She was nervous and the quiet moving and directing of their bodies was comforting. It didn't feel aggressive. But then, Taylor's voiceover began. "Your turn," she'd say, or "Not yet," or worse yet, "Lower. She likes it lower." Camilla began to feel the spontaneity sucked out of it. She didn't know why she followed Taylor's instructions. Audrey seemed to also. Maybe Camilla was afraid not to, afraid that it would have ended otherwise. When Taylor fell asleep and Audrey began her solo act with Camilla, it felt to Camilla like the trailers had ended and the main feature was about to start. That Audrey was telling her, "It's our turn now to show each other what we *really* got."

Now, Taylor said loudly in Camilla's ear, "What took you so long? Audrey's been frothing at the mouth to see you."

Pushing back from her, Camilla said loudly, "Yeah, right. I just saw her."

"Maggie, set us up," Taylor called out to the bartender. "You know Mother Teresa, don't you?" Maggie shook her head, laughing, and moved toward the bottles of liquor.

"You lied," said Camilla.

"What?" Taylor cupped her ear. "What?"

Camilla grabbed Taylor's hand, moving it away from her ear. "You heard me," she said, irritated. "Audrey didn't ask you to call."

Taylor shrugged. "Is it so terrible that a friend wants to spend time with another friend?"

Maggie delivered two beers with shots of tequila. Taylor quickly downed one of the shots. Maggie refilled it.

"You're drunk," Camilla shouted.

"At least I include you in the fun." Taylor scanned across the bar. Camilla wondered if what she was saying meant more than having a few drinks together. Had Audrey told her about their carrying on after Taylor had fallen asleep? Or was Taylor only making a remark about here and now? Camilla didn't know. Nervous, she picked up the other shot and threw it back.

Unsnapping one of her shirt pockets, Taylor reached in, fishing out a small pack of cards no bigger than two inches each way. "I've got a gift for you. Check these out," she shouted to Camilla and fanned them out on the bar. They were all miniature, illustrated women in different lewd poses, naked except for a different military hat or helmet each wore. "The details are fucking incredible," Taylor yelled in Camilla's ear. "They're fucking G.I., girlfriend."

Camilla looked at her. "Yeah, right. They're as much in the army as I am."

Taylor laughed too loudly. "They aren't soldiers, *Earlobe.* They were given to soldiers during the Vietnam War as part of their swag packs. Government issued. G.I. Get it?"

Camilla shuffled them together and slid them

into the small cardholder. "I don't believe it," she said, handing them back to Taylor. "The army doesn't hand out swag."

Taylor snorted. "Your loss, Earlobe," she said as she tucked the pack inside her pocket and made a big show of snapping it closed. "And don't even think about asking me what I have in mind for them for the show."

Camilla almost took the bait and asked, "What show?" Instead, she drank the shot Maggie had refilled and told Taylor, "I can't stay long." But Taylor was ignoring her now, staring at a curly red mop head sitting at the bar. The woman's push up black bra was in full view via a see-through white shirt that she hadn't bothered to button up. "Why waste time?" those unfastened buttons seemed to say.

"Whatever," Taylor said mechanically, smiling at the girl, who smiled back.

Camilla punched Taylor's arm playfully. "Why did you call me if you were only going to leave for another fuck fest?"

Taylor looked at her. "Like I said. I include you. You're my friend, right?" When Camilla didn't answer her right away, Taylor asked her again, "Right?"

"What are you talking about? Of course I am," Camilla said back. Everything Taylor was saying seemed to have double meanings with a lesson on ethics behind it. Camilla glanced over at the girl. "Go on. She's all yours," she told Taylor, trying to get the conversation back on the road she was familiar with and could steer Taylor easily down. She was afraid of this country road they were on where the abandoned houses and burnt trees from out of control fires smelled of trouble. Where they'd surely end up in a dead end, yelling at each other for not reading the map right.

Taylor smiled. "You trying to get rid of me?" Taylor downed another shot. "Whew!" she said, shaking her head to settle the fire in her throat. Then she stared at Camilla.

Camilla looked away. She sipped her beer, hoping the delay would get the conversation on a more even keel. She read once that seventy-five percent of adulterers spilled when their interrogator simply sat across from them in silence. People couldn't stand the emptiness in the air. They needed to fill it with their stories, even those they were trying to hide. Camilla was determined not to be one of those people.

"Hey, didn't you tell me you had a photo of Allison's girlfriend?" Taylor asked, switching the conversation so abruptly that Camilla almost spit out her beer.

"She's not her girlfriend," Camilla told her. "We don't even know how well they know each other. She was an intern. Big deal. It doesn't prove anything, Taylor." Looking away, Camilla stared at an old poster of Bukowski's face, and took a longer sip of her beer. "It doesn't prove a thing," she repeated, as if she was talking to the famous writer.

"Sounds to me like you're not so sure of that. My dad told me repetition is the clearest sign that a POW is lying. Do you have a photo or not? I can't find one on the web. Well, really I found like over two hundred photos of Cindy Hunters in this world and I sure as shit am not going through all those."

"Yes, I have a photo. It's at home with the rest of the stuff Wallace gave me. What difference does it make?"

Taylor shrugged. "I just want to see who I'm

dealing with. What do you care? Afraid I might call her or something? You'd have Audrey all to yourself then." Taylor stared at her for a beat too long. Then she laughed. "Nice coat by the way. Isn't it a little hot for that?" She fingered the end of the suede sleeve.

"I gotta go," Camilla said, turning to get off the stool.

"Hey, come on, don't be like that. I was kidding," Taylor called after her as Camilla made her way back through the crowd.

The air outside was so much cooler as soon as Camilla pushed through the entrance door past a man who was piggyback carrying a woman. Both of them had shaved heads and multiple face piercings, one a matching steel rod two inches long through their nasal septums. The contrast between the duo's hardcore faces and the childlike game seemed like something you'd see at a carnival freak show. Why did she still come here? She and Taylor had started to go there when they were getting their MFAs: Camilla in creative writing and literature, and Taylor in painting. That was almost twenty years ago. The bar had been a font of material for Camilla, who at the time was writing dark stories about odd relationships. She stopped writing fiction, though, when she went back for her PhD, focusing her thesis on the Americanization of Charles Dickens.

Camilla was almost at the entrance to the parking garage when she heard someone calling her name behind her. There was Audrey, running to catch up, still holding the empty tray like a discus.

"Jesus. I have to stop smoking," Audrey said, catching her breath.

"You told her."

Audrey looked confused. "What?"

"Nothing. Sorry." Camilla shook her head and waved her hand in the air. She began to question whether she'd read into Taylor's one-liners too much. "Forget it. What'd you want?"

"Wow. Ice ice baby." Audrey laughed. She raised the tray in front of her face and then peeked around it at Camilla. On the tray, underneath a large picture of a pirate holding up a bottle of rum, was the tagline, "Sorry I Made You Walk the Plank."

"Sorry," Camilla told her. "Taylor just got under my skin."

"She can do that," Audrey said, lowering the tray and cradling it at the side of her body. It reminded Camilla of a mother holding her toddler on her hip. She'd held Nico just like that. His tiny fingers would grip her shoulder. *Don't let go*, those fingers said. It was a possessive and loving feeling at the same time. Never felt before or since.

"I have to go," Camilla said, looking away. She stared at the cars turning into the parking garage. There was a retro bowling alley on the other side of the garage that served elaborate finger foods that were too sloppy to eat with your fingers, and drinks the color of Ty-D-Bol cleaner. It used to be a movie theater where Taylor and she would meet during the college years every Friday for the two o'clock matinee, as neither of them had classes on that day. Afterward, they'd glide over to the bar and chew the movie apart, scene-by-scene. One of their classmates, Bruce, came with them once but never again. "You two are like the quiet police," he told them. "Shushing someone because they're eating popcorn is, like, anti-American."

Everything has changed since then, Camilla thought now. Even her friendship with Taylor, if she could, after last night, still call it simply a friendship. Camilla felt old. She wondered if the carnival couple had made comments about her after passing her in the entrance doorway. Something about the bar offering senior discounts, or imagining that she was another lost tourist seeking out directions to the Pike.

"Hello?" Audrey said, trying to rope Camilla back in. She waved her hand in front of Camilla's eyes. Close up, Audrey looked older, too—at least older than she'd looked when they'd been together in the treehouse. She'd been better in bed than Camilla had expected: smooth, varied, forceful when it counted. Inexperienced lovers would ask for play-by-play consultation. Is this what you want me to do? One finger or two? The thumb, the index? How about this? Do you like what I'm doing? Nine times out of ten, you didn't. Of course, you couldn't tell them that. You couldn't stop them for a lesson to point out that pillow talk was for after sex, not during. Taylor knew what Camilla liked because of their history, but Audrey knew intuitively, as if their bodies had been hardwired to operate with each other on a whole different level. Camilla didn't believe in past lives, though ironically, she did believe in future reincarnation, because who wanted to believe you died and that was it—one big, black, nothingness? But she was surprised that she'd wondered when Audrey climbed on top of her if she and Audrey had known each other before in another life and had been waiting to meet up again.

"Take a photo, it lasts longer," Audrey told her now.

"Sorry," Camilla said, flushing from the heat of her thoughts.

"That makes three times you've said that."

Holding the tray to her chest, Audrey tapped three fingers against the metal. Her slender fingers continued to tap a beat against the metal back. It seemed like some kind of code only meant for Camilla.

"Actually, you said that at least five times last night, too." Audrey smiled. "Look, can I come over later?" she asked Camilla, startling her.

"What?"

A passing car of young boys hanging out of every open window blasted its horn at them. The boys let out a catcall cacophony that washed over Camilla and Audrey and then followed the car down the street to the next female victim they saw walking on the sidewalk.

"Wow," Audrey said. "Nice fan club."

"I think that was all yours."

"So, later then." Audrey turned, not waiting for an answer. She walked away, holding the empty tray aloft as if she was serving drinks on it, throwing her boyish hips out, exaggerating her saunter and showing off her small ass in the sliver of a miniskirt she was wearing.

"Wait," Camilla called out. "You don't know where I live."

Audrey turned around. She walked backward toward the bar. "I Googled you," she yelled. She faced forward again, and without missing a beat with the tray still held aloft, strutted into the bar.

Camilla had heard the phrase hundreds of times from her students. It sounded so different coming out of Audrey's mouth after the night before. Sexual. Intimate. Like an invitation to an exclusive party.

Although Audrey hadn't mentioned when she'd be showing up, Camilla suspected it would be late, probably after the bar closed at two in the morning. It was eleven when she arrived home again. Should she take a quick nap—what her father used to call a "tone-up"? Whenever he said it, Camilla, as a child, envisioned him being slid into their car mechanic's garage bay and hoisted up on the lift. Sleeping was a dicey proposition. Sometimes she didn't wake up well from naps, and ended up crankier than when she'd lain down. Instead, she made herself a double espresso and gulped it down in one swig like the cold medicine she'd taken earlier that evening. She was hoping they would cancel each other out.

She turned her attention instead to the litter boxes that were in the master bedroom closet. Camilla had two indoor house cats that she'd gotten as kittens after she'd left Allison. Now, they looked like Maine Coon cats: big as raccoons with similar coloring. She'd picked them at the Boston animal shelter because they seemed more docile, lethargic even, compared to the other peppy kittens hopscotching in their shelter lockdown cages. It was only when she was paying and the clerk began to recite in a singsong voice how to clean their "wounds" that Camilla's ears perked up.

"If bleeding occurs, just hold pressure there for a bit and tie a clean sock around it," the clerk told Camilla.

"What?" Camilla said. "What wounds?"

The clerk told her that the two boys had been neutered earlier that morning. Their passiveness was a result of the anesthesia filtering through their tiny bodies. Within a day they were clawing their way up Camilla's linen window shades like two rock climbers on Half Dome, their mews of encouragement to each other alerting Camilla to spring into frequent search and rescue missions. Adopting the two brothers seemed at times to have been the wrong way to go. Double the trouble. Double the vigilance that Camilla had to maintain. But, the shelter clerk had told her, "You won't be scratched as much." It was true. They taught each other how much to extend their claws so that it wasn't painful during their rumpuses across her wood floor. It was a lesson she wished she and Allison had learned. Camilla only had been scratched by the duo once in a year. She also liked that they could keep each other company when she wasn't home. She had to admit that they'd given her enormous comfort during that first bleak year.

Scooping up the fouled litter from the two side-by-side kitty porta john boxes, she dropped the clumps into the open kitty genie. She hadn't known about this latest invention for making litter cleaning less repulsive when she'd gone to purchase the litter and plastic trays and cat food from the nearby pet store. The kitty genies were lined up like sentries on the store's shelf next to the gallon jugs of litter and Glade perfumed mixtures. Immediately, Camilla was thrown back to the diaper genie that she'd set up in Nico's nursery. The kitty genie was smaller but operated on the same principles: a flip top that hid a disposable plastic bag, sealing off the abhorrent smells within. Facing the army of the genies, her eyes began to tear. This was during those first months when she had to leave stores or walk in a different direction on the street if she heard a baby crying nearby. The reaction was instantaneous and unbearable. Camilla would have an intense urge to find the mother, shake her, and tell her to love her baby. To not take him for granted. Nico hadn't cried more than usual so she couldn't figure out why another baby's cry had sent her fleeing.

Doris told her, "It's PTSD. You've been in combat." It helped some to hear that she wasn't going crazy, but Camilla also felt like it was unearned. She hadn't really been in a war, like those vets returning home who start to shake uncontrollably when they hear a light bulb explode or too-close thunder. The baby crying PTSD happened less and less now. Still, whenever she cleaned out the litter, the genie seemed to accuse her of something. It was like Sisyphus repeatedly dragging his boulder up the hill only to watch it roll down again. There would always be more litter to clean out. There would always be her memories of Nico. She could hide them under a lid, eventually throwing them into the trash, but there'd always be more.

When she was done with the kitty cleanup, she started on one of her two bathrooms. Cleaning held back the tide of nervousness she felt. Camilla loved her Cambridge condo. After leaving Allison and living with Taylor for those couple of months, it was clear she needed her own home. It was exhausting having her sleep interrupted by Taylor coming home drunk with yet another pick-up. Camilla was a nester at heart. She liked her paintings, her furniture, her dishes that were created by different potters and therefore did not match. Allison was still letting Camilla see Nico every Saturday then. She still believed that this was a phase of Camilla's, that Camilla would return home and their lives would go on as before. But, Camilla could see Nico only under Allison's rules. She could take Nico to the park around the corner, or she could play with him in what had been their house and was now Allison's.

That was it. The restrictions rankled Camilla.

"You probably want me to wear one of those inmate GPS cuffs too," she told Allison, who looked like she'd give it serious consideration. Still, Camilla was able to see Nico, and that was all that mattered.

When she was condo hunting she didn't keep Allison informed. She didn't want Allison interfering or offering her advice on what she should purchase. She ended up buying a much larger condo than she needed—two bedrooms and two baths—thinking that when Nico became a teenager, he would like to have his own bathroom. The condo was also right around the corner from the Montessori school that Allison and she had talked about eventually sending him to. She didn't know that as soon as she bought the condo, Allison would cut her off all visitation.

"You never asked me whether it would be suitable for him," Allison argued with her when Camilla told her about the closing date. "You never told me you were even looking. We're done here. It's your choice. If you want to see him, come back."

At first, Camilla wondered if she should renege on the closing. Maybe Allison would relent then. But, Doris reminded her, "The best predictor of future behavior is past behavior. If you give in on this, she'll just try to control something else."

So, Camilla went ahead with the purchase, secretly hoping that, in spite of what Doris said, Allison's fit of pique would pass as suddenly as her other mood swings had. She imagined a part-time life with Nico in the condo, seeing his tanned baby feet running on the wood floors and oriental rugs, his fingers splayed and twitching as he reached out, cooing, for the scurrying kittens. She saw them years later walking together to

Montessori, where she'd leave him at the gate despite his mantra that she could go home now as soon as the school was in sight down the street. She saw him as a seven-year-old, walking home with his Spider Man backpack, its plastic superheroes hanging by noose threads and swinging in time to his walk. He'd toss it on the living room couch and yell that he was hungry, that the cafeteria food was gross today, that he hated American Chop *Suet*. She saw him as a teenager, that second bedroom his lair full of wet towels, high-top basketball sneakers, boxers, jeans, and T-shirts; his read but discarded paperbacks forming precariously shifting mountains of books; the odor of sweat, and too much cologne used to cover up the bad anti-pimple medication smells.

"It smells like an old lady's perfume and battery acid," she imagined him telling her the first time she'd bring tubes of it home from the CVS.

She saw him leaving for college, saw herself stripping his room of the punk rock poster with Sid Vicious in his torn, magic-markered T-shirt and his iconic porcupine hair next to his quote: *Undermine their pompous authority, reject their moral standards, make anarchy and disorder your trademarks. Cause as much chaos and disorder as possible but don't let them take you alive.* She imagined never really liking the poster in spite of her wanting to do so, imagining he put it up after one of their adolescent-years disagreements.

In his late twenties, he was a wunderkind living in Greenwich Village, whose first novel was a bestseller and the darling of critics, but he always made time for her. She could so clearly see him visiting her in this condo, his forever home that offered him sanctuary and freedom and encouraged his literary passions.

These images continued to swim in and out of Camilla's vision whenever she walked around her home, like the white spots you see when you press too tightly on your eyelids: uncontrollable and yet expected. Sometimes these images comforted her. Sometimes they made her crumple on to the wood floor and weep.

❧❧❧❧

Around one in the morning she'd done all the cleaning she could do without disrupting her downstairs neighbor, Tim. Sitting down at her desk, she brought out a draft of the article Linda had reminded her that she was supposed to be working on over the summer break: "Lady Dedlock: Feminist or Whore?" She'd written the draft a few weeks after the spring semester had ended, energized from having completed grading hundreds of pages of her students' essays. Reading the first page of her own work, Camilla was struck by how god-awful the essay was. Its focus was immature, something one of her students would write about on one of their blogs. Or that Camilla would've written as a freshman undergraduate. Was she regressing on every level?

Opening a desk drawer, she pulled out a pocket-sized, worn leather book that she used to write ideas for future projects in. Her fingers glided over the cover, feeling the leather softened by the years she had had it. Started the year before she met Allison, the book was filled with lined pages, each one from start to finish covered in her notes. She flipped to the last page, its entry dated two years after she'd met Allison. She was already teaching at Tolland. The last idea written down was to do a book, an *entire* book, on the relationship between Dickens and Hans Christian Andersen. After an initial meeting at a party in England of the Countess of Blessington, there had been a smattering of letters between the two men. Two writers of stories that depicted the poor, orphans, and other ravaged characters of the underclass bond. But then, catastrophe. In the five letters Dickens wrote, he consistently invited Andersen to come back for a visit and stay at his country home at Gads Hill Place. Andersen's original two-week stay turned into five weeks. Finally, he was asked to leave. Although Andersen sent letters afterward, Dickens refused to write back, ending the friendship in silence. Why? Camilla had wanted to know the answer. Was it simply that Andersen had overstayed his welcome like so many of us do? Or was it deeper than that? There were insinuations in the scholarly discourse that Andersen's bisexuality might've gotten in the way, that he'd fallen in love with Dickens. The author of *The Ugly Duckling* falling for the creator of *Bleak House*. Imagine.

And then there was the letter Dickens wrote to a friend describing an incident in which Andersen demanded that Dickens's eldest son shave him in the mornings. Camilla had wondered about that, too. They'd been kindred spirits before the rift: admiring each other's work and also sharing a deep love for Rome, although with a deeply felt cynicism about Catholicism and the Vatican, blaming both for the oppression and poverty they'd witnessed all their lives. Both of them would write books set in Rome: Andersen's first novel, *The Improvisatore*, making his name throughout Europe, and Dickens's travel masterpiece, *Pictures From Italy*, convincing people that he wasn't simply a serial novelist. They'd even missed each other in Rome the year before they'd met at the Countess's shindig. It was destined that they'd meet and understand each other implicitly. And yet, the split.

Afterward, Dickens let his feelings be known about the overly tall, seemingly all-bones man by patterning what would become one of his most well-known characters on Andersen: Uriah Heep, the horrible, obsequious, skeletal scoundrel.

Camilla read through her notes. She circled the first item of a list of next steps for the project to proceed: *Go to Rome–the beginning?*

She'd never gone. She forgot about the book. She taught. She lived with Allison. She ate three meals a day. She slept six to eight hours every night. She continued to live with Allison. She published soon to be forgotten articles in academic journals about Dickens and how his traveling was reflected in his novels. *Go to Rome.* Why had she never gone?

She liked to think of Audrey as a step forward, away from Allison and the trapped life that she'd led. She hoped that she wouldn't start to feel those pinpricks people felt when they started to notice details about a lover that drove them crazy—the bit of noisy slurping of coffee in the morning, the over-the-top dousing of perfume, the constant need for reassurance ending in multiple wardrobe changes. She understood that Audrey would have faults and idiosyncratic tics, everyone did. She just hoped that their getting together wouldn't become mundane, centered exclusively on the daily boringness of life, the how-was-your-day conversations.

Camilla envisioned a different life for them. When she was an undergraduate creative writing major, her professors spoke of a life of letters. The first time she heard it, she imagined a graphic illustration of the evolution of ape to man striding across a timeline of eras, with a sky full of a spiraling, out of control alphabet. She learned that such a life, however, focused on reading and writing, where daily genuflections were made to literature and art. That was the life she imagined for her and Audrey. She saw them traveling the country in a van, sending their agents chapters for their books along the way.

Camilla shook her head to change the thought pattern. She often shook her head like that if she didn't want to continue the same thread. She'd done it the first time after she'd seen a grisly movie on television about a young girl who was raped and murdered. The explicit torture scene in the murderer's basement continued to replay in her mind long after she'd quickly turned the television off, shut the light out on her bedside table, and tried to sleep. There was something physically jarring to the repetitive filmstrip if she shook her head as she whispered, "No." It was like those self-defense classes where they teach you to stomp on the assailant's foot and yell, "No!" as loudly as you can. The perpetrator's action is temporarily stopped by the sheer surprise of it. After that first time, Camilla continued to do the Etch A Sketch head shaking whenever she needed to change her thoughts, leaving the "no" soundless.

Who knew what would happen with Audrey? Audrey might be coming over to tell her that what had happened must never happen again. That she didn't have any feelings for Camilla, other than feeling sorry for her. That she really loved Taylor. And Camilla didn't want this to be another "if only" relationship. With Allison, she'd constantly convince herself to stay in the relationship by thinking of all the if onlys that would make everything okay. *If only Allison wouldn't take her frustration from the operating room out on me. If only Allison wasn't addicted to online shopping so she wouldn't feel so much pressure to make money. If only Allison wouldn't be so obsessive-compulsive about where I take Nico, or how I dress him.* The list went on and on. This time around, Camilla wanted to see Audrey and their relationship for whatever they turned out to be, not what she *wanted* them to be.

Camilla realized she was staring at the notebook in front of her. She hadn't made any edits on her manuscript yet. Suddenly, she was tired and slightly irritated. Why hadn't she told Audrey that they could meet some other time at some decent hour? Was this a sign that she'd already begun giving in to whatever Audrey wanted, much as she had done with Allison? There was probably two more hours to go. She'd cleaned the entire house and didn't have the energy to tackle this mess of an essay unless she drank some coffee or had some other kind of stimulant.

Back when she'd done drugs, coke had been her favorite. It had allowed her to stay up dancing all night at the clubs on Lansdowne and then on to the after-clubs. It was fifteen years since the last time she snorted. If she had some now she could stay up to whenever Audrey showed. She worried what it meant that she was thinking of all of this now. Post-Allison, she'd worried if her behavior was regressing. Not like a mid-life crisis, but deeper than that. It wasn't about a new sports car or a younger woman, although she wasn't so sure anymore about that last part. Did a thirteen-year difference in age between she and Audrey pass the litmus test for a classic "younger woman" affair?

In terms of regressing, what she really meant was

this notion that she no longer had anyone to answer to. With Allison and Nico out of her big picture, there was nothing holding her back from doing what she wanted to do. Was that true?

If she did do coke again and Allison found out, wouldn't that be more fuel for Nico to be kept from her? Camilla might have left Allison, but her hold on Camilla was still strong. Doris told her during their session the week before, "You might've left, but you're still *living* with her." During that session, Camilla had confided that she went to great lengths to avoid driving or walking past the Montessori school where Nico went. In spite of withholding Nico from Camilla and there being several pre-schools closer to Allison's home, Allison had gone ahead and enrolled him in Montessori right around the corner from Camilla's condo.

"In spite of? There's no *of* about it," Taylor had said when Camilla had told her about the enrollment. "She did it *in* spite. Period."

Doris made her play out a scene where Camilla would see Nico on the school's playground and what she would do if he called to her through the slats of the white picket fence around the school property. Camilla imagined the scene. Nico would be wearing miniature cargo pants and a long-sleeved T-shirt with an outline of a VW beetle. It was an outfit that Camilla had bought him during the months she was still seeing him. The pants would end at a tiny pair of black-and-white-striped soccer sneakers.

"Well," Camilla said to Doris, stalling for more time as she switched her crossed legs from right to left and then back again. She stared to the right of where Doris sat on her couch, at a beautiful silk tapestry of a vase of Japanese irises. She was probably the only therapist who sat on a couch while her patients sat in two club chairs opposite her. The first time Camilla had seen the office, she'd liked the way Doris had visually turned the whole therapist-patient relationship topsy-turvy. She thought her therapist must have a lot of confidence to put herself in that usually lower power position. Now, she suspected Doris probably just liked the couch better because it was more comfortable.

In the role-play, she told her, "I guess I'd have to say hi to him."

"And then what?" Doris asked.

Camilla didn't have an answer then. Doris asked her to think about it for further discussion at the next session. Camilla walked away like one of her students subjected to a surprise quiz: angry, depressed, and feeling very stupid.

Afterward, Camilla realized that the answer was there was nothing to be gained by starting up a conversation with Nico. It wouldn't change Allison's mind and, in fact, if Nico went home and told Allison about it, Allison might go on a rampage, threatening Camilla with stalking charges or some such nonsense. And Nico would wonder why he would never see Camilla after that. It might confuse him. No, Camilla and Nico would be better off if she simply kept walking after he called to her, as heartbreaking and impossible to bear as that might be. She couldn't stomach the thought, yet alone the reality, of that. But, she promised herself and Nico that there would be no if onlys where he was concerned.

Instead, she simply avoided the block where the school was, often going out of her way when she needed to go grocery shopping or pick up another gewgaw at the hardware store, because both establishments were in a small mall on the other side of the school.

Her essay sat in front of her, silently chastising her. Opening her desk drawer, she threw the stack of paper in and slammed the drawer shut.

She'd resisted making the second bedroom into a roomier office for all of her Tolland work and her own academic writing. It had been a year since she'd moved in and the room still stood empty save for an empty child's bookcase painted in light blue with green dinosaurs on the ends, and a stack of boxes holding the things she'd bought before knowing that it would never be Nico's room: a twin bed frame from Pottery Barn, Spider-Man bed linens, the complete *Winnie the Pooh* and *Harry Potter* series, an art easel, acrylic finger paints, wall posters featuring quotes and illustrations of Christopher Robin, Pooh, Eeyore, and Tigger. A twin mattress still in its delivery plastic leaned against a wall. The stack of boxes seemed to accentuate the emptiness. It spoke of absence. It said: life, interrupted. Taylor had told her one day, "What's next? Piled up bouquets and candlelight vigils? You need to put something in there so every time you pass it it's not a mausoleum. Sell the whole lot on Ebay."

Camilla wondered if Linda had a room just like this one for her daughter. Only her daughter's room was fully realized; it had been lived in, its bed set up, the bedspread clean and covered with stuffed animals and dolls, perhaps an unfinished glass of water still on the nightstand next to a dusty barrette with a sparkly butterfly.

Camilla went to that bedroom now. She opened the door. Without stepping in, she angled her hand around the doorframe to find the light switch on the wall. The overhead blazed on. She stood in the doorway, as if she was sizing the room up for renovations. It was a beautiful room. Or would've been, she corrected herself. She shook her head. There she went again, stepping on the down escalator of if onlys. She snapped the light off. The room had one large double casement window on the back wall that was part of an indented nook. It would be a perfect spot for a built-in seat with storage underneath. There were no shades in this room, although she always kept the door closed anyway so the cats couldn't get in. A large full moon shone a tremendous white light through the window, onto the dusty wood floor. The news had been talking up this moon, calling it a super moon. For weeks, newscasters on every channel described that such moons happen when the moon is at its closest distance to the earth. The shorter distance results in a moon that is thirty percent brighter and fourteen percent bigger than a normal moon. Instinctively, Camilla stepped into the room, drawn by the showy orb like the tide. At the window, she basked in its glow. She wondered if Nico was at his bedroom window in Wilbur at that moment. She quickly dispelled the thought as being ridiculous, another fantasy. Nico wasn't even home. He would be fast asleep, tucked into some stranger's bed in a rented house on the Cape.

The condo's buzzer rang its sharp note, startling Camilla. She hurried from the room, shutting the door behind her. Before she went down the stairs, she glanced in the hallway mirror, and wiped her wet cheeks.

❧❧❧❧

Camilla had purposely not cleaned herself up while she'd cleaned the apartment and waited for Audrey. She didn't shower or change out of the clothes she'd worn to the bar. She reasoned that Audrey would be coming straight from the bar and wouldn't have had time to change herself, and Camilla didn't want her to feel weird or uncomfortable for not dressing for the date. Was it a date? She realized that she didn't know.

When she opened the main house door on the first floor, she was glad to see she'd been right. Audrey hugged her in the foyer before Camilla had a chance to close the door, her clothes reeking of cigarettes and stale beer, and a lingering neck print of patchouli. At least she didn't smell of Taylor's lavender soap. Against her stomach, Camilla felt the hard buckle and metal studs on Audrey's leather belt circling the top of her miniskirt. In spite of the late hour, it was still steamy outside. Audrey's child-sized T-shirt let Camilla feel the fine moistness that covered Audrey's arms. There was an uncomfortable moment when Camilla wanted to let go—she didn't want Tim to come out of his apartment and find them—but Audrey hadn't relinquished her hold yet. Camilla was forced to stay in the position until finally she was let go.

"This is nice," Audrey told her, looking around at the entryway's antique table where packages were left for either Tim or her.

Camilla automatically put her index finger to her lips, giving Audrey the traditional librarian gesture for silence. Immediately, she silently reprimanded herself for doing it. She was always hyper-vigilant, too worried, about how much noise she created in the house. Doris had asked her when the anxiety had started for her, whether it was from the years she'd spent walking on eggshells with Allison. In fairness, Camilla couldn't lob all the blame on Allison. She once told Doris, "I always wanted to be invisible. Even when I was a kid. I was a writer. The watcher." She told her that Allison would humorously kid her about it by asking her when the hovercraft was going to be outside their windows so she could turn on the white noise to block their transmissions. Camilla couldn't say why she cared so much what Tim thought or heard. He wasn't exactly quiet himself. She often heard him and whoever he'd picked up for the night, stumbling downstairs in the entryway, dropping keys on the echoing tile floor, slamming doors both into and inside of his condo, and he was not sparing on his stereo volume either. Although he lived below her, Camilla often heard his heavy footfalls, whether he had been partying or not.

"Sorry," Audrey whispered and bit her lip like a kid called on in class who didn't have the answer. Camilla felt worse. Maybe this was a bad idea.

"No, I'm sorry," Camilla said in a normal voice and began to walk up the stairs to her condo's door.

Upstairs, the first few minutes were spent with Audrey exclaiming how beautiful everything was. She complimented it all: the matching blue sofa and reading chair, the other leather reading chair, the Asian cabinets, the several Buddhas placed in different corners, the high ceilings where the developer had removed the attic leaving exposed beams and new skylights, the flow of the open living room into the dining room into the kitchen, the master bedroom and bath with their walls covered in Mexican milagros and nichos, and paintings by Taylor and other artist friends. As Audrey doled out the compliments, Camilla rushed around the kitchen, de-corking a bottle of white wine from the wine cooler and filling two glasses.

"Are these closets?" Audrey said. She was standing in front of the doors to Nico's bedroom and bathroom. Audrey's hand reached for the doorknob.

"No! Don't go in there!" Camilla shouted and stepped toward her, the wineglasses in hand. Too late. The bedroom door swung open as Audrey jumped back. She stared at the empty room in the moonlight. "Wow," she said. She'd stopped as soon as Camilla had told her to do so, but she continued to stare straight ahead. For a moment, Camilla thought Audrey was commenting on the tower of unopened boxes.

"I haven't had a chance—"

"It's fantastic," Audrey said. She stepped over the threshold. "I've been so sick of hearing about it all week, but I had no idea." She moved toward the window, stepping across the moonlit strip falling across the wood floor. "Do you see this?" she called out.

There was nothing Camilla could do but follow her in. "Here," she said, handing Audrey a glass of wine.

"To super moon. Long may you wreak havoc." Audrey clinked the top of Camilla's glass. "What is the mythology behind the moon anyway, Professor? Is it true about unbridled sex, and the masks and antlers being a must?" Audrey smiled over the rim of her glass and added, "Maybe that's what was going on last night."

There it was. Out in the air between them now, like a scrim of pollen settling down over them. Flustered, Camilla quickly recited, "The goddess of the moon was Selene. She drove a chariot drawn by two horses with wings. The poet Aeschylus called her the eye of the night."

"I thought he was a playwright? She must have been beautiful," Audrey said, looking at Camilla. Then, she turned back to feast on the sight again. The moon was turning an orange-yellow color now. "Although her eye looks a little jaundiced right now."

"Yes-yes, she was," Camilla said, stumbling. She continued to feel unbalanced by the room and by everything that Audrey was saying. It seemed as if there were double meanings to it all, just like with Taylor at the bar. She couldn't have imagined she would ever have another person in this room, yet alone a woman who interested her. "She was unhappy in love," Camilla added. She didn't know why she blurted out this ridiculous stuff. She wanted to leave the room, and yet she was keeping the conversation going.

Audrey faced her. "Oh?" She was so close that for the first time Camilla could see she had a faint horizontal scar right above where her neck ended. It was two inches long and thin as a razor line. For an instant, Camilla wondered if it had been self-inflicted. Disconcerted, she quickly spouted more information: "She fell in love with a beautiful shepherd, Endymion. Cicero says that Selene would put him to sleep every night so that she could come and kiss him."

"That doesn't sound so unhappy to me," Audrey said, giving her a wry smile.

Camilla tried not to look again at the scar. "Others wrote that Zeus gave him a choice of eternal life, but it would be accompanied by eternal sleep. So, Selene could never really be with him."

"I like Cicero's version better." Audrey looked around the room for the first time. She took in the unopened boxes, the bookcase with its painted dinosaurs. The twin bed still in its plastic wrapping, leaning against a wall. She looked at Camilla. "Can we go sit down? I've been on my feet all day." Without waiting for an answer, she walked out of the room. When she followed Audrey out, Camilla fought against closing the door behind her. That might seem like a slap to Audrey. She couldn't, however, quite bring herself to leave the door fully open. Instead, she settled on it being left ajar.

Audrey sat in the leather chair, leaving the couch empty. *That's a bad sign*, Camilla thought, despite her image of the two of them sitting in the two chairs a la Stein and Toklas. Camilla sat down in the blue chair. She especially loved this chair; its bottom cushion was extra long and its back cushion was firm but comfortable. There was a matching hassock, which Camilla swung her engineer boots up on now, wanting to give an impression of her being thoroughly at ease. The problem with the chair was that whenever Camilla sat in it, her two cats would make a beeline for her. She'd gotten in the habit of combing both the longhairs out while she sat in that chair and watched television at night. It was a ritual they wouldn't miss for all the cat chow in the world. They did it now. Up until then, they'd been hidden from sight, under her bed or in the master bedroom closet, or other place known only to them. Camilla had put a hook latch to keep them out of the closet where they tore at her good clothes that she donned when teaching. Within a day they'd figured out how to jostle the folding doors so that the hook bounced out of its eyelet. Now, the brothers pounced at the same time at her, one landing behind her neck on top of the chair's back cushion and the other launching onto her lap.

"Who are they? Your bodyguards?" Audrey

asked and laughed. She drank her wine.

Pointing at the one on her lap, Camilla told her, "This one's Meat. And this one is Ball." She skimmed her hand down Ball's back against his fur grain.

"Cute," Audrey said, but the way she said it, Camilla knew she thought it was stupid. Camilla wanted to tell her that it had been the first word Nico had said, but she decided not to. She didn't want all their conversations focused on Nico. They'd already talked about him that day in the treehouse. And Audrey had just seen his room. Camilla saw her reflection in Audrey's eyes and she didn't like what she saw: a woman obsessed with the son she could no longer have in her life. Christ, she even dressed in all black every day, and while Camilla had thought that was simply a result of her wanting to be invisible, she wondered now if it was also tethered to her grief, like those Greek widows who, according to custom, must wear the black of mourning for the rest of their lives.

Camilla sipped her wine. With her other hand, she pet Meat, who was purring in her lap. "You write mostly memoir?" she asked Audrey to get the conversation back to what Taylor would've called the DMZ—the demilitarized zone. She shook her head. Now was not the time to think about Taylor. *Good grief.*

Audrey sipped her wine. "Yes," she said, drawing the word out as if she was suspicious of where the conversation would lead.

"Are you working on something?"

Audrey smiled. "I'm allergic to cats." Camilla's hand automatically stopped moving on Meat's fur. "It's okay, though," Audrey said. "I'm not going to die or anything. I just start sounding like I have the worst cold possible."

Camilla jumped up, ejecting Meat before he had the chance to claw in. "I'm so sorry. I didn't know. We can go in the kitchen—"

Audrey stood up, too. "Wait. It's okay. Really." She paused. "You apologize too much."

Not really listening, Camilla walked past the dining room table toward the kitchen area. "We can sit at the counter. I don't allow them there. I'll be right back," she said, thinking she could get a couple of Benadryl out of the master bathroom, but when she glanced over her shoulder, Audrey was walking away from her toward Nico's bedroom.

"You keep this door closed usually, right? So they're not in here?" She flicked her fingers at the door, opening it, and stepped in, looking over her shoulder at Camilla. "Bring the bottle." Audrey closed the door almost the entire way behind her.

Camilla stared at the door. She looked over at the bottle of wine where she'd left it in the kitchen on the counter. She imagined taking the bottle and going instead into the master bedroom and closing that door, leaving Audrey alone to figure out her next move. She imagined going into Nico's room and asking Audrey to leave. She imagined pulling out one of the chairs by the kitchen counter and sitting down, pouring herself another glass of wine, and waiting Audrey out. All of it was like a chess game. Move the pawn and the game takes a turn down one path. Move the knight or the queen and other paths are revealed. Which was the right move? Camilla remembered a movie from the sixties in which the Greek gods and goddesses are seen playing chess in heaven, with mere mortals the chess pieces. Every move ended in disaster for the poor humans. Part of her wanted Audrey to leave. Ever since she'd arrived Camilla had been discombobulated, off her game. She couldn't figure out if she liked Audrey's taking control of the situation or not. She swore when she'd left Allison to never, ever give up control over her life again to someone else. Well, this was her chance to show that she was keeping that promise to herself. She should march into that room and ask Audrey to come out of there and sit in the kitchen. Part of her, though, felt a small sense of relief. Here was someone forcing her, finally, to confront what was inside that room. It had become the room in which Audrey demanded she meet her. Camilla could see that was how she'd describe it to Taylor tomorrow or the next day. It had become *Audrey's room*. From then on, it would no longer simply be the room that Nico should have had. It had been transformed from an "if only" room to a "can do" room. It had another story now.

When she touched the wooden door with her fingertips and it slowly swung open, she was surprised to find Audrey sitting back on her ankles, and naked on the mattress on the floor, its plastic sheath balled up in the corner like discarded clothing, along with the miniskirt, the studded belt, Converse sneakers, a black bra, and her child-sized T-shirt. In the moonlight, Audrey looked beautiful. Her short blond hair seemed like a halo. Her small pale breasts were full and perky, with nothing like the slight sagginess of Camilla's that she started noticing when she hit forty. Audrey's breasts were what Taylor called "a perfect handful." Her slenderness seemed like her entire body was on high alert, excited by the prospect of what was unfolding. Surprisingly, she hadn't shaved her pubic area to maintain an illusion of school girlishness like so many lesbians did now. The night before, Camilla had seen that instead Audrey had a downy blond runway strip. Now, Camilla thought of the lines of Christina Rossetti:

> Fair as the moon and joyful as the light:
> Not wan with waiting, not with sorrow dim;
> Not as she is, but was when hope shone bright;
> Not as she is, but as she fills his dream.

Audrey snapped Camilla right out of her literary head, though, when she told her, "All right, Professor. Show me what you got."

Day Five

Camilla, Audrey, Taylor

I'm off tonight," Audrey told Camilla the next morning. "There's an art show I'm going to. Come with me."

They were sitting at the café table on Camilla's deck off the kitchen despite it being overcast. The cloudy scrim permitted only a lifeless light, and the air felt heavy with humidity. Audrey was only wearing one of Camilla's black T-shirts over her own underwear. Her bare legs seemed to mock Camilla's hoodie sweatshirt over sweatpants. It was almost noon and steamy hot. Camilla shivered from what she thought was the damp. She was agitated, torn between wanting to prolong the time with Audrey and wanting to get back to the treehouse. She worried that Audrey would want an invitation to go with her to the treehouse and worried that she wouldn't. Camilla felt like she couldn't win. She could hear Doris asking her, "What do you *really* want?" or "Why the conflict?" Two questions Camilla couldn't answer. She bit off another piece of her cinnamon raisin toast, chewing it rapidly.

"Well?" Audrey said. "Stop looking at me like that." Audrey laughed uneasily, and then picked up Camilla's mug, drinking *her* cappuccino, although she hadn't yet finished her own. The intimacy of the gesture startled Camilla. She couldn't remember the last time she'd shared her coffee with someone, yet alone had it taken from her. She couldn't decide if she felt violated in some way, or felt attended to.

Audrey put the mug back down, a sliver of foam on her top lip. "What? It's not a marriage proposal," she told Camilla. "It's just an art show."

"Sor—" Audrey raised her eyebrow and wagged her index finger at her. "That sounds great," Camilla told her. "What time?" Camilla wasn't sure she did want to go out to a gallery. She'd hardly slept. And it would cut into the time she could be at the treehouse. She'd have to come home early to shower and get dressed. She was nervous, though, that if she didn't go Audrey would think she wasn't interested in art or wasn't any fun. That she wasn't being as nice as she should be after the night they'd spent together.

It had been almost four in the morning when Camilla joined Audrey and they'd broken in the new twin mattress. Any thoughts of the whole thing being weird or disrespectful to Nico were batted away by Audrey's gentle and patience persistence. Audrey focused on undoing the double knot, not on Camilla's boots, but the one *inside* Camilla that would've allowed her to stay removed in those first few minutes. That wasn't happening. Slowly, as Audrey's fingers pulled Camilla's T-shirt over her head, as she unlaced Camilla's boots and pulled them and her socks off, as she tugged on Camilla's jeans zipper, and then her pants, sealing each move with a deep kiss, Camilla felt the knot inside of her coming undone, its loose ends fluttering in her chest, her stomach, below her waist. The same feeling of connectedness that she'd felt the night before when they'd made love as Taylor slept next to them now settled over her as she dropped onto the mattress and felt Audrey's soft skin on top of hers. Camilla came fast this time, with Audrey's lips kissing the side of her neck and her hipbone moving between Camilla's legs, as if Camilla's body knew that if it was going to do *this* in *this* room, it had to be done quickly, in the process once again renaming the room to The Room Audrey Made Love to Her In. For the first time, Camilla understood that this room, like the others in her condo, would have many stories over the years. Stories she could not conceive of yet. Because there would be so many stories, not the one single defining story, the room had become story-less.

When Audrey lifted her face away from the crook of her neck, Camilla traced the thin scar on Audrey's neck. "Back surgery. They went through the front. Don't worry. I asked the doctor up front if I'd still be able to do this." As Audrey kissed her deeply and began to slide down, Camilla felt as if she were free-falling through the sky, parachuteless. She wasn't afraid. Or nervous. She was holding her arms straight out as the ground rose toward her, with the wild, trusting abandon of a child who jumps from a swing, yelling, "Catch me!" She barely knew Audrey. She didn't know what her middle name was, or if she even had a middle name. She only knew that Audrey had come for her. Briefly, she feared that Audrey might be someone who simply defied rules; the room's closed door was to be opened, no matter what the cost, simply because it was closed. But what if it was the opposite? What if by opening the door, Audrey was opening another door, and another and another? As Audrey found her and Camilla's hips rose, she felt like she was being split open and the hard pit inside of her was released and began to roll away across the floor into the tier of boxes with their items that were of no use to Camilla anymore.

An hour later, when their breaths were synchronizing into a deep sleep, Camilla briefly believed for the first time that she maybe *could* make this room into a study. Camilla was half on top of her, her head on Audrey's shoulder. A breeze blew through the room then and Camilla felt the chill of it and shivered, her shudder passing on to Audrey, who shivered too. "Aftershocks," Audrey whispered sleepily, with a small smile. Camilla heard Audrey's breathing get slower and slower until she herself fell asleep, her own breathing hypnotized by falling into step with Audrey's.

It was eleven when they awakened.

"Wake up, sleepy head," Audrey murmured as she slid back on top of Camilla. Camilla put the brakes on that immediately. Her feelings of her life being magically transformed had disappeared the moment she opened her eyes. She should have been at the treehouse by now. She'd lost at least three hours already, and she was still tired from the night before. That would slow her down all day.

"I can't lie around all day," she told Audrey, sliding out from under her. She stood up, grabbing her jeans from off the floor.

Now, at the table on the deck, she fought against feeling guilty about that. Audrey was searching her face, looking like she was waiting for Camilla to say something.

"What?" Camilla asked her.

"You didn't hear a word I just said, did you?" Audrey didn't wait for the answer. "Meet me at seven. Five fifty Harrison Ave."

"What's the name of the gallery?"

Audrey smiled. "I knew you weren't listening. It's a pop-up. I think they're calling it Popped Art or something ridiculous like that."

What the hell is a pop-up? Some kind of tent? She wasn't about to ask Audrey. She could Google it. Like Audrey had Googled her. The thought of that sent a bolt below her waist again. Camilla still couldn't believe that Audrey was here, sitting on her deck with Camilla's plants that drooped from the heat like they were sad from the days of neglect they'd been forced to live under the last few days. Camilla felt her own spirit wane as she looked up at the overcast sky, concerned that it might again rain, further dampening her plans for making headway on the treehouse.

"It's supposed to clear up," Audrey said. She stood, stacking their empty toast plates and mugs. "We can be there in twenty minutes."

The "we" startled Camilla. In spite of the little voice that told her to speak up and shut this down fast, she screwed the top of the strawberry jam back on and dutifully followed Audrey back into the house.

❧ ❧ ❧ ❧

They worked on shingling the roof. It was tedious, slow work, having to line up each small cedar shingle so that they would overlap each other and keep any rain out. Already, from the previous day's work, Camilla's fingers felt raw from the planks' rough edges and the cedar sap. Once again, Audrey was faster at it. She'd measured out two areas for them to work on near each other. Somehow Audrey didn't slip on the steep pitch of the roof's frame either. It was as if her high-tops had those toe suctions that frogs have.

Camilla didn't have such good luck. Her combat boots slipped unless she turned her toes at awkward angles and gripped her soles against the plywood. It seemed as if Audrey had balance in her life, while she did not.

Audrey was still wearing Camilla's T-shirt along with a pair of Camilla's slim jeans that were looser on Audrey than her. Audrey hadn't asked if she could wear them that morning. Camilla had been in the kitchen, making them to-go lattes when Audrey suddenly appeared in them, smiling. "Mine still have bar stink," she said as she balled up and then shoved the miniskirt and Runaways T-shirt into her knapsack that now sat in the back seat of the Mini. At first, Camilla had liked that Audrey was that comfortable with her that she'd wear her things. She liked the intimacy of it, as if she was still wrapped around Audrey. But now, up on the roof, whenever Camilla turned and looked over at her, she felt like she was spying on a thief who had broken into her closet, donned her clothes, and was playing dress-up as part of some weird robbery drag ritual.

Every so often as they hammered away, Audrey would reach out and try to touch Camilla, on the arm or the neck. Once, she touched Camilla's thigh. Camilla told her to cut it out. "I might fall," she said.

Audrey laughed. "Is that an admission of love?"

When Camilla didn't laugh or say anything back, Audrey asked her, "After you left here, did you ever want to leave?"

Camilla stopped hammering. "You mean, Massachusetts?"

Audrey nodded.

Camilla started to hammer a nail again. "My life is here." But even as she said it, she wondered what that meant. She had a job that she loved. She loved her home. She had Taylor. Really, that was it. Was that a life? She thought most people would say yes, but she wondered whether it was.

Audrey resumed hammering, too. "You mentioned the Great American Novel."

Camilla shook her head. "Not going to happen." She paused. "Do you want to leave?"

Audrey looked at her. She shrugged. "I like the challenge of starting over. Makes me feel alive. Didn't it feel that way to you? When you left here?" She pointed her hammer at the house below.

Camilla picked up the pace, hammering nail after nail. She didn't want to remember how she'd felt those first days, months, after she'd left. Alive? No, she hadn't felt alive. She'd felt dead. Numb. And when she hadn't felt that, she'd felt far too much. Everything could end with her crying. A small boy sitting in a grocery basket, picking out Cheerios from a plastic bag his mother had placated him with, popping the small morsels into his mouth, and happily chewing. A song on the car radio, the same song that Allison and she had spontaneously danced to in the middle of an aisle in a drug store one day. The first big snowfall as she sat alone in her new Cambridge home, each flake sealing her away from the life she had once led, away from Nico.

Camilla made sure the sounds of her hammering closed down the conversation.

At five, Audrey called it quits. "Come on. I have to go home and take a shower before I meet you later." They hadn't yet finished the roof, and Camilla was reluctant to go. But Audrey was already down the ladder and jumping onto the ground with a flourish at the bottom.

"Come on, slave driver," she called up, one hand

shielding her eyes from the setting sun.

Again, Camilla heard that voice telling her to take control, to nip anything further with Audrey in the bud. *You're not ready; you know that.* But, she didn't say anything. She slid down from the roof into the doorframe cutout, dropped her tool belt inside the treehouse, and started down the ladder.

☙ ☙ ☙ ☙

After she'd dropped Audrey off at her triple-decker in Somerville, driven back to Cambridge, and taken her shower and dressed, it was six thirty. Camilla wondered why Audrey had suggested meeting at the show when it was just as easy for Camilla to pick her up on the way. Was she meeting someone else in between? There hadn't been enough time to do that, had there? Camilla shook her head to drive away the thought. Why was she so bent on saddling their relationship—if you could call it that—with dreamt up complications?

After parking the car in a resident South End spot, hoping that she wouldn't get a ticket, she walked to the address for the art show that Audrey had given her. Boston parking clerks who walked the beat were the worst. Camilla had heard stories of them slapping on "the yellow boot" willy-nilly without the prerequisite five mandatory tickets.

Once the Bowery of Boston, Harrison Ave was on the cusp of becoming a horizon of renovated warehouses housing art galleries and lofts. At the factory where the show was, there was a line down the street of hopeful hipsters waiting to get in. Audrey was chatting up one of two effeminate bouncers. Camilla wondered when art shows started using bouncers, and felt old again. All three of them were dressed in black as if they were going to a funeral. Audrey was in leather pants and a skintight sleeveless black shirt that from a distance looked like scuba wear. The bouncers were so ballet-dancer-slim they didn't look like they could keep anyone out, yet alone kick anyone out. Audrey waved when she saw Camilla crossing the street toward them. The bouncer closest to Audrey lifted the velvet rope for Camilla and ushered the two of them in before the crowd had a chance to throw curses their way.

Inside the warehouse, the uneven, dirty wood floor was packed with bodies forming a sea of black. Camilla could see that cardboard boxes the size of refrigerators were set up around the perimeter, with cordoned-off lines of people serpentining through and around them, but she couldn't see what was in the boxes. Were they installations? She couldn't tell. Music blasted through a rotation of electronica songs that Camilla didn't recognize.

Audrey hooked an arm over Camilla's neck. "Let's get drinks," she said into Camilla's ear, patchouli sifting through the miasma of sweat and alcohol blown about by industrial fans. The crowd at the makeshift bar of steel doors planked across several sawhorses was four deep. Three female bartenders, all in their twenties with shaved heads and tattoo sleeves stretching from their wrists to their bra straps on their shoulders, jumped from customer to customer like bees flying from flower stem to flower stem. While Audrey sought to catch the eye of one of them, Camilla scanned the crowd for anyone who was at all close to her in age. From behind Audrey, she leaned in and asked, "Is this an underage thing?" Audrey glanced over her shoulder, laughed, and then turned right back to trying to get the bartenders' attention. In spite of their just arriving, Audrey was served faster than anyone else. Camilla noticed that when the bartender handed over their gin and tonics, she winked at Audrey. "What was that about?" Camilla asked as the bartender alighted on the next customer.

Audrey clinked their plastic glasses together, yelling in Camilla's ear, "Drink up. Doctor's orders."

"You're a doctor now?" Camilla said, too loudly.

Audrey drank. "The gin is to make you relax and the tonic is to help your muscles." Then she smiled, but it seemed like her face was angled slightly to the side, at some spot over Camilla's shoulder.

Before Camilla could look back toward the crowd, someone tapped her shoulder. Taylor stood there, a big grin on her face. She hadn't heard from Taylor since the night before when she'd left Taylor drunk at the bar. Camilla hadn't called her, either. She told herself that it was because she was busy with the treehouse and Audrey, but the truth was that she'd been avoiding her. Now here she was, without any warning.

Before Camilla could work out whether Audrey knew Taylor was going to be there, Taylor asked Camilla, "So? What do you think?" Camilla stared blankly at her. Taylor kept grinning at her. Camilla could smell alcohol. A half-full bottle of champagne swayed loosely in Taylor's hand.

Taylor cuffed her on the shoulder. "This is so amazing, isn't it? Who knew I knew this many people?" She waved drunkenly at the crowd.

"What?" Camilla said.

"It's Taylor's show," Audrey told her.

"You didn't know?" Taylor said. She gave a short laugh. "Busted," she said, pointing the bottle at Audrey.

Camilla looked at Audrey. "Why didn't you tell me?"

"You weren't talking to me, remember?" Taylor jumped in. "You got all pissy the last time I saw you."

A woman with waist-long purple hair and wearing a pink bodice and a thong over what looked to Camilla like the fully tattooed body out of Ray Bradbury's story, wrapped her arms around Taylor's neck from behind. "Introduce me to your friends," she cooed, staring glassy-eyed at Camilla and Audrey over Taylor's shoulder.

"I would if I could remember your name," Taylor said, laughing.

The woman smacked Taylor's shoulder, pretending to be miffed, and Audrey took advantage of the interruption to say, "We're going to go take a look." She tugged on Camilla's hand and led her away toward one of the cardboard boxes before she could protest. As they made their way through the crowd, Camilla wondered whether this had been the plan the whole time: to meet Taylor and have a sit-down later on. She tried to say something, but despite their linked hands, Audrey was too far away to hear over the music and the crush of people they were threading their way through. Audrey seemed to be taking it all in stride. Camilla wasn't. She felt again like her life wasn't her own. She was no longer in control of it.

Somehow, Audrey got them to the other side of the packed room. "I don't think there's a sequence to them," Audrey told her. She pulled Camilla toward a box that only had two people in line waiting to walk through. When they joined the line, Audrey leaned over and said in her ear, "This is an adventure." Was it? It didn't feel like that. She should be happy for

Taylor. Why wasn't she? She glanced back at Audrey, who was grinning now. Camilla suddenly wanted to please Audrey. Audrey seemed like she was enjoying it.

When it was their turn to enter the box, Audrey followed behind her, hooking her fingers to Camilla's belt in the back. Camilla was reminded of when she used to go dancing, when girls would form daisy chains as they danced around and through other dancers. There had been something comforting about being in those chains, like she was part of something larger than herself, some place she belonged. She loved the sandwiched confines of feeling the girl's ass in front of her tucked into her hips while from behind another girl pressed into her. Taylor seemed happy she was there. She'd wanted to know right away what Camilla thought of the exhibit. It would all work out.

Suddenly, they were inside the box. The box's walls were painted jet-black, with a cut-out entrance in, and on the other side, exit out. Strobe lights hung from the ceiling and shined down on the floor. A path just narrow enough to shuffle single file through was surrounded on both sides by dolls. On the left, GI Joes were lying on mounds of white rice. The male dolls were in various states of injury with red metallic paint acting as blood. Some of them had gashes in their uniforms. Others had limbs missing. The strobes flashed across the floor like during an air raid. Most of the GI Joes had been cut down before they reached the path, except for one whose hand was outstretched on the border. That wasn't what upset Camilla. The right side chilled her. There, a slew of miniature doll babies was glued to the tops of red Monopoly hotels, their hands and arms open and beckoning to the injured men. An audio track looped on and on in the cardboard hut of children's voices pleading, "Help me. Save me."

"Camilla?" Audrey said, but it was too late. Camilla rushed out of the box and through the crowd. She didn't know where she was going. She simply knew she had to leave there. Halfway through the crowd she saw a sign for restrooms and she made a beeline for it. The bathroom had three ugly green stalls and a row of dirty sinks under a cracked mirror. Two young girls stood in front of the mirror smearing lipstick on each other's lips. A group of other girls stood off to the side, arguing about staying or going. Finding the first empty stall in the crowded room, Camilla locked the door and leaned against a graffiti-riddled wall. She should have told Audrey that they should leave as soon as Taylor found them. Did Audrey know what was in that box? Had Taylor told her about it beforehand? That fucking box. Was that why she had chosen that one first? Did Taylor put those babies in there to mess with her? *Stop. Stop it right now.* Why did she always have to think the worst of everyone lately? Her heart was racing. Thankfully, remarkably, she wasn't crying. She realized she was too angry for that. But who was she fucking angry at? She took a deep breath, and then another, until she felt her heartbeat slow. Why did she have to read into everything? Couldn't she just be happy that Audrey had asked her out, that her best friend was having a successful installation, finally?

"You deserve to be happy," Taylor had told her the night they hatched the treehouse plan. "Out of anyone, you deserve that." Camilla had understood she should be thankful to her for saying that, but she couldn't be. She didn't buy it. It sounded like a false compliment. Besides, it sounded too easy. What had she done to *deserve* happiness? "You deserve happiness" was something that people said to a recently divorced friend, or someone that had lost a leg in a car accident. It meant you've been through so much already that you've *earned* a bye for the rest of your life. You've paid your dues, now it's your turn to win the lottery. Camilla secretly, though, believed in the Buddhist notion that life *was* suffering. Suffering had no end. You couldn't say that out loud, of course. Not in this country at least. Maybe in France. Or Tibet. Here, people would tag you as a pessimist, a fatalist, a Debbie Downer, or, as Taylor called her once, Milly Maudlin.

She stayed in the stall until someone started to bang on it, saying, "Unless you're going to share, you need to get out of there now." When she opened the door, Taylor's forgotten-name woman was standing there. "Oh, it's you," she said in a monotone, and stood back to let Camilla out as if she knew all about Camilla—including not to mess with her.

Back in the main room, Camilla looked around, but couldn't see Audrey. Or Taylor. *Where are they?* Wending her way through the crowd, she scanned everywhere for their faces, to no avail. She came back to the spot where she'd started. They were both gone.

Camilla returned to the bathroom, thinking Audrey may have gone into a stall before she had left. Nothing. She circled the main room again. She wove her way through, this time finding nameless girl once more. "Have you seen Taylor?" Camilla asked her.

"Who?" the girl said, staring off into the crowd with vacant eyes.

"Taylor. The artist. You asked her to introduce us."

"Who?"

Camilla shook her head and went by her. She was no longer simply nervous about being left behind. Now, she felt frantic, as if Taylor and Audrey had been kidnapped. Was this DEFCON 4 or 5 in Taylor's book? She'd prefer a kidnapping, given what else their disappearance could mean. The voice in her head was increasing in volume with each passing minute. *Go home*, it shouted. *Get in your car and go home.*

Running out of options, she went back to the bar area. The crowd had thinned a bit. Scanning the faces, she was surprised to see Audrey and Taylor at the far end of the bar. Miraculously, they were perched on two metal stools in front of several women who were unsuccessfully trying to get any bartender's attention. Audrey was earnestly telling Taylor something, her right hand waving in the air as if making a point. Camilla didn't know whether to interrupt them or let it play out. They weren't, as she'd begun to imagine, in one of the bathroom stalls attempting a quickie under her nose, Taylor's feet making horrible suction noises as they shifted on the sticky stall floor, Audrey up against the metal wall with her legs locked around Taylor's waist, her tight leather pants giving her the friction she needed to get off. They were at the bar, seemingly in an argument. Audrey was clearly telling Taylor something she didn't want to hear. Taylor's face was stubbornly turned down, her eyes fixed on the steel door countertops.

"Are you in line or just a voyeur?" a voice yelled behind her. Camilla shifted over, her eyes frozen on the silent film twenty feet away. Maybe that was what caused Taylor to look up. Audrey quickly glanced over, too. Audrey said something else to Taylor. She leaned in to kiss Taylor on the cheek, but Taylor moved away, her eyes still locked on Camilla. Audrey stood up. She started to thread her way over to Camilla. *You've done it now. Now you're in it.* For a moment, she was torn. Should she leave with Audrey, or should she go over to Taylor and smooth things over?

"Let's go," Audrey told her as she grabbed Camilla's hand and pulled her toward the exit.

Outside, Camilla welcomed the cooler night air, despite the chill it brought because her T-shirt was slightly damp with sweat.

"I had to tell her," Audrey began as soon as they started to walk to the car. She didn't look happy when she said it.

"I don't want to know, Audrey." Camilla held up her hand to emphasize that it wasn't her problem. She understood it was, in fact, partially her doing, but she had enough to contend with. The treehouse. Cindy Hunter. Christ, she couldn't even go to an art exhibit without falling apart. She didn't want drama on top of all of that. Irritated, she told her, "What you tell her is your deal, not mine."

"She had to be told," Audrey said in a flat voice. Camilla could see the Mini a block away. Its tire rims were empty. She almost wished there'd been a yellow boot to discover. She wanted to be angry.

"There goes a twenty-year friendship down the drain," she said harshly. "Sometimes ignorance is bliss. Haven't you ever heard that? I don't get this compulsive need to confess people your age have," she added, switching into the voice she used in the classroom. *Listen up, I'm about to teach you something.* She kept walking, though Audrey had stopped. When Camilla reached her car door, she finally turned around. "Are you coming?" she called back to Audrey. Audrey shook her head. She turned around, heading back to the warehouse. Stunned, Camilla opened her mouth to call to her, thought better of it, and climbed into her bucket seat. She started the engine and drove the car home.

⁂

That night, she couldn't sleep. She'd always had difficulty sleeping since the day thirty-six years before when her father had drowned in a boating accident. Camilla was twelve. Her father was on a fishing trip with five of his friends. A journalist, he was on assignment writing an article for *Troll & Travel*, a magazine that highlighted unusual fishing trips. The idea was for him to weave in Raymond Carver's iconic fishing trip story, male bonding, that sort of thing, but without the dead body that the men find as they do in Carver's story. Except there was one. As her father and the others were crossing the reservoir in upstate New York, the boat, which was overloaded past the weight maximum, began to take on water and capsized. Four of the men scrambled on top of the floating, overturned boat. The life jackets were locked in a cabinet that was now submerged under the water. Camilla's father and one of the others swam for help. It was October. The water was hypothermia-level cold, which was ultimately her father's undoing. The other man reached the shore safely by floating on his back. Somehow the two of them had been separated in the pre-dawn darkness. All the other men survived, too, holding on to the overturned boat like a buoy. Her father, who was Greek on his father's side, would have appreciated the tragic ending of it all.

From that night on, Camilla would fall asleep quickly, only to be jolted awake a few hours later, never to be able to get back to a deep sleep. "Shakespeare called sleep death's counterfeit," Camilla had told Taylor. "No wonder I can't sleep." She thought she sounded erudite when she said it, but Taylor had simply nodded her head thoughtfully and told her, "Yeah, well, that's when those of us who live in the twentieth century pop an Ambien."

In bed, after Camilla returned from Harrison Ave, she stared at the waning moon coming through her bedroom window over her desk. The cats were perched on her desk, two sphinxes staring at the moths that occasionally flew past or battered the screen. The super moon was gone. What was left was an ordinary moon whose grey blotches made it look dirty. Although only twenty-four hours had passed, it seemed as if Camilla had imagined it all: the super moon, Audrey, the carousel of new, happier stories circling in her second bedroom. The ominous red numbers on her digital clock on the bureau now read eighteen minutes past three. She watched the cats swinging wildly at the moths, their claws getting stuck in the metal window screen. Camilla felt their disappointment at never being able to connect with any of the winged insects through the screen. They were there, and then not.

Day Six

Peter

Another hot, cloudless July day. The sun beat down through Camilla's bedroom window onto her desk. Even the cats, who usually loved lolling in the warmth of the sun's rays, stayed under the bed in their cool, dark cave.

Camilla awoke with her T-shirt drenched in sweat. The buzzer to her condo was repeatedly ringing, as if the person outside kept tapping the button like a nervous tic. Whoever it was might have been there for some time. It was ten o'clock. The treehouse loomed unfinished. Time was running out. The buzzer rang again. She wondered if it was Taylor. Then, if it was Audrey. Whoever it was wasn't going away.

Rubbing her sweaty face, Camilla stood up. She'd fallen asleep fully clothed, the creases of her jeans behind her knees now stuck to her legs. The buzzer sounded again. Finally, she gave in to the wasp-like hounding, although she felt suddenly afraid of who was at her door, like she was about to meet a stalker. She went downstairs. When she opened the house front door, she was surprised, to find her brother there.

"Late night?" Peter asked as he brushed by her and his long legs bounded up the stairs. "Bathroom."

Camilla shut the door and leaned her forehead against it. Her life had become that television show during which the host whips out everyone who ever knew you: your kindergarten teacher, the boy who tripped you on the playground blacktop causing your forehead to have a scar forever, the girl you outfoxed in a college tennis tournament, your first employer, and whatever relatives the producers corralled. Peter lived almost four hundred miles away in a small college town in upstate New York. He was three years older than Camilla. Through childhood and adolescence they'd been close. But in her twenties, Camilla, in a burst of wanting her mother and brother to know her—*really* know her—before she or one of them died, had come out to the two of them, and Peter had become distant. It wasn't an abrupt departure, more like he drifted away gradually, like smoke. He still called her every two weeks, as he'd always done. When they did talk on the phone, however, he rambled on about problems at the Wallington Gun Factory where he was in charge of public relations.

"The anti-violence crowd is gunning for us," he told her once. She would've laughed except his tone was so serious.

Ever since she'd come out to him, he filled up the five minutes of airtime with stuff that Camilla either didn't care about or made her furious because of the politics, never once asking her any questions about her life. Nor was there any pause in his gibbering during which she could interject anything. But, Camilla couldn't really be angry. She understood his prattling was born from fear of the unknown. He wanted to connect. Otherwise why keep up the pretense of calling her every other week? He didn't know her language anymore, though. Or that's what she thought he thought. In his eyes, she'd moved to another country, some place where the language was too impossible and difficult to learn easily, like Greece, or one of those nearly extinct rain forest tribal regions.

"Wish we could talk more, but Bonnie's giving me the high sign," he might wistfully tell her just before hanging up. Bonnie, his wife, had no idea what a high sign was, although Camilla and Peter did because they'd watched *The Little Rascals* episode about the he-man women haters club together as kids. Camilla had never taken to Bonnie. She was from a spit of a town near the Canadian border that prided itself on its people being made of, what Bonnie termed, "good stock." Camilla always thought of the town as populated with minotaurs from Greek mythology: bull heads atop thick human bodies. Bonnie's accent grated as well, all hick twang and irritating made-up contractions. She didn't work, claiming taking care of Peter and the house allowed no time for anything else. Camilla knew, though, that her brother was more independent and needed less attention than anyone she knew. He could have originated that old camping saying: If you bring it in, carry it out. If the shit hit the world fan, Camilla wouldn't call on Taylor who talked a good talk but didn't really walk the walk. No, she'd find her brother and hole up with him, living on some mountain, surviving on berries and icy, clean brooks.

Still, when her brother used Bonnie as an excuse to end their conversation, Camilla allowed it. She'd get tired of the nonstop one-sided chatter. During one phone call, she was able to slip in that she'd left Allison only because Peter sneezed, leaving a pocket of air. There followed a larger pocket of air, empty and dead like a no-fly zone. "Gosh," Peter said to her finally. "Do you need anything? Um, like money or anything?"

Now, Camilla shook her head in her downstairs alcove, her forehead still against the front door as she heard her brother racing through her condo upstairs. Doris had told her during one session that there was a Yiddish expression: we plan and God laughs. She'd planned to build the treehouse. God had sent her brother.

When she finally climbed the steps back into her condo, she found him coming out of the bathroom, wiping his washed hands on his jeans. It was an old habit. As a child to avoid their mother scolding him for getting the bathroom towels dirty he dried his hands on his pants or shorts. After their father died, Matilda yelled at them for the smallest infractions. Who could blame her after losing her husband so horribly? Peter had wanted then to be invisible just like Camilla. At family gatherings, Camilla would join Peter in whatever corner he'd scope out. At their father's wake, under the unbearable strain of having to remain next to their mother in the receiving line to greet every person walking through the funeral home's door, the two of them had held hands surreptitiously, their clasped hands hidden behind Peter's back.

"It's our job to make it easier on everyone else," Matilda had told them on the drive over to the funeral parlor. Camilla was twelve, Peter fifteen.

Camilla only released her brother's hand once during the hour they stood welcoming people at the wake. One of the men who worked with their father came through the front door. Immediately, their mother whispered to them, "He was on the boat." He was a big man, doubly so to Camilla and her brother who looked like dwarves next to him. His hair was disheveled, standing up in places it shouldn't and looking like he hadn't combed it since the fishing trip, and his button-down shirt wasn't tucked in. Their mother said quietly to them as he walked into the foyer of the funeral home, "Be nice. He's been through a lot." After crushing Matilda to his chest, the man held out a small pearl penknife to Peter and told him, "He would've wanted you to have this." Camilla could see her brother turning pale. When Peter shook his head, the man added, "It was his—your dad's. I borrowed it that..." His voice trailed off as he started to cry. His hand, trembling, was holding out the penknife, but Peter shook his head even more determinedly, staring down at the man's worn loafers.

"Peter," their mother said quietly. But her brother wouldn't so much as touch the knife. He remained staring at the man's shoes, shaking his head. Matilda, with a pained expression, started to apologize to the man, but then Camilla reached over and took the knife. "Thanks," she said, and hid it in her skirt pocket before her mother could stop her.

"The towels are there for a reason," Camilla now told her brother in her condo. As an afterthought, she softened it with a smile.

Peter shrugged, and stopped wiping his hands on his pants. They stood, staring at each other, near the Mexican dining room table. Peter glanced away first. "Nice," he said, tapping his fingertips on the worn pine tabletop.

"It's old. I don't mean antique," she added nervously. "It's one of the few things I took from the house." No matter how close they'd been as kids, whenever she was around him now she felt as if she had to watch how she worded everything, like he'd get the wrong impression of her.

He looked around the room. Camilla noticed that he seemed skinnier, although he'd always been tall and lanky. His yellow T-shirt, with its black tagline of *Yellow Jacket Tequila: Feel the Sting*, drooped across his waist. His face was thinner, too. Tight like a mask. His brown hair, usually trimmed short, was unkempt and overgrown to the point where his bangs almost covered his right eye, and the back was down past his T-shirt collar. His fingertips unconsciously tapped the table as if he were making a point during a meeting.

"Great place," he said, staring into the living room. He stopped the tapping. "Is that...?" He walked around the couch toward the large Chinese cabinet that Camilla had bought with her tax money that year. Reaching up, he took down a woven fishing creel. His hands caressed the wicker sides. "Huh," he said, smiling. He slipped the strap over his shoulder and opened the creel.

"I *asked* mom for it."

Peter held up a piece of Styrofoam on which were stuck rows of hand tied flies. He raised the white spongy base to eye level, peering at each of the flies as he turned the Styrofoam this way and that. "I can't believe you have this."

Camilla worried that he would demand them. After all, he used to go fly-fishing with their father, she didn't. The only reason Peter hadn't been on the boat that day when their father had drowned was that he had come down with the flu. Otherwise he might not have been here manhandling, as it started to seem to her, what was hers. It hit her for the first time that they might have both been here: her father and Peter. Surely if Peter had gone that day their father would've stayed with the boat with Peter and the rest of the survivors.

He wouldn't have left the boat to swim for shore. He wouldn't have left his teenage son. At the time, she and her mother had been so happy that Peter hadn't gone, that he hadn't died, too, never thinking of a different interpretation. Suddenly, the ground dropped away. Reeling from this thought, Camilla reached out to grab the top of the couch.

"What? What is it?" Peter asked, startled, and put the flies and then the creel quickly back on top of the cabinet. He walked toward her.

"What are you doing here?" she asked him stiffly so that he wouldn't take one more step nearer. She was afraid he'd try to hug her or something. What kind of person was she that she thought so badly of her only brother?

"Okay," he said, scratching his bangs away as if they were itching him. "Okay." He held up his hands in surrender. "Bonnie's left me. For someone else. A friend of mine. My best friend, actually."

He turned away, facing one of the living room windows, pretending to be interested in whatever the sky looked like. It's blue, Camilla wanted to assure him. Like always. It will go on being blue. Instead she said the only thing she could think of. "How are your building skills?"

≈≈≈≈

She told him about the treehouse and Nico and Taylor and Cindy Hunter while she made them their favorite childhood sandwiches of mayonnaise on bulky onion rolls. She left out Audrey. How could she tell him she'd found somebody when he had recently lost *his* somebody?

Peter stared down at his sandwich. "We live in a

time warp," he said, shaking his head, picking up and then putting down the sandwich. He said it wistfully, though. He told her about finding Bonnie in bed with his now ex-friend, and how hard it was to live alone in the house that they had shared together, and that it felt like a prison and not a victory, and that he hated his job but now needed to stay in it for the alimony that he was sure a judge would order him to pay. He told her all this while his sandwich sat untouched, his fingers trembling when he relayed what the ex-friend had said when they were caught: "She's a better lover than you were a friend."

"Stupid shit owes me a thousand dollars," Peter said.

"That what Bonnie's charging these days?" Camilla asked him, mimicking Bonnie's hillbilly inflection.

Peter started to laugh, but then he turned away and stared out the kitchen's glass back door.

"Look," Camilla said softly. "I'm sure if the judge knows the circumstances the alimony won't be as large as you think. Besides, if you quit your job, she can't get blood from a stone. You can stay here as long as you like. Although we'll need to buy a bigger bed for the guest room." Looking at his profile, she saw his jaw clench as if he had a muscle cramp or was about to punch someone.

Finally, he pushed away his uneaten lunch plate. He stood up. "Let's go build that treehouse."

≈≈≈≈

It was Peter who pointed out the obvious: there were no windows in the treehouse. "It's going to be an oven in here with only that cut-out doorway." When he saw Camilla's crestfallen face, he quickly added,

"Windows are a breeze." Then he laughed. "Come on, that was a good one."

Camilla laughed. When they were kids they often tried to outdo each other with their silly puns. Camilla realized now, maybe that was what Peter had been trying to do that time he'd said the anti-gun lobby was *gunning* for him all those years ago. He'd been trying to connect, not *disconnect*.

"Yeah, you really nailed that one," she told him back, holding up her hammer for effect.

"Don't quit your day job," he said, laughing. "The act still needs some polishing. Where's the closest Home Depot?"

They selected a casement window that opened outward and a porthole one that could open out as well and reminded them both of being on a ship. Camilla thought of the poem by Whitman "O Captain! My Captain!," and of *Moby Dick,* and of all the ship stories, like *Treasure Island,* that small boys liked to read. Would Nico read any of them? After he was born and they brought him home from the hospital, on the nights when Camilla was "on duty" and he'd awaken, she'd read *Dombey and Son* to him. Now, looking back, she realized that it might not have been the best book to read him. The son, Paul Dombey, dies by the age of six. But, she'd always loved Dickens's opening lines, especially the first time she'd read them aloud, with Nico burrito-wrapped on her lap at one in the morning.

Dombey sat in the corner of the darkened room in the great arm-chair by the bedside, and Son lay tucked up warm in a little basket bedstead, carefully disposed on a low settee immediately in front of the fire and close to it, as if his constitution were analogous to that of a muffin, and it was essential to toast him brown while he was very new.

"Nico will love this one," Peter said as if reading her mind, as he slid the heavy box with the porthole window onto the store's orange metal platform cart. Camilla felt a tug. Peter had only met Nico once, a few months after he was born. He and Bonnie had come for a weekend. It hadn't been a good visit. Allison was still hormonally hyped and Camilla was a wreck worrying about whether Peter would see through the veneer and would know that all was not right in that house. Bonnie had filled the air with her loathsome silly twattle, making it worse by talking baby talk to Nico who stared at her with his big brown orbs as if she was a creature from another planet sent to kidnap him.

Camilla liked how Peter assumed he still knew what Nico would like, as if he too had not forgotten that Nico was a part of them. Although they were not bound by blood, the cord between them was still there. Camilla felt another tug. She squinted her eyes past his shoulder as if she was searching for something important on the shelves down the aisle that held sample windows of every shape and size.

"You have an electric saw, right?" Peter asked over his shoulder, as he rolled the cart away. She managed to say that she did before following him. Is this what the rest of her life would be like? Seemingly innocent trips to stores weighted down by her memories of Nico. It wasn't always memories, either. Sometimes they were thoughts of what Nico's future would be. What he would do every day. What he'd read. *If* he'd be a reader. What his expression would be the first time he'd open the ship window and stare out at the tree branches and blue sky. What he'd see. Whether he'd ever see Peter again. Whether he'd ever see her again.

At the checkout, Peter insisted on paying. He told Camilla, "It's my birthday present for him." Nico's birthday wasn't for several months yet, and Camilla was certain Peter knew that. He was making sure that she understood that he, too, wanted a part of this right now, right here.

"You know she might tear the whole thing down when she sees it," she said as he handed over his credit card to the clerk.

He shrugged. "Then we'll just have to build it again the next time they go away."

Camilla laughed. She liked the idea of them, and maybe Audrey, and even Taylor, making an annual pilgrimage of it, rebuilding what would be destroyed again and again until they wore Allison down. The treehouse would become those birthday candles that never can be blown out, their light eternal, lasting.

When they were in the car on their way home, Peter said, "That weekend Bonnie and I came? I knew something was wrong. I should've said something."

Camilla focused on the road, her hands moving on the steering wheel into the safe driver ten and two positions, although Mount Auburn Street was an easy straight line with slow-moving traffic due to a slew of stoplights. They were coming up on one of those red lights now. Camilla concentrated on downshifting to second and then to first, rolling to a stop behind a moving van.

"Mills?"

"And here I thought I was so good at subterfuge," Camilla said. She smiled stiffly.

"I am sorry, Mills."

Camilla shook her head. The light turned green, and the moving van in front of them began to slowly roll forward. She sighed. "There was nothing you could've said that would've changed anything. Our fate is a fait accompli." She glanced over at him. Their father would tell them that whenever they bristled under a decision that either he or their mother had made. *Our fate is a fait accompli.* He'd say it holding his hands wide open to show them there was nothing to be done; all had been decided beforehand.

Peter winced. "I used to imagine that those were his last words, swimming away from the boat."

"Did you ever notice how moving vans drive so slowly? Do you think it's to drag out the hourly charges?" Camilla asked, trying to jettison the conversation although she'd been the one who had started it. First Nico and now their father. Suddenly, she found it all overwhelming. She was responsible for bringing them both in to the conversation earlier that day and yet she ended up tamping down any follow-up. She kept opening the closet door only to slam it shut when all the mops, leftover gift wrap, recycled grocery bags, coats and hats and orphaned single gloves began to tumble out.

Peter didn't reply. For the rest of the ride home they drove in silence. Camilla was glad for it. Her brother had only been there four hours and already it felt as if they were headed toward uncharted waters where the only thing that would help them survive would be these few life rafts of silence.

❧ ❧ ❧ ❧

Peter was good at building. Camilla had forgotten how quick and sure he could be with his hands.

Matilda used to say he was born with surgeon hands. And he was strong. He quickly cut out the holes and constructed the two-by-four frames for the windows. The casement on the side would look out to Benji's yard and the porthole on the opposite side would be directed toward the back door of the kitchen. Anyone coming out of the house could be seen before they closed the back door. Neither Peter nor Camilla had to say who they wanted Nico to be able to see coming out of that door, in order to give him a heads-up. Camilla continued to work on the molding around the opening that served as a doorway, glancing over to watch Peter attach the strips of self-adhesive waterproof membrane under, on top, and then on the sides of the cutouts. She helped him place the windows in their new homes, tipping the bottoms in first. She held them steady as he tacked the windows' nailing fins onto the framing with roofing nails.

"They won't have screens, but they will give him air," Peter said as he hammered away. Camilla felt that familiar tug again, only this time it was from happiness. She and Peter were giving Nico air, she thought. He would be able to breathe up here.

"There'll be a nice cross breeze," Peter added.

When they were done, they wordlessly sat down on the plywood floor together, waiting to feel that breeze. For a moment, all Camilla could feel was the stultifying heat. Now that they had stopped working, it seemed as if there was no air in the treehouse despite the new windows. Camilla felt rivulets of sweat wend their way down her back and stomach. She began to say something, but Peter touched her arm and told her, "Wait for it." Then, there it was. Air. She felt it stream past her.

"Anemoi," she murmured. "Do you remember them?" The four wind gods in Greek mythology. Their father had told them about them over a pancake breakfast during a Nor'easter that had cancelled their school day. Their dead end was sealed off behind a ten-foot-tall snowplowed hill of snow. It was as near to seeing an iceberg as they'd ever get, she figured.

"Boreas from the North who brings us the cold," Peter said dreamily, as if he, too, was remembering that snowstorm. His eyes closed as he lifted his face to the crosswind.

"Notus from the south with his storms." Camilla watched her brother's face soften as she spoke.

"Zephyrus from the west, bringer of breezes in the spring and summer," Peter recited, his voice low and soft.

"And Eurus from the east," Camilla murmured, closing her eyes.

They still sat there with their eyes closed after they cooled down. After Peter slipped a hand in Camilla's. After they heard a car drive up and park and a door open and close. They sat there until Taylor's voice called up, "Hello to the house" and the sounds of her feet bounding up the ladder reached them.

Peter squeezed her hand once and dropped it. Then he stood up. And Camilla felt like all the air in the treehouse was sucked out as Taylor's head appeared in the doorway.

Taylor

"Reinforcements!" Taylor said a little too loudly as soon as she barreled through the doorway and saw Peter. She awkwardly hugged him as he was standing up, almost toppling him. "Mills didn't tell me you were coming." Stepping back, she looked at Camilla. She wagged her finger at her. "Naughty girl," she chastised.

"I didn't—" Camilla started to say.

"I surprised her."

"Stealth and deception. Two of the best military strategies according to my father." Taylor held up two fingers, then folded the index one down, leaving the middle one standing alone.

Her brother laughed for an instant. "Same old Taylor."

Taylor beamed. "Why change? You're looking a little POW-campish yourself, Petey." Looking around, she took in the windows. "Wow. How long have you been here? Has she had you locked up in the cellar until today?"

"What are you doing here?" Camilla asked her. The treehouse felt small. Too small. Suddenly, Camilla smelled alcohol. It wafted from Taylor to them, carried by the breeze. She knew that Peter smelled it, too. He sucked his bottom lip in, grabbing it with his top teeth in a mock overbite.

Taylor scratched her head. Then, she pulled out a can of spray paint from her messenger bag. The top was a fluorescent lime green.

"This place could use a little spiffing up," she said, wagging the spray paint can at them.

Camilla was not amused. "Not with that it doesn't."

Taylor laughed. She began to shake the can like a martini mixer, the pea inside knocking against the aluminum can like an ice cube.

"Come on. Lighten up. He'll love it." With her car key Taylor broke the plastic tab securing the lid and popped the lid off, which fell to the floor. "Oops."

Camilla bristled at what she deemed as Taylor trying to take control. Was she that pissed about Audrey that she'd come to destroy what meant so much to Camilla?

"We don't have time," Camilla said. "As it is we might not fin—"

"This puppy's a super fat," Taylor told them. When she saw Peter and Camilla's blank faces she shook the can some more. "The nozzle. It's the fastest, biggest sprayer they have. Watch."

She started to move toward a wall, but Camilla stood in her way. "It's not going to happen, so drop it."

And Taylor did just that, although Camilla had meant the discussion, not the can itself. Lifting her hand away, Taylor let the can fall to the platform and roll away until it thudded against a mound of leftover shingles, lumber, and discarded nails in the corner. "Now look what you made me do," she told Camilla.

"Still doing your artwork then, Taylor?" Peter asked, trying to divert whatever was churning up between them. Camilla saw his hands were turning a hammer over and over.

Camilla was going to pick up the can, but then Taylor laughed and held up her hands, telling Peter, "Peace. Honestly, I came by for the photograph." She looked at Camilla. "You know, the one you have of your accuser? Did Mills tell you about that?" Taylor said, turning to Peter. "About her pesky student?"

"Good thing I did, apparently," Camilla said. "Why would I have it here?"

Taylor shrugged. "Maybe you were using it as a dartboard." She turned again to Peter, this time the movement a little jerky, as if she'd almost lost her balance. "So what do you think about our girl getting herself into all sorts of trouble lately? Shit's getting real, isn't it?" She motioned wildly with her hand at the walls. "She tell you this was my idea?"

"*Our* idea," Camilla corrected.

"Whoever's idea it was, it's great," Peter said, placating. His face still looked tight to Camilla. Camilla was nervous, too. Who knew why Taylor was really here? Maybe to hash out the Audrey question? Maybe to tell her what a terrible friend she was? Maybe to bring her up to date on the latest information she'd found on Cindy Hunter and Allison? Or, maybe it was, as she'd said, simply to add a bit of color to one of the walls or to retrieve the photo. Camilla doubted that. Whatever it was now was not the time to air any of it in front of her brother. He had enough splinters from his own shattered relationship. He didn't need to witness another one being smashed to bits.

"Always the mediator, Petey," Taylor groused, looking around again. She haphazardly crossed over to the porthole and leaned out. "Fucking excellent spy hole by the way, Mills. You going to have Nico report back to you her movements?"

"Are you drunk?" Camilla asked her, smarting. Behind Taylor's back, Peter nodded his head at Camilla, putting his index finger to his lips, but Taylor reeled around and saw.

Taylor stuck her hip out defiantly. "As a matter of fact I am." She faced Peter again. "Did she tell you how she slept with my girlfriend? I'm betting not." She smiled in that knowing way that Camilla hated. "All that fucking stress she's under, you know? That's what *she'll* tell you." She pointed her finger in an accusatory way at Camilla, who stood there, stuck on how she could stop what was happening. Taylor made a waving circle above her head. "Building this fucking treehouse and all. Having some student of hers in cahoots with her ex trying to get her ass fired. I mean why not? Why not fuck your best friend's, your *only* friend's, girlfriend? What a fucking stress reliever, right?"

"She wasn't, *isn't* your girlfriend, Taylor." Camilla turned to Peter, exasperated. "Can we go? I'm hungry."

"By all means," Taylor shouted, motioning toward the doorway. "I'm so fucking glad you have an appetite."

Camilla felt her face get hot. "Can you wait in the car?" she asked Peter as calmly as she could, but her voice trembled.

Peter dusted off his jeans although there was nothing there. "Take care of yourself, Taylor," he said. As he walked past her, Camilla saw his lips were pressed tightly together.

They watched him descend the ladder. Camilla wrapped her arms around her body. She needed grounding. She was so angry with Taylor she felt as if she could throw *her* down the ladder and still that wouldn't be good enough. She felt the treehouse shift with the breeze in its flexible joints.

Taylor said, "Oh sorry, did I break up the family reunion? Where's his lovely wife by the way? She busy at some hog callin' competition?"

Camilla smiled in spite of herself. She dropped her arms. Taylor always found a way to get Camilla to drop the boxing gloves. Afterward, Camilla would think she had been robbed of something. Instead of addressing the weed root of whatever Camilla was angry about, Taylor merely tamped some nice sod over it. Or she'd pull out whatever artwork she was occupied with to distract her, like a magician pulling rabbits and flowers from a hat to divert a pack of demanding kids.

Camilla foraged in her back jeans pocket for cigarettes. Taking a cigarette out, she held it between her fingers but didn't light it. "He came by himself. They're getting divorced. He found her in bed with someone else."

"Hah!" Taylor burst out. "I know the fuckin' feeling. Maybe he and I should form a support group."

"Enough with the pity party. Or don't you remember that it was *you* who planned that fucking threesome? You don't get to control both sides of the chess game."

Taylor waved all of her fingers at her. "Ooh, nice metaphor, Professor. I didn't hear you complaining."

Camilla lit and took a drag of her cigarette and exhaled, hoping the interruption would settle everything down. "Look, I know why I hurt you. It's about Audrey but it isn't. And I know you know that."

Taylor looked away. "So, twenty years of friendship is—"

Camilla reached out with her free hand. Grabbing Taylor's hip, she shook her. "No. It isn't. But you need to stop directing me like some kind of field marshal." She shook Taylor's hip more gently back and forth. "I'm not one of your grunts. I have to go. He needs me now." She gave Taylor a peck on her cheek. "Come on, I'll drive you home and Peter can follow us. You shouldn't be driving."

"Who made you commander in chief?" Taylor muttered, but she let herself be led away by the hand, the runaway can of spray paint forgotten.

❧ ❧ ❧ ❧

After dropping Taylor off with the Volvo, they didn't arrive back at Camilla's until dinnertime. Camilla made a simple meal: salmon, steamed green beans, and red potatoes baked with rosemary and oil. She put Peter in charge of the salmon and the grill outside on her condo deck.

"Slacking off, are we?" Peter smiled as he took the plate with the plain, unadorned fish. He let out an exaggerated sigh. "Well, we're not saving a dime on therapy this month, are we?"

It was a joke they shared. Their mother was a gourmet cook, who was quick to point out at dinner parties that she had gone to Le Cordon Bleu. Matilda had always loved cooking, and after years of having to provide as a single parent for Camilla and her brother by teaching literature in a nearby high school, a job that was at best, as Matilda put it, "a test of endurance as harsh as Anne Boleyn's," she finally pursued her true passion when Camilla was twenty-seven and Peter had just turned thirty. Their mother was in her early sixties then. Five years later she'd die just as suddenly as their father, only from a heart attack. But that day, Camilla questioned her on the phone as to whether that was a wise way to spend twenty thousand dollars for the twenty-one months it would take to complete the cooking course. Her mother told her, "Trust me, this way I'm saving twice as much as that by not needing therapy."

Ever since then, whenever they cooked a bland meal or ate subpar restaurant food, Camilla or Peter would say, "Well, we're not saving a dime on therapy this month, are we?"

What Matilda didn't tell the hosts or the other guests was that she attended the Le Cordon Bleu in

Dallas, Texas.

"What do you say if they ask you what your favorite restaurant to eat in Paris is?" Camilla asked her once after her mother told her about attending a dinner event hosted by their local PBS television channel. Matilda had won two tickets in the town library's raffle. She'd chosen to go solo because she didn't want anyone blowing her cover.

"Oh, that's easy. I simply turn the question back on them by saying I can't possibly choose and what would they say were their favorites? People love to talk about themselves, don't you know?"

Opening the kitchen's screen door, Peter stepped out onto the deck, closing the door behind him.

Camilla pointed the paring knife at him that she was using to cut off the green bean ends and said, "After a good dinner one can forgive anybody, even one's own relatives."

Peter laughed. He looked at her through the screen. "Let me guess. Dickens."

Camilla shook her head. "Not even close. Wilde."

Putting the plate of salmon down on the grill side tray, Peter opened the lid on the small grill. He sang the tune to the sixties Donovan hit, "Mellow Yellow," only changing the first line to "I'm just wild about wild," breaking the last word into two syllables: wile-uld. Growing up, her brother was known to have a remarkable memory of snatches of songs, old and new, that he'd slip ingeniously into conversation. They always were playful snippets that could turn a serious conversation into a more lighthearted exchange. Surprisingly, they never irritated Camilla or anyone else. They seemed to say, *Yes I hear what you are saying, but I'd rather laugh than cry, wouldn't you?*

Smiling, Camilla went back to finishing the tedious task of nipping the green beans ends off. She wondered if his joking and jovial teasing were real, or if they were masking the hurt he must be loaded down with. Maybe it was to make her feel better. After hearing about all her troubles, maybe his didn't look so bad anymore to him. No one was trying to get him fired. No one had taken away his child. And he was rid of hillbilly Bonnie. You couldn't simply say your life was unbearable. You had to compare it to someone else's to really do a proper analysis. Like Jack had always contended, to justify sharing his salacious gossip as a mental health service, there was always someone else who had a worse tale to tell. There was always a worse life to be borne. Once, Camilla told her mother she was sorry that she had become a widow at such a young age, and Camilla's mother had searched Camilla's face and said, "Look around you, darling. How many happy people do you really see?"

The meal was simple, but Camilla and her brother wolfed it down without a word. It could have been the physical labor they had done in the treehouse that was the reason for their fatigue, or it could have been the emotional quagmire they found themselves in between the reason for Peter's sudden visit and Taylor's unexpected appearance. They silently ate everything on their plates and what was left in the serving bowls of beans and potatoes. The silence was comfortable, natural as a silence between close siblings can be. Camilla realized that she no longer felt nervous that he was there with her.

"Guest room okay?" Camilla finally said as they cleared the dining room table and carried the dishes to the sink.

"I'll do these." Peter turned on the hot water faucet. Recently, the town was replacing all the water and sewer lines on Camilla's street and the construction sometimes produced air bubbles that spat out of the faucet. Camilla was used to the Volvo excavators as big as her house that rambled up and down her street, their revolving treads sounding like a fleet of tanks—Taylor called it Beirut when she visited—and the horrendous noise from their diggers smashing holes into the pavement, but the sudden popping and spitting of water always made Camilla jump as if she'd been shot. The water never splattered that far. It was that sudden hissing sound that unnerved her. When it did the same thing now, she jumped.

"Whoa," Peter said, stepping back. He began to scrub one of the plates under the rushing water. "What's up with you and Taylor?" he asked. Stacking the bowls and the pans on the counter, Camilla looked away, back toward the guest room's closed door. Why had she offered him the guest room? The night before she'd slept alone in that room on the twin mattress. The sheets still smelled of Audrey and patchouli. Somehow it cured her insomnia. She didn't notice the void of something missing. It was only the room where she and Audrey had sex. The room where she could sleep now. She began to feel the familiar feelings of guilt and whip of self-reproach then. How quickly she had taken to overlooking—she never quite forgot—the fact that the room originally was to be Nico's room.

"Mills?" Peter was staring at her, his hands dripping water onto the wood floor in front of the sink. His face was grave and worried.

Camilla shook her head, forcing a smile. "Sorry. You'd probably be more comfortable in my bedroom.

The other one isn't really set up for company."

Peter dried his hands on a dishtowel. Crouching down, he began to wipe up the few drops of water on the floor.

"Leave it. The cats will get it," Camilla said.

He stood up, wiping his hands again, this time on his pants. "The couch is fine." He walked toward the living room. "Sit down, okay?"

Camilla sighed. "I'm pretty tired."

He pointed toward the leather chair as he sat in the blue one. "Sit."

Camilla reluctantly did as he told her. As soon as she sat down he said, "What's really up with you and Taylor?"

"You know Taylor."

"What was she talking about? About the girlfriend?"

Camilla pulled her legs up, wrapping her arms around her ankles. "Taylor started something. And she's pissed because I wouldn't let her finish it. Look, you don't want to know, trust me."

"That's the thing. I'm not sure I can right now. Trust you. You seem a bit…"

"What?" Camilla stretched out her legs on to the ottoman in front of the chair, pretending that she was relaxed.

Peter waved in the air. "I don't know. Different. Spiraling. I mean, Christ, you have a lot going on. I thought my life was—"

"Taylor and I had a threesome with someone else," Camilla blurted out, wanting the conversation over with. She knew it was headed to a lecture about her lifestyle, about her mental health being worse than his. The words sounded so simple, so dramatic, so soap opera-ish when they were said aloud. Nothing like the actual act, which had been complicated and confusing. She watched his face for any sign of disgust or anger, but it was a blank board: unreadable and inanimate.

"Taylor's girlfriend," Peter said somberly.

"No. Well, sort of." Camilla pulled her legs back up against her stomach and chest, her fingers laced around the tops of her work boots again. The heels felt solid against the overstuffed bottom cushion on the chair. "You know Taylor. More than a one-night stand is an act of marriage." She tried to laugh to show him that it was nothing to worry about. *Oh, those lesbians,* she wanted the laugh to say. *Always getting into trouble.* "Like I said, Taylor was the instigator."

"What happened?"

Camilla's eyes widened.

"I don't mean that. I mean after. Afterward."

"Nothing. I left."

"And?"

"And what? Yes, okay, I've been seeing her."

"So, you're having an affair with her." He looked miserable then. Camilla realized that it was cutting too close to the bone with him. He tilted his head away, his overgrown bangs falling across the side of his face, like a shield.

"No, listen it's not like that. Taylor's mad at me. Not because of Audrey. Because of me. Do you understand?"

"What are you doing, Camilla?" His calling her by her full name startled her. It was so unusual. Only when he was mad or when they were children and he was frustrated with her. He was staring straight at her now. "Your job might be in the shitter. You're fighting with Taylor, who, let me remind you, was there for you. It's obvious you're still waiting for a miracle to happen and for Nico to be living here with you, and—"

"I am not waiting," Camilla snapped at him. She stood and strode to the guest room, throwing the door open. "See? And by the way, just two hours ago you were happy to help me with the treehouse, so, so much for miracles."

Peter stayed in his chair. He rubbed his face hard with both hands as if he was exhausted and trying to stay awake. "Jesus. I came here to get away."

"Sorry it's not what you expected," she said with an edge.

"That's the thing. I think it was. It is. I think it's exactly what I expected." He stood up. "I'm going to bed." He walked past her toward the guest bedroom and closed the door behind him.

"What happened to the couch?" Camilla said, but he didn't answer.

Later, she turned back and forth on her own bed, uncomfortable in whatever position she landed in. She was too hot. She stripped down to a small tank top and her underwear. Then she was too cold. She sat up and pulled on a long-sleeved T-shirt from the bottom of the bed, huddling underneath the down comforter she'd previously thrown aside. The cats were a nuisance. Nervous with the addition of an unknown person in the other room, they battled each other and then the sheet on the bed, pouncing on any air pocket that formed around Camilla's body curled on its side— behind her stacked knees, in between her elbows, and against her chest.

She felt under attack. What had he meant when he said it was exactly what he expected? Had her life always been so riddled with chaos? Or was it that her life was just that: life? His was barely lived. Why had he come to her with his grieving, his loss of his marriage? Was it because he saw her as the queen of loss? That over anyone else, she would understand what he was going through? Or was it something else altogether? That her life was so screwed up that his looked good in comparison. That hers would be the distraction he needed. But he hadn't counted on hers being such a nightmare. The writer Evelyn Waugh famously said that the only evidence of life was change. Well, pardon her for being open to change, to life.

She decided to confront him in the morning. She would ask him, "The question is, brother, what are *you* doing here?" She thought of him in that twin bed. She wondered if he smelled Audrey's patchouli and intuitively knew it was hers and not Camilla's. She should have insisted that they switch beds. Perfume was probably the last thing he wanted to smell. *Serves him right.*

She stretched her arm across her queen-sized bed. The immensity in comparison to her recent nights— one alone, one not—on the twin mattress accentuated her feelings of separation. She ached for Audrey. She wondered what Audrey was doing at that moment. Whether she was working at the bar or out somewhere else. They hadn't spoken since the night before at Taylor's show. Peter had only been there for a day. That felt impossible. It seemed more like a week. The clock glowed with its red numbers announcing it was almost three thirty in the morning. She needed sleep. She only had one more day to finish the treehouse before Allison and Nico would return. Maybe Peter would agree to stay one more day to help her finish it. In spite of everything. Suddenly, she regretted telling him anything about Taylor and Audrey. Before this, she never would have told him. She would've spent the time masterfully evading all his questions like she did with everyone else. Her mother was right; it was so easy to dodge someone's inquisitiveness if you simply asked him a question back about himself. It was a ploy Camilla used time and again with great success.

But she hadn't done so tonight and now she was paying for it. There was a chink in her armor that frightened her. The threesome had become her Achilles heel that she couldn't hide. She was holding so many secrets now—the breakup of her relationship with Allison, her leaving Nico, Cindy Hunter's allegations, Audrey—they pressed against her skin fighting to escape into the air. To be known. Secrets were like river water, finding a way out through the path of least resistance. She was one of those criminals that fold as soon as he's given the opportunity to spill his side of the story, as soon as the police interrogation begins, confessing to every bad act he'd done since he was five years old. Camilla spooned a pillow, gripping it tightly, as she watched the darkness lift and the sun bleakly come up through her bedroom window. Even the sun didn't have the strength to carry on with this day.

Day Seven

Audrey and Wallace

As soon as Camilla saw the sun's rays inch weakly onto her desk, she got dressed. She pulled on her jeans and favorite Bennington College T-shirt from the day before and double knotted the shoelaces on her work boots. It was still so early that the cats didn't lift up their heads from her bed where they lay on a pile of her discarded slept-in tank tops, two apostrophes curled around each other.

She had a headache that on any other day would have sent her back to bed. Her whole body ached. She didn't want to admit it, but she'd be happy when the treehouse was done and she could return to her life of academia, of reading and occasionally writing soon-to-be-forgotten journal articles about some obscure connection in one of Dickens's novels. Or would she be able to? She thought of Cindy Hunter. She should really call Wallace and find out what was happening. And Taylor. Maybe she had found more out about when Cindy interned for Allison's clinic and whether they had met through that. Not speaking with Taylor on their usual daily basis kept Camilla off-center, uneasy, like the moments before a violent summer storm breaks open the darkening sky, the smell of moisture saturating the humid air.

Peter was already seated at the kitchen island

counter. The counter was more like a peninsula than an island; it was fixed on one end to the sidewall of a closet that hid her stackable washer-dryer. There was a small white shelf over the counter attached to that wall. It housed a collection of Camilla's favorite objects and mementos: a turquoise Buddha, bottles of fountain pen ink with wondrous names like Dragon Red and Kiowa Pecan, a vintage windup alarm clock that had been her father's and was fixed at 10:15 a.m., a dried-up milkweed pod in which Taylor had inked in a naked woman sitting on a rock, pinch pots made by an old school friend, and a bud vase that held a single orange, papery husk from a Chinese lantern. The shelf had been there when Camilla had purchased the condo as if it were waiting for her to arrive with her keepsakes. The only trouble was that its edge was dangerously close to the kitchen stool on that side of the counter. Camilla was always worried when someone sat on it that they would crack their head on the edge if they moved around too much.

Peter was on that stool, eating a bowl of corn flakes without milk. It was a childhood habit that hadn't apparently died out as he spooned the dry flakes into his mouth, crunching merrily away as if it was the best thing he'd eaten all month. He was reading the back of the cereal box, another childhood habit.

"Did you know that a cat has thirty-two muscles in each ear?" he said in between spoonfuls, staring at the box. "Where is the deadly duo by the way?"

Camilla smiled, glad that he wasn't interested in starting the morning by picking up where they'd left off the night before. "They're still in bed."

"You spoil them," he told her without lifting his eyes from the box.

"Cappuccino?" she asked as she turned on the espresso machine.

"You spoil me, too," he murmured.

"There is milk, you know."

He smiled as he crunched a mouthful. "No use crying over spilled milk."

Opening the fridge, she got out the milk. With her back to him, she poured some milk for the both of them into the automatic frother. The cappuccino machine had cost a lot—sleek and fire-engine red. You only had to throw in a capsule from a variety of espressos, hit a button for the espresso side and then another button on the frother, and presto! You had a latte or a cappuccino in minutes. Camilla had spent more money on it than she should have given her academic salary, but it was one of the first things she'd bought when she'd moved into the condo. At first, she'd had another espresso machine that Allison had bought her years before, an over-the-top, expensive Italian number. It reminded Camilla too much of living with Allison, all of the stress and fighting, but she was loath to replace it unnecessarily. Fortunately, the machine suddenly died within a week of Camilla moving into the condo, so she bought the new one. Camilla's father had often told her and Peter, "You cannot love inanimate objects. Love requires life." Camilla wasn't so sure of that anymore. She felt like she did love the new machine. Every morning it gave her pleasure to perform the ritual of preparing her cappuccino and then drinking it while reading whatever author she was currently obsessed with. Ever since she'd been a child, if she found an author she liked she had to read everything she had ever written: good or bad, fiction or non-fiction. It was compulsive. It was as if she thought by reading everything by that writer she would know her inside and out. It always failed. By the last book, Camilla would feel drained, unable to keep any of the books clear in her head. The characters would be jumbled together, imagined stories muddied with real events, a maelstrom of one tragic plot after another.

Yet there was something so civilized, so calming, about the entire morning ritual of drinking her cappuccino. She had felt that with Audrey the other morning, but she remembered she had felt put out when Audrey had casually picked up her mug and drank from it. Even the mug itself was distinct. It was made by Marcella, who threw one-of-a-kind ceramics, including the pinch pots on the kitchen shelf, scratching and painting intricate archeological vases and pillars through the matte maiolica glazes. Camilla's cup had a distinctive painting of an opened book and on the cup's bottom Marcella had painted in small letters: *For Camilla. MS.* On good days, the mug would remind Camilla of how far she had come since those college days, how much she had achieved. On bad days, it made her feel old.

The intense smell of coffee filled the kitchen now as the machine released one shot each into two of Marcella's cups: Camilla's and another one that sported a painted Etruscan vase on top of a pillar. Camilla opened the frother lid and scooped out the steamed foam into the cups. Walking over to the island, she slid one near the cereal box. She sat down across from Peter with her cup and reached for a crumpled pack of cigarettes that lay next to two stacks of already read books.

"This is unbelievable," Peter said, his eyes on the box. "Did you know that a blindfolded dolphin can find a nickel at the bottom of its tank?" When she didn't answer him, he looked up. He watched as she took a cigarette out and lit it up. "I thought you quit."

"Listen," she said, waving away some of the smoke she exhaled that was drifting over to him. "It would be great if you could help me finish it today. She's coming back tomorrow." She took a sip from her cup, the cigarette dangling from her fingers.

"Just tell me now if you smoke crack or something," he said.

"Jesus, sorry I asked."

"I wasn't talking about the treehouse. I was kidding about you smoking again and everything else you've been up to lately. Who knows what else you've gotten yourself into."

Camilla inhaled her cigarette. *Don't respond*, she told herself. Exhaling, she lifted her cup to her lips. It was a strategy she often used with her students when they came to her with their excuses about why they couldn't get an assignment done, or when they asked her questions that they should know the answers to. She simply didn't respond. *Be a river* was an old Buddhist teaching. *Reflect back.* Students, uncomfortable with the resounding silence instead of the expected sympathetic responses, would always then apologize and assure her that the work would get done *tout de suite*, or they would answer the silly questions themselves.

"Of course, I'll help you," Peter said quickly when Camilla didn't say anything. "I thought you said I could stay?" Pushing his empty bowl aside, he lifted his cup, and, eyeing the foam, said, "I could get used to this, you know." He winked at her and took a sip of his drink. When he lowered the cup, there was a fine line of foamed milk resting on his top lip. It reminded

Camilla of when Audrey had done the same thing the morning after they'd slept together. *Was that only two days ago?* Camilla motioned to his lip, but he told her, smiling, "I'm saving it for later." She didn't smile back. His comment about what she had or hadn't gotten into in the last months still stung. Is this what it would be like with him? These side comments sliding into their conversation, throwing her off at every opportunity? Looking toward the kitchen screen door, she finished the last drag of her cigarette. Outside, the basil in a clay pot was in serious need of watering.

"Mills? I can stay, can't I?" Peter paused, thoughtful. "The thing is, it's either here or Motel 6 with Norman Bates. Please," he added.

Camilla looked back at him, feeling awful for his practically begging now. She touched his hand. "Of course you can stay. It's just—"

"We won't speak of it again," he told her. "Unless you want to. I want to be there for you. Really."

Camilla blushed. She stood up so quickly from the stool that she whacked her knee underneath the countertop. She quickly gathered up their empty cups and his bowl and brought them over to the sink. With their backs to each other, she told him, "I'd like to leave in a half hour, okay? And watch your head by that shelf when you get up." She turned on the hot water faucet and began to spray down the dishes, her knee still smarting.

"The past is a killer," Peter quipped, but no one laughed.

୬ଏ ୬ଏ ୬ ୬

In her car, as she stared through the windshield

and turned on the ignition, and Peter was strapping himself in, she told him, "I think I'm in love with her. I know it's bad timing but..."

Glancing over, he said simply, "'If a man insisted always on being serious, and never allowed himself a bit of fun and relaxation, he would go mad or become unstable without knowing it.'"

Camilla shook her head, smiling. "Dad would be proud of you, remembering that." It was a quote by Herodotus that their father would say whenever they asked him if they could go out and play.

Peter laughed. "You remembered, too. It's a wonder we're sane. When you think about it, he really was such an odd duck. The two of them were."

Putting her hand on the back of Peter's seat and turning her head, Camilla concentrated on backing the car down her driveway and out onto the street, but she came perilously close to the house and had to swerve to avoid shearing a side mirror clear off.

"I just wish he'd known how to swim like one," she murmured as she shifted the car into first and drove them away.

"Isn't that water off a duck's back now?" said Peter. Neither one laughed at the puns, though.

⚜ ⚜ ⚜ ⚜

When they arrived at the treehouse, they found Audrey sitting cross-legged inside, reading a hardcover book, her back against one of the walls under the window. Camilla thought again how unexpected everything was about Audrey. Not simply for showing up, either. People her age usually read books—if they read at all—on their smartphones or iPads or Kindles.

Here was Audrey, reading an actual hardcover book in a treehouse that wasn't hers as if it was the most ordinary thing in the world. Both windows were open and there was the breeze again going through the tiny house.

"Hi," Audrey said, putting the book down on the floor. She stood, smiling. She was wearing skinny jeans rolled up her shins with a pair of scuffed purple Dr. Martens high-top boots, and a little-boy-sized black hoodie despite the heat. Her waifish blond hair was standing straight up and out with gel. She could've been on a London poster from the eighties, like the Sid Vicious one that Camilla had imagined in Nico's bedroom when he got older. But, her pixie-like face softened the image.

"You must be Audrey," Peter said, and held out his hand. Camilla watched, speechless, as his long fingers enveloped hers. "I'm," he said, glancing back at Camilla. "I'm her brother. Peter."

"Oh, I didn't know she had a brother. She never said."

Camilla didn't like how she had been delegated to the third person, so she stepped forward from the doorway. "He just came yesterday. It was a surprise. We're going to finish it today," she said in a rush of words.

Audrey stepped closer and hugged her. Camilla felt herself tense up. Finally, Audrey released her, saying, "Great. So, what can I do?" Camilla felt that conflicting mixture of gratitude and violation in her stomach again. She couldn't decide—again—if she wanted to tell Audrey to leave or to profusely thank her for being there. Is this how it would always be with Audrey? The delight and the agony of the unexpected?

You could never count on the unexpected, though. It was thrilling, but there was no saying when the unexpected would end unexpectedly, when it would be on to the next person who would be attracted to the unexpected. The unexpected required you to trust. Trust that once you gave in, once you admitted that you loved the unexpected in your life, that you would go on trusting that it would never end. Did Camilla have that in her?

"The thing about Allison," she'd told Taylor one night years before at the bar, and raised her hand when Taylor began to prematurely object. "The thing about Allison is I know she will never leave me," Camilla had said. "I know everything she thinks, everything she loves, and she will never quit loving *me* no matter what. I don't ever have to worry about Allison finding someone else. There is no *else*. There's only me in her mind. And yes, she's obsessive, and yes, she's controlling, but there's a sense of relief in knowing what to expect. Of what you can count on."

"You're scaring me," Taylor had said back.

"How are you at painting?" Peter interceded now, shattering the treehouse silence. "The trim work around the windows needs finishing. Milly and I are dealing with the door." He motioned over to the door that rested on its side against a wall.

"Michelangelo is my middle name, didn't Camilla tell you?" Audrey said. Smiling, she knocked Camilla lightly on the shoulder and made her way over to the paint can and the brushes. She took off her hoodie, folding it and laying it down on the floor like it was a mink coat. She was wearing a pink T-shirt that had the sleeves cut off. It was from a P!NK concert from a few years before, The Truth About Love tour. The back of the T-shirt sported an image of P!NK upside down, dressed in an almost see-through bodysuit and high heels, hanging from a trapeze, microphone in hand. Camilla remembered seeing snippets of the concert on the news. It was the first time P!NK had incorporated the intensely physical trapeze act into a show and it caused a sensation, especially because her strong voice never wavered as she spun and flew across cables thirty feet over the crowd. Camilla was still living with Allison then. It was after Nico was born. Staring at Audrey's back, Camilla was struck by what a difference there was in their lives at that time: Audrey was leaving the concert, probably grinning from the experience and the drinks she'd consumed; and Camilla was by then making a plan to leave Allison. Their paths to meet had begun then.

She was jerked out of these thoughts when Peter elbowed her and gave Camilla a thumbs-up behind Audrey's back. Then, he walked over to the propped-up door and grabbed an end. "Hey, daydreamer. Ready?"

Camilla shook her body as if she were waking up. Moving over to the door, she lifted her end, and she and Peter carried it like a canoe over to the doorway. Camilla held the door so that Peter could hammer the metal pins into the hinges, connecting it to the frame. As he tapped the first one in, he began to sing under his breath, "The Way You Look Tonight."

"Pay attention before you nail me with the hammer," Camilla groused at him, but inside she was pleased. More than that, she realized, she was happy. No matter what her past had involved, she'd always have her brother.

"Good one, Sis," Peter said.

Camilla glanced over at Audrey. Brush in hand,

she was painting her way slowly around the porthole's frame. Camilla wondered what she was thinking. Whether she was still mulling over what had happened at the warehouse. Whether she was wishing that she and Camilla were alone, so they could talk. That must have been her plan when she decided to show up at the treehouse. Camilla wondered if she felt trapped now. That she'd stayed because to leave after seeing that Peter was there would have been rude or ultimately counterproductive to her wanting to see Camilla, to talk it out.

"Watch it," Peter whispered to her. Crouching nearer to the lower hinge, he was struggling with the lower half of the door to bring the threads of the hinge into alignment. His face turned up to her. He winked. Camilla pushed against the edge of the door so it would line up better. Then, humming the rest of the song, Peter finished driving the lower metal rod through the hinge.

"This is such an incredible view up here," Audrey said. Camilla and Peter looked over at her. She'd stopped painting and was staring out the porthole. Camilla wondered if she'd comment on its position facing the house. Whether, like Taylor, she'd see it as a spyhole. Audrey was smiling, though, when she turned to them and said, "Isn't it fantastic?" Her eyes widened. "I mean, look at this incredible place. I want to live here it's so great."

"Yes," Camilla halfheartedly agreed, for she envied Audrey's ability to be so happy from seeing everything at face value, ignoring the baggage underneath that threatened to destroy it all at a moment's notice. For Audrey, it was simple. They had built a beautiful treehouse for Nico and Nico would surely love it, too. Camilla felt an enormous sadness engulf her. She knew that she could no longer see things so simply, could no longer feel such innocent joy. She no longer had the ability to enter the world every day with wide, open arms. Life with Allison had crippled her in some way. She wanted to tell Audrey that there was no silver lining. That who knew if Nico would be allowed up in the treehouse, ever. She had the urge to recite Longfellow's "The Rainy Day" to Audrey:

> *Thy fate is the common fate of all,*
> *Into each life some rain must fall,*
> *Some days must be dark and dreary.*

But then, just as quickly, Audrey smiled at her, laughed, and said, "What?" The bad feeling passed and Camilla hoped with all her heart that Audrey would never change, would never be changed. Not by her or Taylor or anyone else. Thankfully, Peter made a crack about getting back to work so they could finish this fabulous house, and Audrey went back to painting the porthole frame.

By the time they'd finished installing the doorknob, Audrey was done with the painting of the two window frames. They stood in the center of the treehouse, Camilla between them, all three surveying their work. It was so quiet they could hear the tree leaves rustling outside and their own breathing inside.

"He is going to love it, Sis," Peter said quietly. Camilla felt her eyes begin to tear up. She closed them, praying that he wouldn't say anything else.

He didn't. Audrey did. She added softly, "It's the Christmas you never forget." Then, Camilla felt them both sling an arm around her neck and shoulders from either side. She opened her eyes. The three of them stood in a line like sentries, looking out the open casement window, through the swaying branches, into the empty, blue sky, imagining a small, slender boy standing where they were now, feeling safe and free.

O Captain, my Captain.

❦❦❦❦

"What about furniture?" Peter asked Camilla as they drove away from Wilbur.

"I don't know. That might push her over the edge," Camilla said and felt her fingers tighten automatically on the steering wheel of the Mini. Camilla could hear the plastic straps holding Audrey's bicycle to the roof rack snapping in the wind.

"Definitely a play table with chairs," Audrey suggested from the back. "Max's has a plastic set that would be perfect."

Startled, Camilla turned her head around and looked back at her.

"Hey, watch the road," Peter told her.

Audrey laughed. "I'm in Max's all the time. It's genetic. I love hardware stores."

Camilla looked in the rearview mirror, wondering if she and Audrey had been in Max's at the same time, not knowing that they would eventually collide and end up here, now. Audrey looked the same, but Camilla wondered if she knew her at all. Why would someone like her notice kids' furniture?

"Sounds like a plan," Peter said, smiling.

They drove to Max's and purchased the miniature dining set: a dark blue plastic table and two chairs that were orange.

"It looks like it belongs in an art class on color contrast," Audrey said as they carried it out to the Mini.

"Or he's going to end up a Denver Broncos fan," Peter said.

The table had to be roped down to the roof next to Audrey's bicycle. It looked like they were about to embark on a family vacation. They stowed the chairs in the back after flipping one of the back seats down.

After they delivered the set to the treehouse and drove back to Cambridge, it was dinnertime.

"I think takeout is in order, don't you, Audrey?" Peter asked as they were merging through a rotary onto Fresh Pond Parkway. He'd angled his body completely around so he could face her. Somewhere along the day, the two of them had bonded. Camilla wasn't sure how she felt about that. She realized that secretly she'd hoped to drop Peter off back at the condo so that she could drive Audrey home alone. They needed to talk about what had happened at Taylor's opening.

"Sugar and Spice," Audrey said from the back seat. "Great Thai."

"Yum," Peter said. Since when did her brother use words like "yum"? Camilla felt like he wasn't just referring to the food, either. She shook her head to eject the idea. Was she jealous of her brother, thinking something more had been developing between him and Audrey? She didn't like how out of control she was feeling. How she was so all over the place, one moment happy, the next anxious that her brother was making the moves on Audrey.

"What? You don't like Thai?" Audrey asked her. She'd slipped forward again between the bucket seats so her cheek was resting on Camilla's shoulder.

"She loves Thai," Peter said, and lightly knocked on Camilla's thigh with his fist.

"Good." Audrey kissed Camilla's cheek so quickly before settling back that as Camilla pulled into a parking space across from the restaurant on Mass Ave, she didn't know if it had actually happened or had just been Audrey's shoulder brushing her face before she sat back.

❧❧❧❧

Back at Camilla's Mexican table in the dining room they gorged themselves on the pileup of Thai food: the crispy taro, summer rolls, royal triangles, veggie dumplings, numtok, tom yum soup, drunken noodle, pad thai, lemongrass chicken, virgin garden, choo chee shrimp, and kow moo dang. In spite of her still feeling nervous that at any moment something would happen that would disturb the balance between her and Audrey or her and her brother, Camilla's dutiful eating quickly changed into a food fest dig in. She hadn't realized how hungry she was from not eating breakfast or lunch and then finishing the treehouse. The earthy smells of ginger and curry and lemongrass saturated the condo. Camilla felt the choo chee curry tingling her lips as she chewed a pineapple chunk. None of them spoke until they had cleaned their plates and Peter was going back for seconds. Gingerly lifting some more drunken noodles onto his plate, he told them, "So, if it's okay with you, as soon as I eat everything in sight, I'm going to head over to Kendall. They're showing *Inside Llewyn Davis*."

Startled, Camilla said, "I can go if—"

His mouth chock full, Peter shook his head. Mid-chew, he said, "I'm good. Really. It's the Coen Brothers. You know, the new one about the folk artist. You hate folk music, remember?"

Camilla was relieved. She was grateful that he was making the effort to give them space to do whatever it was she and Audrey needed to do. But what that was, she had no idea.

෴෴෴෴

She never found out. Moments after Peter left for the movie theater, while she and Audrey pretended to focus on packing up the leftovers for the refrigerator, stalling for more time to figure out how to move forward, Camilla's mobile wailed out the ambulance siren ringtone that was set for incoming calls from Taylor. She and Audrey froze where they stood in the kitchen: Camilla by the opened refrigerator door with a stack of full Tupperware in her hands, and Audrey on her way to the sink with the curry-stained plates. Audrey glanced down at the phone that was on the island, but didn't say anything as she placed the plates in the sink.

"You better answer that," Audrey finally said, after the phone continued to ring. "Sounds like an emergency," she joked, but she smiled stiffly. Camilla made a silent note to herself to remember to change Taylor's ringtone. Quickly, she put the leftovers into the fridge and then reluctantly picked up the phone.

"Mills?" Taylor said. Camilla heard the Volvo's ancient muffler in the background. "Listen, I think I found something. Are you home? 'Cause I'm on my way over."

Camilla looked over at Audrey, her eyes widening.

"What?" Audrey turned off the hot water and grabbed for the dishtowel to dry her hands.

Taylor shouted, "I said, I'm coming over. Fuck, I think the muffler just dropped off. I found this photograph but I'm not sure if it's them or not. You have that photo, right?"

Reeling, Camilla said, "What? What photo? I don't know what you're—"

"The *photo*," Taylor shouted again. "Shit, I have to pull over. I'll be there in a few minutes." There was a click and then the black hole of mobile nothing.

Stunned, Camilla tapped her forehead with her cell phone. "Shit. She's coming here."

"Oh?" Audrey said, leaning against the sink counter. She tilted her head like she was taking it all in stride. But then, she circled her waist with her arms.

"God!" Camilla said and dropped the phone face down on to the counter as if it was burning her. "Something about a photo. I don't know." She raked her fingers through her hair. "I think she found something else about Cindy Hunter. The girl who—"

"I know who she is, Camilla. Why didn't you stop her? I mean should I go? Should I stay?" She glanced nervously around the kitchen. "I sound like that idiotic Clash song."

Camilla went over to the sink next to Audrey. Turning on the hot water, she started to wash the dishes for something to do.

"Camilla!" Audrey's hands were suddenly there, stopping Camilla's from washing a plate under the streaming water. "I'm going to go, okay?"

Camilla shook her head. "No, don't." She looked up at Audrey. "I don't know. Maybe yes. Maybe you should go. No, stay."

Before it could be decided either way, her mobile rang again. Audrey nodded firmly. "Answer it. Maybe she's calling back to say she changed her mind."

"It's not her ringtone," Camilla said, twisting around to see if she could see the cell's screen for the caller. But it was face down. With wet hands, Camilla picked up the phone. She didn't recognize the number. For an instant, because she was so off-kilter by the whole thing, she wondered if Taylor's muffler had fallen off and her phone had died and she was now calling from a gas station. She accepted the call.

It was Wallace.

"Camilla? I hope I'm not interrupting you from something important. I'm just leaving your house."

"What?"

"I said I was just at your house. I had a little chat with Allison. Why didn't you tell me you had moved out? Where are you now? We need to talk. That is, if you'd like to. If it's not too inconvenient. If you could make the time?"

⚜ ⚜ ⚜ ⚜

Taylor arrived first, her muffler scraping along the street warning Camilla and Audrey of her arrival.

"This is a nightmare," Camilla muttered, and went downstairs to let Taylor in.

"You might have to follow me to my mechanic," Taylor said as she passed her in the front doorway and began to go up the stairs. Camilla followed her up.

"Audrey's here."

Taylor hesitated as she reached the landing by Camilla's door, but then she opened the door and went in. Audrey was drying the dinner dishes. Camilla could tell by the way she was slowly wiping the plate in her hand that she was doing it so that she'd have something to do when Taylor walked in.

"Do you have anything to drink?" Taylor asked Camilla, and then let out a soft "Hey" directed at Audrey.

Audrey smiled at her. It wasn't exactly a relaxed smile. More like one of those forced smiles that you give in an elementary school photo. A smile to please your parents.

"I'll take one, too, if you're pouring," Audrey told her.

Taylor went over to the small built-in bar and, grabbing a bottle of Scotch, poured out two short glasses. Glancing over, she said, "Mills?" When Camilla nodded she half-filled a third glass. "One cube, right? You, too, Audrey?"

Taylor acted as if it were the most natural thing in the world for the three of them to be standing there, having their drinks on a summer evening. She grabbed the ice tray from the freezer and dropped a cube each into the drinks, handing them to Audrey and Camilla.

"Here's to those who loved us, if only we cared. Here's to those we should have loved, if only we dared," Taylor said and clinked their glasses. Then, she sat down at the island. There were only two chairs. Camilla stood at the top of the island. Audrey slid into the other chair across from Taylor.

"So." Taylor smiled awkwardly. "What a tangled web we weave, huh, Professor?" Reaching into the back pocket of her light blue chinos, she pulled out a folded piece of paper. She unfolded it, smoothed it out, and slid it over to Camilla. Audrey leaned her elbows on the island. It was a copy of a magazine article about up and coming physicians who volunteered their extra time to nonprofit causes.

"Don't read it. Look at the photo," Taylor told them. She pointed her finger to the one photo on the page as if they were having trouble finding it. There was Allison standing between two other girls who looked like teenagers. They were all dressed in white medical jackets, but the two girls looked stiff in theirs, while Allison wore hers as if she had been born in it. Neither of the girls looked familiar to Camilla.

"So? Is this the demon child, or her?" Taylor asked, tapping her finger first over one of the girls and then the other.

Camilla shook her head.

Taylor hit the island with her fist. "Shit. I thought for sure—"

The sound of the buzzer pierced the relative quiet of the condo.

"That's Wallace," Camilla said. "I forgot to tell you. Wallace talked with Allison."

Taylor's eyes widened. "Are you fucking kidding me? Wallace? Here? You asked him to come *here*?" The buzzer rang again. Camilla felt rooted to the kitchen floor. Her heart was pounding. What would Wallace make of the coven?

"I didn't ask," she told Taylor. "He demanded. He'd gone to the house and Allison was there."

The insistent buzzer sounded again.

"Do you want me to let him in?" Audrey asked quietly. She picked at the cuff of her sweatshirt like there was lint on it.

"No, I'll go. Can you both stay here?"

"Oh, damn," Taylor said. "I thought we could make our getaway down the back steps." She paused.

"Kidding."

When Camilla opened the front door, Wallace was about to lean on the doorbell again.

"I thought I might have the wrong address," he said. Under the front porch light, he looked like a gentleman caller out of a Tennessee Williams play. He was dressed in a sand-colored linen suit and brown, very expensive-looking oxfords. A camel-colored Panama with a light blue ribbon around the bottom was perched on his head. It seemed absurdly high in the air on top of his tall, thin body. Camilla was struck again by how he always looked as if he'd just returned from a polo match. How did he afford it on an academic's salary?

"Goodness. Are you going to invite me in or are we to stand on this lovely porch all night?"

She motioned him in. "Sorry. It's the second floor." Closing the door, she hesitated so she could settle her breathing down. Then, she followed him up.

After the introductions had been nervously made, and Taylor had offered and then poured Wallace a Scotch, Camilla and Wallace sat down in the living room. Audrey and Taylor pretended to clean up the kitchen, taking their time drying and then putting away the dinner dishes.

"This is very cozy," Wallace said, glancing around the living room from the leather chair where he was sitting. He placed his hat on the Moroccan tile table next to his arm. "*Très* Gertrude Stein. *Très* Paris in the twenties."

Camilla felt herself bristle every time he pronounced the word *très* with the s. Her body was tense as she sat on the edge of the couch. "I'm sorry you had to find out from Allison. It's just that I don't like to, um, share—"

Wallace waved her away and slurped at his Scotch, sucking in the one cube, which at once marred Camilla's vision of him coming from a cultured background. He might dress the part, but he hadn't lived the life. He crunched on the cube. He *was* Heep, through and through.

"I understand. Sticky wicket," he murmured as he finished munching and then swallowed the ice bits. A small watery dribble landed on his goatee and he quickly brushed it away. He took another sip of his drink. "I came to personally tell you what the status of the case is."

Camilla felt her body tighten up more. He was calling it a case now. Not an accusation. A case.

"So." Wallace took another greedy drink. Camilla realized he was nervous, too. He put the glass down on the table, took out his handkerchief, and mopped the glistening red of his goatee.

"The hearing has been scheduled. A week from today. I asked for it to be delayed until September, you know with everyone taking their last August vacations. But unfortunately the Dean would not hear of it. I did try my best, I assure you. I practically demanded that he reconsider. I mean, it is an *inconvenience* for the committee. They've all made their summer plans. I felt like a heel asking them." He paused, and, as an afterthought, added, "And of course for you, too." He faltered a bit. "You first, of course." He slurped his drink. "One week is simply not enough time for us— you—to prepare."

Camilla couldn't say a word. She found the whole forming-words and using-her-voice abilities to be unavailable, as if she'd had a stroke.

Wallace went on hurriedly. "But it *is* Tolland's policy after all. We must convene the hearing fourteen days from when a request is made. It might be better this way anyway. Get the whole thing over with and we..." he paused, smiled, "*you* can put it behind you. Now," he said, adjusting his legs and getting more comfortable in the chair. "None of your colleagues remembers seeing this girl, this student, at all by your office. Of course, she states that she visited you in the off hours. You do have a copy of that graded paper, right, as well as a copy from your schedule showing the date and time of that one conference you had with her?"

Camilla sat mute. He'd interviewed the other professors in her department. And she knew how these "her word against yours" played out in colleges. There'd be a mark against her forever. They'd have to reprimand her in some shape or form. Show that they treat such claims seriously.

"Camilla?"

"Yes-yes, I have them," Camilla said mechanically back.

"Good. And then there's Allison." He lifted his glass at that and drank down the rest. "Might I have another?" he asked, dabbing at his forehead with his handkerchief again and holding up the empty glass in his other hand as if it were searching for a waiter.

"Allison?" Camilla's heart began to race.

"Yes. She's very willing to testify."

From the kitchen, Taylor yelled, "That bitch!" Camilla and Wallace immediately turned their heads. Taylor and Audrey were both standing by the Mexican table, no longer pretending to be cleaning up anything.

Camilla stood. "She's going to testify?"

Wallace looked confused. "Yes, why shouldn't she?"

Taylor said, "That fucking bitch. I'll testify."

"You're not helping." Camilla glared at Taylor.

Wallace became agitated. He stood. "I don't understand. For you. She wants to testify on your behalf."

"What?"

"I had to tell her why I suddenly showed up at your house. I felt terrible. I caught her while she was unloading the car. It was all sixes and sevens, what with Nico running around. What a darling boy he is, Camilla." He paused, struck by what Camilla could only assume was the look of horror on her face.

"Anyway," he hurriedly went on, "she was very eager to help. She said she knew for a fact that you were home with her during the supposed times that Cindy, er, the student, claims you were doing the hokey pokey around the office floor with her. I'm not saying it's a done deal, but if she does tell the committee that, I really see that everything will go away. In my opinion, that is."

The three of them stared at him as if he were naked.

"Well, fuck me," Taylor murmured.

Wallace winced. "Might I have another drink?" he asked again, holding out and shaking his empty glass. "I thought for a minute the three of you were going to roast me on a spit and eat me for your supper." He laughed nervously and ran his hand down his shirtfront.

"Absolutely," Taylor said. She clapped him on his shoulder as she took his empty glass from him.

"Why?" Camilla was staring at Wallace.

"Why? Well, my dear, there won't be enough evidence and without evidence..." His voice trailed away as he raised his hands and shrugged.

"I don't mean that. I mean, why is Allison—"

Suddenly, Taylor was next to her by the couch holding Wallace's drink in one hand and the bottle in the other. "For fuck's sake, Mills. It doesn't matter *why*. She's doing it. Shut up." She gave Wallace his drink, and then picked up Camilla's glass and topped it off. "I think this calls for a toast. Audrey? Can you bring me my glass?"

"But—"

"No buts, asses, or derrières," Taylor said. She lifted her drink from Audrey's hands. Camilla saw that Audrey looked rattled. She was pale. Her lips were pressed lightly together.

"To good old Allison," Taylor said half-seriously. "Our little stealth bomber."

The rest of them tapped her glass. But the clinking sounded hollow to Camilla like the glasses were about to break. And she wondered if Allison was really and truly their secret weapon or if she'd turn out to be a Trojan horse, surprising them all with what was hidden.

With the surprise of Wallace's visit and his astonishing news that Allison was coming to Camilla's defense, it wasn't until after Wallace left and Camilla was telling Peter upon his return from the movies about it all that Camilla realized she hadn't followed up with Wallace about something else that was important. It was really Peter who pointed it out to her. It was almost midnight by then. They were sitting at the island with Taylor standing next to Camilla's chair and Audrey next to Peter's, everyone eating bowls of Rocky

Road ice cream that had hot fudge on them—another of Peter's childhood favorites that he'd brought home with him. Camilla wondered if he would demand hot dogs and Fiddle Faddle the next day. He'd insisted on heating up the fudge.

"I can't eat this now," Camilla grumbled, but she took the bowl anyway.

If at first Peter had been alarmed to find Taylor and Audrey there, he hid it fairly well, although Camilla could tell by his manic diatribe about how the critics had gotten it all wrong about the latest Coens' film that he'd been thrown a bit by their being in the kitchen when he walked in. As he prepared the sundaes, Camilla told him about Wallace and Allison, with Taylor jumping in now and then to offer her commentary. "For someone so put together, he sure is a sloppy drinker." "How do you think old Wally pays for those thousand-dollar shoes?" And, "What was that about you doing the hokey pokey? Remember that bumper sticker we saw in P-town, Mills? The one that said, 'What if the hokey pokey *is* what it's all about?'"

After Camilla told him everything, Peter swallowed a spoonful of ice cream and asked, "So what did Allison say about the treehouse?"

The other three stared at him, flabbergasted. "Shit," Camilla said, a spoonful of ice cream halfway to her mouth. A marshmallow dropped off onto the counter. "I never asked him. Damn it. How could I forget that?"

"There was a lot going on." Audrey reached across the island to touch her hand. "Maybe she didn't say anything to him about it. I mean, why would she?"

Pulling her hand away, Camilla rubbed her forehead. "I can't believe I didn't ask him."

Taylor was scraping the bottom of her bowl as if more Rocky Road would magically appear. "Will you stop that?" Camilla demanded.

Taylor sucked on the end of her spoon and then chucked it into the bowl. "Don't you think if she was a raving lunatic about it, Wally would've said?"

"Well..." Camilla said.

"Of course he would've," Peter agreed. "Sounds like it was no big deal. Or at least she wasn't upset about it."

Taylor pressed on. "There's no fucking way she would've agreed to be your witness in the box if she was upset about the treehouse."

"Witness in the box?" Audrey said, half-smiling. She'd barely touched her sundae, which now was melting into a thick pool of hot fudge that looked like an oil spill to Camilla.

Taylor shrugged. "Whatever. I'm going home. You want a ride?"

Camilla said, "It's just that I thought she would've called me by now. You know, after seeing it."

"Like to thank you and tell you what a bang-up job you did? And we could all sing kumbaya together?" Taylor exhaled a phut sound. "Not fucking likely. You should be happy that she's focused on helping you out and shut the fuck up. Audrey? You coming?"

Audrey shook her head. She scooped some of the fudge out of her bowl and licked at it. "I have my bike."

"It's past midnight." Taylor pulled out her car keys from her chinos and tossed them from hand to hand as if that would entice her.

"It's only five blocks," Audrey said and glanced across the island at Camilla.

"We can drive you home later if you're too tired to

ride," Peter jumped in. He began to collect everyone's bowls but Audrey's to bring them to the sink.

"I'm gonna jet then," Taylor said. She started to walk away but when she passed the second bedroom, she stopped. "Wow, you finally did it." She turned and looked at Camilla. "'Bout time you cleaned out your A.O." She paused and then clapped her hands. "Bravo. Bet that bed is cozy." Then she left.

"What's an A.O.?" Peter asked as soon as the condo's front door closed.

"Area of operation," Camilla and Audrey said flatly together.

"You owe each other a Coke." Peter chanted the old childhood saying, but Camilla and Audrey didn't smile conspiratorially, or playfully punch each other's arms, as children did whenever they said it. They avoided each other's eyes as if they were both guilty of some crime.

"Well, I'm beat and going to bed," Peter said. "See you in the morning." He went into the second bedroom's bathroom. Audrey slipped into the open seat at the island across from Camilla. Camilla made a show of sliding over a stack of mail from a corner of the island, and began to rip up envelopes that were junk mail. She could hear water running in the bathroom and then Peter brushing his teeth.

"Camilla?" Audrey said.

"In a minute," Camilla said quietly, and proceeded to rip another envelope into thirds and throw it in the nearby recycle bucket.

Audrey watched her and then leaned over to pick up Ball, who was rubbing up against her chair. She stroked his back until he settled down on her lap and purred, although Camilla's sudden ripping of an envelope sporadically halted the purring for a moment before it resumed.

Peter reappeared and then disappeared into the second bedroom, closing the door behind him with a soft, "Night." Camilla shoved the rest of the mail stack to the side. She rubbed her eyes. "Look, I'm sorry about the other night at the show," she said as she continued to rub her eyes. She stood up. "I'm exhausted."

Audrey didn't answer. Camilla dropped her hands on to the counter. Audrey was staring down at the cat curled up asleep in her lap.

"I thought you were allergic to cats," Camilla said.

Audrey lifted her head. "We need to talk."

"Fine. But I'm too tired tonight." Part of her wanted Audrey to stay. She wanted to go to bed with Audrey's body wrapped around hers. But her mind was already racing from everything Wallace had told her and then ricocheting off to wondering what Allison was really thinking about the treehouse. Whether she was concocting some plan around that. Whether she could be trusted to come through for her at the hearing or whether it was all a part of her revenge against Camilla. She thought of Taylor's discovery that Allison knew Cindy Hunter, and while before Camilla had discarded it as an insignificant coincidence, now she wondered if maybe she had been too quick to ignore it. Maybe there was something more to that and Allison was biding her time until the hearing when she could make an entrance and dramatically switch sides, publicly skewering Camilla in the process. Camilla also wondered if Audrey stayed the night, whether feeling her body so close, along with the smell of patchouli, would be an anesthetic, quieting these rampaging thoughts, and lulling her to sleep.

She started to walk past Audrey to the master bedroom, expecting Audrey to follow her. But then, Audrey turned too rapidly on her stool, the side of her head catching the wall shelf's corner.

"Shit!" Audrey moaned so loudly the cat jumped off her lap. She pressed her fingers to her head.

"That damn shelf. Are you okay?" Camilla touched Audrey's shoulder, but Audrey shook her off. She stood.

"I'm going home," she said, her voice trembling slightly. Pushing past Camilla, she grabbed her knapsack from the dining room table.

"It's late," Camilla said. She stayed by the stool that Audrey had been sitting on.

Audrey didn't say anything. She shouldered her pack and walked out of the condo, quietly closing the condo door and then the front door. Camilla stood dumbfounded in the kitchen. The apartment's silence was harsher, more final than if Audrey had stayed and yelled at her. What had happened? Camilla shook her head. Maybe she'd just been embarrassed about hitting her head. It had been a long day. Everyone was wiped.

It wasn't until Camilla was in bed and the cats jumped on the comforter and settled in for the rest of the night that Camilla realized that Audrey hadn't stayed because Camilla hadn't asked her to. In spite of her allergy, Audrey had held Ball simply because Camilla had been unreachable.

Day Twelve

Taylor

All week, Camilla expected Allison to contact her in some way about the treehouse and the upcoming hearing. At first, she waited for her mobile to ring, or the familiar bamboo chirp signaling that a text had been received. She religiously checked it for voicemail messages after a shower and when she'd taken out the garbage. Camilla rarely checked her personal emails. Her friends knew to text or call her. It was enough to have to check her Tolland email mailbox every day for any questions or complaints from her students. But, she began to worry that Allison would send her an email because that was the most distancing of the communication options. After three days, she felt she needed to be more on top of checking just in case Allison did email her. She turned on a sound notification for any received personal emails, a dramatic chord flurry played on an organ. After five days, though, she realized that she wasn't going to hear from Allison, that the first time she'd know anything would be at the hearing.

"Should I call her?" she asked Taylor on the phone Tuesday night. She was sitting on her bed with the bedroom door closed. It was one in the morning. Peter was asleep. Camilla hadn't heard from Audrey, and as much as that hurt, if she was honest with herself she was more worried about Allison than Audrey. Taylor and Camilla had reconnected after the visit from Wallace. With Audrey also out of the picture for the time being, Camilla felt closer to Taylor again. She sensed that Taylor felt it, too.

"Are you nuts? You can't contact a witness." Taylor huffed into the phone, exasperated.

"It's not a court case," Camilla replied with equal frustration. The closer the hearing came, now only two days away, the more on edge they were both getting. "I just think it's weird that—"

"I thought *just* was a minimizing word," Taylor said caustically.

"Very funny. Okay, I think it's straight-up weird. She's living there staring at the treehouse we've—"

"How do you know she hasn't bulldozed it?"

Camilla was silent.

"You've gone there, haven't you?" Taylor asked. "You've done a drive-by to see."

"Okay. I drove by. Once."

"Doubtful, Earlobe."

"Okay, twice. I went in the middle of the night. No one saw me. Anyway, it's weird that she hasn't said a word about it. And why all of a sudden is she willing to do this good deed for me? And what about all that stuff you found out about Hunter working for her?"

"You said that meant nothing. That there are probably hundreds of interns working there."

"Not hundreds. I said a few."

"Whatever." Camilla heard Taylor opening and slamming shut drawers.

"What are you doing?" Camilla asked her.

"Nothing. I'm looking for a cigarette if you must know." She must have found one because suddenly the noise stopped. Camilla grabbed her own cigarettes off the bed table, tapped one out, and lit up. Normally, she never smoked in bed; all those urban stories about people falling asleep and waking up in the middle of a bonfire were more of a deterrent than any surgeon general warning.

"Listen, Mata Hari," Taylor said. "You're going off the deep end, like someone who's about to go AWOL or something. It's going to be fine. What's up with Audrey?"

"What do you mean?"

"Audrey. Remember her? You haven't mentioned her all week, and last night I stopped in at the bar and let me tell you, I wasn't feeling the love, you know what I mean? What's going on?"

"Nothing."

"What'd you do?"

"Don't you think I have enough to deal with?" Camilla snapped.

"Okay, okay. Lower the torpedo. All I'm saying is in war you have to keep your allies happy."

"I thought all is fair in love and war," Camilla said.

"Oh, so it's love now?"

"I have to go," Camilla told her, blowing out smoke.

"Yeah, I thought you'd say that. Listen, when all this is over I need your help. I've got like a million pieces of rice we need to color red with magic markers. It's for another box for the—"

Camilla hung up the cell and dropped it down on her bed next to her. Leaning over, she stubbed out her cigarette, although it wasn't finished, on top of a half-empty can of Diet Coke that was on the bed table. The cigarette had stopped being an instrument of pleasure. It had become, instead, an instrument of death. She remembered that someone had once told her that twenty-four percent of the thousands of fires started in the home began in the bedroom. She stayed stretched out on her bed, irritated and cranky. It bothered her when Taylor intuitively knew what she'd been up to. That she knew she'd been driving by the treehouse. Camilla didn't think of herself as so obsessive, and she hated that Taylor did. She wiggled her toes so that her feet wouldn't fall asleep. One of them tensed up as if that foot was about to have a cramp. She hated that she let Taylor get under her skin like that. She moved her toes rapidly to ward off the cramp. *Who cares what Taylor thinks anyway?* If their roles had been reversed and Taylor had been the one that hadn't heard from her ex, Taylor would be driving by that house every night with goddamn night goggles. Except she'd spin the whole thing. "It's not stalking. It's justifiable reconnaissance."

Camilla picked up her cell. No messages. Why hadn't Allison tried to contact her? She flipped onto her side, staring at the cell's screen covered in app logos. When had she downloaded so many apps? She had the ridiculous thought for a moment that maybe there were so many apps that somehow they were blocking any texts, emails, or phone calls from coming in. She touched the small phone icon to make sure there were no recent calls from Allison. There were none.

For the first time, Camilla wondered if in those first months after she'd left Allison, when she'd been so distraught, that maybe she'd blocked Allison's number and forgotten about it. Allison had called her repeatedly that first year, had left her hundreds of voicemail messages, emails, and texts, most of them yelling at her for abandoning them. Maybe Camilla *had* blocked her and forgotten about it? She went into her contact list and pulled up Allison's info, and inadvertently, before she realized what she was doing, she'd dialed Allison's number. As soon as it started to ring, Camilla grasped what she'd done and quickly pressed the red button to hang up. *Shit! Shit!* She jumped off the bed. She paced around the bedroom. She held her breath. Cradling the phone in her palm, she stared at the screen, willing it to remain silent. Surprisingly, it did. Camilla sat back down on the bed, her back against the pillows, her knees up, as she continued to stare at the cell's screen, her heart racing as if she was expecting someone to jump out of her walk-in closet that was next to the bed. Ten minutes passed. Then thirty. She relaxed her legs, letting them fall against the comforter.

As if they sensed a change in the air, Meat and Ball appeared from under the bed and jumped up onto the mattress. Meat curled up on Camilla's thighs and Ball found a spot by her ankles.

Maybe Allison had been in the middle of something when Camilla's accidental call went through and Allison hadn't seen it. Maybe Nico had awakened from a nightmare, crying out for Allison. Or a bird had flown into the window of Allison's study where she'd been sitting working on a new article for a medical journal. Allison had been down in the basement taking the opportunity while Nico was sleeping to put in another load of laundry. She hadn't heard the phone ringing. Camilla shook her head. She didn't want to be in that house with them. Nothing good would come from those thoughts. She'd end up missing Nico so painfully that she'd want to run down the back stairs, jump into her car, and drive over there. Did it really matter why Allison hadn't picked up? Camilla shook her head again. She turned off the retro bedside lamp that looked like it belonged on Ben Franklin's desk. Fully dressed, she got under the covers, sliding Meat next to her. The two cats began to breathe deeply in sync with each other. Camilla slowed her breathing to match theirs.

She fell asleep, only to be awakened an hour later by her mobile's loud ringing. The cats scampered back under the bed, scared by the sharp noise. Camilla was still holding the phone in her hand. Disoriented, she looked at the bright screen. Allison. Panicking, she froze. By the time she pressed the Ignore button, the call had vanished. She let out her breath. Then, a voicemail message popped up. Shaking, Camilla pressed Play, praying that she wouldn't somehow touch the Call button instead. Allison's voice was quieter than she remembered it being. Over the years since Camilla had left, whenever Camilla heard in memory Allison's voice, it was that cutting, shouting one from their fights. She'd forgotten that the majority of their lives together, Allison's voice had been calming and often sweet. Camilla immediately had the image of Allison lying in their old queen bed with Nico asleep and tucked in next to her, keeping her voice low so that Nico wouldn't be disturbed as she left the voicemail.

"Hey," Allison said. Her voice was sleepy, tired. "Not sure if you were trying to call me or you butt-dialed me, but, well, if you were trying to call me about the...well, you know I obviously heard about what's happening at Tolland. You know Wallace came here, right? You don't have to worry. About what I'll say, I mean. It's the right thing to do. That girl should be shot for the lies she's saying about you." She paused. "It's just the right thing to do," she repeated and paused again. "I'll never forgive you. He's so beautiful you can't...it's just, well..." She paused again. Then she ended the call.

Camilla was reeling. She wanted to throw the phone against the wall and she wanted to kiss it. She hated Allison for everything she'd done to her, for keeping Nico from her. And she loved Allison for being able to do *the right thing* in spite of how angry she still was. She'd never understand Allison or what had happened between them. She'd never understand how she could have loved someone so much to stay for a decade in a place where she allowed almost everything to be out of her control. She'd never understand why she gave up that control. Sure, she'd never understand Allison, but she also thought that maybe she'd never understand herself, either. And that was far worse.

"Sometimes there is no closure, or at least not the kind you're wanting," Doris had told her during one of their first sessions together. "Sometimes there is simply forgiveness and moving on, and that's closure of a sort."

"You think I should forgive *her*?" Camilla had asked, bristling. She'd been ready to call therapy quits right then. It was immediately after Allison had given the ultimatum, *come home or you can't see him anymore.*

"Not *her*," Doris told her. "You. You need to forgive yourself."

Camilla had the urge to call Allison back. To thank her for being willing to testify? To hear that sleepy voice again? To ask her, "Please, can you put the phone next to his mouth so I can just hear him breathing as he's sleeping?" To tell her, "I'm sorry. I am. I'm sorry that your whole life came crashing down because I chose to live again." The urge passed as Camilla started to cry. She didn't hit redial. Instead, she got out of bed, still crying, and reached underneath her bed, pulling out both cats. She held them close, then got back into bed and continued to hug them both to her chest until they started to purr.

Day Thirteen

Audrey

In the morning, her phone ringing on her nightstand awakened Camilla again. Panicking that Allison was calling back, she leaned over to look, without touching the phone. It was Audrey.

"Did I wake you?"

"No, I was just about to get up." Camilla sat up. Meat and Ball were still fast asleep at the bottom of the bed, curled around each other.

"Catching up on your sleep?"

"I didn't get to bed till late," Camilla said defensively.

"I meant, now that the treehouse is done. You must be exhausted."

"Oh."

"Are you all right?"

Camilla rubbed her eyes. The truth was she felt shaky like she had a fever. Her clothes were drenched with sweat. Her throat felt scratchy. Her head throbbed. She wondered if all the wretchedness from the night before had metastasized into the flu, infecting her body. She remembered how for an entire week after Taylor returned from her life-changing Miami trip, Taylor had espoused the benefits of a cleansing fast.

"You cannot believe how much our bodies are riddled with toxic shit," she'd told Camilla. "It's like we manufacture our own Agent Orange with all these anxieties and shit we give in to." Her cult-like obsession with *getting the shit out*, as Taylor had called it, had only lasted a week, though, before Taylor had insisted again on gulping down greasy burgers and getting drunk at the bar. Still, Camilla questioned now whether there had been something to what Taylor had been saying. Maybe she was toxic. Ever since she'd started to build the treehouse, her life had taken a turn for the worse.

Except Audrey. Audrey had been the one good thing that had happened. At least before Camilla had fucked that up, too. And Peter. *Don't forget Peter*, she thought. She was glad that they had reconnected. And she and Taylor were talking again, or at least sparring like they used to.

"Camilla?" Audrey's voice startled Camilla out of her listing everything that was working, like one of those affirmation mind/positive body exercises in a self-help book.

"I'm here. Sorry, what were you saying?"

"Are you all right?"

Camilla hesitated.

"I'm coming over," Audrey told her. "Don't leave."

"No!" But it was too late. Audrey had already hung up the phone.

Camilla swore under her breath. She pressed redial but the phone went straight to Audrey's voicemail. Why hadn't she simply told Audrey she was fine? She heard sounds coming from the kitchen. Cereal clattering into an empty bowl. A spoon scraping the bowl's sides. She imagined she could hear Peter munching his dry corn flakes. She wanted nothing more than to turn over in the bed and go back to sleep, using the cats as earmuffs to block out all sounds. Audrey would be there in minutes on her bike. Camilla got out of bed.

Peter looked up from the island as she came out of the bedroom.

"Well, you're up early," he said, but his voice was edgy enough to tell her that it wasn't early. The stove clock told her it was noon. Peter wasn't eating cereal. He had a bowl of cocktail peanuts in front of him. He raised a spoonful and began to munch happily.

"I think we need to go food shopping," he said through his crunching. "The cupboards are bare, Mother Hubbard."

"You eat like you grew up in an orphanage," Camilla said, looking at the bowl with disgust. She went over to the refrigerator, grabbed the milk, and turned toward the counter with the cappuccino maker. She turned the machine on, emptied the last espresso capsule, dropped in a new one, and began to fill the frother.

"Please, sir. I want some more," Peter said with a fake cockney accent. He was holding out his bowl toward her.

"Very funny. You're no Oliver Twist, trust me," Camilla said back, frowning. She spooned the rich foam into her cup on top of the espresso.

"What?" Peter stood up, his eyes widening. "Am I to make my own coffee, too, then?" he bellowed, slamming down his bowl. He began to laugh. But Camilla wasn't having it. She went to the back screen door and stared out to the deck and the trees beyond, sipping her cappuccino.

"What's up?"

"Audrey's coming," Camilla told him with her

back still toward him. Cosimo the squirrel flew from the deck's railing into the cascade of tree leaves three feet away and miraculously nabbed a thin branch, hung on, recovered, and then dashed away along the slim wood as sure as a tightrope walker.

"I can make myself scarce," Peter said. The sounds of his stool scraping back made Camilla finally turn around.

"No, you don't have to. Let me make you a coffee," she offered as a way to make amends. She didn't want to take out on him whatever it was that was making her seesaw between resentment and reconciliation. He was on her side, she reminded herself. She was all over the place, that much she knew. It was all too much, that's all. Cindy Hunter, the treehouse, Allison, Nico, Taylor, Audrey. *When it rains, better reach for the wellies,* she heard her father say. He said it one night while watching a television news clip about Bill Clinton and Monica Lewinsky.

"Mills?"

Camilla shook her head. Mechanically, she began to make his cappuccino, the simple routine of the steps providing some comfort.

"I don't know why she bothers," she said with her back to him. She spooned some sugar into his mug, while the espresso streamed in. "My life is so fucked up. *I'm* so messed up. She must be a sadomasochist." Camilla scraped some foam out of the steamer into the cup.

Peter laughed. "You try to hide it under a boatload of crap, but you're the ultimate optimist. Yes, you are. So stop smirking. She's got your number." He surely would have gone on, but the buzzer rang.

"We'll finish this later, missy," he said, smiling

and grabbing up his mug, and headed for the deck.

When Camilla opened the front door downstairs she was struck again by Audrey's lightness. Her short blond hair reflected the sun. She was dressed in a short, cotton, sleeveless pink dress that had a print of intersecting white triangles. On her feet were ankle-high, lace-up black Dr. Martens with Victorian pink, red, and yellow roses imprinted on them. Camilla stood there awkwardly, feeling underdressed and dirty in yesterday's black jeans and T-shirt. The side of the T-shirt was partially covered in cat fur where Ball had slept.

Camilla rubbed her forehead. "Sorry, I didn't take my shower yet."

Audrey kissed her on the cheek as she passed by, heading up the stairs. "I woke you, remember?"

When they got into Camilla's condo there was an uncomfortable moment when Audrey asked if Peter was home and when Camilla pointed to the deck, Audrey ducked into Camilla's bedroom. Reluctantly, Camilla followed her in. Audrey sat on the bed, immediately unlacing her boots. Camilla made a show of looking for the cats under the bed, in the walk-in closet.

"Don't worry about the cats. Close the door, okay?" Audrey dropped one boot, then the other, onto the floor. Something about the thudding sound of that made Camilla more nervous. It felt like an ending, not a beginning. She closed the door. She sat down on the bed with her back against the pillows, her knees cradled against her chest with her arms wrapped around her ankles. Audrey swiveled on the bed to face her, her legs crossed. Her dress hitched above her thighs. Camilla caught a glimpse of black underwear.

Audrey cleared her throat. "So, what's going on?"

Camilla shrugged. "Nothing. Everything."

"You go tomorrow?"

Camilla gripped her ankles tighter and nodded.

"What time?"

"Ten." Camilla looked away toward the louvered closet doors. Her breathing was shallow. She felt almost lightheaded for a moment, and then it passed. When she looked back, Audrey was watching her.

"Can I come?" Audrey asked softly. "I'd like to come."

Camilla shook her head. "That wouldn't be a good idea. Besides, I think it's closed. Victim's rights and all."

"You could waive those rights." Audrey was smiling.

Camilla let out a short laugh. "I think they see Cindy Hunter as the victim here, not me."

"Can't I testify or something? You know, be a character witness?"

Camilla smiled, feeling her breathing slow down. "It's not that kind of trial. It's on campus and—"

"I know," Audrey said. "I want to help, that's all."

"Our fate is a fait accompli." When Audrey looked confused, Camilla waved at the air and said, "Something my dad used to say. It just means—"

"I know what it means." Audrey sighed. Camilla couldn't tell if she was frustrated or sad. "Where is he? I mean, are your parents still together? You haven't really mentioned them."

"He died. A long time ago." Camilla glanced toward the window. She hadn't noticed that it was a grey day. It looked like it was drizzling. She started to move off the bed, saying, "I should tell Peter it's all right for him to come in. It's raining."

But Audrey's hand on her shoulder stopped her. She'd leaned over so much the dress was now near her hips. Camilla had the overwhelming urge to push her down and make love right then and there. To forget everything.

"He's a big boy, Camilla," Audrey said. She dropped her hand from Camilla's shoulder. Camilla wanted to put it back on her shoulder. She leaned back against the wall of pillows.

"Are you ready for tomorrow?" Audrey asked her. Pulling her dress down, she shifted her legs so they were curled to the side. She lowered herself on the bed and leaned down on her side, propping her head up with her hand, her elbow on the comforter. She looked like a magazine pinup.

"How come you aren't sneezing?" Camilla asked her. "The cats sleep there every night."

"Drugs." Audrey smiled. "I popped a few before I came over." She paused. "What does she look like?"

Audrey switching up the conversation like that startled her, but Camilla stood and walked over to her desk. Rifling through the folder, she found Cindy Hunter's photograph. She was glad for the interruption. She'd been afraid that Audrey would want to talk about Camilla's father, how he died. It was far easier to talk about the case. In the photo, Cindy Hunter had a get-it-over-with smirk on her face for whoever was shooting it. She handed the photograph to Audrey.

Audrey stared at it, her face immediately changing, disconcerted by something. "Wait. This is Allison?"

Camilla startled. "What? No. That's Hunter. The girl—wait, you were talking about—"

"I know her," Audrey said. "I've seen *her*."

Surprised, Camilla's heart started to race. "What? When? How—"

Audrey looked up at her. "At the bar. Taylor. She came in with Taylor one night."

"What? When?" Camilla touched her own throat. She could feel her pulse throbbing under the skin.

Audrey stood up. "Six months ago, maybe." She paused. "Did you show this to Taylor?"

Camilla shook her head. "I kept forgetting to. She asked me for it. Fuck. I can't believe Taylor didn't tell me. I'm going to kill her. She's the one who told—"

Audrey touched her arm. "She doesn't know. She would've said. Who knows what name that girl gave her anyway."

Camilla shucked Audrey's hand off. "I can't believe this." She started to pace in front of her desk and bureau. "Taylor told her everything about me. Fuck."

"Camilla, stop." Audrey grabbed her by the shoulders. "We should call her or go find her right now. We need to find out—"

Camilla twisted away. Opening the bedroom door, she walked out. She grabbed up her keys and wallet. She ran down the stairs, not knowing whether she had closed the condo door behind her or not, and not really caring, either. Outside, it was a dark day. The wind was picking up. She was already starting the Mini when the passenger door opened and Audrey slid in.

"Jesus," Audrey said, breathing hard. She was bending over tying her Dr. Martens when Camilla heard her mumble, "This is so fucked."

❧❧❧❧

They drove straight to the bar after they tried calling Taylor and kept getting her voicemail. They both knew that the only times that Taylor didn't pick up was when she was home painting, at the bar, or... otherwise involved.

"She could be home, you know."

"I don't think so," Camilla snapped.

"Please slow down," Audrey said quietly as Camilla sped the car along Storrow Drive, zipping in and out of the cars in the two lanes. Leaning slightly forward, as if to calm her nerves, Audrey looked through the windshield at the Charles River on the left. Camilla glanced to the left, too, as a reflex. The Charles had always reminded Camilla of the Ouse River where Virginia Woolf had drowned herself. She'd never seen the Ouse, didn't even know if they really resembled each other, but during the months of her deepest depression after leaving Nico, Camilla would sometimes imagine herself walking off the footpath and wading into the Charles, her winter coat loaded down with big stones like Woolf's had been.

During those months, she had become obsessed with reading the stories of famous people who had drowned. Of course there were all those poor *Titanic* victims, or Natalie Wood the actress, or the poet Shelley, who drowned in a sudden storm while sailing off Italy, but Camilla wasn't interested in them. She was fixated on those who had committed suicide by drowning, from the poet Hart Crane in 1932 back to Qu Yuan of China, who killed himself in 278 BC as a form of protest against corruption, a sacrifice still celebrated during the Dragon Boat Festival. Woolf was the queen, though. Camilla's own father's drowning had been an accident, but she often wondered what his final moments had been like, whether he had thrashed about for some kind of purchase, or had simply and gracefully let go.

"Hey!" Audrey's voice snapped her back. The Mini had swung across into the next lane. Camilla wrenched the steering wheel to get back in their lane. The rest of the way, she kept her eyes straight ahead and tried to keep her mind blank.

Taylor wasn't at the bar. They searched both rooms and the bathroom. When they saw Taylor wasn't in the back room either, Audrey went to the bar and flagged down John, the night's bartender, asking him if he'd seen Taylor. Camilla saw him shake his head, and immediately turned on her heel and marched out of the bar toward the car. Audrey ran after her.

They drove down Boylston toward the South End in tense silence. When they couldn't find a parking space near Taylor's condo, after circling twice, Camilla said, "Fuck it," and double-parked the car in front of the brownstone.

"You can't—"

"I'm not staying long." Camilla cut Audrey off and jumped out of the car.

Camilla was already leaning on the buzzer by the ground-level gate entrance to Taylor's apartment when Audrey came up behind her. When that didn't bring a response, Camilla began to rap on Taylor's bedroom window that was to the left the gate. They couldn't see through the window because of the darkening shades that Taylor had taped to the inside. Camilla had always loved the black iron six-foot gate and the small grotto-like outdoor space that was between the gate and Taylor's front door. In the grotto, the white paint was peeling off the brick walls and there was an

orange Eames plastic chair to sit in if you had to wait
for Taylor to show. On the brick wall by Taylor's front
door was a small metal sign that Taylor had stolen
somewhere in Paris that read, "Chez Bizarre." Now the
gate made the place seem like a fortress built solely to
keep Camilla out. The grotto looked dark, damp, and
menacing.

Camilla's rapping turned into a thumping that
rattled the pane. Flecks of white paint sifted to the
ground like flour.

"Stop it. You're going to break it," Audrey said.

"Good. Maybe she'll come then."

"Maybe she just isn't here."

They heard the front door open.

"Christ, are you crazy?" Taylor said on the
other side of the gate as she stepped into the grotto. "I
thought someone was trying to break—"

"You fucking told her everything," Camilla
yelled.

"What? Who?"

"Open the damn gate."

Taylor fumbled at the lock on the doorknob. In
the best of times, the gate was prone to sticking and
you had to pull or push it hard to get it to open. Now,
without waiting, Camilla kicked at the bottom as soon
as she heard the lock click, making the gate fly open.

"Jesus. Make my fucking day, Terminator,"
Taylor said, but no one laughed as Camilla shoved past
her into the house.

Camilla thrust the photo at Taylor when she and
Audrey joined her in the darkened bedroom. "Cindy
Hunter. All this time..." Camilla couldn't finish the
sentence. She was so angry she thought she was going
to cry. She felt her hands trembling. She was all twisted

up inside. She looked away from Taylor and Audrey, her eyes roving around the room for something she could land on that would ground her. Finally, she focused on the television that was in the corner. It was an older one that Taylor had found years ago on garbage day in front of a brownstone down the street. Taylor had been so happy that day, calling Camilla to tell her about it.

"You cannot believe what these yuppie college students throw out at the end of every semester," Taylor had told her. They'd hooked up a game player to it. For months, the two of them had played every game they could borrow from friends, lying on Taylor's bed, joysticks in their hands. Hours passed with the only drama enfolding on the television.

"This is Cindy Hunter?" Taylor finally broke the silence.

"Oh please," Camilla said, and looked at her. "Like you—"

"I didn't. I swear. I kept asking you for the photo, don't you remember?"

"Why?"

"Why what?"

Camilla stared at the TV again. "I think somewhere you realized you might have been with her. But you just kept it to yourself."

"I didn't. I would've told you." Taylor paused. "Mills, I swear I didn't."

Camilla looked at Taylor, but had to look away again. She couldn't bear it. Dickens knew the devastation left behind in the wake of betrayal and deceit. It's what had attracted her as an academic to his novels in the first place. Dickens understood that intimacy inevitably led to betrayal. Nell and her grandfather in *The Old Curiosity Shop. Oliver Twist.* The worst ones were those where mothers betrayed their children. All that academic understanding had been worthless, though, for here she was anyway, betrayed by Taylor. *We forge the chains we wear in life,* Dickens had said.

Camilla shook her head clear. She'd be damned if she accepted the blame for this. "You didn't what? Know it was her? Tell her about me and Allison? All those things she claimed I told her in that bunch of lies she wrote? You were the one who told her."

Taylor moved closer to her. She raised her hands. "Okay, okay, can you just calm down? I slept with that girl. But she told me her name was Denise or Diane or something. It was not Cindy. She never said Cindy. I slept with her once. I was drunk. She came into the bar and sat down next to me. She told me she was an art student at the Museum School. We talked about the school and about me going to our school and how I was a painter. I think she told me she was a painter, too."

Camilla snorted. "So when was it exactly that you told her about me?"

Taylor pushed her fingers through her curly hair. "I don't know." When Camilla gave her a look of disgust, Taylor threw her hands up. "Look, I was drunk. I don't remember." Taylor glanced away. "Wait. She saw that photo." Taylor pointed to the framed photo on the bookcase of Camilla and her. "She asked me who you were and I must've told her." Taylor rubbed her head. "Look, I'm sorry. I had no idea. She lied about who she was. Clearly, she was bat shit about the grade you gave her and she planned this for a while. She's graduating this year, right? It's probably the only C she got in her life. Probably fucked up her application to med schools."

Camilla had forgotten Audrey was in the room until she said, "Obviously she was out to get you, and when she saw the photo, she used Taylor to get information."

Camilla stared back at the television. Her entire body was rigid except for her hands, which were shaking more violently. She tightened them into balls. Still staring at the television, she asked Taylor, "What did you say about me?"

An uncomfortable silence fell on the three of them as if a lid had been quickly placed on a bubbling pot that was spewing its liquid contents all over the stove. *Enough*, the lid says. *Enough mess. Shut the hell up.*

But sometimes the pressure of the boiling pot is too much. Sometimes the lid is put on in so much haste it's not securely battened down. Sometimes the lid is shoved away by the spewing water. There's no stopping the course of the water that wants to move up and out of the pot. Out into the open, scalding everything in its path. Apate unleashed.

"Well?" Camilla pressed on. She focused on looking at the veneer of dust that was across the top of the TV. She had the urge to write "Fuck You" across it.

"That you were my ex. My best friend." Taylor paused. "Probably the love of my life."

Camilla looked at her. Taylor shrugged. Camilla teetered on the brink between smiling and wanting to throttle her. But then Taylor bit her bottom lip and looked away, saying, "Oh shit." And Camilla knew in that instant that Taylor had said much more than that short and sweet version of their relationship. Like most professors, Camilla had never been a fan of CliffsNotes for literature. "Sure you get the action, the plot," she'd tell her students. "But Oliver Twist is more than a boy holding an empty plate out and asking for more gruel, and Scrooge is more than a bitter skinflint. For the real story, you have to dig deeper."

"That wasn't the end of it though, right?" Camilla prodded Taylor. "It's all coming back now, isn't it?" Her fists had stopped clenching.

Surprisingly, Taylor began to cry. She scuffed her flip-flop back and forth on the hardwood floor. She sniffed hard and rubbed her nose. She tried to square her shoulders, but ended up looking awkward and stiff. Her voice cracking, she told Camilla, "She asked me why we weren't together anymore. I told her we'd been through too much. I told her about Allison. About Nico. It was right in the middle of all that. I was upset. For you." Taylor began to cry again. But instead of going to her and telling her it was going to be all right, Camilla turned away and took a step.

"No, Camilla!" Audrey said loudly as she stepped toward Camilla. Picking up the game player, Camilla ripped it from its cable connection to the TV and threw it as hard as she could against the bookcase, spilling over with books. Her aim was dead on. The photograph's glass was smashed into shards. A gash ran across Camilla and Taylor's faces as if a stalker had taken a knife and tried to cut it in half.

Stunned, they stood where they were without saying a word. Audrey broke the silence by telling them she'd get the broom and leaving the room. Taylor walked over to the photo in its glassless black frame, and, touching the photo's surface, began to lightly wipe away the tiny glass crumbs. She'd stopped crying, the suddenness of Camilla smashing the glass to bits shutting it down.

"You know," she said with her back to Camilla. Her index finger kept brushing the surface, getting snagged on a shard here and there, which left pinpricks that began to bleed and just as suddenly dry up. "Out of all the stuff in this room, this is the only thing I really cared about." She turned to Camilla. "Now what?"

Camilla had no idea. The rush that had overtaken her was subsiding. She felt tired and slightly nauseous. Before she could say anything, Audrey was there again, broom in one hand and dustpan in the other.

"Can you move over there?" she asked Taylor quietly, as she slipped by her between the bookcase and the bed. Taylor sat down at the foot of the bed, still holding the photo.

Camilla felt her body start to shake. She tried to latch on to the sound of glass being scraped into the pan. "I should do that," she told Audrey. As if in answer, Audrey stooped down, her head bent over the mess.

"You never did like this picture, did you?" Taylor said, her head tilted down toward the photo in her hands.

Audrey stood up and walked toward the doorway. "Just going to empty this out," she said quietly as she left and went down the stairs to the lower level.

Camilla sat down next to Taylor on the bed. She suddenly felt the urge to apologize, but then that slipped away as she looked at the photo. Taylor was right about that photo: she hadn't ever liked it. The photo brought home to her every way that she and Taylor were unalike. She had known even when the picture was being snapped that she and Taylor were not going to last. Taylor had been ogling some other girl at the party when the shutter had clicked. But she now lied, telling Taylor, "No, I liked it."

Taylor's fingers moved over their faces again, across their foreheads. "You thought it only showed how different we are. I think it shows how we're the same."

Camilla laughed harshly. "We're nothing alike."

Taylor shook her head. Her index finger lingered on the top of Camilla's head in the photograph. "We both can't believe someone could love us." When Camilla opened her mouth, Taylor said, "I mean really love us for who we are, not because we're the flavor of the month, or in your case, as a thing to own or control. I'm so tired. Aren't you tired, Mills?"

Camilla lay back on the bed. She rubbed her face.

"Aren't you?" Taylor asked again. She turned to face Camilla. "You know, she's gaga over you."

Camilla snorted. "Give me a break." She covered her face.

Taylor laughed a little. "No, she is. I could tell right away. That morning you got up and left, you know the morning after—"

"You don't have to say it. I know what morning, trust me," Camilla said. "Ugh! How did this all happen?"

Taylor shook her head. "Don't ask me. The first thing she asked me was if I thought you liked her. I mean, come on. We'd just all been in this bed—"

Camilla groaned. "Please."

"I didn't stand a chance," Taylor continued. "There you were. Smart. Beautiful. A classics professor. Someone whose job it is to figure out when people have behaved like decent human beings and when they haven't."

"Someone whose own life is a monumental train wreck," Camilla interjected.

"Someone whose life," Taylor went on, ignoring her. "Has been a shit storm of tragedy and death, and still you get the fuck up out of bed every morning. You build a fucking treehouse in the hottest summer on record for a boy who you, in all likelihood, will never see again. You stick by me for twenty years. Like I could compete with that? Audrey told me you were the most loyal person she'd ever met. No matter what hits you, you come out the other side. It's like you have this secret weapon that we know you have, but you never lord it over us."

Camilla groaned again. "Enough with the military metaphors." Camilla was flattered but it was all too much coming on the heels of finding out that Taylor had spilled the beans to Cindy Hunter. The entire mess was at Taylor's feet. How could they come back from that?

Taylor snorted then, opening her mouth to say something back, but it was Audrey, coming back into the room, who replied, "You know, you two are the loneliest people I know on this earth."

❧ ❧ ❧ ❧

Camilla drove Audrey home. They hadn't stayed much longer at Taylor's because there wasn't much left to say, and the next day Camilla had to be ready for the hearing. On the way home, Audrey tried to get Camilla to talk about how she was feeling, but when Camilla switched the radio on to a call-in show about fixing cars, Audrey let it go.

"Will you call me and let me know how it went?" Audrey asked her after she'd gotten out of the car, and as an afterthought, had leaned back in.

"Sure," Camilla said, but even as she said it, Camilla wasn't so sure she would.

Inside her kitchen, she told her brother that she had a splitting headache and needed to lie down. It was four o'clock in the afternoon. Camilla hoped she would fall asleep and stay that way until it was time to get up for the hearing.

That didn't happen. Lying in her bed next to her, Meat and Ball obsessively cleaned each other, licking each other's furry backs and faces. She felt their rhythmic motion through the covers. It started to irritate her until Ball, frustrated that Meat wasn't giving it up, jumped off the bed and slumped down against the closed bedroom door. Lying there, Camilla began to think about what had happened at Taylor's and what would happen the next day. She kept coming back to Audrey, though, and what she had said about her and Taylor being the two loneliest people she knew. Camilla knew that she kept people at arms' length. But lonely? Was she? She connected with people. She simply did so on her own terms. Who didn't? Everyone gave what they could. Opened themselves up to what they were able to. No more, no less.

She thought of Audrey as naïve and innocent then. She imagined Audrey rushing to gather the world in her arms, never stopping to think of the consequences. Like someone who runs into a field of sunflowers, egged on by their beauty, not realizing that their heads are covered with bees, the bees' colors camouflaged against the petal colors. You could get hurt. You could hurt someone else. No one ever loved each other in the same way at the same time. That's why couples therapy was a booming business. Audrey was too old not to know that. For the first time, Camilla thought that Audrey was not as sophisticated as she was. As knowledgeable about people. *But she said I was one of the loneliest people she knew. Me and Taylor.* Audrey was wrong. *Just because we choose to be by ourselves doesn't mean we're lonely.*

Don't fool yourself. You're a self-contained unit, one of Allison's emails to her had read. She'd sent it in the first weeks after Camilla had left. *You didn't leave out of some altruistic notion of saving Nico. You left because you want to be alone. Plain and simple. You'll die alone and lonely. I hope you're happy.* For days after she'd received it, Camilla had obsessed about whether Allison was telling the truth. That Camilla had fabricated the entire story of their increasingly violent relationship, of Allison being a control freak, as some kind of psychological salve for the real wound she carried inside of her: that she wasn't cut out to be a mother. That, when it came down to it, she didn't have the staying power needed to stick out the relationship. Any relationship.

Camilla began to cry. Had she been fooling herself all this time? *We forge the chains we wear in life,* she thought again. She kicked at the bedcovers, feeling overly hot, and accidentally flung Meat off the bed. It was not lost on her that by doing so, she was alone once more.

❧❧❧❧

At seven that night, there was a light rap on her door and then it opened. Peter carried in a tray holding all of Camilla's childhood favorites: tuna fish salad with melted cheddar on two lightly toasted hotdog rolls, two small cans of Pringle potato chips, and two glasses with ice and root beer. He set it down on the comforter and sat down next to it.

"Big day tomorrow. You have to keep your strength up," he told her solemnly. It was so theatrical, she almost laughed. "How's your headache? Come on, eat." Closing the hotdog roll sandwich up like a clam, he stuffed one end in his mouth.

Camilla sat up. "I can't believe you remembered." She shook her head, smiling a little, and, separating the two halves of the roll without thinking about it, she began to eat one side. She appreciated that he had spread extra mayonnaise across the bun the way she liked it.

"Who could forget tuna boats? I never understood why you chose them every year for Mom to make on your birthday. I mean, here's a graduate of the Cordon Bleu and—"

"The *Texas* Cordon Bleu," Camilla corrected, talking with her mouth full.

Peter waved her way, finishing his sandwich in one bite. "Yes, yes. Whatever." He shook his head. "Tuna boats and Pringles. Every year."

"The Pringles were for you, remember?"

Peter shrugged. He picked up a can, emptied the potato chips onto the tray, and placed the lid back on top of the canister. "Choose your weapon," he told her.

Camilla emptied her chips as well and smoothed the lid down again on top.

"Ready," Peter said. They both raised their cans and looked down them as if they were using a riflescope. "Aim, fire!"

They squeezed the cans so hard the pressure blew the lids off across the room. The cats leapt off the bed, scurrying for cover underneath as one lid blasted into the walk-in closet and the other hit the window over Camilla's desk.

"What ho, sailor! You've struck their bow!" Peter shouted, laughing. He jumped off the bed to retrieve the lids.

"That's enough," Camilla said, laughing in spite of herself. She took another bite of her sandwich and sipped her root beer. "Root beer always reminds me of Dad."

Peter threw himself down on her bed. He picked up a few of the chips and tossed one into the air. It floated down perfectly over his nose and his mouth snagged it. He chewed it thoughtfully.

"Me, too," he said finally. "Friday nights. Pizza and root beer. The only night Mom didn't cook. Are you going to eat that?" Sitting up, he pointed at the half of sandwich lying on Camilla's plate. The melted white cheddar was hardening into a darker yellow.

Camilla picked it up and shoved the whole half into her mouth. Then she grinned.

"Beastie girl," Peter said, smiling. "Well, there's enough tuna for another. I'll split it with you." He got off the bed, and, walking through the doorway, added, "If you're lucky."

Camilla listened to the sounds of him making another tuna boat: the refrigerator door opening and closing, followed by the creaking door of the toaster oven, the spoon scraping the sides of the bowl to get every morsel of tuna salad, the sharp sound of a plastic bag being opened and closed as she imagined him placing the cut cheese slices on top, and finally the creaking toaster oven door again.

Ball jumped from the floor onto her lap, and she stroked him until he shifted into a purring machine. The clatter of her brother in the kitchen made her feel nostalgic. She realized that she was getting attached to him living there, that sometime during the last week she had stopped counting the days until he'd leave and she would be alone again, to now, when she dreaded his leaving. Dreaded the silence she knew would settle as soon as his car pulled away. She heard him raggedly whistling a random tune. She was struck by how much he seemed to be getting younger the longer he stayed, while she felt so much older with each passing day. He seemed to be shedding the weight of years gone by, as she was shouldering more and more of a burden. But maybe she couldn't fault him for that. The hearing tomorrow was weighing her down. She knew that was the true cause of her unhappiness.

But that wasn't all of it. She would see Allison tomorrow, for the first time in almost two years. Taylor would probably be there as well. Before Audrey and Camilla had left Taylor's apartment, Taylor had insisted on being at the hearing so that she could testify how Cindy Hunter had really found out about Camilla's life.

Camilla thought of Audrey. She didn't deserve Audrey. Camilla had told Doris once, "How can I possibly bring someone else into my life, when *I* can't even stand being in it?" Doris had smiled thinly. She'd replied with a question, a strategy that sometimes irritated Camilla, because, after all, she was paying her for the answers, not more questions. Doris had asked, "What is it about your life that you can't stand?" As Camilla stroked Ball's back now, a dark box began to open up, but at the same time, Peter suddenly opened up her bedroom door and was there again in the room, with his too-long hair that needed to be cut and another plate with a tuna boat on it, the smell of the cheese and the tuna salad bringing Camilla back to warmth and goodness.

Day Fourteen

Camilla

She didn't sleep at all that night. The cats, sensing that something was off, were up as well, pogoing on and off the bed repeatedly. The thought of seeing Allison again had kept her wide awake. She still didn't trust that Allison would come through for her. By four in the morning, Camilla started to worry that Allison might even show up at the hearing with Nico in tow, further evidence for the panel to consider as they judged whether Camilla was fit not only as a teacher, but as a mother as well.

By seven, she knew sleep was impossible. She slipped a hoodie over her head and pulled on jeans from the floor. She went into the kitchen where the morning sun was finding its way through the gaps on either side of her window blinds and the tapestry curtain that covered the glass back door. The brilliance of the sun sneaking in offended her. Shouldn't it be a downpour outside? Would she feel any better if it was?

Meat and Ball followed her out, mewing for their breakfast. "Shh," Camilla told them as she began to wash out their bowls and mechanically began the feeding ritual: popping the vacuum-packed lids, spooning out the tuna chunks with gravy, rinsing out the cans for recycling, placing the full bowls on the turquoise plastic floor mat next to their water bowl, followed by Ball's licking only the gravy off both bowls and leaving the chunks for Meat to eat. The normalcy of it all calmed Camilla a little.

She wanted some more time to herself before Peter came out. As opposed to last night, this morning she wished that he wasn't here. She knew he would insist on coming with her to the hearing, too. She didn't want that either. She wanted to go by herself. To get it over with, with as few witnesses as possible.

Her shoulders were tensed. The sounds of turning on her espresso maker would wake her brother, but she needed the comfort of her daily rituals. This was her life, as tattered as it was. "Save the ribbons, save the ribbons," she heard her mother saying in a mock Julia Child voice. "You never know when you'll need them." It was said in reference to cleaning up the shredded gift-wrap and discarded boxes after Christmas, but Camilla understood now that it might be a useful code to live by.

She poured the milk into her frother, turned on the espresso maker, and slid an espresso capsule into the machine. As she batted the lid down on the capsule and pushed the On button, the sound of the machine reminded her of mechanical iron gates closing over a storefront. She felt the familiar feeling of not being in herself, but of watching herself. Not from above, but as if she were standing in a corner of the kitchen. Invisible. The watcher. This isn't happening to you. It's happening to *her*. The feeling comforted Camilla. She could, would, get through this day as long as she stayed removed.

Miraculously, despite the noise, the guest room door stayed shut. Grabbing her filled mug, Camilla opened the back door and shut it behind her. She turned to see Cosimo running along the railing and launching himself into the nearest branches. Section after section of leaves shook and then fell quiet. She sat down on the iron chair by the café table in the corner of the deck farthest away from the door. It was already sweltering hot at eight a.m. She pulled the hoodie off, letting the sun bake her arms, her black T-shirt immediately catching and absorbing the warmth, too. The air was dead still, a few leaves shaking as the squirrel moved farther away from the house. Then silence. It was so deathly quiet that Camilla imagined she was the last person on earth. *That would be one way of getting out of the hearing.*

Then, the back door opened. There was Peter, with a coffee mug in his hand and his brown hair matted with sweat on one side of his head and standing up on the other side. His hair wasn't the only thing off-kilter. He slumped down in the other chair at the table across from Camilla, and from his other hand he unveiled a new pack of cigarettes. Lucky Strikes. Their father's brand. Peter began to unwrap the cellophane.

"What are you doing?" Camilla asked.

He cleared his throat, took a sip of his coffee, and coughed. "I slept like shit," he said hoarsely. "How about you?"

"Since when do you smoke?"

He shrugged. "The day calls for it, don't you think?" There were purplish pillows under his eyes and his face looked pale. Gone was the brother who ate their childhood foods and spun puns out of air. He rubbed his eyes.

Camilla felt compelled to tell him everything was going to be okay, but Peter simply cleared his throat again and lit a cigarette, drawing deeply on it. As he blew out the smoke with one of his eyes squinting, he asked her, "Do you want one? Breakfast of champions." He raised his mug with the cigarette laced between his fingers holding the handle. She shook her head.

"So, little sis, what's the plan?" he said as if he was asking about the departure time for a trip to the beach, but his voice cracked and Camilla knew at once he wasn't simply tired—he was scared. It irritated her at first. Didn't she have enough to worry about? She wanted to stand up, to shout at him to cut it out. To buck up. Then, she was scared again, too. She picked up the cigarettes and tapped one out, put it to her lips, and stretched over the table so that Peter could light it for her, although he stayed slumped in his seat as if he was conserving his energy for something bigger. Camilla leaned against the back of her chair, her head resting against the deck's railing as she looked into the tree branches overhead. She took a drag and blew the smoke straight up into the sky.

"I see you, you know," Peter finally said.

She raised her head, squinting at him. "What does that mean?"

"You're not invisible. As much as you want to be."

She scowled. She took a long drag on her cigarette.

"That might've worked when we were kids. Christ, after Dad, Mom didn't care if we were there or not. Or at least if *I* was there. But we're not kids anymore, Milly."

She scowled again. "Really? *You* could've fooled me."

He sipped his coffee. He sat up in his chair. "Remember watching that movie, *The Invisible Man*? *Science Fiction Theater*? Saturday mornings? Channel eleven?"

She smiled meanly. "You're so transparent it hurts."

He laughed harshly. "Good one, Sis." He pointed his cigarette at her, then took a drag and blew out the smoke. "Do you remember what happened in it? The movie?"

She shook her head, dropping her half-finished cigarette butt into the remains of her espresso. "I'm not playing this game." She stood up, but Peter grabbed her wrist.

"Griffin, the scientist, didn't fool anyone. In the end, the townspeople found him and killed him. They didn't need to see him to *see* him."

Camilla wrenched her wrist away. She picked up her mug. "Sorry, I don't have time for Siskel and Ebert. I need to get ready."

She walked away, but as she opened the kitchen door, her brother called out, "Don't even think I'm not coming with you, either."

Turning to him, she said, "It was *Creature Features* and it was channel five, not eleven, and it was his best friend that betrayed him to the police." Then, she went into the kitchen, closing both the screen and glass doors behind her.

"I'm still coming," her brother yelled after her, his voice muffled by the glass door, seemingly coming to her from a long way off, a bad connection with a foreign country.

⊷⊷⊷⊷

The hearing was to be held in the Dean's conference room in Edgar Hall. Camilla knew the department chairs within Arts and Sciences met there monthly, the agendas mostly centering on money matters and occasional reports from the chairs on student issues and achievements. The room was a paean to gothic architecture. A rounded bank of skinny eight-foot windows looked out onto The Green, mahogany paneling on the other three walls, two of which had floor-to-ceiling bookcases jammed with first editions. The other wall was covered with austere oil portraits of the current Dean and every one of his male predecessors dating back to 1880, all posed on the same gothic throne, which sat empty in one corner of the room. In the center, there was a large, oval, walnut meeting table and its twenty matching high-backed chairs, covered in deep red velvet damask. Farthest from the door was a fireplace large enough to contain a cot, swept clean for the summer months, and two large merlot-colored velvet chairs. Nearby, a soft sofa of candied-apple-colored velvet sat. Along its back stretched a large mahogany desk, clean except for a black desk pad and a stand of fountain pens, and a matching mahogany chair.

Camilla had never been in the room before, although she had taught at the college for eight years. When she entered it for the first time that morning, it looked to her like a room in which a bloodbath had taken place, there was so much red everywhere. In her classes, she taught her students how important colors were in literature and that colors like red could have multiple meanings: passion, energy, love, versus anger, war, danger. She often took a poll the first day of class on what they felt red meant as a barometer for what type of class she would be facing in the coming months. What, she wondered, was the designer of this room hoping to convey to anyone meeting with the

Dean now?

෴෴෴෴

Earlier, she and Peter had driven to the college in silence, stymied by everything they wanted to say but couldn't broach. When Camilla pulled the Mini into a parking space by Edgar Hall, Peter had stared through the front window and said, "You've been through worse and survived, you know."

Camilla shook her head. "No, I didn't. I escaped. I never fought, not really." She looked out her side window. "Every minute I'd repeat to myself this mantra. Make a plan. Make a plan." Her eyes began to tear. She forced herself to look at her brother. "Make a plan," she said again, very quietly. "But I didn't. I couldn't. It was like I'd fallen into a lake and there was this thick coating of ice over me. I could see everyone reaching out to me. Yelling at me to get out, but I couldn't move. I was so scared."

Peter touched her arm. "But you did. You got out."

She nodded. "Something happened when she pushed me against that wall with his blanket and Nico was crying. It was like I was suddenly seeing myself. I hated it—me—so much. All the times I swallowed, I gave in." She shook her head free of the image. "We should go in," she told him.

She clicked her door open. Peter grabbed her arm, stopping her.

"You'll get through this. You can fight them. You've been through so much worse," he said again.

Camilla smiled painfully. "Don't think I was courageous or noble or anything like that, okay? I saved myself, and maybe by leaving I saved Nico, but some days I'm not sure which came first."

She got out of the car.

As she and her brother crunched their way across the gravel toward Edgar's main doors, there was the sound of running footsteps behind them. Taylor jogged up to them.

"Didn't you see me?" she asked, breathless as she caught up to them. "You walked right in front of me as I was pulling in. How you doing, Mills?" She patted Camilla's shoulder. Camilla thought she'd start to cry if Taylor continued to touch her, so she moved slightly away.

Taylor was dressed up in a cream linen pantsuit and a crisp white shirt. She looked stunningly beautiful. Camilla wished she had dressed similarly instead of the black suit, black oxford shirt, and black shoes she was wearing. She was ready for a funeral, Taylor for a baptism. Camilla's eyes welled up again, she was so touched by Taylor's dressing up. She turned away, facing Edgar Hall.

≈≈≈≈

The building was one of those noted in a recent *New York Times* article that compared the gothic architecture of Tolland to Hogwarts, the famous and fictional school for wizardry in the *Harry Potter* books. Edgar, with its sky-reaching turrets and an actual parapet that ran along the roof, complete with gargoyles, either gave you comfort by its very grandeur, or left you feeling cold and imprisoned. Camilla had always loved it, seeing it as more Dickensian than Rowling-esque. The first time she'd seen it, eight years before, she half-expected Pip and the beautiful Estella to step through the doors with Miss Havisham beseeching them to stay. Camilla still felt consoled by it. At least the hearing wasn't in Carey Hall, one of two buildings that had been built in the seventies and looked like bomb shelters. There was talk that those buildings would be razed in a year and rebuilt in keeping with the gothic elements everywhere else.

Now, Taylor stepped next to her and grabbed Camilla's hand. "Come on. Courage." For a second, Camilla wondered if Taylor had overheard her conversation with Peter. As the three of them walked toward the main doors, Camilla thought that maybe the Chinese poet Lao Tzu was right: Loving someone deeply gives you courage.

But just as quickly, as soon as the three of them filed into the waiting room leading into the Dean's suite on the first floor, any romantic notions of love and friendship evaporated. Allison sat in an empty row of chairs on one side of the room. Her head was down. She was reading, with a highlighter in her hand, from a stack of papers on her lap that perched on a half-full red folder, the accordion legal file that she used for all her medical journal reading.

The Dean's secretary was at her desk. She picked up the phone, and, punching in a few numbers, said quietly, "She's here."

Allison lifted her head and saw Camilla. "Hi," she said simply. It seemed like she wanted to say something else, too, but then she closed her mouth.

The year before, Doris had ended their first session abruptly, or so it had seemed to Camilla at the time when Doris said, "I'm sorry but that's all the time we have for today." As Camilla was putting on her coat, she asked her, "Don't you want to ask me why I left?" When Doris had stared at her blankly, Camilla added, "Why I left Allison?"

Doris smiled that thin smile that Camilla would come to realize meant that Camilla had missed the mark, missed the point of whatever they'd been discussing. "The more important question is, why did you stay?"

Now, seeing Allison for the first time in two years, it all rushed back to her. Why she had stayed. She'd stayed because Allison was loyal to her. Yes, she was obsessed with Camilla, had put her in an ever-tightening box of rules that Camilla was suffocated under. Yes, Allison could lose it Titanic-ally whenever her anxiety flared up and screamed. And yes, those times had happened more and more frequently with each passing year, positively exploding after Nico was born. "Are you trying to kill him?" Allison shouted at her when she saw those flammable socks that Camilla was dressing him in. Camilla knew that Allison had harbored an overwhelming fear of fire ever since she was six years old when her family's home was partially destroyed by a fire from an electrical problem in the kitchen. Allison, her two sisters, and her parents all escaped to safety, with Allison never forgetting being carried out in her pajamas into the icy winter air by her father while three fire trucks barreled into the driveway, sirens blaring. They'd had to move out into a cramped rental apartment for a year while half of the house was rebuilt. Afterward, Allison had made her parents complete an emergency fire plan so that everyone would be fully informed about where the emergency exits were in the house.

She was neurotically worried about all disasters,

really. Her family had seen it all: flooding in the basement of their house, which unfortunately was located at the bottom of a hill; a one-hundred-year-old oak tree struck by lightning and falling onto their garage; one of her sisters being knocked unconscious by ice spikes falling from one of the gutters she was walking under. Camilla had called the house Amityville Horror after the movie depicting the true story of a possessed house in Amityville, Long Island. Allison hadn't found it funny.

"You think life is easy because you never had to suffer like I have," Allison told her. "Nothing bad ever happened to you." Camilla didn't bother to correct her by reminding her about her dad's drowning or her mother's sudden death, leaving Camilla parentless, rudderless, in her thirties.

All of that was true, yes. But, Allison had always been loyal to Camilla. Had never wanted anyone else. Had never looked at anyone else. And after her relationship with Taylor, Camilla had craved that. Why had she stayed? She stayed because Allison wanted her to stay. She stayed because Allison wanted *her*, no matter what. She stayed because in the evening, as Allison walked through the door, she would greet Camilla with a "Where's my humanity?" and in the morning as she walked out the door, she'd tell her, "See you tonight, humanity." And Camilla had, during those moments, felt like it was what she'd longed for during the years after her parents had died: a family. And she should stop thinking of herself and what she needed besides that. Because she was part of something bigger. She stayed because Allison, after all they had been through, was still loyal.

Thankfully, before Camilla could look for

other telltale signs of which of the two Allisons had shown up that day (Was her jaw tightening? Was she sweeping the highlighter fast and furious across the page?), the secretary stood and walked toward a large, shut wooden door. She told Camilla, "You're early, but they're ready for you."

Camilla followed her toward the door. She felt as if she was going to throw up. Her fingers were trembling. Her legs ached. Just before she passed through, though, she looked over her shoulder. She didn't know why she did it. Reflex? Hoping to get some last-minute strength transfusion from her brother and Taylor? Peter gave her a thumbs-up and Taylor saluted her to make her laugh. But it was the image of Allison that stayed with her throughout the hearing: Allison, standing up so suddenly, the file and its papers falling to the ground, unnoticed. Allison, who touched the tips of her index and middle fingers to her lips and then blew across the tips of them in the air toward Camilla.

Then the door closed between them.

✺ ✺ ✺ ✺

The committee members were all at the long conference table in the middle of the bloodbath room. At the head of the table, in a chair that was closest to the door and slightly larger than the rest of the twenty matching ones, sat Dean Wilkins. Camilla had met him several times, knew that he was a widower and had a cat named Bootsy that he revered because she had been his deceased wife's beloved pet. She had talked with him for a long time at one of the school's faculty holiday parties—she remembered it was a drunken conversation first about Bootsy, and then about whether Shakespeare was dyslexic—and yet she always felt compelled to introduce herself anew ever since he'd called her Cordelia once when she'd passed him in the hallway. Maybe it was a leftover consequence of the Shakespeare discussion and combined with his hazy memory that her name began with a C, he'd settled haphazardly on King Lear's favorite daughter.

In addition to the Dean, Camilla saw a few other familiar faces around the table. Wallace Fields, of course, and there were two other female professors from her department, both Joyceans. She wondered if that would make a difference. She'd never finished *Finnegan's Wake*, but she seemed to remember it was a freewheeling account of sex between a Molly somebody and a Joyce stand-in. Maybe they'd be more forgiving because of it.

"Please, have a seat, Professor Thompson," Dean Wilkins said. He gestured toward the other end where the only open seat was. To the right of it she recognized her former pupil, the newly appointed student representative on the committee. He was still wearing the familiar Tolland Swim Team jacket he'd worn religiously in her classroom although he'd graduated the year before. Despite Wallace thinking he'd be her ally, Camilla worried he'd have to choose between siding with Cindy Hunter out of a public commitment to represent student concerns, and wanting to stay on the good side of faculty. There was also the question of how he and the other eleven men in the room from various departments would come to terms with faking a pro-feminist stance, knowing full well that many of them might have been in the same exact position as Camilla was now with countless of their female students in the past. Camilla didn't recognize any of

them. She should've been able to. The school prided
itself on its small size fostering a close-knit family
amongst the students as well as the faculty. It was her
own fault. She'd always kept herself separate from the
school, rarely attending any of the faculty events, never
joining in on the informal get-togethers at nearby bars,
barely attending mandatory department meetings. She
was the same with her students. In spite of the annual
letter from the Dean encouraging and providing money
for faculty to host end-of-semester dinners within
their own homes for their students, Camilla preferred
to have pizza delivered to the classroom on the last day
of each term.

On the way to the open chair, Camilla scanned
the last four women who sat on one side of the
table, looking like the Soviet bloc at an international
gymnastics meet. Their faces were unreadable, although
one, whom Camilla recognized as Peggy Huggens,
a faculty member in the Peace Studies department,
smiled wanly at Camilla, as if she'd had second
thoughts on remaining cement-faced and felt that if
she was going to walk the walk and talk the talk on
compassion and forgiveness, she should start showing
some at home. The other three women Camilla vaguely
remembered meeting in a slapdash way at the only
luncheon hosted by The Women's Tolland Faculty
Association that Camilla had ever gone to in the past
eight years. She hadn't wanted to go to the luncheon,
but Linda, wearing a matching leopard print scarf and
faux leopard fur bracelets and earrings, had insisted.

"If you want to get anywhere in this school you
have to have allies," Linda had told her.

"Couldn't they have come up with a better
name?" Camilla asked her. "WTF? I mean, come on.

It's begging for ridicule."

"The acronym is WTF*A*, Camilla," Linda retorted brusquely.

Now, Camilla seemed to remember that the three other women were all tenured professors from the Mathematics and Science departments, although who belonged to what department she wouldn't have been able to say. She'd hated the luncheon. The main speaker, brought in at considerable expense, was an infomercial-plastic-female whose main message was that women were paid less than men, received fewer academic promotions than men, and were more often the butt of cruel postings on student faculty reviews than men. "Tell me something I don't know," Camilla had mumbled to her table companions. One of the table sitters had surprised Camilla when she'd raised her index finger, like a librarian, to lips tightly buttoned up in a grimace. Camilla had stood then and strode out, disgusted. She wondered now, as she sat down and crossed her legs, whether any of the women would remember her from that luncheon, or worse, if any of them had been at her table when she'd walked out.

On the other side of her seat was Wallace. As she glanced at him and muttered a quiet hello, he winked at her. She saw that he had left behind his usual dandy look and was wearing a dark blue suit with a white shirt and a blue-and-yellow-striped tie, not one from his usual bow tie assortment. Leaning over, he whispered in her ear, "You look like you killed Bootsy. Steady on, it's all good," all the while patting her leg under the table. *It's all good.* Another student salve said to heal all wounds—a forgotten homework assignment, a job interview gone wrong, a messed-up boyfriend who cheated with a best friend. It really meant: I'm fucked.

No, dude, Camilla thought. *It's not "all good." And get your bloody hand off me.*

She realized, however, that Wallace's hand wasn't patting her leg at all. It was trying to hold her leg *down.* The leg that was jiggling from her crossed foot tapping in the air. She willed it to stop. Wallace immediately removed his hand, and folded his hands on the table, on top of the file she recognized as the one he'd brought to her house.

"Professor Thompson," the Dean said loudly from the other end. "As you know, there has been an accusation"—he looked to her right at the student liaison—"a very serious accusation, from a past student of yours." The Dean looked back at Camilla. "The Chair of your department has advised the committee that you are apprised of the contents of that accusation. Is that correct?"

Camilla knew that the Dean did not particularly like Wallace, hence his calling him out by his title, as if Wallace wasn't in the room with them. Would that affect the hearing's outcome?

"Professor Thompson?" Dean Wilkins was staring at her. She wanted to say yes but she was afraid that her voice would crack under the strain. She'd hoped that she could adopt her watchful pose, stand in her corner and observe the proceedings untouched, unfazed. But her throat was tight. Her foot had started to jiggle again like a patient who has restless leg syndrome.

It was Wallace's tight grip again on her thigh that brought her back and she was able to say a quiet, "Yes" and nod in case Wilkins didn't hear her.

The Dean nodded back. "We have heard from the student as well as"—he broke off to look at the paper in front of him—"an Allison Whitmere."

Camilla jerked automatically at the mention of Allison's name. So, Allison had already given her testimony. That was shocking in itself. Why had they spoken to her before they spoke to Camilla? Even more surprising was that Allison had stayed afterward. Had she stayed so that she would force Camilla to see her? Had she done it to be kind, or to throw Camilla off her game even more? But before Camilla could sort through it, the Dean was reading from the paper that he'd picked up from the table.

"It appears that Ms., or should I say, *Doctor* Whitmere, is a surgeon, a highly regarded one, and she discounts the student's testimony in its entirety and I quote, 'On the dates in question I can unequivocally state that Camilla Thompson was at home with me and our son, Nico Thompson Whitmere. Furthermore, the claimant's argument that my relationship with Dr. Thompson had ended is not true. As a doctor and as a mother, I am torn between suing the claimant for libel and suggesting that she receive the mental health support she is clearly in need of.'" At this Dean Wilkins placed the letter back down on the table. "You all have received a copy of this letter so I do not have to read the rest. And Doctor Whitmere is at our disposal should we want to question her further. I am told that she is in the waiting room outside, at considerable expense to her patients." Here, the Dean nervously began to dog-ear the page in front of him, and pushed down on it. Camilla had the sensation that his thumb and index finger were pressing her throat.

One of the Joyceans spoke up. "Excuse me, Dean, but are you saying that there may be a question of the school being sued?"

Wilkins raised his hand from the table. "Doctor Whitmere assured me during our pre-hearing conference call that she hoped it would not come to that." He paused, fiddling with his papers again, creasing the dog-ear more definitively. "But, of course, we cannot say that for certain, given the nature of the student's accusations. For now, I'd like to hear from you, Professor Thompson."

Camilla was still reeling from trying to keep up. Allison hadn't testified yet. And now the committee wanted to hear what? Her response to Allison's veiled lawsuit threat? Or her response to Allison's letter? The letter that she hadn't seen herself. *Isn't that against the rules?* she thought petulantly. Shouldn't she have received it as well? Why hadn't Wallace shared *that* with her? There was no time to sift through it all, though, as the Dean was staring at her again. Someone in the room coughed. Wallace pinched her leg.

"Yes?" Camilla's voice eked out. She cleared her throat. She should stay clear of the lawsuit question; of that much, she was sure. "I haven't seen that letter, so I'm not sure what I can add to it."

"Professor Fields, will you..." Wilkins gestured impatiently at Wallace, who slid his copy of the letter in front of Camilla. She tried to read it, but the letters in the words moved around like fleas. She couldn't concentrate. Here was a letter, on hospital stationery, that Allison, or maybe her secretary, had taken the time to type out and mail in. No, not mail. Allison would have paid to have it couriered over to be certain it was delivered and signed for. Camilla tried to remind herself that it was, according to the Dean, a supportive letter. There had been no hidden accusations, no double entendres, no ulterior motives. Camilla focused on reading the first sentence again. *My name is Allison Whitmere, and in addition to being a surgeon in the Urology Department at Massachusetts General Hospital, I have been in a loving and committed relationship with Camilla Thompson, Assistant Professor of Literature and Writing at Tolland College.*

Camilla noted the "I have been." Allison had walked the tightrope between offering support and outright lying. *I have been.* The present perfect continuous form. It can mean a duration from the past till now, or recently. Even the sentences that Wilkins had read treaded a line very carefully. Camilla had been in Wilbur with Allison and Nico on the dates that Hunter had claimed she'd been with her—that was true. But she'd been *visiting* Nico. She was still allowed to see him then, but she hadn't *lived* there then. And yes, you could say that their relationship hadn't really ended yet as it was mere weeks after she'd left Allison. Allison still thought it was a blip and that they'd get back together. But Camilla had known even then, she'd never go back.

She heard people getting restless around the table. Papers were being shuffled, one of the men was whispering to Peggy Huggens, who was nodding her head enthusiastically.

"Can you corroborate that Doctor Whitmere's account is true?" Camilla heard Wallace say next to her. She glanced at him. His face was pale and looked tired, as if her delay in responding was sucking the life out of *him*.

"Yes," Camilla said, staring at him. She turned back to the Dean and said more forcefully, "I can."

"Thank you," Dean Wilkins said, his fingers now un-creasing the dog-ear entirely. "Would you like to add anything to your own written statement that Wallace has provided us?"

Camilla took it as a sign—a good sign—when he called Wallace by his given name. If it was, she didn't really want to add anything else. Who knew if she did that she'd mess it up somehow? Time and again, she admonished her students when she handed back their papers, "Less is more." Allison's letter had caused them to have doubt about Hunter's testimony. Shouldn't she leave it at that?

But then she imagined Allison waiting for her outside. She'd wait as long as she could for Camilla before she'd finally have to return to work. There would certainly be patients waiting, phone calls to make, perhaps she had a surgery that afternoon she'd have to prepare for. As much as Camilla was thankful for the letter, she didn't want to have to speak to Allison in person. That might start it all up between them again. Her being indebted to Allison. That's how split couples came together again, with one of them showing an act of unexpected kindness, a vestige of what they once had together. Suddenly, all the dissension, all the fights, the insults, the shouting and more, were blown away by the power of that one small act. But while it was okay to forgive, it was not okay to forget. Because eventually, the couple's differences would raise their ugly heads again like Cerberus, the hellhound who guards the entrance to the underworld to prevent the dead from escaping and the living from entering. It was better to leave the dead where they belonged. It was better to thank Allison via a short email, or better yet, to not thank her at all. So, it would be best to delay leaving this table until Allison, frustrated, would pack up her red file and leave. *I've given up so much to separate from her*, Camilla thought. Yes, she must force her to leave.

"Professor Thompson? We're still waiting," the Dean said to her. Frustrated, he clasped his hands on the papers. Wallace pinched her thigh again, whispering, "For goodness sake."

"Sorry," Camilla said. She uncrossed her legs, throwing Wallace's hand off, and sat up straight. "Yes, there is something else." The Dean's right eyebrow shot up. Everyone was looking at her now. "There is somebody—" Wallace gave her right ankle a kick. Still, Camilla plunged ahead. "A witness, I guess you would call her, that can testify to how Cindy"—Wallace gave her another hard kick—"how the student, came up with the story, and it is a story, a fabrication, that never happened." Camilla wished she had dragged her speech out longer. But, Wallace gave her another kick. She kicked him back. She didn't know why he was kicking her. Maybe it was simply because she hadn't filled him in about Taylor. Maybe he simply had been more than ready to pack up and head to the nearest piano bar for a triple Scotch.

"Oh?" said the Dean. He examined his papers, adding, "I was not aware—"

Camilla cut him off. "I'm sorry. I just found out about it myself."

Wilkins looked at her. "And this person...what is her name?"

"Taylor Johnson."

"And Taylor Johnson has information that is pertinent?"

"Yes," Camilla said, but as she said it, Wallace kicked her one last time and Camilla's voice rose and said, "Shit."

Peggy Huggins spoke up. "I think there is time to hear from this additional witness, don't you, Dean?"

Camilla smiled. "Thank you." She was somewhat comforted for the first time that day. After Taylor testified, Allison would be gone. Allison wouldn't allow herself to be on Taylor's time.

But then something happened. Something that Camilla hadn't planned on. Dean Wilkins spoke. "Thank you, Professor Thompson. Can you please tell Ms. Johnson to come in on your way out?"

There it was. Nothing had been gained. She was being sent out. She wasn't, as she thought she would be, allowed to stay in the room as Taylor gave her testimony. Surely, Allison hadn't left yet. She'd come all this way. She probably had enough work with her to take up another hour.

"May I stay?" Camilla said, weakly.

"I'm afraid that isn't possible," Wilkins told her. "Thank you, Professor Thompson. Just send her in please," he added dismissively.

Camilla was miserable as she stood. Wallace wouldn't look at her and again she wondered what he was upset about. She walked slowly to the door, not saying good-bye to any of the committee. She slowly opened the door. There was her brother and Taylor who, head down, was busy twisting pipe cleaners into some sort of gun. Allison's seat was empty. She was gone. Camilla could've wept from the sheer relief she felt. She addressed Taylor. "They'd like to speak with you."

"Great," Taylor murmured, but she said it uncertainly, didn't stand up, and Camilla realized that Taylor, in spite of her declarations to Camilla and Audrey the day before that she wanted to make amends and admit to the committee that it was she who had provided Hunter with all the private information about Camilla, the truth was Taylor hadn't really thought the committee would want to hear it. Taylor hadn't expected to testify. She packed up the pipe cleaners in a small box and stuffed it into her messenger bag. She stood up.

And then something else happened.

Taylor said with false bravado, like one of her father's grunts entering a firefight for the first time, "I'll give 'em hell, don't worry," but as she passed by Camilla through the open door and into the room, Camilla realized with horror that she'd made a horrible mistake. Taylor would tell the committee that she'd confided in Cindy Hunter that she was worried about Camilla because her relationship with Allison had ended. *Had ended.* If she told them that, it would call into question everything that Allison had stated in her letter that their relationship was good. Once the seed of doubt was laid, who knew what else the committee would begin to disbelieve? Cindy Hunter wouldn't be the liar anymore.

It was too late.

Taylor closed the door behind her, her nervous smile disappearing completely behind the door.

Without a word, Camilla strode past Peter. By the time she was outside she was already crying and hitting her head with her fists in frustration.

"Camilla?" Suddenly, there was Audrey walking up the steps toward her. She was dressed all in black. She could have been Camilla's twin except she didn't have a black jacket on, only the black oxford shirt and pants. Camilla shook her head and made a beeline for the Mini. "Hey, Audrey," she heard Peter say behind her. Their footsteps crunching on the gravel quickened to catch up to her.

"I can't," Camilla said over her shoulder, not having it in her to complete the sentence. At the Mini, she clicked open the doors. As soon as she sat inside, she banged the vinyl dashboard above the absurdly large odometer that was as big as a pie plate. "Shit!" she yelled. "Fuck me." She smacked the dashboard a few more times and then leaned back into her chair, closing her eyes. By then, her brother and Audrey were in the car. Audrey, leaning forward from the back seat, was trying to console her with platitudes of how it was going to be all right, no matter what was upsetting her. In the passenger seat, Peter repeatedly asked her what had happened.

Camilla started the car. Her brother's hand punched the ignition off. "You can't drive. You're crying for fuck's sake."

Before Camilla could argue, Peter spoke sternly. "Get out. I'll drive." Camilla started to shake her head, but he was already out of the car and then opening her door, ordering her to get out.

Halfway down the school's ribboning road around the campus and out on to Commonwealth Avenue, he tried to ask her again what had happened, but Camilla only told him, "I can't," twisted her body away, and stared out the window. The car fell silent again.

The whole ride home she tried to calm down. She kept replaying the moment when she'd told the committee about Taylor. How stupid she'd been. How blind. She was so scared of Allison, of facing Allison, that she lost her compass. Her ability to think straight was jettisoned. Two years later, and her fear of Allison could still cause her to react in ways that only made life worse. She was still looking for that escape hatch that she couldn't find in all the years of their relationship. All that time and she was no different. There had been no growth. No change. She drummed into her students that unless literature ended in a different place than it started, it failed. "Without the character changing, either for good or bad, why waste your time reading it?" She'd write on the chalkboard: *character flatline = sudden story death.* Any idea that she'd recovered from their relationship and was free, living her own life, was a lie. And now she'd thrown away her career because of it. She'd shown everybody what a weak fool she really was. Everyone knew she was a fraud now.

They were parked in her driveway. Camilla didn't remember the last half of the trip. She put her fingers on the silver door handle. Immediately, Audrey reached around the passenger seat and put her arms around Camilla. Peter hit the automatic door lock. Camilla heard the click of her door.

"Let me out."

Her brother shook his head. "Just tell us what happened."

Audrey asked, "Did they fire you?"

Camilla shook her head. "Not yet." She paused and breathed out. "But they will."

"What happened?" Peter asked again.

Camilla bristled. "Christ, can't you think of something else to say? You're a fucking broken record."

Audrey hugged her tighter. "We're just—"

Camilla pulled Audrey's hands away. "I know. Don't." She ran her fingers through her hair. It was damp. Without the air conditioning on, she was sweating. Her oxford shirt was stuck to her back

underneath her suit jacket, and her pants were stuck
to the vinyl seat. A dull brown bird landed on the hood
of the car and immediately took off, the metal too hot
for a landing strip. Simultaneously, as if reading each
other's minds, Camilla and her brother both reached
over and pressed the metal levers on the central console
to open their windows.

"Owe me a Coke," Peter said.

Camilla sniffed. "You're supposed to *say*
something at the same time, not *do* something."

"Next you're going to be telling me the rules to
Red Rover."

The image of cleaning out her office at Tolland
came charging in. Camilla began to tear up. She looked
out her window. How would she do any of it? No matter
how confidential the hearing was supposed to be, she
knew that word of it would snake along the department
corridors. She'd be marked. They'd look away as they
passed her in the halls. They'd talk about how they
never had a problem with Cindy Hunter. How Camilla
had always kept apart from all of them, as if she was
trying to hide something. Well, now we know, they'd
say, nodding in agreement with each other. Now we
know what her secret was. Camilla remembered Emily
Dickinson's famous poem: Our little secrets slink away.
She unconsciously shook her head. *No, they don't. They
gallop away, bursting with their freedom, excited with
their scandalous, wicked news. Hear ye, hear ye.*

"Just start in the middle, Homer," her brother
said softly next to her. It was another of their father's
sayings. Homer had begun so many of his epic tales—
The Odyssey, *The Iliad*—*in medias res*. In the middle of
things, rather than at the beginning of the plot. Their
father would interrupt them whenever she or Peter

were dithering around and trying to formulate some cockamamie excuse for one of their screwups. "Just start in the middle, Homer," he'd prod them.

Camilla missed her father so much then. Could she ever have told him about the committee? She'd never even come out to him.

"Mills?"

"We should have waited for Taylor." She really didn't feel bad about that, but she wanted to put off telling Peter and Audrey any of it because it all led to her confessing that she'd fucked up the outcome. Beginning, middle, or end, it didn't matter where the story started. The lot of it would end the same way. Aristotle knew that an ending naturally follows another thing. There had to be a well-earned closure. Like Chekhov said, in a play where one of the characters shows he has a gun in the first act, it must go off by the third act. Or something like that.

"Taylor's fine," Audrey said from the back seat.

Camilla waited a beat. Then, she told them everything.

๛๛๛๛

Audrey and Peter were on their first glass of wine and Camilla was almost finished with her second when Camilla's cell phone rang, startling all three of them. Camilla and Audrey were on the couch together. Audrey's bare feet were curled to the side up on the couch. Settled into the leather chair, Peter sat with his shoes up on the ottoman. On any other day it would have looked as if they were enjoying a relaxing visit amongst family and friends. They were all worn out. Camilla was on her way to being drunk. It was only eleven thirty in the morning.

She'd tried to stick to the highlights when she'd filled Peter and Audrey in on the hearing. As much as she struggled to control it, she couldn't stop her voice from shaking with emotion. Her storytelling wasn't exactly *in medias res* either. It was more like some experimental narrative jacked on steroids that messed about with temporal sequence so much it took the concentration of a medieval translator to understand it at all. She started out with telling them that it had been going so well, and then she jumped to Allison's letter, interrupting that with five minutes on who was on the committee and how there were so many wild cards of people she didn't know. Mostly, she kept coming back to that fatal moment when she'd come up with the idea of stalling by bringing in Taylor as a witness. "I fucked it up," she repeated throughout.

When her brother and Audrey finally understood what had happened, they'd been sitting in the car for another thirty minutes.

Audrey insisted that they still didn't know anything, not until they could talk to Taylor to see what she had said exactly. Maybe Taylor hadn't told them explicitly the part about Camilla and Allison's relationship sinking into nonexistence.

"You have no idea how they'll vote, either," Audrey offered.

"You need a drink," Peter said to Camilla, and opened his door. "It's not over till the fat lady sings the death aria."

"Please stop quoting Dad. It's too weird." Thankful for the excuse to get out of the hot car, she obediently followed him up into the house.

Now, in the living room, her cell phone kept

ringing on the coffee table between the couch and where Peter was sitting. Camilla leaned over to see who it was.

Stretching his hand out to Camilla, Peter gestured for the phone. "Let me answer it."

"It's Allison," she said. Before she could stop him, her brother reached over and grabbed the phone, accepting the call.

"Don't!" Camilla yelled too late.

"Hey Allison, it's Peter," he said smoothly into the phone. He gave a thumbs-up to Camilla and nodded. "She's sleeping right now." He paused. "No, not really." Covering the bottom of the phone, he whispered, "She asked if you slept at all last night."

"Tell her good-bye," Camilla whispered harshly.

He held up his index finger to her. "Yeah, no we really appreciated that, Allison…yes, the committee mentioned it."

Camilla stood up. "Hang up the phone," she told him. "Don't tell her any—"

Peter kept his index finger up as if he were bidding at an auction. "I will. I will tell her that…I'm not sure about that…um, okay…Thanks, Allison." When he disconnected the call, he told them, "She wanted to tell you she hopes the committee does the right thing and if they don't, she thinks you should appeal."

Camilla scoffed at the idea. "It's not a lawsuit. There's no appeal."

"So, that's it then, right?" her brother asked, but Camilla could tell from the way he said it he was making fun of her. "What'll it be: poisoned Kool-Aid or razor blade?"

"What were you and Allison and Taylor doing when I was in the hearing?" Camilla asked.

"Not whatever it is you think we were doing," Peter said back. "It was unbelievably awkward."

"Poor you. Now you want me to feel sorry for you?"

Audrey touched Camilla's leg. "What?" Camilla said. "Stop telling me to shut up or whatever it is you're trying to tell me. Do you understand I've just lost my job?" But when she saw Audrey wince, she rubbed her forehead and added, "Don't listen to me. I'm fucked up."

Peter told her that the three of them had sat in silence in the waiting room after brief hellos and how've you beens. Taylor had said nothing, focusing on scrolling repeatedly through old text messages as if they were new and hadn't been read yet.

"All you could hear was Allison's highlighter scratching frantically across the paper. Oh, I almost forgot the best part," he said, and took a sip of his drink.

"There is no best part," Camilla told him. "It's all shit."

He smiled. "You'll love this. Guess what else Allison asked me to ask you on the phone?"

Camilla stared at him.

"She wanted to know if we installed a lightning rod somewhere in the treehouse." He started to laugh. "She's still a neurotic mess."

"Taylor must be done," Audrey said, trying to divert the conversation. "You should call her," she told Camilla.

Camilla shook her head. "Not yet." She stood up with her empty glass. "Who wants another?"

❧ ❧ ❧ ❧

Within the hour, Taylor was there. Camilla was drunk by then. Audrey had tried unsuccessfully to get her to eat something. Peter had made tuna boats, whispering loudly to Audrey in the kitchen as he took out the mayonnaise from the refrigerator that that would do the trick. But Camilla left hers untouched on the plate that perched on the stack of books that was piled on top of a long bench in front of the couch. The whole thing was so precarious Camilla wondered if the tuna boat would fall off and sink. Right before Taylor showed up, Peter leaned over from the leather chair and lifted the hotdog roll to his mouth, stuffing half of it in his mouth. Audrey gave him a look of exasperation, while Camilla seemed disgusted by it.

"What?" her brother said, his mouth full. "You weren't going to eat it."

"What are you, twelve?" Camilla asked him.

Then, the buzzer sounded and Taylor was there in the living room with them, throwing off her linen suit jacket, kicking off loafers, and making for the kitchen, all the while saying, "I hope to God you left me some." Grabbing the bottle of Scotch that was half-empty from Wallace's visit from days before and a glass from the bar counter, she came back to the living room, plopping down in the blue chair.

"Jesus. How can people dress and go to work every day like this? It's fucking ninety degrees out," she told them. "I'd go insane. Do you have a T-shirt and shorts I can change into?" She poured herself a hefty drink and drank most of it down. "Stop looking at me like I'm a freak."

"What happened?" Audrey said, nervously glancing at Camilla who was sitting on the edge of the couch as if readying herself to pounce.

Taylor rubbed her forehead with the hand holding the Scotch. "What do you mean what happened? It was not pleasant, let me tell you. How can you work with those people? Do you actually *like* working with them? When I walked in there I felt like they were the firing squad and so I asked them if I could have a last cigarette, but you know how well that went over. I mean, Mills, I'd rather give up smoking, drinking, *and* sex than be in the same room as them again. Jesus. They're worse than the living dead. They are the dead living. It's going to be my next series." She made a sweeping motion with her hand to signify a marquee. "Academically speaking: The Living Dead. Can't you see it now? I mean—"

"It wasn't about *you*," Camilla snapped. "What the fuck did you tell them?"

Taylor jumped. "Jesus, Mills. It was fine. I was fine. Have a little faith in me. It's going to be okay."

But it wasn't. That was confirmed as soon as Taylor recounted to the committee how she'd told Cindy Hunter not only about Camilla, but also about Allison and, worst of all, about Nico. She'd even told them about the treehouse.

"So they'd see how great of a mother you could be. Are. Wait, why are you crying?" she asked Camilla. "You should be happy. Or is this one of those times you're crying for joy?"

"Shut up, Taylor," Audrey said quietly. She told Camilla, "You don't know yet how they'll—"

Camilla stood. Without a word, she walked to her bedroom and slammed the door behind her.

※ ※ ※ ※

The Dean called Camilla at six that evening. By then she'd already heard from Wallace, who had informed her that the vote was very close, but in the end she was going to be suspended for one term.

"You shouldn't have brought Taylor in," he said quietly. "I'm sure it would've been a different outcome. It's just my opinion but...you had convinced them, I'm sure of it." He paused. "Well, it's only for one semester." He sighed. "Think of it as a sabbatical. You can write. A whole semester off, I cannot imagine it! I envy you. What I wouldn't give to have an entire semester off. What a gift."

"It was good of you to warn me, Wallace," Camilla said back, her voice flat, before she hung up.

The Dean was more overbearing, laying it on thick about how the school didn't take such accusations lightly, that she should be happy that the Committee hadn't penalized her further, that she would need to be more careful—"more judicious" were his words—with her power over students in the future, that they were the protectors of students, not their adversaries, and that he hoped she would reflect on this while she was home the next semester. Camilla didn't say a word throughout the call, even when the Dean asked at the end, "Is there anything you want to say?" When the phone remained silent he told her that she'd receive a formal notice in an overnight package, said his quick good-bye, and the phone clicked and went dead.

"Well?" Audrey said as Camilla curled back into a fetal position next to her on the bed.

"Tell Chekhov the gun went off," Camilla told her, closing her eyes and dreading the hangover that had already begun to worm its way in.

❦❦❦❦

She slept for a while, but awakened suddenly from a bad dream involving a pack of rabid cats that had run her down in an alley, pouncing and tearing at her clothes. She'd taken a couple of Tylenol PMs and was totally disoriented. The room was pitch-dark except for the white sheet twisted in a gigantic corkscrew around her legs. Her cheek was wet with sweat. Her hair was matted down. Audrey was gone. She heard low voices from the kitchen. Struggling out of the sheet, she got up and went out of the room.

They were seated around the kitchen island, Taylor and Audrey sharing one of the stools and Peter on the other. The Formica was covered with empty beer bottles, the almost empty bottle of Scotch, and their glasses, some more full than others.

"She lives," her brother shouted, pointing at her with fingers that loosely held a lit cigarette. He was squinting his eyes from the smoke that filled the air. All three of them were smoking, and from the pile in the ashtray, it looked like they had been at it for some time.

Taylor sloshed the rest of the Scotch into a glass and held it out to her. "Come on, take it. You have to catch up."

From there it was straight downhill with the four of them finishing that bottle and Camilla finding another behind cans of kidney beans, diced tomatoes, and corn in a cabinet.

She wouldn't be able to remember exactly when they had come up with the idea, or who had proposed it first, or why they thought it would somehow make

them feel better. She'd only remember that someone—
her brother? Taylor?—said they needed to go on a beer
run because a nearby package store was the only thing
still open, and who wanted to go along?

At eleven in the evening, all four of them piled
into the Mini. Camilla drove, insisting, "It's my car,
dammit." Camilla and Audrey sat up front and Peter
and Taylor crashed into each other in the back. They
never made it to the liquor store. Somewhere on
Brattle Street, the siblings and Taylor were suddenly
agreeing that it was more important that they drive
to the treehouse, Taylor arguing they would never get
this chance again to do it together.

"We need some fucking closure," Taylor said.

Camilla almost told her that there would never
be closure no matter how many times they went to
the treehouse, but she didn't say a word. Truthfully,
she wanted to see the treehouse one last time. In her
drunken state, part of her wanted to destroy it after
the day she'd had. A fucking lightning rod. Leave it to
Allison not to give one complimentary word. She had
to find the one thing that Camilla hadn't thought to
do. She wanted to tear it all down to show Allison that
she could build the treehouse *and* she could demolish
it, wiping it away as if it never existed. But part of her
wanted to go one last time for something else: to leave
her mark on it. She'd built it, but she hadn't taken the
time to leave a sign that it was her creation, built out of
her love for Nico. As if it were the most natural thing
to do, Camilla turned right onto Fresh Pond Parkway
toward Wilbur.

Audrey's initial silent acquiescence wore off the
longer they drove. "Do you think they'll be home?"
she nervously asked Camilla as the Mini turned off the

parkway at the Wilbur exit.

"I hope she is," Taylor said from the back. "This is all her fault."

Craning her neck around toward the back, Audrey stated, "No, it's not."

Hunched over the steering wheel, Camilla told her, "Please don't defend her. I'm not drunk enough for *that*."

Taylor leaned forward through the gap between the two front seats. She held up a finger. "One. She drove Milly crazy. Two." She added another finger. "She hounded Milly like crazy. Three." Her hand was in a Cub Scout's honor pledge gesture. "She drove me so fucking crazy that I fucked a girl I ordinarily wouldn't give the time to if she stopped me on the street, and I then made the spectacularly poor decision to confide in her, thereby handing over the secrets of my best friend to the enemy. And four." She tucked her thumb down as she raised her pinky. "She *is* crazy." As if the speech had been too tiring, Taylor fell back into her own seat. Peter clapped lazily next to her.

"Can you all just shut up for a minute? Shut up, shut up. We're almost there," Camilla said.

"Go dark, Mills," Taylor whispered. "Turn off your lights."

"We're not a fucking drone," Camilla replied, but she did click the lights off and the car rolled slowly downhill toward Allison's house.

"Ssh, keep it down," Taylor whispered. "Go around the side."

"Stop acting like we're on a fucking search and rescue mission," Camilla whispered loudly, looking in her rearview mirror at her.

"We look more suspicious with the lights off,"

Audrey said in her normal voice. Taylor shushed her again.

Peter started to laugh, drunkenly. "I haven't had this much fun since Tommy Loney and I broke into the motorcycle gang's clubhouse when we were twelve."

Camilla snorted. "It wasn't a motorcycle gang's clubhouse, you dumbass. It was a shack that the train watchman lived in."

That made Peter laugh harder.

"Shut it," Taylor spat.

"Yeah, maybe in the eighteenth century," Peter said loudly, still laughing hard. "It was where the fucking gear heads hung."

"Yeah, right. And by the way. You were sixteen."

"You're high," he said, his voice squealing in delight.

"I'm going to kill you both if you don't shut up," Taylor said.

"Ooh, I'm scared," Camilla said, looking in the rearview again. "Guess what? You already did that this afternoon."

She parked the car crooked on the side of the house's lot, next to the tallest section of the surrounding wooden fence. The right front tire was against the side garden's railroad tie border while the back tire was a good foot away.

"That's okay. I'll take a cab to the curb," Peter said, laughing as he got out of the car.

"Shut the fuck up," Taylor slurred over the roof of the car. "She'll hear us."

Peter smiled. "Losing your nerve, captain?"

"Shh," Audrey said quietly, and because she hadn't said very much up until then, they all quieted down.

"Did you hear something?" Camilla whispered. Her heart was racing now that they were standing outside the car, vulnerable on the street in their small circle near the back gate. She hoped that the streetlight on the corner wasn't illuminating them too much.

Audrey shook her head.

"Right," Taylor whispered. "Let's do this thing."

That started Peter laughing again, but Camilla clamped a hand over his mouth, whispering in his ear, "Shut up." He nodded. She let her hand drop.

"What exactly is it we're doing?" he said very quietly.

Camilla opened the back gate slowly. Still drunk, she felt that every sound was absurdly loud. There was a stiff breeze blowing through the tree and she could hear the treehouse bolts attached to the platform shifting and groaning with the wind as it had been built to do. Some kind of unseen animal was scratching at the ground under the rhododendron bush. She put her finger to her mouth and went into the garden. They filed through after her.

It was dark in the garden. A thick cloud cover was moving in rapidly, hiding the moon and most of the stars. The house was dark, too, except for the stove overhead light, which Camilla knew Allison left on every night in case she woke up and needed to get a glass of water in the middle of the night. What used to be their second-floor bedroom—now only Allison's—was at the front of the house, while Nico's dark bedroom looked out from the back onto the garden. Allison would have left the sound machine on in Nico's room, though. The peaceful hum of a waterfall would be keeping him asleep through the night. Camilla was sure of it, as if she still lived there.

Now that they were there, Camilla didn't know what it was she wanted to do. She only felt that there was something she had to do. She needed to deposit some sign that she was there, would always be there, in that treehouse. Nothing would be able to take that away. She knew the others were now following her lead. She could feel their tension. They must be wondering what they were doing there, too. The alcohol would be wearing off as their anxieties about getting caught took hold. Who knew what Allison was capable of if she found them? She could easily have them arrested for trespassing without a second thought. What had before seemed like a lark, a drunken adventure that they'd joke about in the future, was now a stupid, juvenile gambit that they might be ashamed of in the morning. They weren't fueled, like Camilla was, by a buried desire for visibility, for an intense longing to finally be seen. Alcohol and their loyalty to her, Camilla thought, would only push them so far.

They climbed the ladder silently, following her lead, one after the other.

Inside the treehouse, they stood close by each other, their arms touching each other. The room was awfully stuffy as if the windows hadn't been opened in weeks. They huddled together as if they were children afraid of the dark.

"I can't see a fucking thing," Taylor whispered.

"Wait," Audrey whispered back. "Our eyes will adjust. What's that smell?"

For a moment, Camilla was brought back to the night when she'd slept with Audrey and Taylor, and in the dark bedroom had struggled to see their faces. She broke the spell of the huddle by walking over to the porthole. She looked down at the house. The wind was picking up even more, and the porthole window rattled slightly. She and Peter should fix that. Then, she remembered that they couldn't. Allison was back now. Time had run out for any more work on the treehouse.

There was a star in the sky above the house and to the right. The thick cloud blanket quickly extinguished it. Camilla felt the same feeling of emptiness she felt when she was on her annual beach vacation and fog rolled into Provincetown, wiping the slate of docks and boats and houses so that it seemed as if the entire town disappeared and your life was snuffed out, too.

Below, the house was still quiet. The stove's light reminded her of all the gourmet dinners she'd cooked. Allison had two specialties she occasionally made: vegetarian chili, and pancakes. Now *she* had the gourmet stove. Camilla wondered if it was ever used. She didn't miss the stove, as they'd hardly had it before she'd left. She would, however, sometimes be cooking in her Cambridge condo and would go to get something she needed out of one of the kitchen cabinet drawers—a lemon zester, the small silver ladle that was perfect for gravy—and she'd realize that she'd left whatever it was behind in the Wilbur house. Allison and Nico's house. An overwhelming feeling of loss would overtake her then. Sometimes she couldn't even finish cooking the dish, or in the gravy's case, eat it, she'd be so upset, and she'd empty her plate into the sink, turn on the noisy garbage disposal, and get rid of it as fast as possible. She'd try to calm herself down and talk herself through it, telling herself she would buy a new peeler, but it was no good. She liked *that* zester, the one she'd left behind. And now it sat in a drawer below, some twenty feet from her, probably ignored and unloved.

Suddenly, the gusty wind threw the porthole window open against the wall. Camilla shut it firmly and did up the eyehook to keep it closed.

"So, what's the plan, Mills?" Peter whispered. He rubbed his pale arms. Aside from the noises the treehouse was making because of the wind, it was so quiet they heard his skin-on-skin, sandpaper-like rubbing.

"Stop being so nervous," Camilla told him quietly as she walked back to the group. "She can't hear us from where her bed is."

"What *is* that smell?" Audrey said.

"I'm cold." Peter shivered.

"Me, too," Taylor whispered. She laughed nervously. She pulled out a crumpled pack of Lucky Strikes and lit one up.

"It didn't smell like this the other day," Audrey said, going over to one of the windowsills she painted. She sniffed at it.

"Put that out!" Camilla told Taylor. She was suddenly colder, too. The wind was picking up now. A stronger gust shook both windows. Camilla's T-shirt that had been sweaty in the car began to cool off, and she shivered. They all listened as the treehouse's groaning got louder. They felt the platform swaying. She felt Audrey's hand slip into hers at her side.

"Camilla?" Audrey whispered, tugging on her hand. "Do you smell..."

The darkness outside lit up in momentary whiteness and went dark again. They heard a thunderclap nearby.

"That's not good," Peter said.

"No shit, Sherlock," Camilla said. She pulled her hand out from Audrey's clasp.

"Camilla," Audrey said again, but the sky exploded with lightning that was followed almost immediately by thunder crashing. Camilla tried to remember what the mathematical formula was to measure how far away lightning was.

"Shit, it's almost on top of us," Taylor said.

The lightning and thunder cracked simultaneously. Still, there was no rain. The wind was now battering all the walls. The treehouse was in full sway, its bolts screeching with the movement. They all heard a large tree branch crack and crash in Pecksniff's yard. Camilla and Peter raced to the window to see.

"Stay away from the windows!" Taylor cried out.

"We have to get out of here. Now!" Camilla shouted and grabbed Peter's hand, rushing toward the doorway. "Come on!" she yelled at Audrey and Taylor. "Go!" she directed Peter at the landing by the top of the ladder. "I'll be there in a minute." When he hesitated, she pushed him toward the first rung, and then grabbed Audrey and shoved her through the doorway, too.

"What are you doing?" Audrey yelled, but she had to go down as Camilla was forcing Taylor down next as if she was that person on an aircraft who grabs fearful parachuters and gives them a push into the open sky.

"Mills!" Taylor shouted. A streak of lightning that opened into thin tributaries flashed over the Bishops' house across the road.

"I'll be there in a second!" Camilla quickly took out the penknife from her jeans pocket. As she went through the door, another thunderclap made her gasp. She closed the door on the landing and started down, but on the third rung down, she leaned over and, holding on to the tree, began to carve into the tree trunk as fast as she could. The wind was full tilt now, jostling the ladder. Camilla gouged the wood quickly, her fingers confidently holding the penknife and pressing down for just the right amount of pressure so that the blade wouldn't get stuck. She smelled smoke and wondered for a moment if Pecksniff's tree had caught fire, but the ladder jostling underneath her brought her right back to what she was doing and she forgot all about Pecksniff and his tree. All those years of her secretive carving were paying off. They had all been for this moment. Because of the wind, she had to rush it. She knew the N-T-W and the C-T below it were all crooked and different sizes, like a child's scrawl. She couldn't do any better than that, though. The wind was rocking the ladder. Then, it started to rain. The third act had begun. The rain picked up force, soaking her clothes. There were fewer streaks of lightning, and the noise of thunder slipped farther away, the low rumbling continuing in the distance, the audience's clapping fading.

Slipping the knife into her pocket, Camilla scrambled down the ladder, the rain pelting her. As she ran to the car, she saw the house lighting up, starting with Nico's bedroom, and then room after room downstairs. She raced through the gate, knowing that Allison had possibly seen them, or at least, her. She didn't care. She only cared about getting to the car where the others were waiting. Someone opened the driver's door as she got there and she jumped in, shutting the door against the wind and rain.

"Are you fu—" Taylor started to speak but was cut off by a loud explosion. "Jesus, we've been hit!" she yelled.

The four of them peered through their windows.

The treehouse was engulfed in flames. Immediately, the treehouse was cleaved in half, the side with the porthole window crashing to the ground, the remaining side, hugging the tree, smothered in flames and smoke. The orange-yellow smear was the only thing they could see through their foggy car windows and the rain reaching a full pitch.

"Holy shit!" Peter shouted.

They all watched, paralyzed in their seats.

"Go out, go out!" Camilla cried to the fire, her heart racing.

Suddenly, the flames died, the deluge smothering them out like a fire hose. A huge plume of smoke rose, like from a waste factory, above the tree. Then, as suddenly as it had arrived, the rain began to move away, on to the next town as if it had tired of this game, lessening to nothing.

"Fuck," Taylor muttered. "We could've been killed!"

Camilla and Peter simultaneously opened their doors.

"Get back in!" Taylor yelled. "We need to get out of here!"

Peter looked at Camilla. They both got out of the car.

"Milly!" Taylor hissed.

They walked to the gate, which was swinging lazily in the soft breeze the storm had left behind. The air was warmer and smelled of rain and earth and the acrid smoke that was still funneling into the sky from the treehouse. Camilla heard a car door close behind them. Audrey came toward them. The three of them walked through the gate, into the side garden with its trampled irises and rhododendrons, glistening with wetness, still alive. They stopped on the bluestone pathway. Water was gushing noisily down the gutters. Pieces of lumber were strewn with tiny branches and sodden leaves across the garden and the brick patio leading to the kitchen door. Shards of the porthole's glass lay shiny on the bricks, its splintered frame flung to the side, just missing the house.

Camilla gripped the top of her head with both hands as she felt Peter's hand touch the small of her back. The skies had cleared, leaving a bright three-quarter moon and a landscape of stars. Audrey stood there, with her hand over her mouth. Taylor walked through the gate opening, her arms hugging her stomach. "I can't fucking believe it," she said. "What's the chances of that happening?"

Camilla stared at the smoky devastation. The treehouse was lost. She imagined all the losses in her life—her parents, Nico, in a sense Taylor, her job, and now, the treehouse—piled up like a garbage bin filled to capacity, and still more was being piled on and overflowing because there was nowhere to put it all. As soon as that first real loss came into your life, it didn't matter if you were a girl of twelve or an adult of forty-eight, it opened a locked door to let more losses in. You could never shut the door again, either.

"I mean it must be like a thousand to one for lightning to strike next door and then right here?" Taylor continued. "Shit."

"What?" Camilla turned around to face her.

"Maybe even a million to one." Taylor kept prattling on, as if she were in shock.

"But, there wasn't any lightning," Peter said. "It had stopped, remember?"

"What are you talking about?" Taylor said.

"What did you do with that cigarette?" Camilla asked Taylor.

"What?" Taylor said.

"What did you do with the cigarette?" Camilla practically hissed.

"I threw it away," Taylor said.

"Where?"

"There's no way, that fire—come on, did you see that thing? It was huge."

"The spray can," Peter said.

"What?"

"The spray can," Camilla bellowed, her voice rising. "You left it there. You must've fucked up the valve when you dropped it. The vapor's fucking flammable, you idiot. It's been leaking for days in the heat."

"No way," Taylor said, defensively. "I didn't—"

"That's what I smelled," Audrey said, slowly. "Aerosol propellant."

"No way," Taylor repeated, but less sure of herself.

Camilla grabbed her by the shoulders. "You fuck up everything," she yelled. But then they heard the kitchen door open behind them. Camilla let go of Taylor. She turned around.

Allison walked out onto the brick patio, leaving the door wide open, holding Nico, who was staring, wide-eyed. He was so much bigger than Camilla remembered. The baby she had left was no more. He was a boy. He was wearing a Batman T-shirt and matching pajama shorts. His legs were long and spindly, wrapped tightly around Allison's hips. There was so much of his life that she didn't know about anymore. Yet, she would have recognized him anywhere. The sight of him startled her more than seeing Allison. Allison was murmuring in his ear. Nico bit his lip and sucked on it. With his fist, he rubbed one of his eyes. Allison smiled weakly at them. Tilting her head back, she looked up at the shorn off section of the treehouse that seemed to be gripping the tree trunk for dear life.

"I was just telling Nico," Allison said, her voice faltering. She took a deep breath. She angled her face down again so she could look into Nico's face. "I was just telling you, wasn't I, Nickel, that the fairies who built it the first time built it wrong. They didn't make it fireproof. But tomorrow we'll go talk to the fireman in town and ask him how it should be built so we can write a letter to the fairies and tell them all about it, right?" Nico nodded his head. He burrowed his forehead into her neck. Allison looked at Camilla. She opened her mouth to say something, but the sounds of sirens could now be heard in the distance.

"You need to go," Allison said. When no one moved, she reiterated. "Go home, Camilla. Just go home." Turning around, she headed toward the open back door, Nico's large brown eyes bobbing over her shoulder the whole way. Allison closed the door behind them with a soft click. They watched as Allison and Nico walked through the kitchen, shutting off lights along the way, and although Peter led Taylor, despite Taylor's weakening protests, out of the backyard, Audrey stayed with Camilla, holding her hand, as Camilla watched all the lights in the house except for the stove light being extinguished and the house falling into slumber once more.

"Time to go," Audrey said quietly next to her. And then she led Camilla down the path, out through the gate, and back to the car.

❧❧❧❧

They all slept in the next morning. Taylor was sound asleep on the couch, a pillow firmly held over her head, and Peter's bedroom door was still closed. Camilla and Audrey made cappuccinos. They carried them, along with plates of mini croissants and a jar of blueberry jam on a metal tray that showed a scratched illustration of a Paris café, to the back deck. Camilla had bought the tray at a yard sale for twenty-five cents the first summer after leaving Allison. She thought at the time that she would see Paris before the year was up, but she hadn't gotten around to it. So many of the plans she originally thought she'd do after regaining her freedom had fell to nothing. Her life had continued as before, only without Allison and Nico. The treehouse had been the only new thing she'd tried to finish. And now, that was gone.

"What will you do now?" Audrey asked her as she took a sip of her espresso at the table on the deck.

They'd been gentle with each other when they'd arrived back at Camilla's house at one in the morning. Holding each other all night, they'd turned over from side to side in unison, first one spooning the other, then vice versa. Camilla had finally fallen asleep by syncing her breathing to Audrey's slow, sleep-filled rhythm.

Camilla shrugged. She watched Cosimo run along one of the deck railings and launch onto the tree. She picked up a piece of toast and then laid it down again. They watched the squirrel fly from branch to branch, sometimes falling if the branch was too thin to hold his weight, but always grabbing another offshoot at the last minute before he would have plunged to the ground.

"How do you feel about Rome?" Camilla asked her.

"What?"

There was a small white thread snagged on one of Audrey's short bangs. Camilla plucked it off absentmindedly and then realized what she'd done. It was the automatic gesture done hundreds of times by a couple that had been together for a long time. She had the urge to put it back so she could pluck it off again.

Camilla shook her head. "I'll tell you some other time."

They sat watching Cosimo as he dove and recovered, jumped and hung on, averting disaster by a fraction of an inch, continuing his precarious trapeze act from branch to branch, emergency landing to emergency landing.

One time when he missed and was caught by a lower branch, Audrey gasped, "Oh, no."

When he launched again, they began to hold their breaths and then slowly release them together.

But he finally made it to the ground.

Audrey murmured, "Safe and sound."

"Yes," Camilla said, smiling. "Safe and sound."

About the Author

Randi Triant spent ten years as a documentary and medical education writer and producer before receiving her MFA in creative writing and literature from Bennington College. Her fiction and nonfiction have appeared in literary journals and magazines. She has taught writing at Emerson College and Boston College, and lives in Massachusetts.

Other book's by Sapphire Authors

Razor's Edge (American Yakuza) – ISBN – 978-1-943353-81-1

Luce Potter lives by a code of honor. Push her and she shoves back, harder. There's only one problem: Luce has just found out that revenge is a knife that cuts both ways. Now that her lover Brooke has survived the attack on her life, Luce has only one thing on her mind, and his name is Frank. Unfortunately, someone walks into her life that she didn't see coming.

Brooke Erickson has survived an attack so brutal it's left a permanent scar on her soul. All she wants to do now is go home and finish recuperating with her lover, Luce Potter, by her side. An unexpected event puts Brooke at the head of the Yakuza family. Can she command the respect necessary to lead it through the crisis?

Luce and Brooke's worlds are upending. Can each do what's necessary to survive and return to a new normal?

Meet Me in The Middle – ISBN – 978-1-943353-63-7

Veterinarian Aislin O'Shea runs a busy clinic. She wasn't looking for a relationship. She'd already had the perfect one. She certainly wasn't attracted to fancy pants executive, Ms. Zane Whitman - she wasn't her type.

Zane Whitman had it all. Stellar career, wealth, exclusive social circle, and models vying for her attention. Impulsive, emotionally charged Aislin was not her type.

Two women from the opposite side of the tracks.

Neither one expects meddling from an unexpected source on the Other side.

Neither one knows the train is coming.

Four of a Kind – ISBN – 978-1-943353-61-3

Tess Whitcomb is a struggling artist who has to work a second job at The Sloop to pay her bills. Upon her aunt's death, she is given a sealed envelop by her aunt's doctor and instructed to hand deliver it to N. Hamilton Esq., a maritime lawyer. Neither one understands why Tess has been sent to her firm. The whole meeting is odd and confusing. The only thing that is clear to each of them is that there is a strong and immediate attraction between them. Tess leaves the office certain that they will never meet again.

A valuable necklace owned by Nikki's deceased mother shows up in the most unexpected way and the truth about their entwined past is revealed. Nikki is intrigued by Tess but dismisses the meeting as ridiculous. She suspects that Tess is part of an office scheme by some of her staff trying to set her up on a date. Her heart was closed tight since the death of her beloved Jo.

Can these two women handle the truth? Can they accept that love can happen anytime and anywhere?

From the start, Avery knows winning Catherine's heart will be no easy feat. When curve ball after curve ball is thrown her way, does she scrap her design or make it work.

The Dreamcatcher - ISBN - 978-1-943353-67-5

High school is rarely easy, especially for a tall, somewhat gangly Native American girl. Add a sprinkle of shyness, a dash of athletic prowess, an above-average IQ, and some bizarre history that places her in the guardianship of her aunt. Then normal high school life is only an illusion.

Kai Tiva faces an uphill struggle until she runs into Riley Beth James, the extroverted class cutie, at the principal's office. Riley shows up for a newspaper interview, while Kai is summoned for punching out a classmate.

Riley is the attractive girl-next-door-type whom everyone likes. Though a fairly good student, an emerging choral star, and wildly popular, she knows she'll never live up to her older sister. She makes up for it with bravery, kindness, and a brash can-do attitude.

Their odd matchup is strengthened by curiosity, compassion, humor, and all the drama of typical teenage life. But their experiences go beyond the normal teen angst; theirs is compounded by a curious attraction to each other, and an emerging, insidious danger related to mysterious death of Kai's father.

Their emerging friendship is tested as they navigate this risky challenge. But the powerful bond forged between them has existed through past lives. The outcome this time will affect the next generation of Kai's people.